Thurmond's First White-Knuckle Adventure!

Thurmond's Saga

Hoping to escape the poverty and tedium of village life, Thurmond dreams of joining the Brotherhood of Underworld Adventurers, an elite fraternity of warriors dedicated to the destruction of vampires, trolls, and goblins—the natural enemies of mankind. But since he has no battle experience or combat skills, it looks like he's out of luck.

This all changes when he steals a treasure map and embarks with a group of misfits on a daring quest to win fame and fortune or die trying.

Action-packed, funny, suspenseful, and unpredictable, **Thurmond's Saga** is a heroic tale of loyalty and courage set in a haunting medieval world.

Available at
robertjmackenzie.com
and
amazon.com

CASTLE OF THE RED CONTESSA

Chronicles of the Medieval Underworld, Book 2

ROBERT JOHN MACKENZIE

Distributed by Bublish, Inc

ISBN: 978-1-64704-172-4 Paperback
ISBN: 978-1-64704-173-1 eBook

TO SAM, LARRY, AND CHARLIE

CASTLE OF THE RED
CONTESSA

CONTENTS

GLOSSARY OF CHARACTERS

Lady Agnes de Roache: dead witch

Baidan: self-styled king

Bess: Bodo's wife and Roscoe's household servant

Bodo: Roscoe's man-at-arms

Bombardo: leader of caravans

Dollop: well-fed gaoler

Fishbone: surprisingly knowledgeable river rat

Florio: elf of many talents

Gavin: not the real name of a most mysterious character

Ghleet: shaman of some skill

Giles: butler to Lord Percy Staynes

Father Hieronymus: not-so-humble village priest

Jarvis: purveyor of used and unusual items

Lars: Roscoe's man-at-arms

Lord Torgul Bonelip XXIII: doughty dwarf and Adventurer in good standing

Maybelle: Bess's sister and Roscoe's household servant

Baron Sir Melgwyn de Pudni: cruel despot

Murd: Roscoe's serf

Leticia: luckless victim

Old One: witch of Castle Sathas

Ouichi: Baidan's enforcer

Pozi: plucky village girl

Roscoe Franklin: Thurmond's mentor and Adventurer in good standing

Sarah Staynes: young witch and Thurmond's closest friend and ally

Skrot: Roscoe's serf

Thurmond: would-be Adventurer and our hero

Vilnos: captain of mercenaries

Xortai: bringer of changes

PART 1

A THEFT OF OLD BONES

CHAPTER 1

WEIRD TIMES IN GORGONHOLM

Thurmond was worried. Sarah was up to something, something he probably would not like. For three days now she had been distant and preoccupied. When he asked her about it, her response had been vague and evasive. When she announced at breakfast that she intended to go on a stroll through the forest, he had offered to accompany her, but she declined. She needed, she said, a chance to be alone, to collect her thoughts, to find her feelings. Thurmond did not believe any of this and had followed her at a discreet distance. As he suspected, her steps had taken her not to the forest but straight to the city of Gorgonholm and then up Castle Wynd toward Market Square.

This was the heart of the great city. The outer edges of the square were given to respectable semi-permanent booths from which reputable merchants sold their wares, but the center was a wild labyrinth of crude wooden stalls and shabby canvas rainscreens tied to farm carts. Here peasant families sold their radishes, cabbages, and leeks. Itinerate tinkers plied their trade, and fishwives sang the praises of the day's catch. A group of screaming boys fought a merry battle with horse turds.

Citizens of all castes and professions picked their way through the maze of guy ropes and wagon tongues in search of bargains. Pompous nobles and blustering guildsmen pushed through crowds of sullen apprentices and loud, drunken laborers. The prostitutes did a good bit of business, as they did on every Market Day. So did the deft and canny cutpurse.

Actually, it was quiet for Market Day. No caravans had arrived recently, so there were no swarthy foreign merchants with exotic spices and fine silk cloth from the lands to the east. There were neither dwarves nor elves, though members of those races were sometimes present as they passed through the city on some business or other.

The Blue Friar's cathedral rose on the left, monstrously huge, like a great stone fist demonstrating the supreme authority of the church. Gargoyles gaped open-mouthed along the rooftop. Imposing stone statues flanked the massive, iron-bound doors and frowned with grim disapproval at the bustling Market Day scene before them.

Thurmond concealed himself in the structure's shadowy portico and watched as Sarah made her way to the far side of the square. She was typically quite open about her personal business, so her duplicity made him uncomfortable. What could be prompting her to deceive him in this way?

Sarah was, he knew, entitled to her privacy. He had no control over her comings and goings, no right to thrust himself into a matter from which he had been deliberately excluded. She was not his ladylove. She was just … well … he had no idea how to accurately define their relationship.

The previous summer they had joined forces with an old Adventurer named Roscoe to pillage a hoard of gold from a nest of goblin river-pirates. They had faced deadly peril side by side and saved each other's lives multiple times. They had suffered terrible hardships and defeated fearsome enemies. Such experiences had forged an indelible bond between them.

Trusted friend and ally? Boon companion? Partner in crime?

Certainly, she was all these things, but his feelings for her went well beyond that. It was just that he could not explain, even to himself, exactly what those feelings were. They had been through so much together—why would she deceive him in this way?

Thurmond shrank back further into the dark recess of the portico. Sarah would be furious if she discovered he was following her, but he had to take that chance. Maybe she was in trouble. Maybe something she was afraid to speak of. If so, he would be on hand to come to her aid.

Sarah seemed distinctly nervous as she pushed through the throng of merchants and shoppers. She kept turning her head, scanning the crowd, obviously looking for someone, and growing increasingly agitated when that person failed to appear. Thurmond was more and more positive something was deeply amiss.

She suddenly stopped pacing, stared intently on a small street that opened into the far end of the square, and strode briskly in that direction. Something in her gait seemed unnatural, as if she had to refrain from running toward her assignation.

ᚱ

Sarah was happy. Happy like hell, in fact. She had met someone, someone who could give her what she had been needing for so long. His name was Gavin, and despite his youth, he was a highly skilled magician. Actually, he was not all that young. She guessed his age to be perhaps five-and-twenty, about eight years older than herself. More importantly, his soul seemed old and wise.

Gavin was tall and muscular, which pleased her well, for she too was tall and broad-shouldered. He had shaggy, dark brown hair that fell nearly to his shoulders and even darker eyes—eyes filled with mystery. Not that his appearance was of any import—*nay, nay, nay*. Sarah wanted him to be her mentor in the occult sciences. As a master magician, his thoughts would be far removed from anything like dalliance.

Sarah's most fervent desire was to become an expert practitioner of the magical arts—that and to have her skills recognized through admittance to the local sorcerers' guild, The Most Sacred Fellowship of Spell-casters, Alchemists, Diviners, Sorcerers, Philter-Mixers, and Thaumaturgists of Gorgonholm. Such distinction would enable her to live without having to ask aye or nay from a father or husband.

As the illegitimate daughter of Lord Percy Staynes, Sarah had enjoyed a comfortable, perhaps even pampered, childhood. Her keen intelligence was recognized at an early age, and she had been educated, even in the use of letters. This was indeed an unusual attainment for a girl, and it had been a significant turning point in her life. She became a voracious reader and advanced her learning far beyond the limited scope provided by her tutors.

Late in his life, her father had become an avid collector of ancient books and manuscripts. This was fortunate for her, as it allowed access to scores of moldering volumes stacked on the shelves of his library. There were works of geography, history, philosophy, even poetry. But mostly there were grimoires, treatises on a wide array of arcane subjects—sorcery, divination, even the dreaded and forbidden practice of necromancy. Yellowed papyrus scrolls explained the summoning and controlling of infernal entities. A massive tome with greasy leather bindings provided hundreds of detailed formulas for philters and potions. Another listed the secret names of imps, demons, cacodemons, and archfiends.

Sarah knew from the start she had found her true calling. She was to be a great enchantress, a witch, a *magicatrix*—or whatever a female magic user was called. She set out to read every book in her father's library and was making good headway when, just over a year ago, her studies were interrupted by the sudden need to flee her childhood home.

Her father, Lord Percy Staynes, had experienced a steep decline in health. He was an extremely aged man, and no one expected him to live long. It was no secret that Sarah's half-brother Bartholomew awaited his sire's demise with gleeful anticipation. He lusted for the prestige and wealth that would descend to him along with his father's title. And he had made it plain that his lusts extended in Sarah's direction as well.

So she had fled into the night with a young housebreaker she had caught in the act of pillaging her father's home. This turned out to be Thurmond, who had been hired to steal a magical mirror from her brother. Ironically, they had become friends, and Sarah joined him on his quest for goblin gold.

She, like Thurmond, came away from that adventure with several hundred gold sovereigns, most of which she was currently carrying in a bag tied beneath her skirts. The rest she had invested toward the advancement of her occult skills and knowledge. This entailed the purchase of many odd and unpleasant materials magicians always deem indispensable. There were foul-smelling incenses and even worse essential oils. Then she had needed some liver of sulphur and milk of lead, some goat gall, and a pair of howlet's wings.

The problem remained that Sarah was only a self-taught novice. She was a quick learner, and her magical intuition was quite good, but her workings often went wrong. An ill-conceived spell involving the mummified thumb of a drowned ship-captain had resulted in a terrific blast of wind that nearly sucked her up the chimney. On another occasion she had summoned, entirely by accident, an infestation of small invisible creatures that scratched, bit, and pinched unmercifully, forcing her to flee her workshop for several days until the spell dissipated.

It was clear that if she wanted to advance to mastery level, she would need formal instruction. This typically involved serving as an apprentice and enduring years of abuse at the hands of a magus. Thurmond, who had once been apprenticed to a dyspeptic carpenter, was adamant in his condemnation of this option. Sarah had been dejected, frustrated, and angry over her inability advance in her craft. She had spent a year dabbling on her own but made no real progress. Then she had, by great good fortune, met Gavin, who was to be, it seemed, the answer.

CHAPTER 2

THE COMING OF GAVIN

Sarah's happiness turned to stomach-fluttering nervousness as she entered Market Square. She had first encountered Gavin three days ago on the cramped little street known as Spellcaster's Wynd. Absorbed in her thoughts as she exited a shop of arcane wares, she had not seen him until she bumped into his back.

Instead of the expected rebuke, he had offered her a smile, which led to an extended conversation. She was delighted to learn he, too, was a magic user. Though young, he had studied sorcery, alchemy, and divination under the great masters of the east. Now he had come west to make his fortune. New to the city, he had not as yet made many personal or professional contacts.

Sarah instinctively knew that Gavin could be trusted. She had learned to rely on her intuition, which had never yet led her astray. He was so easy to talk to, to confide in, to trust that she had revealed her unhappy situation. His eyes shone with sympathy as he listened.

Then he made her an astonishing offer. Perhaps they could have a less formal relationship than the traditional binding servitude of apprentice to master. He could not, of course, commit himself until he had time to consider the situation more carefully. They had agreed to meet in three days to finalize the details of their arrangement. She was now on her way to that meeting and was prepared to agree to whatever conditions he might require.

Searching through the crowded square, Sarah spotted Thurmond lurking in the shadows of the cathedral—rather, she spotted his hat. It was conspicuously patterned after the black campaign hats traditionally worn by the Adventurers, though not nearly so broad of brim. As Thurmond was still only a Prospect in that organization, he was not entitled to a genuine Adventurer's hat. This one came as close as he dared.

She should, she knew, be angry with him for following her. Whom she met was none of his business. But her excuses had been feeble—a sudden need for a solitary walk in the forest. Thurmond was far too perceptive to fall for that. Her deception probably hurt and worried him, so she really could not blame him for tagging along. At the same time, she was relieved he had the good sense to hold back. It was almost time for her meeting with Gavin, and if Thurmond were to insist on accompanying her, it would be awkward.

Thurmond was, beyond question, her closest friend and ally. They had an indestructible bond, having repeatedly saved each other from deadly foes and their own folly. They had kissed more than a few times, and she still recalled the intense feelings those moments evoked. But that had been before she met Gavin, so maybe those feelings were somehow less important now.

Sarah made her way across the square, passing an aged beggar with no feet and a young girl with a basket of dried pansies. Someone tugged at her sleeve—a lean, bent man with a thin, squeaky voice and a blind, milky eye.

"Tell your fortune, girlie? Only two farthings."

She pulled away, angry.

"Hands off! Right now! Or you'll regret it!"

Sarah was only a novice witch, but she was certainly capable of dealing with a street huckster. The man released her sleeve but pushed his face into hers, pointing at his ruined eye.

"This sees the other side real good, girlie, sure it do! You wanna find out if your sweetheart really loves you? Half price for you—only one copper farthing!"

Sarah spun away and quickened her step. Market Square teemed with pitiful charlatans claiming to be skilled in the magical sciences, preying upon ignorant farmers who came to the city to peddle their produce. Such swindlers sold useless luck charms and love spells, offered fraudulent séances with dead loved ones, and removed non-existent curses. Sarah was uncertain whether to be appalled or amused.

At the far side of the square, she paused at an inn called The Golden Eunuch, just where Spellcaster's Wynd began its narrow and twisty passage toward the city's east wall. Also known as Street of Spells or simply Spell Street, this was the lane in which Gorgonholm's respectable magic users, those possessing legitimate psychic powers, kept their shops and laboratorii.

Each of the many crafts and professions in the city had its designated section. There was a street of jewelers and one for cordwainers, an avenue of weavers and another for milliners and haberdashers. Armorers and weaponsmiths were up along the north wall.

Beyond the city's west wall ran the great Mad River, where riverboats of all types and sizes were tied to the docks and quays that lined its banks. Slaughterers, tanners, and tallow boilers were relegated to the narrow strip of land between the city wall and the river. The stately townhouses of the city's gentry sat atop the great hill that rose in the city center, happily beyond the worst of the stench produced by the noisome streets below.

Sarah was familiar with the shops and people of Spell Street. Madame Gorko could read the future by staring into a bowl of water. For a silver penny, Master Samwise Twist would cast a fair horoscope. Shops large and small sold every nasty item a witch or wizard might need.

Sarah disliked being made to stand and wait on a corner, but Gavin had refused to reveal the location of his residence, claiming that she not yet sufficiently advanced in the Art to enter his personal spiritual sanctuary. Her raw psychic emanations would, he claimed, disrupt the ethereal harmonies. He did, however, agree to meet her on Market Square.

Sarah tried to amuse herself by watching the ebb and flow of the crowd, but she grew steadily restive as the minutes ticked by. She figured she must look like a bumpkin who had come to town for the market. To amuse herself, she contemplated the signboard swinging above her head—a fat, large-breasted, effeminate male with faded vermillion skin. The Golden Eunuch. She did not understand why inns always had such disgusting names. Thurmond, Roscoe, and Torgul frequented a horrible place called The Severed Head. There was also The Drowned Rat and The Randy Bear. *Ugh!*

Men, she decided, must take pleasure in such disturbing names, but she knew not why. She favored a more dignified appellation, something like The Quill and Scroll. But nay—that was a bit staid even for her. The Rose and Hare perchance…

Then Gavin stood before her, and all such trivial considerations evaporated from her mind.

"Hello Sarah, I'm happy to see you."

His speech, as before, was subdued, hardly above a whisper. And there were those eyes again, so dark as to be almost black and so very penetrating. Sarah felt as if they could see right into her soul.

"Oh, Gavin…aye. I'm here. I mean, I'm happy to see you too. I was just…"

Her voice trailed off. She felt foolish and childish and angry with herself. She always seemed to get tongue-tied at times when she most wanted to appear intelligent and poised.

She could not help being impressed by him. Most magic users were gawky, scraggly, ill-mannered buffoons. They boasted of their great and terrible powers, yet acted more like petulant children than spiritual masters. Their outlandish robes, habitually embellished with absurd charms and unsavory symbols, were perhaps intended to seem exotic or glamorous. Sarah found them singularly unbecoming.

Gavin was different. He was elegantly and neatly dressed. His tunic, a rich dark green trimmed with blue, revealed muscular legs in tight black hose. Straight of back and deep of chest, he was indeed remarkably well formed in comparison to other magicians. His hands were large and looked powerful. He was almost *too* attractive. It was distracting.

Sarah was here to discuss a serious professional issue, not to moon over him like a love-struck housemaid. He would, in any circumstance, be far too cerebral to take an interest in such base sensual concerns. It was, she felt, a mark of immaturity to allow herself to be so consumed. Fortunately, Gavin seemed not to notice her discomposure.

"I pray you weren't forced to wait long. I came as soon as I could. You see, I was engaged in a most delicate operation. Please try to understand."

Sarah regained her composure and her voice. She was not one to remain befuddled for long.

"Of course I understand. And you aren't late. I have just now arrived as well."

"Excellent. Then may I suggest we move to a place more private to discuss the matter that lies between us. I would as lief not have every shopboy and housewife know of my private affairs. Let us enter the cathedral. It should be standing empty, with everyone so intent on the market."

Sarah nodded, and they started across the square toward the huge, glowering edifice. Gavin's stride was brisk and determined, just the opposite of the slinking shuffle affected by most in his profession. Sarah liked that. She saw no reason why magicians should sacrifice proper deportment or render themselves unattractive.

Men often found her comely, and for good cause. Her features were clear and regular, her brown eyes large and bright with wit. Her hair was also brown—though not as dark as Gavin's—and lustrous with a slight natural curl. Though not particularly vain of her looks, Sarah did not conceal or deny them. She was wise enough to know that beauty is transitory, that age and ugliness must eventually arrive.

Sarah and Gavin entered the vast, yawning cavern of the cathedral. Sarah was glad to discover Thurmond was no longer in the portico. He must have sidled away when he saw them coming. As Gavin had predicted, no one was inside. Even friars enjoyed the market days. The light was dim, and the air smelled vaguely of mold. The ancient and imposing edifice always filled Sarah with a sense of morbid dread, which she supposed was exactly what it was designed to do.

The long nave led them between rows of sarcophagi, each topped with a remarkably lifelike effigy of the deceased—presumably the cathedral's former bishops. Their faces bore identical looks of sour condemnation. Small side chambers held the tombs of the noblest families of Gorgonholm. Their heraldic achievements—dusty shields, rusted swords, and dented helmets—hung above the crypts of knights long dead.

Gavin led Sarah to one such chamber. When he spoke, his voice was low and gentle.

"Here, I think, we can speak our minds openly and without interruption. Now, Sarah, I have pondered well the possibility of taking you as my—I don't really know what you would be—not an apprentice but neither a colleague. Perhaps you'll simply be a pupil and, I suppose, something of an assistant. I consulted my minions beyond the Veil. You will be pleased to learn they are favorably disposed toward you."

Sarah was glad to hear this but could only guess as to who or what these *minions* might be. She wished he would hurry up and get to the point. Unfortunately, he was not yet ready to do so.

"Have you considered well, girl, just what it really means to align yourself with one such as me? I appear much, much younger than I am in years, for I have studied the forgotten wisdom of the east and learned many of its most closely guarded secrets. The path is extremely difficult. The degree of discipline and courage required is almost unimaginable. Knowledge and power such as mine come only with great sacrifice. Are you certain you are prepared for that?"

Sarah replied with only the slightest hesitation, just a tiny catch in her breath.

"I am certain. This is what I've wanted for as long as I can remember. I am willing to devote my life to the pursuit of knowledge under your tutelage. When can we begin?"

Gavin stared hard into her eyes.

"It's not that simple, girl. You must first prove yourself. Show me your resolve is firm, your spirit clear, and your body strong—that you are truly as devoted as you claim to be."

This time her response was immediate. There was no catch in her breath. "What must I do?"

"You are familiar, of course, with the occult properties of the number three?"

Sarah was aware all numbers had magical associations, but she had no detailed knowledge of such things. She only knew *three* was quite common in the old tales told to children by their grandams—there were always three evil witches or three helpful fairies granting three wishes—but she was not about to admit her ignorance to him.

"Aye, I know the meaning of that number."

Gavin continued as if she had not replied. His voice rose. It was the first time she had heard him speak in anything but a low, controlled tone. The words resonated from the chambers stone walls.

"It is the eternal triad, the equilibrium of the unities. The number of ambition, magic, and intuition. Of spirit, mind, and body. Of birth, life, and death. Creation, preservation, and destruction. Past, present, future. And as such, it is the number of new beginnings."

He now paused, regaining his typically subdued demeanor.

"You, Sarah, must face a test of three. Did you attend to the matter we previously spoke of?"

"Aye, I have it with me now."

"Then consider the first trial already completed, for you have amply demonstrated sincere resolve."

He leaned close, taking her shoulders in both his large hands.

"Now I will impart to you the exact nature of your second test."

CHAPTER 3

SARAH'S BARGAIN

Thurmond left the cathedral and positioned himself behind a cart loaded with sacks of giant beets. From there he had a good view of Sarah standing across the square in front of The Golden Eunuch, and he was pretty sure she could not see him. He was growing ever more suspicious and distrustful of whatever business had brought her here.

Thurmond had no intention of interfering with her dealings. He had no desire to control her, and she would not permit it if he tried. But something in her recent behaviors made him uneasy. What could possibly be so sensitive that she would keep it from him? Seeing her in the square, he resolved to keep a watchful eye open, just in case.

One look at Gavin was sufficient. Thurmond took an immediate dislike to the tall, handsome stranger. Something in the man's self-satisfied smile and stylish garb aroused Thurmond's ire. He looked like a man with something to sell. Nay, that was not exactly right. More like a man *hiding* the fact he had something to sell. Thurmond looked on in a state of great discomfort as the couple entered the cathedral. Knowing Sarah would be furious over any interference, he suppressed an urge to follow them in. He suddenly felt childish and ashamed, as if he were betraying her somehow. But hell, should he just abandon her to the machinations of some fancy fellow?

Or maybe he was just jealous.

He left the beet wagon and took a seat on some steps by Castle Wynd.

The cathedral's huge doors were still in his sight, so he would know when they emerged. If she headed home afterwards, she would come upon him, and he would let her think he was merely dawdling at the market. But if she and that wretch went off together, he was unsure *what* to do.

The wait was painful and seemed interminable. As he sat, he recalled the unlikely events of the past year, the fantastic turn of Fortune's Wheel that had put him on the threshold of fulfilling a lifelong dream, of accomplishing a goal that had once seemed so distant as to be unachievable. A year ago, he had been nothing more than a runaway apprentice, a young man of seventeen with neither useful skills nor social connections.

But he had been driven by an abiding desire to win wealth and renown as a member of the Brotherhood of Underworld Adventurers, an elite warrior fraternity sworn to the destruction of fell creatures such as ogres, vampyres, goblins, trolls, and their ilk. Because such species possessed an instinctive hostility toward humankind, slaying them served the common good. Adventurers were supreme fighters and utterly fearless. They had to be, for they boldly invaded the creatures' subterranean lairs, slew whatever inhabitants they found within, and availed themselves of their accumulated treasures.

The risks were enormous, but so were the rewards, for fell creatures, like humans, had an innate need to amass great piles of gold and other valuables. Adventurers lucky enough to survive often became rich and famous. Such was Thurmond's greatest dream, and it looked like it might be coming true. Thurmond had begun as a lowly hang-around, a casual associate with no official status within the Adventurers. But after proving himself in a number of deadly encounters—and especially after securing a pouch of rare gems— he had been promoted to the rank of Prospect, or prospective member. Two seasoned Adventurers, Roscoe and his companion Torgul Bonelip, a doughty dwarf, became Thurmond's designated mentors. The day could not be far off when he would be awarded full membership into the Gorgonholm chapter.

Thurmond's musing came to an abrupt end when Sarah and the fancy fellow exited the cathedral. He was relieved to perceive no degree of intimacy between them. They neither touched nor exchanged yearning looks. Sarah spoke briefly, nodded, and turned in the direction of home. She walked directly toward where Thurmond reclined on the steps, so he stretched out his legs to affect the attitude of casual loiterer. He had, he would tell her, grown bored of the market and decided to rest here awhile before heading home. The story was plausible. She would have no reason to disbelieve it.

Drawing closer, Sarah waved and smiled. He returned the gesture, still feeling a bit guilty for his snoopery. Her smile broadened as she approached.

"I see you're keeping an eye on me. How do you like Gavin? He's an attractive man, don't you think?"

Thurmond was caught entirely off his guard.

"What? You don't think...I mean...I'm not..."

"Not spying on me? Come on, I saw you lurking by the cathedral and then peeking out from behind that beet cart. Now you're pretending to be lounging on these steps like a drunken market day reveler. I know you better. You want to know what I'm up to."

Denial being pointless, Thurmond cast all pretenses aside.

"That's right. I was worried about you, and I don't like the looks of that fancy fellow."

"Then you're lucky you won't be having to deal with him, but never mind that. I'm glad you're here. I have a task to fulfill, and I need your help."

Sarah explained her test, but she was careful not to reveal the full details of her bargain with Gavin for fear Thurmond would misunderstand and disapprove. He was very protective of her, as she was of him. He might not fully appreciate how important this opportunity was to her. She also knew he would be jealous of Gavin, though for no reason. Her relationship with her mentor was by necessity spiritual rather than physical.

In sooth, Sarah was equally jealous of Thurmond's affections toward other girls. He had named his horse Millie, and their village blacksmith had a daughter of the same name. She could well imagine the transactions Thurmond was having with her. Nonetheless, she decided to set his mind at rest.

"Look, Thurmond, trust me in this. You have naught to worry about. Nothing—nobody—is going to come between you and me. My association with Gavin is strictly that of student and teacher, and will remain so. Nothing more, ever. I give you my word."

Thurmond was visibly relieved to hear this.

"I do trust you and take you at your word. Thank you. You have released me from some most unpleasant thoughts."

"Wondrous! You'll help me then? I came with you on your adventure, after all. Will you come on mine?"

"When have I ever refused you?"

"Never, my friend, but it would be wrong to take you for granted, would it not?"

"What must we do?"

"Nothing much, only break into the cathedral at night, find the secret entrance to a forgotten crypt, and bring back some old bones."

"Grave robbing! Old bones! Necromancers use old bones! If we get caught, they'll hang us for certain."

"Calm yourself. Old bones have lots of magical uses, not just for necromancy. And they'll not catch us. The goblins and kobolds couldn't catch us last year. We were too good for them. This job won't be any riskier, and I have a new spell that will create a perfect distraction."

Thurmond remained skeptical.

"I dislike the idea of stealing from the Church. That must be a great sin, don't you think?"

"I think the Church has gained all its wealth by stealing from other people. The Blue Friars were certainly prompt to demand their tithe of gold from our adventure, as I hope you recall. Anyway, we're not taking anything valuable, just some moldy old bones."

"I don't like that either. What about the spirit of the dead person? I don't want to be haunted by an angry ghost."

"That person has been dead far too long for the spirit to be still lingering about or fretting over its bones."

Thurmond remained uneasy, unconvinced.

"When, pray tell, would you have us do this desperate deed?"

"Tonight."

"Tonight? Nay! Too soon! Let us wait a bit and devise a thoughtful plan."

"I'd rather not wait, Thurmond. I…"

She knew she had to tell him the whole story. He had a right to know.

"Look, I want no secrets between us, so there's something I must tell you. Gavin placed a *geas* upon me."

Thurmond was shocked and offended but did his best to keep himself in check.

"And what would that be?"

"It's a spell of command. I have to follow through with my task or I'll start to suffer ill effects."

"He bewitched you? I will go find him at once! Either the spell will be lifted or his head will…"

"Nay, nay, please listen. I allowed him to do it. It's to ensure that I carry out my part of the bargain. I had to agree to it. It was the only way."

Thurmond, angry and frustrated, waxed sarcastic.

"Your word alone was not sufficient for this supreme master of all wisdom?"

"Please, Thurmond, great magi have earned certain privileges. They're not like you and me."

"What will happen if you fail to complete your task, Sarah?"

"From what I've read about geas spells, I'd probably start having horrific dreams, followed by bouts of the vapors, then a brain fever, and finally, I imagine, a painful, lingering death."

"Then we really have to do this thing?"

"Aye, and the sooner the better."

"What does it feel like, this spell?"

"Like naught, nothing at all, neither now nor when he cast it. But should I begin to neglect my obligation, it will take effect. Once I finish the task, the spell dissipates."

"Is there anything else you haven't told me? Any other little details you've left out?"

"None I can think of, perhaps only that I gave Gavin most of my gold."

Sarah read the look on her friend's face.

"I know what you're thinking, Thurmond, but please don't jump to conclusions. Gavin is new in Gorgonholm and out of coin. He needs something to get himself established here. He's my teacher, so he's entitled to payment."

Thurmond again fought to keep his anger under control. He had grown up in poverty and was always careful with money—that is, until his newfound wealth awakened a hunger for acquisition.

As a hang-around, Thurmond, like Sarah, had received several hundred golden sovereigns after their previous adventure. Unfortunately, this wealth, immense as it was, seemed to run through his fingers. His first purchase had been a simple, practical broadsword, nothing too expensive. Next he bought a new suit of clothes, then several more. Was he not, after all, entitled to flaunt his success to some degree? And did he not look fine in his new broad-brimmed hat?

Then there had been a horse. Not the prancing warhorse he had always wanted, but a sturdy, broad-chested cob of great endurance and far more practical for his purposes. Of course, there had to be a saddle, bridle, and other associated tack.

It had been the armor that took most of his coin. He had always lusted for a complete harness of shining plate but settled for a light open-faced helmet, a mail coif, and a thigh-length mailshirt known as a habergeon. Even such basic gear was expensive because the people who typically bought armor—nobles, Adventurers, mercenaries—had the coin to afford it. Thurmond had been so thrilled to possess his own armor that he spent the last of his gold without a second thought. Acquiring it was, after all, the fulfillment of a lifelong dream. He could not, therefore, find fault with Sarah for squandering her coin on the vile fancy fellow who had promised to fulfill her greatest aspiration.

He shrugged in resignation.

"Surely the cathedral will be well guarded."

"Most likely, but I have something in mind."

CHAPTER 4

INTO THE CATHEDRAL

The great doors of the cathedral were locked after the final evening service, and most of its interior lights were extinguished. Only the candles surrounding the massive stone idol of Charon the All-Father still burned. A porter was on duty throughout the night, should anyone seek entrance beyond routine hours.

The cathedral's defenses were the same as those of any fortified building. Make no mistake, the cathedral was a fortress as well as a place of worship. In addition to the porter, a dozen young friars were stationed in a guardroom just inside the main doors. Though permitted to sleep, these men remained clothed and kept their weapons close at hand. They were ready for immediate duty should the porter ring the alarm bell.

The cathedral was designed to withstand a determined assault. Its stone walls were thick and strong, its heavy oaken doors braced with iron. The large stained-glass windows were crisscrossed with heavy iron bars, and narrow openings in the walls provided shooting ports for friars armed with crossbows. The structure was rumored to be guarded further by an array of subtle, spiritual defenses. No one knew what these might consist of, and it would have been remarkably unwise to inquire about them. The business of the Blue Friars was best left to the friars themselves.

Charonism was by no means a pacifist religion. Clerics were well versed in the use of weapons and quick to use them in defense of their own interests.

Over the centuries, much blood had been shed as the various denominations—the predominant Blues, the ambitious Blacks, the conniving Whites, and an array of others—had contended for wealth and power.

At present, the sectarian rivalries had subsided into a resentful truce. The Blues, being the largest and most influential denomination, controlled the cathedral and received an annual tribute from the others. The Blues also held sway over a great many farms, villages, and even entire towns throughout the kingdom.

r

Thurmond and Sarah huddled in a dark niche of Market Square. It was now largely deserted, the merchants and farm families having long since packed up and gone home. They sat swaddled in ragged blankets, disguised as poor peasants stranded in the city. It would not do to be recognized while lurking about the cathedral on this night. When the lights of the Golden Eunuch were extinguished and the last drunkard staggered off toward home, they moved.

A large courtyard surrounded by a high wall extended from the cathedral's north side. A pair of tall wooden gates surmounted with sharp iron spikes opened into the large cathedral complex. There were dormitories, a refectory, a scriptorium, and an armory, as well as kitchens, stables, storerooms, and workshops. The cathedral was in many ways a self-contained community.

Sarah produced her wand from beneath the blanket tied around her shoulders. Gripping it in both hands, she chanted a brief incantation and then touched it to the lock of a small, man-size door built into the courtyard gates. The lock gave a sharp *click*, and the portal swung silently open. This was one of Sarah's new spells—a knock spell. She was pleased it functioned so well, for it was her first time applying it to a real purpose. Spells cast in actual field conditions rarely worked as they did in the workshop.

She whispered to Thurmond.

"See how well it went? I told you so, didn't I? Now be quick. I don't think guards are posted in the courtyard, but be careful. You know what to do while I get my other spell ready."

Thurmond did indeed know what to do. The courtyard gates had stood open during the day, allowing friars to come and go without hindrance, but also giving him a good look inside. Two large hay wagons, obviously a delivery of fodder for the cathedral's horses, had been driven inside and parked. Thurmond now used flint and steel to strike sparks to this hay. Being bone dry, it leaped into a jolly blaze.

Then the screaming started. This was Sarah's doing. Her spell invoked the bone-chilling shrieks of children in mortal terror. She had a natural talent as an illusionist, so this spell was easy. The knock spell, requiring psychic manipulation of material substance, was a much more challenging feat.

The two ran across the courtyard to conceal themselves behind an ornamental shrubbery by the cathedral's side door. They assumed the friars, alerted by the screams, would leave a door open as they rushed out to fight the blaze. Sarah and Thurmond could then enter through the unguarded entrance. It seemed like a good plan.

Alas, even good plans often go awry. Unbeknownst to Thurmond and Sarah, the hay was not the only delivery the friars received that day. Concealed beneath the burning hay, lay a consignment of *uisge*, the potent distilled beverage produced by the Keltin tribes on the opposite side of the Mad River. Though highly popular, uisge remained illegal. Thus, Bishop Boniface's consignment had arrived clandestinely.

With darkness falling, the cellarer, a thin-faced friar named Hubert, had elected to wait until morning to unload the heavy casks. He knew there was to be pease porridge for supper that evening, and he did not want to be late—he liked his hot. Friar Hubert was entirely unaware that one of the casks, in its journey over rough roads in a springless wagon, had sprung a leak. A steady drip of the precious liquid was now making a puddle in the bed of the wagon. When sparks from the burning hay reached it, the entire cargo erupted in a furious ball of fire.

So intense was the heat that the branches of overhanging trees took flame and spread the fire across the courtyard. Various wooden storerooms and workshops were set alight. The gates blazed lustily. Burning bits of hay floated in the air. Thurmond and Sarah feared they might be roasted alive.

Aroused by the high-pitched wailing, the leapt from their beds. Doors flew open on all sides as they ran to fight the conflagration, but the flames were too big, too hot. They could only stand and stare, utterly dumbfounded by the terrible sight of the courtyard engulfed in flames. Sarah had assumed the friars would be moved by the squeals of frightened children and would at once run to their aid. But instead the superstitious clerics took the screams for the shrieking of demons and believed themselves under attack by the legions of Hell. They immediately ran back into their rooms and locked the doors behind them, praying for divine intervention to stifle the flames.

Luckily, the young friars of the guard detail were made of stouter stuff. Roused from their cots by the porter, they charged through the side door exactly as Sarah had hoped. The porter came last and, in his excitement, neglected to shut the door behind him. Thurmond and Sarah went through it in an instant.

They crossed the nave and entered the chamber holding the tombs of the de Roache family, one of the oldest and noblest in Gorgonholm. This was the very room in which Sarah had her conversation with Gavin earlier that day. She now moved to a large stone sarcophagus on which rested a full-size bronze effigy of an armored knight with a dog beneath his feet.

While Thurmond lit a candle, Sarah fiddled with the dog's paws. There was a *click*, and a panel opened on the side of the sarcophagus. She and Thurmond recoiled from a blast of dank air, before bending to look into the opening. There was just enough room for a person to crawl inside and descend a set of iron rungs set into the side of a vertical shaft that resembled a well.

Sarah started toward it, but Thurmond pulled her back.

"I'll go first."

The rungs were cold, damp, and slippery. He held the candle in his left hand, making the descent even more treacherous. He glanced up and saw Sarah right behind him, her foot on the rung just over his head. The distance to the bottom was perhaps four times the height of a man.

They dropped into a narrow passage cut into the solid limestone that formed the bedrock of the city. The citizens of Gorgonholm had for centuries mined this stone for building purposes. The city walls, the cathedral, City Keep, and the large mansions of the aristocrats were all constructed with this material. As a result, the city sat upon a labyrinth of winding tunnels. Some sections served as storerooms, but most were blocked off and forgotten.

Trespassing in the tunnels was strictly forbidden. The authorities did not allow thieves and rebels such a convenient and efficient hideout. Nonetheless certain groups, those requiring privacy for forbidden rites and clandestine business transactions, knew the secret entrances. Dark rumors swirled of unspeakable activities carried out beneath the city streets.

Sarah had received specific instructions from her mentor. He told her how to open the hidden panel on the side of the crypt and where, once they arrived below, to find the tomb they sought. His instructions were explicit—*Go straight to the end. Do not turn off right or left.* The tunnels, he emphasized, were dangerous. Not only did unpleasant creatures reside within, it was quite possible to become lost in the endless maze. Many people had disappeared forever within its inky depths. Gavin refused to tell Sarah how he knew so much about the Catacombs, but his information was clearly accurate. The spring-catch opened the false tomb exactly as he had said, and the underground passage ran straight and true, just as he described. Other passages branched off at irregular intervals, which Sarah ignored as instructed.

They came at last to a doorless chamber that held a single marble sarcophagus inscribed with the name Lady Agnes de Roache. The atmosphere was thick and clammy. Fat drops of moisture seeped through the porous limestone ceiling, falling with uncanny accuracy on the backs of their necks. Thurmond had to fight an urge to flee.

He whispered in Sarah's ear.

"Why was this woman buried down here instead of up in the family vault?"

Sarah was every bit as frightened as her companion. Something about the chamber, something indefinable, inspired great instinctive dread.

"She was a notorious witch. The friars denied her burial in the cathedral, but her family was so powerful they were permitted to put her down here."

Thurmond recoiled in horror.

"We're stealing witch bones? Have you gone entirely mad?"

"That's why Gavin wants them. They have special properties. Come on, we're here. Let's get the damned things and get out."

Together they pushed the heavy marble lid of the sarcophagus to one side, revealing the naked skeleton of Lady Agnes. A gold medallion, heavily embossed with mystic symbols, lay where her neck had once been. Beyond that and bones, the sepulcher was empty.

Sarah spread her blanket out on the floor. She scooped up the bones and medallion, placed them in its center, and tied up the corners in a beggar's bundle. Intent on this task, neither she nor Thurmond was aware of the entity manifesting behind them and cutting them off from the doorway. Its attack was both sudden and strong. Thurmond and Sarah were seized by debilitating stomach cramps that doubled them over and dropped them to the floor. Thurmond struggled to rise, to draw his dagger, but his limbs had lost all strength. Vomit rolled listlessly from his open mouth.

Sarah fared no better. She sprawled on the floor deathly ill as the thing sucked the life-force out of her. Her mind blurred, making it was impossible to cast spells. She knew she was dying. The air grew colder and colder. The assailant was naught but a thin shred of luminescence floating by the door, a faint smear of pale light, a mere wisp of radiance in the darkness, yet deadly as a viper.

It was Thurmond who saved them. Knowing naught of spectral entities, he could think of nothing else to do. With the last of his strength and with his consciousness slipping away, he groped in the bundle of bones until his fingers closed on the medallion. Perhaps it had some kind of power over evil spirits. He thrust it toward the glowing thing and wheezed out a single word.

"Begone."

And lo! Quite unexpectedly, the thing was no more. The attack was over.

Thurmond felt his blood once more flow through his veins. Soon he was able to raise himself on hands and knees. Wiping the puke from his lips, he reached out to his companion.

"Sarah...Sarah...are you still alive? It's gone...I think it's gone ...."

"Aye, it's gone. I'll be all right. Just give me a moment. Oh, God's curses! I think I've soiled myself."

"What was that thing?"

"Don't know. Can you get the bundle? We must get away."

The pair tottered from the chamber as quickly as they were able, returning the way they had come. Though their strength was slowly coming back, they were left exhausted and enfeebled by the psychic attack. The specter, whatever it was, had come very near to sucking out the last of their vital energy. The encounter had been a damned close-run thing.

Sarah was about to scale the rungs when Thurmond stopped her.

"What do we do if the cathedral's full of friars? What will we tell them?"

"I don't know, but we've got to get out of here. I can feel that thing behind us somewhere. It's following us. Let's go!"

When they re-entered the cathedral, they found it teeming with people, not only friars but also dozens of townspeople who had assembled to fight the blaze. Men and women ran up and down the smoke-filled nave. They carried buckets, wet blankets, and long-handled hooks—the traditional weapons against conflagration. No one paid any mind as Sarah and Thurmond, coughing and choking as if afflicted by smoke, exited the main doors, which now stood wide open.

Once in Market Square, Sarah took the bundle from Thurmond.

"I must take this to Gavin. He lives just up Spell Street."

"I'll come with you."

"Nay, I must go alone. But wait here. I'll be back directly, I promise. Please just trust me. I won't be long."

And with that, she disappeared into the dark.

Thurmond was very unhappy about being left behind. He did not trust this Gavin, whom Sarah seemed to find so wonderful. It hurt to be excluded, particularly after what he and Sarah had just been through together, and especially considering he had just saved her life. But there was nothing for it but to wait, so he resumed his previous position on the steps and did just that.

True to her word, Sarah soon rejoined him. She, too, was annoyed.

"I don't know what's going on, Thurmond. Gavin told me I could get word to him at this place down on Spell Street. It's some kind of private alehouse, a dark little hole of a place. Didn't even have a signboard. They responded very strangely when I asked for Gavin, like they didn't want to admit knowing him. When I persisted, they finally sent the potboy to fetch him. They refused to tell me where he lives."

"You gave him the bones?"

"Aye, and the medallion.

"The medallion too? Why? It was probably pretty valuable."

"That was the deal—to bring back whatever was in the tomb."

"What happens now?"

"I have to meet him tomorrow night for test number three."

"A test in three parts? I like this not at all."

Thurmond had heard that line before. He had once been subjected to a similar triple test that had been nothing more than a devious scheme to deceive him. He wanted to scold Sarah for being naïve, but he knew that would be pointless. She was determined to go forward, so there was nothing for it but to go along with her.

He also thought her ambition was keeping her from seeing the truth about her fancy fellow. Then again, maybe he was just jealous.

GRIM TIMES IN GRIMSGARD

Roscoe was unhappy. His distress stemmed partially from his awareness that he *should* be happy. He had everything he had always wanted. He was, though a commoner, the de facto Lord of Grimsgard. He had attained a degree of comfort, security, and respect that few men of his station ever hoped to achieve. He could, should he so choose, spend the rest of the day sitting in the shade with a tankard of ale in his hand. No one could say him nay. So why was he not happy?

He had many reasons to rejoice. Though he was no longer a young man—his once auburn hair and beard were streaked with gray—he was sufficiently active and healthy to revive his career as an Adventurer. This had been curtailed several years ago by a savage blow to the hip that left him with a profound limp. It had seemed at the time that his monster-slaying days were over, so he resigned himself to a dreary existence selling fruit on Market Square. But then an eager young lad named Thurmond had lured him back into a life of adventure.

Their quest had been long and difficult. After a series of desperate encounters, they had won a great store of gold only to lose it again. But their luck had turned when Thurmond discovered a small packet filled with gems. These were not ordinary gems but the heirloom jewels of the powerful

Mortimer family. Earl Ralf, Roscoe's feudal overlord, was a Mortimer, so was Tancred, King of Poitiers. In a complicated and rather duplicitous bargain, the gems were returned to the Mortimers. Roscoe was rewarded with a deed to a small towerhouse and the village of Grimsgard, where Roscoe, Thurmond, Sarah, and Torgul now resided.

The adventure had brought him a life of ease and privilege. He was now a franklin, a man of common birth who had won wealth and become the proprietor of a small feudal fief. But instead of bursting with pride, Roscoe was filled with dark dismay. His problem, he realized, was that he could not act like a noble. He cared far too much for the prosperity of his property and people. Nobles, those born to gentility, took their holdings for granted and cared less for their tenants than they did for their livestock. Their land and tenants were naught but a source of income. Roscoe, born to poverty, did not share their inborn nonchalance. He was harrowed when his affairs did not go well.

And things were *not* going well at Grimsgard. The winter had been long, the spring late, and the summer cold, so the fields yielded far less than expected. His hogs did not fatten properly. The milk of the cows was thin, and the cheese it made was sour. Many of the fowl died of a mysterious pip. People whispered of a curse upon Grimsgard.

Roscoe's larger problem was with his serfs. A contingent of serfs—forty bedraggled men, women, and children—had come with his parcel of land, which had been owned by the despotic Lord Drakar. He found them in a deplorable state, half-starved, diseased, almost naked.

As a man of humble station, Roscoe would not continue the dire oppression the upper classes routinely inflicted on the lowest. He was the son of a fruit vendor and a cider maker, and had expected to follow the family trade. But he had, through his own courage, skill, and resolve, given himself a much better life. He was determined to give the same chance to his tenants.

He felt great pity for these poor blighted souls and set about to improve their dismal condition. Those who showed aptitude were allowed to enter a trade—blacksmith, cooper, tanner, thatcher. Children possessing wit were sent, at Roscoe's expense, for lessons at the cathedral school. Most important, he derived an entirely unprecedented scheme in which workers who displayed initiative or diligence would receive more than a customary share of the fief's annual yield.

This was an unheard-of innovation. By custom, all but a small percentage of a fief's crops and livestock belonged to the lord of the manor. To share it with the brainless drudges who tilled his soil was to flout a thousand years of tradition. According to some, it was to defy the will of God, the great bald-pated Charon, and God's will was strictly enforced by the nobles and priests, who owned and controlled almost everything.

Roscoe's problem did not, however, come from resentful nobles or clergymen. His great scheme had been disrupted by his own tenants, the very people he sought to help. Once freed from the cruelty of Lord Drakar de la Pole, they lapsed into lethargy and surliness.

No amount of gentle admonishment or even slightly forceful prodding made them see how much their lives had changed. Their souls, it seemed, were dead after so many years of crushing oppression. There had been too many generations with no hopes, no dreams, no future. By law and custom, if one was born a serf, one lived and died a serf. They knew no reason to hope for anything else. Their one prayer was for an early death as an escape from their earthly sorrows.

Roscoe's tenants were too broken. They could not grasp that they could benefit from working hard. That they might aspire to something beyond the hauling of dung and plowing of fields. That their children could learn their letters and find gainful employment in the city. Such thoughts were not even in their dreams. Accustomed to the driving force of the lash and club, the serfs fell idle when such motivations were no longer offered. Hardened by the brutality of Drakar, Roscoe's benevolence was mistaken for weakness. Thus, they stole, lied, and shirked.

Things in Grimsgard were not going well. Roscoe's grand scheme had been expensive. He had paid the tuition for students who never attended a day of lessons. He had provided tools and materials to would-be craftsmen who sold them for whatever they would bring and spent the proceeds on ale. Roscoe watched in dismay as his field hands lazed rather than plowed.

Autumn would soon arrive with winter not far behind. The year's scant harvest meant he would have to buy food to keep his people fed. There was no other way to keep the gray wolf of starvation from their doors. The problem was, he did not have the coin to buy the required victuals. Perhaps he, he thought, could borrow from Thurmond. The lad was always so good about lending him a bit of gold. The old Adventurer was certain he could count on Thurmond.

Torgul, unlike Roscoe, was a noble by birth. His name and title, Lord Torgul Bonelip XXIII, was duly inscribed on the Roll of Peerage of the dwarves of Spear Mountain. He was a lineal descendent of the legendary Torgul the Great, whose name he bore, and Borik the Bold, whose name was celebrated with almost equal acclaim.

But despite his prestigious lineage, Torgul, like Roscoe, had known hardship. Almost all dwarves could claim some sort of illustrious ancestry, so a title of nobility carried no special privilege or advantage. In Dwarf-land, possessing rank did not typically translate to possessing wealth.

Torgul had, long ago, been forced by desperation to seek his fortune in the lands of men, where dwarves were generally disliked and often refused admittance even at humble inns. Despite the narrow attitudes of humans, his fierce loyalty, and indomitable fortitude had led to his admission to the Adventurers. He was the first and only dwarf to win the black campaign hat.

In this role, he had met Roscoe, who, being of liberal mind, had no objections to befriending a non-human. Together they joined Thurmond and Sarah on their quest, during which he had proven himself a most worthy companion. But now Torgul was frustrated and angry. As a dwarf, he was by nature diligent and creative, consumed by an inner need to build, devise, and repair. When he arrived at Grimsgard, the village was in a lamentable state of dilapidation, as the previous owner had taken no interest in the well-being of her tenants or the upkeep of her property.

Torgul fell to work on the instant. His first task was to refurbish the decrepit blacksmith shop and produce tools for the idle serfs. With this accomplished, he set them to work replacing the rotted timbers of the huts and outbuildings. Loads of clay were hauled up from the river, mixed with straw and dung, and slathered over the crumbling wattle and daub walls. Roofs were re-thatched with bundles of river reeds.

The dwarf was dismayed by the serfs' lack of motivation. Even when repairing their own homes, their work was slipshod unless he was standing over them, directing their every move. They seemed not to care if their roofs were leaky or if the doors sagged in the frames. Such carelessness was incomprehensible and deeply troubling to the industrious dwarf.

Then there had been the affair with the Brown Friars. Torgul took great pride in his reputation as a brewer of fine mead. He purchased several hives of bees and established them in a clover field. There he regularly retired after his evening repast to croon such old ballads as dwarven lords used to win the hearts of dwarven maidens. These filled the hearts of the sleeping bees with such poignant melancholy that their honey was infused with a provocative tang. It produced a mead Roscoe declared to be the best ever tasted.

The problems started when word of this delicious concoction spread to neighboring villages, finally coming to the attention of the Brown Friars in their monastery several miles south. They were driven to a frothy rage and immediately dispatched an envoy with haughty and indignant instructions to cease mead production at once and destroy all stocks of such beverage.

The Friars were in possession of a certain warrant given to them by some distant forbearer of the present earl, said document granting them the exclusive right to make mead within a defined radius of Gorgonholm. Roscoe, as lord of the manor, was in clear violation of their ancient concession.

Torgul, as volatile as he was assiduous, was ready to remove the officious envoy's head from his shoulders, but Roscoe restrained him and assured the friar that all would be made right. He then sent a large cask of the mead to their neighbor Lord Drakar, along with an explanation of the problem and a request for his advice in the handling of the matter.

Drakar, the most fearsome noble of Avincraik County—some said the entire kingdom—responded directly. He appeared at the Brown Friars gate, sword in hand, and demanded an audience with the prior. He then brandished that weapon beneath the nose of the aged cleric, announcing, *Here is my warrant to make mead!* and proceeded to chop up the furniture of the monastery's rectory.

In sooth, Drakar's antipathy toward the Brown Friars stemmed entirely from an ongoing boundary dispute. They had accused him of moving the boundary stones delineating their property lines. Drakar had, in fact, caused the stones to be moved, but that was irrelevant. These pathetic, knee-scraping clerics had challenged him, Lord Drakar de la Pole, and that was not to be borne. They had to be taught to know their place, and the dispute over the mead gave him his opportunity to do so. Sufficiently schooled, the friars quietly withdrew their complaint, and Torgul was permitted to go on producing mead.

And then there had been the issue with the mill. The southern boundary of Roscoe's holding was Snake Creek, also known as Little Mad River. Someone had, many years ago, built a grist mill on the banks of this stream, but it had, like the other enterprises of Grimsgard, been allowed to fall into disrepair. Torgul, ever a dwarf, was appalled at this slovenly neglect.

He rebuilt the mill, enabling Roscoe's tenants to grind their own grain and thus avoid the hefty tithe demanded by the Gray Friars, who operated the only other mill in the region. This, of course, was the bone of contention. Within a very short time, an angry delegation of Gray Friars arrived in Grimsgard, demanding the destruction of Torgul's new mill.

They too produced a warrant issued by some long-dead earl, granting them exclusive rights to the milling of grain within a certain radius south of the city. It was a battle Roscoe knew he could not win. Drakar had no interest in the Gray Friars, and so there was, in the end, nothing for it but to throw the millstones into the river. Torgul had wept long and bitterly as he sang to his bees that night, so the mead was even more pungent than before.

All this was unsettling, but Torgul knew he and his companions now faced a problem much more serious than lazy peasants and peevish friars. They were out of coin. Roscoe meant well, certainly, but he had no aptitude at the managing of an estate. The dwarf watched in consternation as his friend squandered his gold on one foolish scheme after another. When Roscoe's funds were exhausted, Torgul offered his own—dwarves could be surprisingly generous with trusted friends—but now his was gone as well.

If their financial situation did not improve, the taxes would go unpaid, and Roscoe would lose his holding. Earl Mortimer would simply replace him with someone more capable. That would be a terrible turn of events. As Torgul saw it, only one option existed. They would very soon have to undertake another adventure to bring in sufficient treasure to refill their coffers.

But he had no idea where such a treasure might be found.

CHAPTER 6

FLORIO ARRIVES AT GRIMSGARD

Roscoe's tenants were all in a hubbub. They stood in a tight mass on the village green, not unlike a flock of sheep, discussing the most exciting event in many a season. A traveler had brought word that the Blue Friars' cathedral had been attacked by a swarm of demons and nearly consumed in a holocaust of hellfire. Only the fervent prayers of the friars, coupled with the fire-fighting efforts of the citizenry, had kept the entire complex from being engulfed.

Several storehouses and workshops, along with the big courtyard gates, were total losses. The kitchen and privies were badly damaged. The cathedral, rectory, and dormitories were foul with soot and smoke. Two newly arrived wagons carrying casks of holy water were believed to have been the target of the infernal assault.

Thurmond and Sarah joined Roscoe and Torgul at the edge of the crowd. They said nothing of their involvement in the business. Some things were best left unsaid. Roscoe and Torgul smelled the smoke in their clothes and came to their own conclusions, but they kept their thoughts to themselves, for they, too, understood that some things were best left unsaid.

Roscoe looked at his people milling about on the green and wondered how he could get them to return to work. They dropped their tools and chattered like drunken goblins at the slightest distraction. With such a sensational story to talk about, they might be off work for days.

It was time to face the sad fact that he was a piss-poor franklin. He lacked the aptitude for managing people and keeping accounts. He was a skilled and valiant warrior, a competent expedition leader, an experienced scout, a resourceful woodsman, and a decent horseman. Hell, he even knew how to make good apple cider and operate a fruit stand. But he did not have the knack for running a village.

The old Adventurer was broke and could not buy the supplies needed for the coming winter. Torgul had already given him the last of his coin. Unless he got a loan from Thurmond, the serfs would starve. He had not yet made the young man aware of his desperate plight, but he would have to tell him this very day.

Immersed in gloomy thoughts, Roscoe failed to notice the lone figure walking up the trail from the Royal Highway. Sarah spotted the stranger first and drew the attention of the others.

"Isn't that a girl? Look at her lithe build and the way she walks. It's a girl, for sure. Why would a girl be coming out here all alone?"

Actually there were many reasons a lone girl might come to Grimsgard, but Sarah was still jumpy from the previous night, so the approach of a stranger made her nervous. As the figure drew closer, however, it proved to be not a female, but a male and an elf. He was lean of build and a bit taller than Torgul, though not quite of Sarah's height. The gigantic Roscoe, of course, towered above the elf. His ears grew to slight points, and his eyes carried a subtle slant. He carried a small valise in one hand and a lute in the other.

He stopped before Roscoe and offered a low, sweeping bow.

"Have I the pleasure of addressing Roscoe Appleman, master of this village?"

"I am indeed Roscoe, but an apple-man no longer. I'm now called Roscoe Franklin, in accordance with my new station."

"As you wish, gracious lord. My name is Florio."

"Florio? Not an elven name certainly. What can I do for you, good Florio?"

"I come in the hope of securing a situation."

"A what? Please speak in plain terms a humble Adventurer might understand. I'm but a simple man, so I am."

This was far from the truth. Roscoe possessed a fine gift of gab and was quite capable, when the situation called for it, of using the high diction customary in formal conversations. He was testing the elf a bit, gauging his responses.

Florio remained polite and discreet.

"Employment, sire. I seek a position by which I might earn my daily bread."

Roscoe had suspected this, for the elf looked quite out at elbows. His once-elegant green tunic was faded and threadbare, his hose were patched and mended, and the tips of his toes poked through the ends of his pointy boots.

The old Adventurer scowled and poked at Florio's lute with his thumb.

"I've no need of a bard at present—sorry."

"Good milord, 'tis true I possess the skills of a gleeman—singing, capering, plucking a lute—but I can offer much, much more."

Florio fixed his eyes on Roscoe's great round belly and knew exactly the right thing to say.

"I am a cook of the first order. I can roast a fat goose or boil a mutton stew. I'll mince a tartare of larks and nightingales, fricassee squabs in a savory sauce, or fry up a scramble of leeks and calf brains."

This got Roscoe's attention. His meals were presently prepared by Bess and her younger sister Maybelle. The former was the wife of Bodo, who had become Roscoe's man-at-arms during their last adventure. This personal connection made it difficult for Roscoe to dismiss the sisters from his kitchen, though in sooth both were unskilled and indifferent cooks.

"Can you do a black pudding?"

"Naturally—a hearty one with extra marrow fat. Do you find quince tarts agreeable as well?"

Roscoe mentally licked his lips.

"As a fact, I do. Are yours toothsome?"

"Superlative, and my blancmange is beyond compare."

Florio observed the serfs milling on the green and sensed their lack of motivation. He looked about the village and recognized that ordinary tasks were not getting done.

"And I could be your village reeve, freeing your lordship for more fitting pursuits. Give me leave, and I will make these lounging yokels fear me more than death itself. I'll have them stepping to their work with a zest. I have that special flair, so they will dance to my tune.

"I'll keep your accounts in such order that no man could find a fault, and tally your beeves, milk-cows, sheep, swine, and poultry down to the last egg. I can augur from the flights of birds the coming yield of your farm-fields."

Roscoe's face split into a wide grin.

"That's all? Naught else? I seem to recall you saying you could do *many* things."

"I can dress your wounds, let your blood, clip your pate, and shave your chin. And I can write and read in five languages. Is that not enough?"

"Nay, not nearly enough! Surely there must be something more."

"I can draw up a legal and binding contract, and …."

Florio's voice dropped as he looked shiftily from side to side.

"…I can forge a signature so well the earl himself could not distinguish it from his own."

Roscoe was now laughing aloud at the elf's recitation.

"Certes, 'tis sufficient. But peace, as much as I could use a reeve of your talents, a great obstacle stands in the way of your employment. I am in a state of financial embarrassment—wholly destitute you might say. Not a single copper farthing to spare. I must bid you seek elsewhere for your situation."

Florio refused to be discouraged.

"I have made no mention of remuneration. Allow me a period of trial— say, a month and a day—during which I will labor at no cost to you. At the end of that time, you may judge my worth and set my wage as you see fit. What could be more fair?"

Roscoe drew back a bit. He ran his eyes up and down the elf's thin frame, and then stared deep into his eyes. Elves had a reputation for deceptiveness, flattery, and manipulation. Many people despised them. Was this one attempting to ingratiate himself for some concealed purpose?

"I must consult with my companions, good Florio. Prithee, be so kind as to stand apart a little so we may converse freely."

As Florio moved off, Roscoe, Torgul, Sarah, and Thurmond went into a huddle. Sarah was the first to speak.

"I like him. He's smart, perceptive, and persuasive. He'll do a better job running this place than any of us can. Let's hire him."

Thurmond had stopped listening to the conversation as soon as Roscoe mentioned his penniless state. Could it be true?

"Roscoe, are you really broke, or did you just say that to get the elf to go away?"

"Nay, laddie, I'm sorry to say it's entirely true. My coffers are empty. Torgul's are, too."

"God's great grasping fingers! I'm broke as well, and so is Sarah or nearly so. This is terrible news. I was going to ask you for a loan to hold me over to our next Adventure."

Roscoe gave a great sigh.

"Lady Fortune must be havin' a laugh at our expense. I was going to ask the same of you. What about the elf?"

"I don't know. I've never met an elf before, but lots of folks don't like 'em."

"True enough, but the same folks tend to feel that way about dwarves. Our good friend Torgul aptly proves such people to have shite for brains, don't you think?"

"True enough, and I could do with some better victuals than we've had of late."

Roscoe turned to Torgul. This was a potentially sensitive issue, for there was no love between elves and dwarves. The former saw the latter as boorish, blustering, and unkempt. Dwarves thought of elves as prissy, foppish, and self-serving. Roscoe did not want to distress his friend.

"What say you, my brother?"

"Hire him! If I can learn to put up with you humans, I guess I can get used to an elf. But I fail to see how that scrawny little runt can goad your slothful serfs to work."

Roscoe beckoned Florio back to their group.

"Pray tell, sir elf, why it is that such an accomplished individual as yourself would be seeking employment in my humble fief and willing to work for no wages? Can you explain that?"

"Most readily, good franklin. I left my ancestral homeland after a personal misunderstanding between myself and my father. No longer in his good graces, I decided to try my luck in the company of humans. But I have found those of my race are not as well received as I had hoped.

I heard that you, good sir, are brother-in-arms with this sturdy dwarf-lord, so I thought, prayed really, that you might be more open in your views than some others. So here I am."

Roscoe was tempted to ask about the nature of the dispute between Florio and his kin, but he decided to hold off. The elf had stammered when he spoke on the subject. If pressed he would either lie or refuse to answer, and neither response would be useful. Roscoe took a more indirect tack.

"Florio is not an elven name. What were you called by your family?"

The elf reddened and balked.

"I'd rather not say. Good taste dictates otherwise."

Roscoe expected this. Everyone knew that to share one's true name was to expose oneself to magical attack. The old Adventurer wanted to gauge Florio's reaction to his demand—would he refuse, equivocate, or lie?

"Out with it!"

"Good milord, I don't mean to be contrary, but…"

Roscoe spoke sternly, wanting the nervous elf to feel his authority.

"None of that! If you want the position, you'll tell me. I've got a right to know whose livin' under my roof. And no shilly-shallying—our sorceress will detect anything that ain't complete honesty."

Florio said something in the sing-songy elven tongue that sounded as if he were choking on cheap wine, something vaguely akin to *carrots and onions*.

Roscoe's good humor returned. He could never keep it suppressed for long.

"And what would be the meaning of those words in the common tongue? Pray, enlighten us."

"The Man with the Bloodstained Fangs."

The others broke into a roar of spontaneous laughter. Florio stood silent for a moment, looking humiliated, and then joined them in a jest at his own expense. Roscoe placed a hand on the elf's shoulder. His eyes twinkled, but his voice was steady and serious.

"A month and a day it is, Florio. After that, we may all find ourselves on the highway in search of a job of work, so we might. And I think you're going to need those bloody fangs of yours to get my lazy serfs up and going."

CHAPTER 7

IN THE CIRCLE OF STONES

There was good eating at Grimsgard that night. Florio brought out a great platter of ox livers stuffed with pickled heron-eggs. This was followed by river eel flambé, lentils and dandelions in a pungent sauce, and a curiously crunchy snack that turned out to be toasted crickets. No one could recall a finer repast.

Thurmond ate until nearly bursting. His normally insatiable appetite was for once fully glutted. With such food in his belly, Torgul dismissed any lingering qualms about associating with an elf. Roscoe was in a veritable transport of delight as he contemplated fine dining on a regular basis.

Only Sarah refused a second, third, and fourth helping of everything. She found the cuisine excellent but was too nervous to gorge herself. She was slated to see Gavin at midnight to learn the nature of her third and final test. If she could complete it, he would become her official mentor.

They were to meet at the Stones of Dhrughi, a ring of ancient standing stones on a bluff overlooking the Mad River. About halfway between Grimsgard and Gorgonholm, it was an isolated place and reputedly haunted by evil spirits invoked by the pagan priests of yore. Sarah had no idea why Gavin chose such an untoward location, but it was not her place to question his decisions.

Thurmond, of course, was forbidden to accompany her. He had tried to insist, and she had to admit that his arguments had merit, but she could not allow it. This meeting was too important to her. Should Gavin discover Thurmond's presence, he might disassociate himself from her altogether. She had to see this through on her own.

She knew Thurmond would try to follow her in spite of her prohibitions. Well, let him. She would slide into the shadows and leave him casting about in the dark until he got discouraged and went back to the tower. When she returned, she would find him swilling mead with Roscoe and Torgul. Much better that way.

Slipping away turned out much easier than anticipated. The heavy meal, coupled with copious quantities of Torgul's mead, put all three of the menfolk into a deep torpor, sprawled upon the benches of the great hall, surrounded by the empty platters and drained goblets.

Perfect! This made it ever so easy for Sarah to grab her cloak and steal away. The night was cold and wet, but the evening drizzle had stopped, and the light of a nearly full moon was beaming through the dissipating clouds. The distance from Grimsgard to Stones of Dhrughi was about a half-league, so Sarah wasted no time. It was important to demonstrate her sincerity and maturity by being punctual. And she was eager to see Gavin again. Holding her cloak closed with one hand, she scampered off into the darkness.

Thurmond, as it turned out, had not drank deeply of the mead, nor was he as slumberous as his companions. He only feigned sleep so he could follow Sarah to her assignation with the fancy fellow. He gave her a head-start, took his cloak and sword from the pile by the fireplace, and set off after her.

Sarah, he knew, would be expecting him to follow and would try to disappear into the darkness. She was certainly smart, but sometimes she forgot simple details. Because the night was bright with moonlight, Thurmond had no trouble finding her footprints in the wet grass and damp mud. The ground was open, so following was easy. Her path led to the west and north. She could only be heading toward that old stone circle—there was naught else in that direction. It was a bad place. Nothing good could happen there.

Local legends attributed the Stones of Dhrughi to various ancient peoples—the savage Attaboaii and Attabrinii, the ruthless Etrusians, or the horrific Vanarians. These were all incorrect, for the construction was actually much older than any of those ancient civilizations. The legends, however, were uniform—and much more accurate—in declaring it a place of madness and ruin, a place to be avoided.

The Stones of Dhrughi, Thurmond thought grimly, would be the perfect spot if you wanted a meeting to seem spooky and mysterious. And the perfect spot for the fancy fellow to work his will upon an unsuspecting young girl. He quickened his pace, hoping to shorten Sarah's lead.

In his haste, he lost his footing in a patch of mud and rolled down a steep embankment, coming to rest in a bramble bush. By the time he extricated himself, scratched and bleeding from the prickly thorns, Sarah was far ahead.

When the stones finally hove into sight, he was thoroughly winded, for he had run most of the remaining way. The muscles of his legs burned, and a sharp pain pierced his left side. He paused briefly to catch his breath and rest his weary legs. He crept forward as silently as he could. Though the moon was still bright, he could discern no movement within the darkness of the stone circle.

Suddenly a high-pitched squeal tore through the night, the scream of someone in agony or mortal fear. *Sarah!* He sprinted forward, reckless of what might await him, shouting her name as loudly as he might.

"Sarah! Sarah!"

Several more screams emanated from the center of the stones. Thurmond drew his sword and crashed blindly through the night, shouting like a man demented. Then Sarah appeared, not running in fear from some unseen pursuer but with the unwavering step of extreme anger. She stopped in front of Thurmond, livid with rage, her eyes burning like coals of fire.

"That bastard! That poxy, conniving maggot! May God rot his eyes! I'm glad you found me, Thurmond. Please take me home. I'll tell you all about it as we walk."

But Thurmond was not listening at that moment. He advanced into the stones, sword raised. Sarah, seeing his intention, caught his arm and pulled him back.

"Nay, Thurmond, don't do it. I took care of him—don't worry. Please, now stop. I just want to get away from this horrible place."

"I heard you scream. *Nobody* hurts you like that."

"That wasn't me screaming. It was him. I made him scream. See? I'm all right. Let's go."

The young man lowered his sword and caught Sarah by the arms.

"Not until I see that prick's blood. What did he do to you? If he hurt you, he won't live to see sunrise."

"Nay, unnecessary. Don't kill him—he's hurt enough. You don't need to carry the burden of his death. Take me away from here, and I'll tell you what I did to him."

Thurmond heard a low moaning from the ring of stones.

The girl offered a small, brittle chuckle.

"Hear that? He didn't hurt me, I hurt him. He told me that tonight he would assign me the final test. If I passed it, he would become my mentor in the magical arts. Well, do you know what that last test really was? He wanted to screw me. He spouted some shit about it being the ultimate spiritual bond…but I know better."

"And what happened then?"

"I said *nay*, naturally, and I really meant *nay*. But he didn't listen, he just kept trying to fondle me. I pushed him back and said again *nay*. He kept trying to put his paws on me, and I didn't like it. I felt he had betrayed me. I thought he was far too evolved to be interested in matters of the flesh."

"What happened then?"

"He pushed me to the ground and pulled up my skirts."

Thurmond's eyes lost focus when he heard these words. Two silent tears began to drip down Sarah's cheeks as she continued.

"Then he jumped on top of me and tried to force my legs apart, but I brought my knee up and gave it to him right in the balls."

"Did that stop him?"

"Certes! I must have knocked them clean between his ears, for he started flopping and gagging. Then I gave him a few good kicks in the ribs, just to make sure. And I took this—it was hanging around his neck. It is rightfully ours, after all."

She produced the gold medallion they had removed from the tomb of the dead witch.

"As you said, it's probably valuable, and right now we need money.

Gavin—I don't even want to say his name—that poxy maggot has no right to it, so I took it back. I looked for my coin, too, but he didn't have it."

Thurmond had listened to as much as he could stand to hear. He again started into the stone circle, and this time there was no holding him back. Gavin writhed on the ground, acting just as a man should when his gonads have been knocked up between his ears.

Sarah may have intended for her kicks to land on his ribs, but one had taken him square on the sternum, knocking the wind from his lungs. Another had broken his nose, which now streamed with blood.

Thurmond put the tip of his sword to the side of Gavin's face.

"Hear this well, fancy fellow—I am always with Sarah, always nearby. I was there when you led her across Market Square to the cathedral, and I was there when you came out. I was outside when she took the bones to you. She's never without me. If I ever set eyes on you again, that day will be your last."

When Gavin did not respond, Thurmond dragged the tip of his sword along the line of his jaw, producing a long, shallow cut.

"Every time you see that scar, remember what I told you."

Thurmond left the circle and rejoined Sarah. They set off for home, their arms around each other. She was trembling and kept wiping her nose on her sleeve, but her fear was far outweighed by her anger. She leaned her head on her friend's shoulder and talked while they walked.

"Damn his foul soul to the deepest pit of Hell. He's ruined all my plans. Do you know what it's like to grow up and never really know who you are or where you fit in?"

Thurmond did not. He had grown up in a small farming village, where his identity had been very much defined and very confining. As a poor peasant, he had been expected to remain in the life he was born to.

He had been called Wido, or more specifically *Marge's Wido*, to distinguish him from the many village men with the same name. His mother Marge always claimed he was sired by the local lord, one Beaufort de Oinque. Thurmond, however, doubted this, well aware that his mother enjoyed the companionship of a great many men.

At age fourteen he had been apprenticed to an aged and choleric carpenter, who beat him regularly and severely. Fed up, Thurmond had stolen his master's tools and made his way to the great city of Gorgonholm to create his own destiny. He renamed himself Thurmond after a legendary hero of old and set about to win wealth and renown as an Adventurer.

Thus, Thurmond's past was quite different than Sarah's. He rejected the role of peasant villager that he had been born to, but he had at least been given a role to reject. Sarah had never had that. She was reared in the household of Lord Percy Staynes, her mother being one of the housemaids. When her mother passed, Sarah's care was left entirely in the hands of servants. There were no words of solace, no explanation of what her future might hold. She had been permitted the bounty of Staynes Hall—good food, a soft bed, fine apparel—but she was denied the human warmth every child craves.

Sarah seldom saw her alleged father, and such contact as she did have remained cold and formal. Her half-brother Bartholomew had been a cruel boy, whose company was best avoided. As Sarah approached womanhood, he expressed to his sibling the most vile and unwholesome of intentions. Such alienation during her formative years instilled in the girl an abiding need to belong, to enjoy the security of a guaranteed place in something large and permanent.

Where could she find such a place? Men certainly had plenty of options. Commoners could swear allegiance to their lords and be taken into their service. Nobles took oaths of fealty binding them to the king. Friars made unbreakable vows when accepted into the church. Roscoe and Torgul were members of the Adventurers, and Thurmond longed to join them. Craftsmen and merchants formed guilds.

But what was there for Sarah? A nunnery? Domestic service? Those options would entail a loss of independence, and that was a sacrifice she was unwilling to make. She had no desire to become some man's wife. Women were little more than servants to their husbands. With few rights by law or custom, they could be ignored, abused, or beaten with impunity. It was not a life she aspired to.

Certainly, her life with Thurmond and the others was a good one. They treated her as an equal…well, nearly so. They did not expect her to pick up the bones they routinely threw on the floor during meals. And they took her seriously, respecting her intelligence, courage, and loyalty.

That was well and good, but she still longed to be part of something larger, something established, something recognized as legitimate. As an adolescent, she had found in her father's book collection a copy of the meeting-minutes of the local magicians' guild. It had become her greatest ambition to join this august organization.

As the moon set, it became more and more difficult for Thurmond and Sarah to stay on the path. When they began to trip over the roots and rocks thrusting up from the ground, they took a break and sat propped against an old log.

Sarah was still angry.

"May Gavin's bones rot. I trusted him. I thought that with his help I could finally get the skills I need to really establish myself and be allowed into the magicians' guild. It's not easy, especially for women. The guild only ever admitted a few. Mostly it's just a bunch of self-satisfied old men, but I wanted to feel accepted somewhere. But now I don't know. I think the magicians' guild is really just a gaffers' eating club. I wouldn't ever be welcome really, and I probably wouldn't like them if they did let me in."

Thurmond understood her feelings of deep disappointment. He could imagine how he would feel if the Adventurers suddenly slammed their door in his face.

He was suddenly struck by an unsettling thought.

"What about the geas? Aren't you still under its power?"

Sarah's response was bitter.

"There was no geas. It was a lie, just like everything else Gavin told me. He's no magician."

"How can you be sure? From what you said—"

"Don't worry. After what I did to him, if it were real, I'd be feeling its effects by now."

The night grew chill. Thurmond unfastened his cloak and wrapped it around Sarah's shoulders so it encircled them both.

PART 2

THE WITCH'S MEDALLION

CHAPTER 8

BREAKFAST WITH ROSCOE

The first light of dawn was just starting to trickle through the thick, wavy glass of the window, bathing Roscoe's bedchamber with a weird, greenish tint. The lord of the manor was not an early riser by nature and would have preferred to remain snug beneath his counterpane until the sun had fully established itself in the sky. But on this morning, he was not permitted this luxury, for he was awakened by a loud and strident voice coming from the lower levels of the towerhouse. It was followed by an angry female voice that he recognized as belonging to Maybelle, the assistant cook. He could not distinguish what was being said, but it was clear that a rancorous confrontation was taking place downstairs.

Maybelle's voice ceased, and a door slammed. There was a brief pause, and then came the sounds of a woman—Roscoe assumed it was Maybelle—weeping. The old Adventurer rolled over and drew the covers up around his ears. He just wanted the noise to end so he could go back to sleep.

The strident voice began again, this time from outside—loud, sharp, authoritative, and completely unfamiliar. Who could it be? Who would be so determined to disturb his rest? Roscoe was highly displeased. Whatever churl was causing such a ruckus was about to catch the sharp edge of his tongue. He dragged himself from bed, the counterpane wrapped around his shoulders like a cloak. Pushing open the casement, he looked into the yard below. *Florio!* The elf stood before a huddle of serfs, belaboring them for their laziness and ingratitude. He held a large wooden spoon, with which he gestured menacingly.

To Roscoe's surprise, the normally surly and uncooperative serfs appeared crestfallen and subdued. They endured the tongue-lashing with complete deference, and set off submissively to tend to their chores. Now *that* was a sight worth seeing.

Thoroughly awake now, Roscoe pulled on a tunic started down the spiral stairs, gimping along on his bum leg, which had stiffened overnight. He wanted to find out what was going on between Florio and his workers. What he next encountered drove all previous thoughts from his mind. Up from the ground-floor kitchen wafted the most wonderful aromas. A plethora of scents—delicate, robust, poignant, exotic, and profound—summoned the old Adventurer most seductively. Roscoe's bare feet skipped lightly over the stone steps to the bottom of the staircase.

In the large chamber called the great hall, a most marvelous surprise awaited him, a breakfast even more magnificent than the supper enjoyed the night before—minnows sautéed in sow blubber, owl eggs poached in red wine, thinly sliced goat tongue garnished with capers, great slabs of warm bread smeared with a conserve of yodelberries. Nearby was a pitcher of clabbered ass's milk strengthened with a generous measure of uisge. *What a breakfast!*

Roscoe fell to with the zeal of a true Adventurer. He had not been feasting long when Torgul appeared, rubbing the sleep from his eyes with one hand and combing the snarls from his beard with the other. Roscoe tried to greet him, but his mouth was too crammed with food for coherent speech. The dwarf assessed the great spread with obvious delight.

"What ho, brother Roscoe! This looks to be some right fine eatin'! Does it taste as good as it smells?"

Roscoe swallowed hugely and took a deep draught of the fortified milk.

"By God's great round belly, aye—it tastes even *better* than it looks or smells. Come, join me. This is far too wonderful to experience alone. We must savor this meal and talk about it afterward. Eat! You must eat, my brother!"

"What about the young'uns? It don't seem right to deny 'em their share. Do they know about this feast?"

"Nay, they're still abed, so they are. If they choose to sleep the day away, am I to go hungry in the meantime?"

The old Adventurer caught the look of reproach in his friend's eye. He turned to Maybelle, who stood silently by the sideboard.

"Maybelle, do you mind fetchin' down Thurmond and Sarah so they may join us?"

Maybelle, like her sister Bess, was a sour woman, whose face was drawn into a permanent scowl. Though still young and not unattractive, she seemed perpetually filled with a deep dissatisfaction.

Both women had been hired as cooks and housemaids, but they performed their duties in only the most cursory fashion. When asked to carry out the most basic of tasks, their responses were invariably rude and disobliging. Only Roscoe's regard for Maybelle's husband Bodo, his man-at-arms, kept them in his employ.

Maybelle was about to offer an ungracious reply when she caught sight of Florio watching her from the kitchen door, his hand holding something behind his back. He said nary a word, merely revealed the wooden spoon. That was sufficient.

"At once, Lord Roscoe."

She gave a slight curtsy and scurried for the stairs.

Roscoe found this change of behavior even more shocking than the unexpected feast. What could have wrought such a change of attitude? Why was she suddenly so subdued and polite? Roscoe glanced over at Bess, who stood attentive with folded hands as if awaiting his beck and call. What the hell was going on?

Maybelle reappeared.

"Good milord, I am sorry to say neither the young lady nor the young master is in their chambers. It does not appear either bed has been slept in."

So now here was another mystery. What had become of Thurmond and Sarah? Certainly, they were of an age to come and go as they pleased, but both Torgul and Roscoe were concerned. They were obviously up to some hijinks. The night before they had been involved in the cathedral fire. What was it now? Were they in some kind of trouble?

Roscoe's mind was soon set at ease when the truants entered the great hall.

They were damp and disheveled, looking a bit sheepish as if embarrassed by the belated homecoming. Roscoe burst into laughter, and even the typically dour Torgul permitted himself a slight smile. Roscoe could not help teasing them.

"Well, now there's a fine pair of lovebirds, sneaking in after a night of… well, I guess we all know what. I hope you've strength enough left for the day's chores, that you're not so exhausted as to be unfit for an honest day's toil. Thurmond, laddie, have you saved at least a wee bit of energy to attend to your duties? You look plumb wore out, so you do."

Both Sarah and Thurmond blushed to the color of red wine. They chimed together.

"Nay, you but misunderstand. It's not that. We but fell asleep by a fallen log. Nay! Nay! Nay! Not what you think…"

Roscoe was relentless in his joking.

"Sarah, darlin', are those grass stains I spy upon your dress? You must have Bess attend to them at once, lest they set and leave permanent marks."

Thurmond started to renew his protest, then shrugged and sat down with join his friends. Mortified, frustrated, and tongue-tied, Sarah was about to storm off to her chamber, but when she caught sight of breakfast, she took a place beside Thurmond.

Roscoe now affected his best stern, penetrating stare.

"So, Prospect, it's time to reveal to your mentors just what you and the lassie have been up to the last couple of days. You've been out late two nights in a row. First you came back carrying the stench of a burning cathedral. Now you drag in here with muddy clothes and leaves stuck in your hair. There's more goin' on here than a little light love. No double talk now—tell us."

When addressed in this formal manner, Thurmond had no choice but to open to Roscoe and Torgul. As a mere Prospect in the Adventurers, he was obliged to obey the commands of full members. If he were instructed to eat a horse turd, he would have done his best to choke it down and make it look like he enjoyed it. He shrugged and related the events of the last two days— Sarah's bargain with Gavin, the raid on the cathedral vaults, the fire, the gold medallion, the abortive meeting at the Stones of Dhrughi.

However, he held back the details of Gavin's assault on Sarah. If she wanted that part told, she could do so herself. He said only that she had been disgusted by his untoward advances and negated their agreement with a kick in the nads.

Roscoe exploded in laughter, and Torgul gave a chuckle. Sarah smiled along with them, but Thurmond knew she was being disingenuous. The event was too recent, her pain too fresh, to be an occasion for mirth.

Roscoe laid his hand on the girl's shoulder.

"That was well done, lassie. You gave that little shite exactly what he had comin'. A worthy deed, so it was. Now, you say you found a golden medallion. Let's have a look-see."

Sarah took the requested item from her pouch. It was a heavy gold disc nearly as wide as the palm of his hand. Around its edge, nine interlaced serpents squirmed in a circle, each swallowing the tail of the one before it and being swallowed, in turn, by the one coming after. The burnished gold gleamed with reddish highlights.

Roscoe took the medallion from Sarah and examined it closely, his brow furrowing in displeasure.

"You say you stole this trinket from the dead witch? I wouldn't want her vengeful shade comin' to call. That would be very bad, so it would. What do you say, brother Torgul?"

"I ain't seen the like of this before, and I've a fair knowledge of goldsmithery. A strange style, to be sure—and not what I'd call pleasin'. Just lookin' at it fills me with a cold dread. The sooner we're shed of it the better."

Roscoe was quick to agree.

"Certes, you are correct. The thing's plainly evil, and I'll rest easier when we're rid of it. But I imagine it's of value, and right now we're in dire need of funds. Let's find someone to buy it, and let's do it today."

Torgul lifted the item in question with a toasting fork, as if unwilling to touch it with his bare hands.

"Right you are, brother Roscoe, but this enchanted doodad will fetch a higher price if we can learn who made it or what its properties are."

Sarah spoke up.

"I'll look in my sorcery books. Maybe I can identify that snake design, but I don't think so. I've been through my books time and again. I'd remember something so unusual. And I think all of you are wrong! The medallion's not evil. It has an energy you don't like, but I don't feel the same way about it."

Roscoe shrugged.

"Well, whatever it be, we're hurtin' for coin. I think we can agree we need to sell it as quick as we can."

Thurmond had an idea.

"Let's take it to a diviner, someone who can identify magic stuff."

The old Adventurer shook his head.

"Too expensive. Them kinda guys always want more than an item's worth. I have a friend called Fishbone, who might be willing to help us. He ain't much to look at, certain enough, but he's like a walkin' library, so full o' facts he is."

Thurmond was intrigued.

"Who what is he? A scholar? A priest?"

Roscoe chuckled and took a swig of milk.

"Fishbone ain't like no other person, and that's a fact. Lives alone in a little hovel on the riverbank. Speaks in this low twangy kinda voice that makes him hard to understand. But a smarter man you ain't goin' to find, nor one who knows so much about so many different things."

"Why is he called Fishbone?"

"He had an unlikely experience as a wee laddie. He was out on the river in his papa's coracle when some great water monster comes up from bottom and swallows him whole, coracle and all. Well, it seems he got stuck in the beastie's throat—him or the coracle as it may be—like a fishbone in yours or mine, and the thing commences to thrash about, tryin' to shake him loose. And when he come unstuck, he was spit out, and the monster dove back to the deeps.

"After that he wasn't ever the same again, changed somehow. All his brothers grew up to be fishermen, but not him. I don't rightly know how he lives or where he learns so much. He said somethin' once about listenin' to the stars and the wind and the flow of the river, but I think he was just spinnin' a yarn.

"A man of mystery, so he is, but a good man to know when you got to find out somethin'. I'd bet he'll help us if we bring him a flask of Torgul's good mead."

"How do you know him, Roscoe?"

"Smugglin' days."

At one time, Roscoe was involved in the illicit importation of uisge. This fiery drink could only be obtained from the Keltin tribes across the river. Aware of its great popularity among the citizens of Gorgonholm, the tribesmen demanded nothing less than the finest steel weapons in exchange.

Such transactions were a capital offense, for the Keltins were the traditional enemies of Gorgonholm. There had been innumerable raids and wars over the years. Thus, the arming of these dangerous foes was strictly forbidden. But the trade flourished in defiance of the law because everyone from Earl Mortimer on down—the bishop, the sheriff, everyone—liked his nip of uisge.

Another thought struck Thurmond.

"Say, what's going on with your serfs?"

Roscoe frowned.

"What do you mean?"

"They're really working out there, not like normal. When we were coming across the common just now, they were working harder than I've ever seen 'em. That Florio guy is keeping 'em at it by threatening 'em with a wooden spoon."

The old Adventurer raised his hands in a gesture of bewilderment.

"Haven't the faintest idea, but I'm right pleased about it. Florio's worked a miracle, so he has. Even Bess and Maybelle are actin' like proper servants—no more sour faces and back talk."

Thurmond took a giant bite of goat tongue.

"God's mighty thighs! This food is *really* good."

Sarah had to agree. The sow's blubber had begun to congeal and the owl eggs had grown cold, but both dishes remained quite delectable. The yodelberry conserve was sheer divine bliss. Unfortunately, Roscoe and Torgul had drained the pitcher of fortified milk.

CHAPTER 9

THE RIVER RAT'S TALE

Roscoe was right. Fishbone wasn't much to look at, and his speech was almost impossible to understand. When presented with the gold medallion, he muttered something akin to *wall—thars niddin ta beh gi'in twa aleedy*.

Sarah grew impatient.

"Roscoe, tell us what he just said."

"Only that this particular trinket would not be a proper gift with which to win a maiden's heart."

Fishbone spoke again, very low and without pause, and much too rapidly for Thurmond or Sarah to follow. From time to time, Roscoe interjected an occasional remark in the same unintelligible dialect.

Fishbone's language was actually the common tongue of the citizens of Gorgonholm and the other subjects of the Kingdom of Poitiers. But his impenetrable dialect was that of water folk—boatmen, fishers, smugglers, and pirates who lived their lives on the river. It was a unique and clannish community, largely closed to outsiders. Over the generations, they had developed their own vocabulary and pronunciations. This fostered a strong group identity and allowed them to exclude others from their conversations.

Thurmond examined this odd man. Fishbone was tall and wizened, his skin burned brown from a lifetime spent outdoors. His hair was long, matted, and nasty. His mouth held very few teeth. He wore no hose or breeks, and his ragged, too-short tunic exposed things best left unseen. His watery blue eyes seemed to gaze off into another reality.

Fishbone's one-room hovel stood just downstream from where the accumulated sludge of the tanneries and knackers oozed out into the river. The stench was abysmal, even to those accustomed to the stink of human and animal waste.

Roscoe produced a large flask of Torgul's mead, which the old Adventurer and scrawny river rat passed it from hand to hand. The young people were not invited to partake. They began to fidget as Fishbone droned on and on and on. Bored, Thurmond cast about for a distraction. Peering through the open door of the decrepit shanty, he saw a tangle of blankets on a pallet of bracken. A ragged cloak hung from a peg on the wall. A basket held what looked like dried fish-heads. But no books, no scrolls, no implements of any kind that might be associated with learning. So where did the old gaffer's vaunted knowledge come from?

The conversation came to a sudden stop. Fishbone drained the last of the mead, rose abruptly, entered his hovel, and shut the door.

Sarah was concerned.

"Is he angry? Did we offend him?"

"Nay, lassie, that's just his way. He had his say, and now he's done, that's all. The mead made him a tad drowsy. He don't mean to be rude."

"Did he tell you anything about the talisman?",

"Aye, he told an interestin' tale. Seems this little bauble was once worn by a Sister of Sathas. It was a cult—or I guess a coven, more properly speakin'—of a particularly evil bent. Always eight adepts and a leader—all women. They was witches of the most dark and deadly kind. One member for each one of the snakes on the thing."

The mention of witches got Sarah's full attention.

"What's Sathas?"

"Not a what, girl, but a who. There's a story from the olden times—I'm surprised you haven't heard it before. I remember my grandam tellin' me some of the story, sittin' by the fire on a winter night. Sathas lived in a castle on a tall mountain in a faraway land. She was a countess, or what they called a *contessa* where she come from. She was also the most powerful witch in all the realm, reigning supreme for many a year.

"She was beautiful too, so she was, with big blue eyes and golden hair and soft pink skin, but never was a woman more vain of her looks, and when she grew older and the wrinkles began to crisscross her flawless skin, she turned to demonic arts to hold the years at bay.

"Her way of doin', it was terrible cruel, for she took to bathin' in the blood of young girls. She butchered her poor, innocent housemaids and bled 'em out in a big bronze tub like they was hogs. She was always sendin' out her henchmen to find new girls. People started callin' her the Red Contessa 'cause she was always wantin' more blood.

"And so it went for a power of years, with her needin' more and more girls as the weight of the years grew heavier and heavier. So many girls did she kill that it was too hard buryin' 'em, so they took to flingin' 'em from the mountaintop into the river far below. Many a poor father was grieved to find the floatin' corpse of his own beloved daughter who he'd been proud to send to work for the great lady.

"Aye, the Red Contessa was a bad one, so she was. So bad that the people of the land finally rose against her in spite of her powers. Her castle was strong, and her guards were tough and loyal, and the attackers died by the score. But the time had come to bring the witch down, and they managed at last to breach the gates.

"Then Sathas, the Red Contessa, bein' a witch and all, called down terrible things from the sky and brought up even worse things from her castle's cellars. But so great was the rage of the common folk that they fought on regardless of loss until all the monstrosities lay dead.

"They wrapped her in chains and hung holy symbols around her neck so she couldn't work her magic. Then they held a quick trial, and naturally she was condemned to death. But what do you think they found out? They couldn't kill her. Her magic and all that blood had put a charm on her life so nothin' could hurt her—not iron, nor fire, nor water, not even being hurled down from a great height. She just laughed at their efforts and refused to die.

"Not knowin' what else to do, the people finally bricked her into the walls of her own castle, sealed her right into a tiny space with neither air nor light nor even any way to move around. Well, she didn't like that, not one bit. She began to scream and scream, and five years later was still screamin'. Most of the people in the nearby village packed up and left 'cause they couldn't sleep at night for all the racket.

"Then one day, the screamin' suddenly leaves off. They knew she couldn't die, so why'd she stop? Not one of 'em was about to go up to the castle to find out. Nobody ever went there. But finally somebody gets a thought. Maybe she wasn't dead exactly. Maybe somehow her spirit was still there but had left her body so it didn't scream no more. Maybe she was now free to come down and haunt them, or maybe her spirit had become part of the castle itself.

"That's how things stood until, many years later, a coven of witches moved in and conjured the shade of the Red Contessa to infuse themselves with her great and frightful powers. Called themselves the Sisters of Sathas, so they did. They grew as rich and powerful as their namesake ever was, and they was just as feared. They've been there ever since, at least as far as Fishbone knows.

"This necklace of yours used to hang around the neck of one of 'em. It's an evil thing and might have a little piece of Sathas's wicked soul locked inside it just like the rest of her is trapped in the walls of her castle. Least ways, that's what Fishbone thinks, and I've learned to rely on his judgment."

Sarah was thoroughly intrigued.

"Your friend believes this story is true and that this place really exists?"

"Aye, for a fact he does."

"Where is it?"

"He didn't say, but I seem to recall my grandam sayin' it was somewheres far away."

"If we could find out where, we could go there."

The color drained from Roscoe's face and his mouth hung open.

"Are you mad, girl? Why, by God's twelve toes, would you want to join up with such an evil brood as them witches?"

"Nay, you mistake me. Not join them, never that. Not at least if they're as evil as Fishbone claims they are. But who knows?"

Thurmond was as unsettled as Roscoe by Sarah's idea.

"What you suggest is impossible. To help you, I'm ready to fight with men or goblins, maybe even a troll, but I don't want to tangle with a bunch of evil witches. Also, I'm not going to stand by while you try to join 'em. I didn't stop you from making your deal with Gavin, and that was a mistake. This would be a lot worse."

"Nay, I swear to you both I don't seek to join them. I'm not skilled enough even if I wanted to. I just thought…well…that there might be something useful there. I don't know, it was just a thought."

In fact, Sarah had been having many strange thoughts even before she heard Fishbone's tale. Ever since she took the talisman from the tomb of Dame Agnes, the medallion had been calling to her. Nay, that was a lie! It had been *commanding* her, haunting her every moment both awake and asleep.

Delivering it to Gavin had required all of her strength and willpower, and since getting it back, its hold on her had grown steadily stronger. Now that she had heard Fishbone's story, the medallion's demands were irresistible. It wanted her to take it home.

Sarah turned kind eyes to Thurmond.

"Thurmond, I know you mean well. That you have my best interests foremost in your heart. I love you, but that does not mean that I will not allow you to make my decisions for me. If I elect to undertake such a quest, you are under no obligation to accompany me, and neither is Roscoe nor Torgul."

These words hurt the young man. They felt like a betrayal of the absolute affection and loyalty he had always given her. But Sarah always made it clear she valued her independence more than his friendship. He had no choice but to accept her for who she was.

But it still hurt. And it angered him because he knew that his feelings for her would never allow him to stay behind while she went off on some perilous, probably unholy, quest. He would have to go with her, even though he knew it to be a fool's errand. *God's holy molars!*

Roscoe handed the charm to Sarah.

"I have to see a man about a bit of business. I might be off for a day or two or three, but if all goes well, I'll come home with some coin for our coffers. Don't ask no questions, just do as you're told.

"You two need to go talk to Jarvis. He's the only one I know who might purchase this piece of bric-a-brac without too many pryin' questions as to where it come from."

The old Adventurer was referring to a local purveyor of used and unusual goods. Jarvis's combination shop and warehouse was a dark, cavernous edifice, stuffed floor to rafters with countless articles acquired during decades of trade. On his dusty shelves, one might find anything from a pair of well-worn riding boots to the petrified egg of a dragon.

In his years as an Adventurer, Roscoe had had many dealings with Jarvis. The merchant was always ready to offer a fair price for exotic items seized from the treasure hoard of werewolves or ogres. Most recently, Jarvis had brokered the deal with Earl Mortimer that led to Roscoe's possession of Grimsgard.

Roscoe continued his instructions.

"Try to get at least a thousand gold sovereigns. Somethin' this rare ought to be worth that much. Don't seem too eager to sell. Act like maybe we got somebody else interested. And don't tell him what it is right at first. Get his curiosity up a tad. Then maybe let slip about the Red Contessa, kinda by accident. Try to make him feel like he's putting one over on you.

"On your way now, you two. Give Jarvis my best regards. With any luck, I'll be back with some money in my purse."

With that, Roscoe turned and trudged up the bank in the direction of the city docks. Thurmond and Sarah headed into the city through the West Gate, also known as the River Gate.

CHAPTER 10

A Conversation with Jarvis

Jarvis's shop was as cluttered and uncomfortable as usual. The narrow aisles were jammed with oversize items too large for the long rows of shelves. There were racks of swords, bundles of old cloaks, and a bushel basket of preserved bats. An entire corner was filled with a pyramid of rusty helmets. Wooden crates bore inscriptions in strange, unknown tongues. Carved furniture of ancient design was stacked higher than the head of a tall man. The air carried an aromatic blend of dust, mold, incense, and exotic spice.

Sarah and Thurmond carefully made their way around a precarious stand of pole-weapons that looked ready to clatter to the ground with the slightest touch. They approached a large cage of wrought iron bars within which the proprietor sat on a tall stool behind a high counter. An older man, Jarvis was small of stature, round of shape, and gray of hair. He was using a rag to rub an ointment into what looked like a human nose. Seeing the young people, he put down the rag and placed the nose in a small silver box. He snapped the lid shut and looked at them with heavily lidded eyes.

The medallion was tearing as Sarah's soul, but she forced herself to speak.

"Good day, Master Jarvis. Do you recall us? We were here with—"

Jarvis interrupted, his voice was unusually high-pitched.

"With Roscoe the Adventurer. I do recall you both. It was a fine bit of business we did together, he and I. I expect he is well pleased with the outcome. So why is it he chose to send his minions this day instead of coming himself?"

Neither Sarah nor Thurmond considered themselves to be Roscoe's minions, but they let the slight pass. Jarvis was typically condescending and abrupt, even to Roscoe.

Now Thurmond spoke, deciding to play along with the merchant's misapprehension.

"Our master sends his compliments and his profound regrets that he could not come in person. He is, this day, engaged elsewhere on urgent business. He has recently come into possession of a very unique and potent talisman. He wanted to show his gratitude for your past kindness, so he sent us posthaste to give you the opportunity ...."

He let his voice trail off as if unsure what to say next.

Jarvis's face remained expressionless.

"Is that right? Let me see the item."

With the greatest reluctance, Sarah placed the medallion in the merchant's outstretched palm. His brow puckered at its touch, and he dropped it on the countertop.

"Well, young man, you are correct. It is an ensorcelled piece. I felt the tingle right down to the soles of my feet, but I must have it assessed before I can go any further. You may wait on the street in the meantime."

"How long will this take?"

"No more than a few minutes. You will be summoned when the examination is complete."

Thus dismissed, the pair left the shop to wait until sent for. As soon as the door closed behind them, Sarah grabbed Thurmond's hand. She was in a high state of agitation.

"Did you see what was on the floor next to the counter?"

Thurmond had no idea what she had seen or why she was so excited.

"Nay, what was it?"

"I'll tell you exactly what it was—the bones we stole. The bones of Dame

Agnes, still wrapped in that old blanket I carried 'em away in. The bones I gave to Gavin."

"Why does Jarvis have 'em? I thought Gavin needed 'em for some important magical thing. Isn't that what you said?"

"That's what he told me. He said he needed them for a most difficult operation that would allow him to ascend to an even higher ethereal plane. Look, he was lying to me all along. I thought he was so much more advanced in sorcery than I am that I should believe everything he said. I guess I *wanted* to believe him."

"Why does Jarvis have the bones?"

"I don't know, but I might have a way to find out."

Jarvis had been truthful when he said the examination would take no more than a few minutes. The door opened, and he summoned the two back into the shop. Resuming his place behind the counter, Jarvis placed the talisman on the counter and pushed it toward Thurmond.

"I'm not interested. Tell your master I am not able to make an offer for this item."

Thurmond was dumbstruck but quickly recovered his poise.

"May I ask why not? My master will want to know."

"The piece is cursed. It is charged with unholy magic that can bring nothing but woe and destruction. It should be thrown into the river, or, better yet, dropped into the depths of the sea."

"Were you able to gauge its particular properties?"

"Nay, we did not try, nor do I want to know. You will now remove this item from my premises. Good day."

While these words were said, Sarah took a great chance. Everyone said Jarvis's shop was guarded by supernatural entities that had, in the past, torn would-be thieves into small pieces. One unfortunate housebreaker was literally turned inside out. So even the small transgression Sarah contemplated entailed significant risk.

She had decided to try her truth spell on the shopkeeper. If successful, he would be compelled to answer her questions in complete candor. When the spell dissipated, he would have no recollection of the conversation. Of course, he might be protected against such magical attack, and if he were to become aware of her attempt, it could go badly for them.

While Jarvis's attention was fully upon Thurmond, Sarah quietly murmured the required incantation and pointed the spell in the old man's direction. She saw the will depart from his eyes and knew the spell had worked. It would be of a brief duration, so she began at once.

"Master Jarvis, what is bundled in that old blanket by the counter?"

"The bones of the celebrated witch Dame Agnes de Roache."

"Why do you have these bones?"

"They were requested by a valuable customer who I am happy to please."

"Who would that be?"

"Master Asmodeus."

Asmodeus was the mightiest wizard in Gorgonholm. People young and old, rich and poor, lived in dread of his name. He was said to be as vindictive and capricious as an evil god. Fortunately, he seldom ventured into the streets of the city, so few ever had the misfortune of crossing his path.

"For what purpose did he desire said bones?"

"I know not."

"By what means did you acquire them?"

"By the hand of a young thief I hired for the purpose."

"What is the thief's name?"

"He calls himself Gavin, though I doubt it is his real name."

"You say he is a thief. Is he not a magician?"

"Nay, not a magician—a thief, and quite skilled for one so young."

"Why do you say so?"

"He invaded the cathedral and retrieved the bones from its crypts. Such a deed calls for great skill and daring."

Jarvis blinked as the spell wore off, his eyes regaining their recognition. As instructed, Sarah gathered the cursed talisman, very relieved to have it back in her own hand.

Back on the street, she gave vent to her burning rage.

"Oh, that big lump of goblin shit! That scabby prick! He used me from the start, used me like some high and mighty lord might use his housemaid. He lied to me, told me what I wanted to hear, stole my money, sent me on a dangerous job so he wouldn't have to do it himself, and then tried to screw me on top of everything else."

Thurmond tried to comfort her, calm her down.

"Let it go, Sarah. It's over. He's gone. There's nothing more for it."

She was, however, in no mood for soothing words.

"I will *not* let it go! By God's holy elbows, nay, I will not! Let's go find him right now. I want my money back!"

"Find him how? You don't know where he lives, do you?"

"I don't know where he lives, but I know who does—the people at the alehouse where I contacted him before. They sent their potboy for him. I'll tell them I have something of his I want to return. When they send the kid, you can follow him to wherever he goes."

"Then what, Sarah?"

"Then we'll force him to return my money."

"And what if he refuses or doesn't have it or if he fights back or has friends with him? I might have to kill him. Are you ready for that?"

"I'm ready for almost anything right now. Let's go!"

They soon stood at the door of the strange little alehouse. As Sarah had reported, it was quite unlike a typical tavern—very small and narrow and dark. The door was so low they would have had to duck to enter. It had neither signboard nor any other indication that it was a place of trade.

Sarah was about to step through the door when Thurmond suddenly clutched her shoulder and pulled her back. He had spotted a small figure, a fearsome tentacled creature, painted on the beam that served as the door's lintel. It was the sigil of the Brethren, Gorgonholm's dreaded crime cult.

This fearsome organization controlled the smuggling, thievery, extortion, and murder-for-hire that occurred within the city walls. Such activities were conducted only with permission of the cult's leader, a mysterious figure known as the Patron, who demanded a sizable cut of each take. Freelance criminals were summarily butchered, their eviscerated remains dumped in a public square to demonstrate the Brethren's sincerity.

The city's tradespeople were generally left to conduct business unmolested as long as they dutifully paid the boot tax to the Patron's collectors. Those foolish enough to refuse experienced such runs of bad luck and ill health that they were forced to reconsider their rash decision. For the average citizen, there was no advantage in declining the Brethren's demands.

All this was well known to Sheriff Brandon, the city's official keeper of law and order. He, however, found it prudent to ignore the complaints of wealthy travelers and foreign merchants who came to him with tales of kidnapped daughters and pilfered inventories. In exchange, the Brethren kept random street crime to a low level.

The only area where mayhem and pillage prevailed was Old Shambles, the city's poorest quarter. Neither the sheriff nor the Patron was equipped to bring this squalid section under control. Within its narrow confines, a throat could be cut with little concern for official consequences.

Having lived on the street during his first two years in Gorgonholm, Thurmond was quite familiar with the sign above the door.

"Hold it! See that thing with all the legs?"

Sarah paused.

"That black kraken?

"I don't know what you call it. Just take a good look at it"

"It's a kraken, an aquatic monster that—"

"None of that matters. The only thing that signifies is that it's the sign of the Brethren. You've heard of them, right?"

"Aye, from you. Of course."

"That's their sign. That creature over the door means this is one of their dens. You were right, this isn't a regular tavern. These people are in league with the Brethren. Your fancy fellow must work for them."

"What?"

"Listen, when you were living a pampered life in your father's mansion, I was just trying to survive. I had to know about things like this if I wanted to stay alive. I should have thought of this before—that sorcerer Asmodeus wanted the bones from the cathedral. He would be rich and influential enough to get the Patron to sanction it. Jarvis was in on it too. He must have hired the thief, but he has no idea Gavin used us to do the stealing."

"So what? What does this have to do with getting my money back?"

"It means you *don't* get it back. If we interfere with the Brethren, we're dead, plain and simple. I don't think your fancy fellow intended for you to leave the stone circle last night. It would have been much better for him if you weren't alive to tell the story. That's the way the Brethren does business. We might both be dead right now if he told the Patron about what you did to him, but he's probably too ashamed to admit a girl took him down. We have to stay out of the city for a while."

CHAPTER 11

IN THE HANDS OF
LADY FORTUNE

In a small tenement room just few doors away from where Thurmond and Sarah were standing, Gavin readjusted the bloody rag tied round his lower face. Never in his life had he felt so angry and humiliated. His plan had been brilliant, its execution perfect. How could he have failed so miserably? There must be a reason.

He thought back on the events that brought him to such a sorry pass. He had been hired to steal some old bones from the cathedral. He knew neither why these bones were wanted nor who required them. All arrangements had been made through an intermediary, the man called Jarvis—safer that way. It had been a simple contract. He had fulfilled his end of it and been paid accordingly. And how clever he had been when he convinced that little witch to do his work for him. She had actually paid him with good coin to be allowed to do so. That was the way he operated—let others take the risks while he took the gold.

Gavin was not his real name. He revealed that bit of information to no one, for names carried too much power. He told no one where he had been born nor offered any true details of his personal history. And he never shared his real thoughts. He had no friends. His familial connections had been severed long ago. He slipped in an out of his identities easily—a new one for each new circumstance. A master of disguise, he could, as the occasion called for, portray a rich young dandy or a dull-witted, weather-beaten rustic. He could affect the dialect of any of the kingdom's provinces, and alter his gestures, gait, and stance to match his every persona.

He had become Gavin specifically for the young witch. It was a name that bespoke honesty, dependability, and strength—qualities all girls wanted in a man. His garb and grooming had been carefully contrived to appeal to her uncultivated tastes. It had been too easy. She had succumbed to his charms within moments of their meeting. The dumb little harlot never suspected she was all part of his plan.

He had been well pleased when she brought him the bones, but then something had happened that immediately rendered their importance secondary. That silly slut, trusting him implicitly, had given him the golden talisman she found in the tomb. What a stroke of great good fortune! Gavin had immediately recognized the medallion as an item of value, but he did not learn its true worth until he showed it to a debauched and degraded wizard he met in a tavern. The besotted imbecile had, for the price of a drink, identified the symbols as those of a powerful witch cult residing in the mountains of Carpat, a kingdom far to the east. Having found out what he needed, Gavin followed the wizard into a privy, broke his neck, and left the body—drawers around ankles—slumped on the wooden seat.

The witches, the Sisters of Something-or-Other, might be willing to pay handsomely for the medallion's return, but it would be much more profitable if he used it to penetrate their stronghold. If they allowed him to pass through their front gates, he could steal the rings from their very fingers. They were women as well as witches, after all, and they would be as susceptible to his charm as any of the myriad wives and daughters, nuns even, he had used and discarded.

But that stupid little witch had caused a problem. His soul burned with rage as he recalled the events in the circle of stones. She had grown willful, refused his advances, and denied him something she should have been eager to give. Then, to his great consternation, the bitch had kicked his ballocks and broken his nose. Still worse, she had taken the medallion from around his neck.

He could not understand it. All the wenches loved him. All of them! He made it so easy for them with his warm smile and caring eyes, the hint of a soft heart beneath his manly strength. They would perform any deed, absolutely anything, in order to please him. They would, at his command, violate marriage vows, steal from their elderly parents, betray their own children. What made this Sarah think she was better? By what right did she refuse his demands?

It occurred to him why he despised her so much—she reminded him of Mother. She was willful just like Mother had been. And like Mother, the witch failed to recognize how special he was. Well, Mother had lived to regret her willfulness, indeed she had. In her final moments, the total truth had been revealed—that her son was a semidivine being to whom lesser men and women were as cows and sheep. He would see to it that the witch soon enjoyed a similar moment of revelation.

The silly little doxy could have made it so much easier on herself. He had not intended for her to suffer. Just one quick twist of the head, and she would have died without so much as a whimper—no fear, no pain, just sudden oblivion. Gavin was, after all, quite skilled at delivering a quick easy death. Her willfulness had changed all that. The selfish little whore had to die soon, die slow, die hard. So did her dolt of a lover, the one who had slashed his face while he lay helpless on the ground.

But above all, he must get his medallion back! It was the key to his fortune.

It suddenly occurred to Gavin that he needed a drink. He did not often indulge in alcohol, but his neck hurt, and he craved an escape from the unrelenting torrent of his own dismal thoughts. The Black Kraken, the private alehouse around the corner, would have a goodly supply of uisge on hand. It was just what he needed.

As he stepped into the street, Gavin realized his sudden urge for a drink did not descend on him by chance. It was the work of the always benevolent Lady Fortune, whose favorite he was, for he saw, just ahead and entirely unaware of his presence, the witch and her bumpkin making their way toward Market Square.

He would have preferred a much more painful end for the pair of them, but this was too great an opportunity to miss. It was obviously a gift from Lady Fortune, and he must accept it graciously. He stepped up his pace and drew his dagger from its sheath. He could, if he hurried, catch them from behind and cut their throats before they knew he was there. If Good Lady Fortune continued to smile, the slut would have the medallion on her person. If not, he would contrive a way to ransack her quarters.

Gavin's plan might well have come to fruition had Lady Fortune been as constant and loving as he believed. Unfortunately for him, she chose that moment to display her zeal for the unexpected.

A black rat, scurrying along the edge of the street, was spied by a feral cat lurking in the gloom of an alley. The ensuing chase led the panicked rodent directly beneath the hooves of an oncoming cart horse, the hungry feline close behind. The horse, old and nearly blind, remained unaware of the creatures underfoot until its right forehoof came down squarely on the cat's furry back. The crunch of bone so alarmed the superannuated equine that it reared as sharply as its old, worn muscles would allow. This maneuver caused the rickety, overloaded cart to tip backward and spill the contents of a large open-topped barrel onto the street.

The owner of the cart was a *gong farmer*, a man whose unenviable occupation was the emptying of privies and cesspits. When caught in this distressing series of events, he had been bringing his load of *gong*—human waste—to a gong broker, who then sold it to gong dealers, who in turn delivered it to farmers to fertilize their fields. It was, all in all, a tidy business arrangement.

The falling barrel, filled to the rim with ordure most foul, landed squarely at Gavin's feet. This could have been bad for him had he not been blessed with such exceptional reflexes. Instead of being drenched with gong, he skipped back so lightly that not one spoonful fell upon the toes of his boots.

Yet Gavin was not destined to escape unscathed. Even before the toppling of the barrel, two apprentice stonecutters had singled him out for some well-deserved abuse. Dressed in the dirty, ragged smocks of their trade, they resented the young dandy in his tight hose and short, embroidered tunic. Their hair and beards were filthy and matted, while his were clean and neatly trimmed. They hated him on sight. The graceful backstep by which Gavin dodged the spilled shit was not to be endured. This mincing fop had to be made to suffer.

Gavin was still standing on tiptoe, congratulating himself for escaping the cascade of waste, when a meaty hand struck him hard between the shoulder blades and sent him face-first into the muck. He rose at once, dagger in hand, but by the time he wiped the filth from his eyes, the two laughing apprentices had disappeared.

Up ahead, Sarah and Thurmond proceeded on their way, unaware of the drama unfolding behind them.

CHAPTER 12

RETURN TO
STAYNES HALL

Sarah was reluctant to heed Thurmond's words of caution. She was at that moment too consumed with ire to fear the Brethren or the Sisters of Sathas or even the Red Contessa herself. Seeing that she was temporarily beyond reason, Thurmond took her by the sleeve and pulled her away from the doorway and on down the street. She resisted a bit at first, but then acquiesced.

Back in Market Square—not being Market Day, it was largely deserted—Sarah regained her composure.

"I know you're right, Thurmond. But it's hard having to accept what that pig did to me. If I don't at least try to get even or get my money back...I don't know...I'll lose respect for myself or something. I can't just let it go by."

Thurmond understood her point of view. He felt much the same way but was a bit more circumspect about how to proceed.

"Bide your time. Wait for a better opportunity. Maybe it will never come, but be ready to strike if you see the chance. Then you're not giving up, only picking a more effective moment. It's not being weak, just not being stupid."

His words cheered Sarah.

"That's a good way to look at it. Thank you. You pulled me back when

I was determined to be stupid. It seems like you're always saving me from something these days."

"I seem to recall you doing the like for me."

Sarah smiled.

"Maybe so, but I'm still grateful. And you're right, we should remove ourselves from the city for a while."

"True enough. But...?"

Thurmond knew Sarah very well and discerned from the lilt in her voice that something more was in the offing.

"Before we go, I want to pay a visit to my father."

"Him? Why do you want to see him?"

"I don't want to see *him*. I want to use his library. He's got far more volumes of magical lore than I can ever hope to own. There are some things I want to try to look up."

"Like what?"

Sarah did her best to sound offhand, but in reality she was suffering from a mounting anxiety. The medallion's demand was unrelenting—she must dig through the musty piles of books and scrolls to discover the whereabouts of Castle Sathas.

"Just some occult things. What difference does it make? Will you come with me or not?"

As always, Thurmond followed along in spite of his misgivings. The pair soon stood before the massive portal of Staynes Hall. It was Thurmond's third visit to the premises but the only time he had come as something other than an intruder in the night.

On the first occasion, he had been a common burglar. This was when he first encountered Sarah, and she ran away with him to escape the incestuous inclinations of her brother Bart. It had been quite a night. The second time, Sarah had led him into the library through a secret passage. Their intention was to appropriate a document declaring Sarah to be Lord Percy's natural child. But to their surprise, they were confronted by Lord Percy himself, who, far from being offended by their clandestine incursion, seemed mildly pleased to see his daughter and gave over the desired document with a good will.

Sarah raised the heavy iron ring of the knocker and gave the door a series of vigorous raps. She smiled at Thurmond.

"That ought to wake them up a bit."

They waited several minutes before the ponderous oaken portal swung open. To her surprise, it was Giles, her father's butler, who answered her call. She had never before seen him lower himself to such a menial task. Door-opening had always been duty of lackeys or housemaids. His demeanor, however, had not altered. Giles remained as cold as ever.

"Miss Sarah."

Sarah returned the hauteur the butler had always shown her.

"Giles, I've come to see my father."

When Giles stood unmoving in the doorway, as if uncertain what to do, Sarah glowered.

"Well, Giles, are you going to admit us?"

The butler shifted to one side.

"Of course, Miss, but you will be pleased to remain in the entry while I announce your arrival."

The entry was a long, wide, high-ceilinged room, bare of furnishings save for a series of large decorative urns running along each wall. This was the very room in which Thurmond had effected his first larcenous invasion of the property. A second-floor balcony ran across the far wall. It was from this point of vantage that a plucky ten-year-old had nearly skewered him with a crossbow bolt, the missile whisking the hat from his head.

Sarah's gave the butler to a dismissive look.

"Do that, Giles, and tell him I'd like to use his library for an hour or two."

The butler returned a slight nod and left them. Sarah noticed the residence was unnaturally quiet. A year ago, her father had maintained a large household staff. There had always been people coming and going, arguing and gossiping, laughing or weeping. Now she saw no one, heard nothing. Why were there no sounds of normal human existence? A pall of death seemed to hang over the house.

Giles reappeared as silently as he had departed.

"His Lordship is indisposed and regrets that he cannot receive you this day. The library, however, is at your disposal."

Thurmond was very pleased to hear this—he dreaded another meeting with Lord Staynes. The man was obscenely old and was enduring the consequences of a life spent in pursuit of depravity. His face oozed with open sores. He trembled continuously as if consumed with ague. His breath was a gurgling wheeze. He reeked of age, stale urine, and sin. How Lord Staynes could continue to live was mystifying. That someone so decrepit could still draw breath defied all decency and logic. Sarah believed he was kept alive by a spectral agency.

He had, in his younger days, been an infamous rakehell, concerned only with gratifying his own carnal appetites. But then, late in life, he had become a collector of ancient books, particularly those concerned with the occult. This had at first been puzzling to Sarah. She was certain her father, like most of his social class, had no skill at letters. She believed Lord Percy had purchased the books in a desperate effort to extend his decaying life. He had undoubtedly hired a master magician, perhaps an entire college of them, to scour those venerable tomes in quest of a rite, a potion, a spell to convey longevity to his cadaverous body. Sarah thought again of the dwindling household staff. Many had been quite young. Where could they have gone? She could only imagine the depraved practices and ghastly sacrifices used to infuse vitality into putrefying tissue.

Giles led the pair down the corridor to the library and unlocked the door with a key from a large ring on his belt. He turned to leave, but Sarah brought him up short with her most imperious tone.

"My friend and I require refreshment. A cold chicken would do nicely, along with some bread and cheese—the soft, creamy kind with the green strands. And two bottles of wine."

Giles acknowledged her commands with a brief nod and was gone.

Sarah entered the library and examined the familiar shelves with their long rows of bound manuscripts. Along one wall, racks held ancient vellum scrolls. Her father's desk was cluttered as usual with random papers and artifacts. Beside it stood the cabinet from which she had taken the document affirming her parentage.

Many of the library's volumes were in the abstruse language of the ancient Etrusians—a tongue Sarah learned as a young girl. She quickly scanned the shelves for the books she needed. Some works were blasphemous grimoires of the blackest magic—the revolting *Ritus et Ritulia Obscena* and the forbidden *Compendium Spirituum Tobiæ*. She considered a crumbling tome with a wooden binding but then recalled that its author, a desert-dwelling nomad, was said to be mad, so she left it on the shelf. She already had enough craziness in her life.

Giles returned with the food and drink. This time, his departure was so quick he seemed to evaporate. Thurmond was starving and fell to at once. Sarah perused the shelves while gnawing a chicken leg. Finally, she selected Sinestre's *Sorores de Obscuro Dea* and Aquinas Magus's *Historia Cultum Maleficos*.

A full bottle of strong red wine coupled with the past two nights of little sleep soon caused Thurmond's eyelids to droop. He stretched out across two chairs and was instantly asleep. Sarah sat at the desk with her books, eating with one hand, turning pages with the other, and taking an occasional sip of wine. From time to time, she rose and drew down another book from the shelves or unrolled one of the scrolls.

While reading *Geographia Prohibitum Silvestri*, her efforts were at last rewarded. She sat up straight, took a deep drink of wine, and drew furiously with quill, ink, and parchment taken from her father's desk. She paused, leafed through several pages, and drew some more. A look of satisfaction crossed her face. She set down the pen and drained the last of her wine, her task complete.

Crossing the room, she shook Thurmond's shoulder.

"Wake up, Master Slugabed, I have something to tell you."

Thurmond sat up abruptly, completely disoriented and unable to remember where he had fallen asleep.

"Whaaa…are you all right? What's the matter? Where am I?"

"Listen to me. This is important. Here, have some wine—there's still a little in the bottle. Now listen, I've got an idea. Maybe you'll like it, maybe not. But it might bring us enough gold to get us through these hard times."

"Argh…no more wine. Please, by God's holy arse…"

"Stop complaining and just listen. I've found Castle Sathas, the place

Fishbone told us about. It took some reading and thinking, but I'm sure I found it. We can go there."

Thurmond was now awake.

"And why would we want to go to such a horrible place?"

"Because we have the medallion, the emblem of the Sisters of Sathas. I don't think they're as bad as Fishbone says. Maybe they've changed since the old days. You never know. If I'm right, perhaps they can teach me what I need to know, help me become the adept I've always wanted to be. But if they're really as bad as we heard, I'll pose as an eager apprentice and apply for membership. That way, I can get inside and find a way to let you and the others in. Then we can steal everything they have. What do you think?"

"I think your brain has gone soft. That is way too dangerous."

"More dangerous than going down into a cave full of goblins and kobolds with absolutely no idea what we were getting into? More dangerous than having assassins, and imps, and evil witches coming through our door? We seemed to be able to hold our own. What's different here? You're not afraid of mere women, are you, Thurmond?"

This last taunt was unfair. Their greatest nemesis had been Lady Renata, a powerful witch.

Thurmond felt caught in a bind and was unsure of how to respond.

"I don't like it, Sarah. It just sounds too dodgy."

"Because I thought of it? How sound was *your* plan during *your* adventure? All you had was a map, but no real idea of what it might lead to. How is my plan any less practical?"

"I don't know. Maybe I'm wiser now. But I'll tell you what—explain your plan to Roscoe and Torgul. They're a lot more experienced than either of us. They'll know what to do. If they go along, so will I."

"That's fine. That's what we'll do. But I'm telling you straight up, Thurmond, if they say no, I may well go anyway on my own. I really want this."

"Do you want this for the good of us all or just for yourself?"

That was a question to which Sarah could not afford to give an honest answer.

"Come on. Let's get back to Grimsgard. If we leave now, we can get back for supper. I'm betting Florio has laid on another of his spectacular meals. Shall we go out through the front door or the secret passage? Oh, I know, let's take the passage. Giles will think we're still in the house and have to search it top to bottom trying to find us."

CHAPTER 13

SUPPER WITH TORGUL

It was the grandest meal yet. Smoked beaver tail enlivened with a comfit of tadpoles and lizard roe, served on a bed of turnip leaves. Broiled snails so fattened on beer they could no longer retreat into their shells. A light puree of liver, kidney, heart, and lung. A score or so of whole thrushes baked in a large pie. Roscoe was still off on his secret business, but Torgul, Sarah, and Thurmond gorged until their stomachs felt fit to burst.

Torgul filled their goblets with another round of mead. He had drunk copiously and was feeling expansive.

"'Tis pity Roscoe ain't here to join us in this fine meal. That pie was dainty enough to lay before a king. A feast like this oughta be sung about. Maybe I should play the bard and compose a verse in its honor."

The young people braced themselves. They found dwarven poetry exceptionally tedious. Compositions took hours to recite and tended to consist mostly of long lists of who was begat by whom. Torgul, however, considered poetry the highest expression of dwarven culture and, in an effort to instill in them an appreciation of the art form, often insisted his friends endure his endless recitations.

They were therefore relieved when Florio entered the great hall and stood before them, looking humble and submissive.

"I trust the repast is acceptable."

Torgul rose from his seat, came round the table, and stood before the elf.

"Master Florio, I'm sure you're aware us dwarves are a plainspoken race. We don't much care for dressin' up our words with a bunch of frippery that takes away from what we truly mean…"

Thurmond and Sarah rolled their eyes, having endured interminable sessions of dwarven frippery.

"…so I'm just goin' to tell you—that was the best food I've ever ate, and you are the greatest cook that ever lived."

That said, he delivered a bow so deep his beard swept the floor.

Florio was taken aback. A strong tradition of distrust existed between dwarves and elves, so he did not expect such a demonstration of courtesy. He understood Torgul was making an exceptional effort to show his appreciation. He chose his response very carefully, trying to be as direct as his exaggerated sense of decorum allowed.

"I am very gratified you find my efforts to your liking, Lord Torgul. I have been trying to make myself useful…to you and the others. I hope you find my other exertions on your behalf equally satisfactory. I am happy to report that the house servants and field workers have gained a better understanding of the benefits of honest toil. There will be no more slacking or shirking of duties."

Thurmond was amazed. He had believed nothing short of divine intervention would inspire the serfs to work.

"How did you manage that, Florio? None of us could get 'em moving. What's your secret?"

"My father was the majordomo in the household of a great elven noble. I was brought up to take his place and instructed from early childhood in the management of servants. I suppose it's in my blood."

"Come on! There's more to it than that. I've seen you with your wooden spoon. The serfs and servants are scared to death of it. Is it magical?"

Florio's passive expression hardened slightly, as if he found the question somewhat offensive.

"Nay, milord—it is a perfectly ordinary wooden spoon I found in your kitchen. No different, I assure you, than the one your mother used to stir your porridge as a child."

"Then why are they afraid of it? A wooden spoon can't hurt them—can it?"

"In sooth, it cannot, nor would I do them any injury even if I could."

"Then why does it hold such power?"

The elf shifted from one foot to the other, clearly reluctant to reveal his secret, but Thurmond persisted.

"Tell us, Florio. Shouldn't we know what's going on with our people in our own fief?"

Florio sighed.

"Very well—I've been playing upon one of their buried fears, a dread so deep most of them have forgotten it."

The young man was puzzled.

"What are you talking about?"

"Your mother, I assume, had such a spoon in her kitchen when you were a child."

"Aye, naturally, all mothers have such implements."

Florio turned his eyes—they were green and slightly slanted—straight into Thurmond's. They seemed to bore right into his brain.

"Did she ever use her spoon for a purpose other than cookery?"

The memory slammed into Thurmond like the heavy fist of a blacksmith. Indeed she had, and the thought of it made him cringe. He stood silent, his mouth agape, transported back to the grim days of his childhood. He could smell the greasy reek of his mother's ragged, unwashed clothing.

The elf spoke again, his voice sharp, as if addressing a naughty child.

"You will answer my question. To what other purpose did she put her spoon?"

"To rap my knuckles when I was bad—sometimes the top of my head. It hurt terribly."

Then the spell was broken, and Thurmond was again in the great hall at Grimsgard. Yet something of the moment remained—the awful fear of the wooden spoon.

Florio at once apologized.

"A thousand pardons, milord, but I know no other way to explain save through a brief demonstration. Every human mother, it seems, threatens her children with a wooden spoon, and that fear digs deep into their souls. They may forget it later on, but it lingers still. By showing the serfs and servants the spoon, I revive their old dread. They now fear me as they once feared their own mothers. It is a harmless trick to ensure obedience."

Thurmond was distinctly peeved.

"Harmless my arse! Am I to go through life afraid of wooden spoons?"

"Nay, nay! Your mind is much too strong. You had but the briefest of recollections, and it will fade away quickly. It should be fading already."

That was true. Thurmond no longer feared his mother's spoon—or any damned spoon.

Now Sarah spoke.

"You are truly an elf of many talents, Florio, but I never suspected you were also a magician. How advanced are your skills?"

Florio seemed astonished by the question.

"Magician? Nay! I have no occult power."

Sarah was not satisfied.

"How do you it, then—this touching of people's minds?"

"It's simply a skill some elves are born with. I learned it from my father, who found it quite useful for managing his master's household."

Sarah could well believe this. Elves had a reputation for being tricky and manipulative. Now she knew why.

"How do you do it?

"When I look into a person's eyes, I can cloud their mind so memories buried deep inside come to the top. Sometimes I can arouse certain feelings, like I do with the spoon—that's all."

Sarah became entirely serious.

"You must never, Florio, under any circumstance, try your trick on me. Is that clearly understood?"

"Ay, milady, I understand entirely. In any case, your will is far too strong to be affected by my small power. I was barely able to penetrate the mind of milord Thurmond—yours would be quite impossible to touch. The simple minds of the serfs, you see, are much easier to influence."

Sarah wanted to believe him, but she needed to be sure. She rose as if to excuse herself from the table, then turned quickly and spoke her truth spell into the elf's ear. His eyes grew appropriately blank as the magic took hold.

The young witch wasted no time.

"Have you been entirely honest with us, Florio?"

"I have, entirely."

"Can we trust you to be faithful and true?"

"Indeed, you can."

"Are you considering any deed or misadventure that could…"

The elf's eyes cleared as the spell wore off. It was never long lasting, but its duration in this case was unusually brief. She had to wonder—were elves resistant to the effects of my magic? Was he truly under the influence of her spell? She could not be certain. He would bear watching until she knew him better.

She resumed their earlier conversation as if no interruption had occurred.

"One more question, Florio. You've fed us snails fattened on beer, owl eggs, beaver tails. There's nothing like this in the larder. Where are you getting such exotic foods?"

"Elves are children of nature, milady. We treat the earth with due respect, and it offers its bounty in return."

The elf bowed to the group and left the room.

With their bellies stuffed and no other business at hand, Sarah finally broached the subject that had occupied her thoughts all afternoon.

"Torgul, I have an idea. Something Fishbone talked about has inspired me."

She gave the dwarf a quick rundown on the medallion and Sisters of Sathas.

"I got curious. Thurmond and I went to my father's library this afternoon to see if I could learn more about the cult. Well, I found what I was looking for, and I located Castle Sathas. I made a copy of a map that shows where it is. I want to go there. If they're truly as evil as Fishbone claims, then they're worthy of whatever destruction we can bestow upon them. And if they're as rich as he says, our money problems will be over."

Thurmond chimed in, clearly agitated.

"Sarah, by God's great hairy shoulders—how can we overcome a cult of such supreme witches?"

The girl remained unruffled.

"We'll use the medallion to our advantage. It has real power. It even scared Jarvis."

"Aye, real evil power. You heard him. He said throw it in the river."

"I don't think he understood what the medallion actually is. It's charged with female energy. Men always fear such things. Woman magic doesn't feel natural to males, so they assume it's evil. This is a potent charm, to be sure, but I don't feel anything malevolent about it."

"I do! I get a strange sick feeling every time I hold it."

"That's the woman magic. It might not sit well with you, but that doesn't make it evil. Remember how you used the medallion to drive off that horrible crypt ghost? It had to exude positive energy to do that. It even worked for you—a male.

"Thurmond, I'm not saying the charm's *not* dangerous. We don't even know its purpose. But I'm certain it is powerful and that I can control it once I learn its properties. What do you think, Torgul?"

The dwarf was silent for a long moment, pondering. When at last he spoke, his tone was measured and thoughtful.

"I'm thinking we're desperate short of funds and that Roscoe will lose the fief unless we come up with something soon. I'm thinking that it's a perilous and even outlandish idea you're proposin', but right now, I don't have a better plan. I'm thinking we have to give it a try. Where is this Castle Sathas located?"

Sarah brightened, her voice eager.

"In the kingdom of Carpat, a mountainous land far away to the east. Have you ever been there?"

"Nay, missy, but I've heard tell of it. Supposed to be a haunted land, a realm of blood-sucking nightgaunts and shape-shifting wizards. No sane person would ever go there. It sounds like our kind of place."

"You will go?"

"Aye."

"What about Roscoe? Do you think he'll go along?"

"Pretty sure. He's not one to hold back, especially with things so critical."

Thurmond re-entered the conversation.

"Speaking of Roscoe, do you know where he is, Torgul? He went off, but he wouldn't tell us where or why?"

"I've a fair idea, but I'll not be sharin' it.

"Why not?"

"If he wanted you to know, Prospect, he would've told you himself."

The reminder of his lowly Prospect status was always sufficient to ensure Thurmond's compliance. When he fell silent, Sarah took up the conversation.

"Maybe you can silence Thurmond that way, Torgul, but I'm no Prospect. I'm not trying to join your Adventurer's club. Tell us where he is."

"If you want the details, missy, you'll have to ask him when he gets back… if he gets back. I'll only say he's out trying to raise some coin. Something so risky he wouldn't even take me along. He's out doing his best for all our sakes. All right?"

"All right, Torgul. I didn't mean to be disrespectful."

"No offense taken. Say, I think it's time for me to go sing to my bees. If you'll excuse me…"

The dwarf rose and left the young couple alone in the great hall. Sarah touched Thurmond's hand.

"Did they ask you about last night?"

"Aye, they did. I told them only…"

"What did you tell them?"

"Only that we fell asleep by a log."

"Good! I was afraid you might embellish your tale with a lot of fanciful details."

"Nay, I wouldn't do that."

"I thank you for that. It's hard enough living here with three blustering men without becoming the subject of everybody's lurid gossip."

No matter how vigorously Gavin scrubbed himself, regardless of the scented water he lavished on his skin, the foulness of the gong still lingered. Its greasiness clung to his fingers, its odor to his hair, its flavor to his tongue. Humiliated and befouled, he had at first been tempted to throw himself into the river—better to drown than to endure the laughter of the townspeople and the taste of gong.

Now he was in an inconsolable funk. Good Lady Fortune had forsaken him. She had thwarted his desires and brought him misery. How could this be? He was her favorite. She had always before granted him his every whim. There must be some reason behind her change of heart.

He thought and thought, striving to discern her purpose, searching for the cause of her disapproval. *Lust! It has to be lust!* His problems had all started in that accursed stone circle, where he tried to use the witch for his carnal pleasure.

He should have quietly murdered the bitch when she brought him the bones and dumped her body in the river, but he had allowed her pretty face to tempt him. And that had caused him to neglect his own cardinal rule—never take unnecessary chances.

The Good Lady had tried to counsel him, had sent the kick in the nuts to remind him to control himself, but he had failed to heed her warning. Instead, he had allowed his anger to cloud his judgment. Trying to knife the witch in the street had been foolhardy, a rash act inspired entirely by wrath. There had been far too many pain-in-the-arse bystanders who would have gladly told the authorities what they had seen.

And then, of course, there was his overweening pride. Pride was such a dangerous and destructive emotion, and it was the real cause of his problems. The witch and her lover had not injured only his body, they had wounded his pride. Trying to strike them down in the street had been a desperate attempt to restore it. In his pride, he had grown too confident in his own abilities, had forgotten that his successes all stemmed from Lady Fortune. She had sent him a barrel full of gong to remind him to stay humble.

Yet she had not truly forsaken him, for even her punishments revealed her unrelenting love. His misfortune had kept him from being arrested and hung on the city gallows. The significance of the gong incident was not lost upon him. A murder in broad daylight on a busy public street would have landed him in a far deeper puddle of shit.

Not that he intended to forgo vengeance—not at all! He still intended to take his revenge on the witch and her paramour. He could not afford to let such an affront go unpunished. But he must be more circumspect, must not take his great good luck for granted, must always show his appreciation to the Good Lady.

He would therefore choose a more secluded place to murder them, one that allowed him to fully enjoy the experience.

CHAPTER 14

THE LAYING OF PLANS

Roscoe returned on the third day. The others were enjoying a delightful snack of pickled mooncrawlers in aspic when he burst through the doors into the great hall. He smiled his broadest smile as he tossed a leather wallet onto the table. It gave off a heavy *thunk*, the unmistakable sound of coin.

In spite of his good humor, the old Adventurer looked extremely weary. His face was drawn, a deep scratch ran down his left cheek, his right arm was bandaged, and his limp was more pronounced than usual.

Thurmond jumped from his seat and brought his mentor a bench. Sarah pushed the bowl of amazingly long worms toward him, and Torgul poured him a large measure of mead. Roscoe nodded in appreciation.

"Thankee. I'm plumb worn down, so I am. A bit carved up, too. But there's enough in that wallet to see us through the winter, perhaps a bit longer if we're chary with it."

Sarah spoke up.

"We are very glad you're back. I was worried. You were so mysterious about whatever it was you were doing. Can't you tell us about it now?"

"When I choose to keep a secret, young lady, I generally do it for good reason."

Sarah was never one to back down in a battle of wills.

"No doubt your reasons are excellent. Nonetheless, could there not be even more compelling arguments for revealing the source of this gold? Your wounds proclaim it was won at sword-point. Will not the former owners seek to reclaim it? Do we not have a right to know what we might expect?"

"Calm yourself, lassie, no one will come for that gold."

"How can you be so certain?"

"Because they…have no more interest in it."

"You mean they're all dead. All right then, but will the sheriff not take an interest in their demise…or perhaps the Church…or the dead ones' friends? How can you be so sure all of us are not to be threatened by some unforeseen danger?"

She had him. The task he had undertaken had been extremely dangerous, and there was just the slightest chance that things could yet go badly. He had to tell them, but he decided to delay a little, downplay it by making a game of it.

"By the fangs of God, Sarah, you are, in sooth, a deadly foe in a battle of wit. I must yield and declare myself defeated and disgraced."

Sarah was not to be outdone in a duel of either reason or diction.

"Then I accept your surrender, Master Adventurer. So gallantly did you proffer it that I must respond in kind. I am now pleased to return to you your honor entirely intact and unblemished. And whilst I revel in my newly won glory, *will you please now just tell us where you've been for the last three days?*"

These last words were delivered with such exaggerated emphasis that Roscoe and Thurmond burst into laughter. Torgul may have smiled behind his beard.

"Aye, so I will, lassie. I've been off on a little adventure with my old comrade Scrymgeour."

Scrymgeour was a veteran waterman who operated a small flatboat on the Mad River. These days, his business was mostly confined to hauling legitimate goods and passengers, but in years past, he and Roscoe had made a good living running sword blades and spearheads to the Keltins in exchange for casks of uisge.

Roscoe continued his story.

"There ain't many freelancers bringin' in uisge anymore. The trade is all controlled by the Brethren, and woe to anyone they catch dealin' on their own. Of course, there's always a few brave enough to do a little business now and again. Scrymgeour's a fearless old rooster, so he is, and he knows where to find the best product, so he does.

"Well, what with him havin' a new young wife, and her bein' fit to burst with a new baby, I figured he might could use a bit of extra coin. And right I was. He was most eager to make a run. The job should've been quick and easy, and all would've gone smooth and fine had we not encountered a bit of difficulty.

"We was on our way back with a goodly stock of the best drink ever known to man—no offense, Torgul, as you brew a fine mead, but I'm talkin' a beverage infused with real hellfire—when who do we meet but a crew of Brethren men with a load of their own.

"Now this was a bad moment, for they saw our faces clear, which meant the Patron's bully-boys could track us down later. But we had a bit of luck, for they believed themselves entitled to our supply as well as theirs. This led to a disagreement in which they were less than fortunate."

Sarah interrupted.

"You killed them over a load of uisge?"

"Nay, we slew them in the defense of something that was rightfully ours—namely, our very own lives. For they were set on having them as well as the uisge. Don't forget—these was all red-handed killers. It ain't like the old days, when me and Scrymgeour kept our dealin' small and friendly. Back then, almost nobody got hurt. But it's all big time now, with cold-blooded murderers behind it."

Thurmond interjected, his voice tinged with excitement.

"How many were there?"

"Only five."

Thurmond beamed.

"Five! You two old-timers dispatched five Brethren toughs? That's a real feat of arms! And Scrymgeour lives still?"

"Aye, he's as hardy as he ever was, though a tad sliced up just as I am."

Sarah remained dubious.

"This is a bad business, getting on the wrong side of the Brethren. Suppose they find out it was you. Won't they come here?"

"And how would they be findin' that out? We left no one to carry the tale."

"I don't know. Maybe your friend Scrymgeour will get drunk and talk too much. Or he'll spend his coin too freely and someone takes notice—someone sent to watch for that very thing."

In sooth, this was a concern, for Roscoe's friend was sometimes given to boasting when in his cups. But he did not want to alarm the others, so he dismissed the possibility.

"Nay, lassie, Scrymgeour's too canny for that...and too tight-fisted to spend any coin he doesn't absolutely have to. If they did find him out somehow, he's much too loyal to give me up."

"You say he has a young wife who is big with child. What if they hold her toes over a fire? Wouldn't he talk to save his family?"

This was Roscoe's greatest worry. What would Scrymgeour do if forced to make that choice? There was no way to know for certain, and he was unwilling to continue deceiving his friends.

"Let us hope, lassie, that question remains unanswered. In the meantime, you will please recall that I am an Adventurer, and that we Adventurers earn our living by accepting risks other men quail from. We needed funds, and I have procured them. Naturally we added the slain miscreants' load to our own, thereby doubling our profits."

Sarah realized further discussion was pointless. She was still deeply concerned about her own brush with the Brethren, and the thought that Roscoe might also draw their ire sent chills through her bones.

Torgul, in typical dwarfish fashion, remained dour and silent while the humans bantered among themselves. Finally, he spoke.

"It seems to me, Roscoe, you've done a fine deed. You've brought us gold, saved your own life and that of your companion, and made the world a better place by riddin' it of five louts who most certainly deserved to die. I say, well done."

"Thankee, my brother. I knew as a fellow Adventurer, you would see things in the proper light. And I might add that I've also provided our city with a soothing beverage to slake its ardent thirst, so I have."

"Aye, that you have. But since your fine deed might bring Brethren killers to our door, maybe we oughta disappear for a bit. What think you?"

"I do indeed concede to the wisdom of your words."

"That's mighty good, because Sarah and Thurmond have thought up an adventure that'll get us out of town and with any luck fill our purses with gold enough to last for years. Want to hear about it?"

"Most certainly."

Sarah explained her plan to journey east in search of the Sisters of Sathas, always careful to downplay the danger while describing the potential for glory and treasure in the most enthusiastic terms. They knew that Roscoe was typically receptive to such outlandish schemes, the possibility of wealth and excitement outweighing the danger of suffering and death.

When her proposition was complete, Sarah sat holding her breath, nervously awaiting the old Adventurer's response. Whatever doubts Thurmond entertained, he kept to himself. They expected that Roscoe would ask many questions and consider deeply before rendering a final decision.

To their surprise, he immediately embraced the idea, for he was quite eager for a break from the dreary responsibilities of running his fief. He proclaimed himself Adventure Captain, as on their previous outing. In his capacity he would make all important decisions and would receive for his efforts the greatest share of whatever treasure they recovered—three-eighths after expenses.

Torgul, next in line in experience and, like Roscoe, an Adventurer in good standing, would again serve as lieutenant and earn a customary two-eighths. Sarah and Thurmond, still lowly novices, would receive one-eighth apiece. Though a much smaller cut, it was considerably more than non-Adventurers typically received. Any other servants or fighters they needed would be hired for a fixed rate.

The remaining eighth would be retained for unexpected expenses, such as a funeral service, or compensation for the loss of a limb or eye. Anything left over would be divided between the four of them.

They started making plans, for there were many details to attend to. Roscoe turned control of Grimsgard over to Florio. The elf had been with them for only a matter of days, yet they all agreed he seemed entirely trustworthy. He certainly possessed administrative skills far greater than any of them.

Their destination was deep in the northern mountains of Carpat, a terrible forgotten territory that was, in winter, buried in deep drifts of snow. With that season coming, they needed to be in and out quickly before the temperature fell, or they would not get out at all.

The trip would be long and expensive. They would need heavy cloaks, thick wool blankets, and sturdy felt tents. Sarah clamored for special occult supplies that were, she claimed, absolutely essential. Thurmond argued for a dozen hired swordsmen. Roscoe, however, chose to keep their adventuring company as compact as possible.

Bodo and Lars would come along as men-at-arms. Both had a smattering of military training, and had proven themselves brave and loyal on their previous adventure. They would have to be outfitted with armor and weapons. Two serfs would be recruited as camp servants and baggage handlers. All would require horses. Two mules would be necessary for provisions and equipage.

It was obvious such expenditures would so deplete the available funds that there would be little left to feed Grimsgard's population in the coming months. But Roscoe remained unconcerned. Florio's ability to exploit the bounty of the natural world afforded him every confidence that the elf would find a way to provide for his people.

The group should, with any luck, be back before winter set in. And if all went according to plan, they would return so laden with treasure they could spend the year feasting and reveling. His tenants would have plenty to eat, and he could leave off worrying about crops and debts and indolent serfs.

Roscoe spread Sarah's map on the table.

"Sarah, would you be so kind as to tell me what all this means?"

The girl moved to his side and explained all she had learned about Castle Sathas and its location.

CHAPTER 15

An Encounter at the Goddess Spring

Thurmond sat in a green glade deeply shrouded by the thick surrounding forest. He watched as a small spring forced its way through a crack in the rocks and rolled down to fill the pool beneath. The stones of its lip were slick with moss. This was the Goddess Spring, a place venerated since ancient times. The spirals, quarter moons, and wriggling serpents cut into the surrounding stones were symbols of She-Who-Abides.

Grimsgard's villagers, particularly its women, came regularly. Small food offerings around the pool's edge offered ample evidence of their devotion. Strips of cloth dangled from overhanging tree branches, tied there to attract the spirits of the air as they wavered in the breeze.

There was, Sarah claimed, an awesome and potentially terrible power in the lazy, peaceful spring. Here was the limitless energy of the natural world— power far greater than that wielded by the most accomplished human wizards.

Thurmond knew Sarah would appear shortly. She liked to come to this cool spot in the heat of the day to tend to Whisper, a benign woodsprite she had rescued by transplanting a tiny root sprout from the decaying oak he had formerly inhabited. As a mere sapling, Whisper had lost most of his previously formidable powers, but his spirit lived on. Sarah claimed she could feel his gratitude whenever she brought him water from the sacred spring.

Thurmond had no particular interest in tree spirits or ancient goddesses. He came today to speak to Sarah away from the others. Something was not quite right with her, and he meant to find out what it was. Something to do with that damned medallion.

His thoughts were interrupted by a quiet rustling in the undergrowth on the far side of the spring. Somebody or something was coming. Not Sarah—she would arrive on the path. Perhaps a boar coming down for a drink? Nay, the approach was too slow and stealthy, too cautious. A large stag? Nay, the rhythm of the movement was wrong. The sounds grew closer, and he recognized them as the footfalls of a man proceeding with a remarkable degree of grace and restraint.

Thurmond slipped into the shadows, where he could watch the spring without being seen. Instinct told him to be careful, to let the other fellow show himself before he made his own presence known.

He saw him then—a man crouching behind a large tree on the opposite side of the glade, obviously taking care to conceal himself. The figure seemed familiar, but the light was too dim for a good look at his face.

Sarah emerged on the path from the village. The man left his hiding place and blocked her path. Taken unawares, she stepped back in complete surprise.

"Gavin, what are you—"

The man uttered not a word but struck her on the side of the head with his fist. She went down without as much as a whimper.

Thurmond sprang from the shadows to confront the attacker.

"You, leave off! Stand away from her!"

Unintimidated by these words, the man placed his hands on his hips and gave a malevolent grin.

"Come on, boy! Let's get this done so I have my way with this wench."

Gavin prodded the unconscious girl with the toe of his boot. When she stirred not, he drew a long dagger and advanced on Thurmond. The latter at once produced his own blade, a short, single-edged knife designed as a tool rather than a weapon. He had not anticipated having a fight on his visit to the spring.

Thurmond was reasonably well trained with sword and shield. He knew the basics of the battle-axe, glaive, and spear, but he had not practiced much with a dagger. Roscoe believed in keeping one's enemies at a greater distance. No one, the old Adventurer claimed, came out of a knife-fight entirely intact.

Gavin was an expert in close combat with daggers. As a professional thief, his dexterity and reflexes were excellent. He had received the best of training and developed his skill with years of diligent practice. He glided toward his opponent with supreme confidence in his superiority.

Thurmond attempted two ineffectual feints, but these drew no response. He realized that his opponent's knife-fighting ability was far superior to his own. Then with one swift move, Gavin was upon him. He shifted slightly to one side, drawing Thurmond's blade in that direction. Spinning back, he caught the young man's knife-hand in an unbreakable grip. His own blade lashed out, slashing Thurmond straight across the chest. Simultaneously he kicked Thurmond's feet from beneath him, throwing him backward to the ground.

The fight had lasted no longer than the flash of a serpent's tongue. Thurmond lay flat on his back, gasping in pain and shock, bleeding heavily from a chest wound. The thief's foot was grinding his knife-hand into the soft loam of the forest floor.

Gavin chortled in sardonic glee.

"I've been needing to kill you, so I'm quite grateful you made yourself available to me today. I…"

At that moment, Sarah rose from the ground, her magical dagger, her anthame, in hand. She aimed a strong underhand stab at Gavin's left side, just below his short-ribs. But the thief's fighting instincts were too keen. Maybe he caught her motion in the corner of his eye, or perhaps he merely sensed her presence. He turned so suddenly that her blade, rather than piercing his vitals, raked diagonally across his hip before digging deep into his left buttock.

He shouted out in pain. His leg gave way, and he sank to one knee. But even in falling, he lashed out with his fist, striking the girl square in the face with a backhand blow that left her, once again, stretched out on the ground.

Finding himself released, Thurmond sprang at the injured man and sank his blade to the hilt into the base of his adversary's neck. The man tried to scream but was unable. His arms flailed as he toppled over the mossy rocks and into the pool, his eyes expressing a profound disbelief. Blood flowed like a river from his wound to mix with the sacred water of the Goddess Spring.

Holding his hand to his injured chest, Thurmond was relieved to see Sarah attempting to rise. He looked into the pool, which was now stained red. Then a wave of dizziness passed through him, and he toppled down next to the dead man.

Thurmond grimaced as the needle was pushed up through his skin and the thread pulled snug. The big Adventurer with the great round belly chuckled.

"You felt that one, didn't you, boyo? Better take another drink. We've got a deal more to go."

The young man took an obedient slug from the goblet in Roscoe's hand. The harsh flavor of the uisge was somewhat ameliorated by a generous measure of addleberry juice. He gritted his teeth in anticipation of the next stitch. Leaning against a pile of bolsters and soft fleeces in the glow of the great hall's massive fireplace, he was as comfortable as his friends could make him. But his offended flesh was a howling agony.

Roscoe chuckled as he slowly closed a gash that extended nearly shoulder to shoulder.

"You're lucky, boyo, so you are. This cut's a big one, to be sure, but not deep. Must sting like the very devil though, I'll warrant."

Indeed it did, more so now than back in the woods when as he lay beside his attacker on the edge of the Goddess Spring. At first, his perceptions had been dreamy and unfocused. The pain had yet to set in. But when it came, it came hard.

Sarah, too, was splashed with blood. Most of it was Thurmond's, for he had bled freely during the long, dreadful walk back to the towerhouse. She had persevered in spite of her smashed nose, pulling Thurmond along on shuffling feet, holding him up by one limp arm hung across her shoulder, and delivering him to Roscoe. Then she had gulped a mug of fortified uisge.

Torgul left to remove the corpse from the pool. It would not do, Roscoe said, to leave such things lying about where they might be found.

Roscoe continued his patter. Thurmond knew he was trying to distract him from the on-going stitchery.

"You've no need to worry. I'll have you good as new in a trice, so don't be gettin' twitchy. Take another drink. Got to get you up and about—we'll be leavin' here pretty damned quick."

With his wound closed and the uisge taking hold, Thurmond felt the dreaminess edging back. Perhaps it was the addleberries, which were notorious for provoking bizarre dreams and wondrous visions. Thurmond was scarcely awake when Torgul returned from his task. As he sank into slumber, he heard the dwarf's voice, low but filled with tension.

"I found a big puddle of blood, sure enough, so he was sore hurt, and a trail of it leading off into the bushes. But he was gone. Not dead enough."

The big man's reply carried no less concern.

"Now that's not good, not at all. If he's with the Brethren, we've bought ourselves a power of trouble. The boy's first scrape with that rogue was bad enough, so it was. But the Patron ain't about to forgive him for cuttin' up one of his own like that. We'd better fade right soon."

CHAPTER 16

THE THIEF AND THE SHAMAN

Gavin awoke from a terrifying dream in which he re-lived the excruciating knife fight. He still felt the coldness of the blade entering the flesh of his neck, the pumping of his blood from the torn vessels, and the gushing spring water as it filled his nose and mouth.

The meaning of his defeat was nearly as painful as the wounds he had suffered—Lady Fortune had abandoned him again. He had tried so hard to amend his sinful ways, to curb his lust and anger and pride, just as she wanted. What had he done wrong?

He sifted through the details of the last few days, seeking an explanation. His plan had been excellent, each step executed with meticulous care. It should not have failed.

He had presented himself at the witch's dreary little village in the guise of a diseased and noisome beggar. All had gone exactly as expected. Transient vagrants were common enough in rural villages, so he had attracted no undue attention. His pox-ridden countenance—a testament to his skill with face paint—and the persistent gong-ish stench had kept the villagers at bay, allowing him to set about his task without interference.

He had spent two days loafing about the cottages, all the while watching as the stupid girl went about her daily routine. He had quickly learned when she rose in the morning and retired at night, when she took her meals, and how often she visited the privy. He had watched as she took afternoon walks down a woodland path to visit some supposedly sacred spring.

Killing her should have been so easy. Even the unexpected appearance of the bumpkin lover should have presented no problem. Both had been helpless at his feet. Yet Lady Fortune had again turned against him. *Why?*

Then another thought struck him—had he really been that unlucky? The bumpkin's knife had opened the veins in his neck. He should by all logic be dead, and yet he lived! Something special in the spring water had stanched the flow of his blood and preserved his life. That had been pure good fortune! The Good Lady had not wholly abandoned him.

There could be only one answer—he had been impatient. Such a childish fault. A skilled and experienced professional such as himself strikes only when the ideal moment presents itself. He had been careless in trying to take her so close to home.

Then another realization came to him—the bitch would not have been carrying the medallion during her walk in the woods. It was too valuable. It would have been tucked in a secret place in the towerhouse. Had he killed her, he would still have had to sneak in and find the damned thing.

A new plan formed in his mind. During his visit to the village, he had used his ears as well as his eyes. Though few of the thick-witted peasants had deigned to speak to a scabby beggar, they had jabbered incessantly with one another. He had learned their master—a great tub of guts called Roscoe—was preparing for a long journey. That could only mean one thing—the witch and her companions had discovered the nature of the medallion and were preparing for a journey to Carpat. They, too, intended to raid the castle of the witch cult.

Gavin would go with them, unseen, of course, until the perfect moment. This time the stupid flirt-gill would be dead before she even saw him coming. He would be on her like a snake on a hapless rabbit. So far from home, she would be certain to have the medallion on her person, probably hanging around her neck.

Gavin knew the journey to faraway Carpat would be long and arduous, so he set out at once to make the needed preparations. First of all, he needed someone with firsthand knowledge of the desolate kingdom, someone who spoke the language, preferably someone with occult skills. And as always, someone he could safely dispose of afterward.

Only one person in the city of Gorgonholm, the Patron, could bring him such a minion. As head of the Brethren, the Patron had at his disposal a wide circle of kidnappers, extortionists, thieves, murderers, smugglers, renegade magicians, and fallen priests. No one knew the identity of the Patron or dealt with him directly, but his henchmen carried out their tasks quite openly. He must, therefore, locate such a person.

Though the hour was late, Gavin made his way to the Black Kraken, where the tavern keeper introduced him to a scar-faced man with the appropriate affiliations. For a certain fee, Scarface accepted Gavin's note and promised to pass it to a second man, who would send it up the chain to a third.

The next afternoon, Gavin received word that his request had been approved and that, for a rather large sum, a suitable individual would be provided. Thus, he received Ghleet, a stoop-shouldered, bleary-eyed villain with the long arms of a monkey. His skin looked like badly tanned leather. His teeth were but blackened stumps, causing his breath to reek of rot. He stood no taller than a dwarf.

Ghleet was a native of the mountains of Carpat, who had been captured, sold into slavery, and brought west, where he eventually found himself the property of the Patron. The loathsome captive was permitted to live because he possessed one valuable attribute—he was a shaman, something like a priest of the natural world. The shaman's powers were derived not from a divine entity but directly from the currents of energy found in all living things— mighty forests, grass-covered steppes, and life-force of animals.

Shamans enjoyed the unique ability to meld their own spirits—their personal energy—with those other currents, allowing them to feel what a tree feels, to know the swaying of branches in an evening breeze and the rush of sap in a warm spring afternoon. A shaman could soar overhead in spirit form, looking down on the earth with the eye of a hawk or swim with the grace of an otter in the cool waters of a mountain stream.

Because shamans could influence the natural currents, they could also cast spells that manipulated certain aspects of the physical world. They could summon or disperse wind, rain, and snow. They commanded the obedience of feral creatures from wrens to bears. And they could predict natural occurrences, such as earthquakes, landslides, and floods. Like clerics, shamans could heal or at least remedy disease and injuries. The most advanced were rumored to speak the language of the dead.

Unfortunately, Ghleet had proven to be far more bother than he was worth. His nature-based abilities were not in high demand in urban Gorgonholm, and much to the Patron's disappointment, he lacked the ability to commune with the dead. Moreover, he was troublesome and had to be kept in close confinement. At one point he summoned a legion of rats that overwhelmed and consumed three of the Patron's henchmen, stripping their flesh right down to the bones.

Wizards were then dispatched to block his psychic emanations, but they had become infested with a sudden plague of fleas and were forced to withdraw. Snakes found their way through cracks in the stonework and sank their fangs into whichever gaolers piqued Ghleet's displeasure. Given such tribulations, the Patron was quite glad to sell the ugly little shaman to Gavin for only slightly more than he had paid for him.

Gavin examined his purchase with disgust. The wizened runt was dreadfully filthy, his bald head and shoulders covered with oozing sores. His breath was horrid. Wanting to win the shaman's loyalty, Gavin began with a conciliatory tone.

"Would you like to see your home again, to go back to your home in the mountains? Be free? I can make that happen."

Ghleet said nothing but began to hop up and down on one foot. A spark brightening his lifeless eyes. Gavin's distaste for his new acquisition grew.

"I'll take your little jig for an *aye*. Good. Now here is what you must do to earn your freedom. I have a matter of business in those mountains of yours, and I need an assistant with your unique abilities. If you serve me loyally and well, I will set you free at the completion of my quest. Fail or betray me, and your soul will be fed to demons. Do we have an understanding?"

Again the hopping, this time accompanied by the slightest nod of Ghleet's head. Gavin suspected that the man was a mindless idiot, but he pressed on.

"Excellent—then you will gladly submit to being placed under a geas to assure your compliance. You do, I assume, understand what a geas entails. You will obey my commands and complete your tasks dutifully or you will endure spiritual torment beyond description. Are you agreeable? A geas can only be placed on a willing subject."

Ghleet hopped and nodded some more, a drop of saliva running from the corner of his mouth. Gavin was now regretting his purchase of this imbecile.

"While I must commend your aptitude for nonverbal communication, I would appreciate a more specific response. You possess the power of speech, do you not?"

Hopping, nodding, and drooling, Ghleet managed a froggy croak.

"Ghaaagh."

"Speak up, sirrah. You are of no use to me if you cannot speak intelligibly."

Ghleet said something in what at first sounded like a foreign tongue but upon more careful consideration was found to be a heavily accented version of the common trade language.

"Ah zavve mazder on well doe yuer will."

"Oh, my—so you can speak. Then we have an understanding."

In actuality, Ghleet understood every word spoken by Gavin and was entirely capable of responding in a coherent manner, but years of subjugation had taught him the wisdom of duplicity. Never admit to knowing anything. Always play the fool. Function beneath the expectations of your tormentors. Gavin was entirely taken in.

"According to your, uh, previous owner, you have the power to heal. Is that correct?"

"Ghaaagh."

"Well, if that is so, why haven't you attended to those ghastly sores on your head and body? By God's bald pate, man, they're revolting."

Ghleet shook his head vigorously from side to side.

"Cand hell mezelv."

This was a common problem for clerics of all types. A healing spell that worked perfectly well when cast upon others most often malfunctioned if applied to oneself.

"I see. Now that you mention it, I've heard tell of that. But you can heal others, correct?"

"Ghaaagh."

"Then come lay hands on me now. I have nasty wounds in my neck and, uh, upper leg. They must be attended to before the rot sets in. Let this first task serve as a test of your ability to obey my commands. You may impress me with your skill."

"Ghaaagh."

The next morning, Gavin examined his neck in a reflecting glass and was surprisingly satisfied with the results of Ghleet's healing. The light in his little room was dim, but he could see the wound had closed, and the festering had ceased. The throbbing pain had abated to a dull ache.

He looked at Ghleet curled up like a sleeping child in a far corner and apparently comfortable on the bare floor with nary so much as a blanket. Once rest and nourishment had restored the shaman's powers, Gavin would demand a second treatment. After that, or perhaps a third, he should be fully recovered.

There was much to attend to before beginning the trek east. He and Ghleet would require suitable equipage. He had to find a magician to set a genuine geas to secure the shaman's allegiance, and he must pay a cleric to cure the oozing sores that covered the little man's head and body. He could not tolerate such a disgusting sight on a daily basis.

Ghleet was a truly vile creature. As soon as his usefulness ended, he would be disposed of.

PART 3

A LONG DANGEROUS QUEST

CHAPTER 17

WITH BOMBARDO ON THE GOLDEN ROAD

The heavily laden caravan moved with grinding slowness, the pace set by the plodding hooves of the oxen. These immense brutes, bred for strength and endurance rather than speed or intelligence, drew low-slung drays, sideless wagons of extremely stout construction, specifically designed to carry vast cargoes over rough terrain. In the event of an attack, the drays were chained together in a large square that afforded excellent protection to the caravaneers. When rivers had to be crossed, the wheels could be removed, transforming the drays from wagons to rafts.

Roscoe had known that it would be slow going when he made his bargain with Bombardo the caravan master, yet it galled him as the days flew by so much more quickly than the leagues beneath the wheels. Time mattered. They must enter the Carpatan mountains, complete their business, and make their escape before deep snow began to fall.

Gavin's stabbing and subsequent disappearance had dictated immediate departure of the adventure party. There had been no time for Sarah to purchase occult supplies. Tents and cloaks remained on the merchant's shelf. The companions had simply gathered whatever equipage was at hand and set out. Thurmond's wounded chest still pained him some, but Florio had instructed Sarah to brew a tea of certain leaves, roots, and berries. This vile-tasting concoction permitted the young man, though injured, to ride with the others. It also made him seriously loopy and slurred of speech.

Florio had been given complete authority to manage the fief as he saw fit until their return. He was left with the keys to all the doors, the strongbox, everything. Though Roscoe had known him but a short time, the old Adventurer trusted Florio. The elf was amazed. These humans seemed to genuinely like him—even the dwarf. Incredible.

Bodo and Lars were lucky to be alive, and they owed that to Roscoe. Both had been menial laborers before becoming the armed retainers of Sarah's half-brother, Bartholomew Staynes. They had faced almost certain death when their ill-fated adventuring party was nearly annihilated by goblins. Fortunately, Roscoe came to their aid and subsequently recruited them into his service.

Bodo was the elder of the two, somewhere in his mid-thirties. Years of hard physical labor had made his lean limbs exceptionally strong. He was a quiet man, not much given to bawdy songs or strong drink, but steadfast and capable in a fight. Lars was a lusty, muscular fellow of perhaps five and twenty years. The old Adventurer suspected that the man's enthusiasm for the new adventure was largely inspired by his desire to flee Bodo's sister-in-law Maybelle, with whom he had shared a brief involvement.

Both now wore rusty hauberks and carried cheaply made swords and crossbows that had been purchased in haste just as the adventuring party was leaving the city. Roscoe promised to provide helmets, shields, and other vital equipments at the earliest opportunity. Their mounts—another last-minute acquisition—were of equally spurious quality.

Two serfs completed the party. Murd was a large, placid man with roughly the intelligence of a sheep. He was, however, extremely gifted in the handling of animals, and was always content when in their company. Skrot was younger and smarter. Roscoe hoped that the latter trait would prove to be a virtue rather than a problem. Skrot had volunteered for the journey and was put in charge of the baggage.

Bombardo, as master of the caravan, had been eager to add the two seasoned Adventurers and their retinue to his contingent of armed retainers. Adventurers were widely known for courage, reliability, and skills at arms. The mere sight of their broad black hats might deter would-be raiders. In exchange for their service, the Adventurers would join the caravan free of charge and receive a small stipend.

Thurmond's chest wound healed quickly. Sarah applied a paste made of a greenish powder that reminded him of mold. It caused the cut to itch unmercifully, and he was tempted to wipe it off, but Sarah insisted the itching was a sign of healing and warned him to keep his hands off it.

The first leg of their journey was the easiest. They traveled the broad Golden Road, a royal highway stretching from Gorgonholm in the west to the city of Vistu in the east. This major trade route brought caravans of exotic goods from far distant lands. It was, by royal decree, well maintained and protected. Bridges spanned rivers and gorges. Landslides and fallen trees were quickly cleared away. Royal Road Guards were commissioned to defend travelers from the deprivations of bandits or marauding goblins.

All this was well known to Thurmond, though he had never before been in this part of the kingdom. He often sat in the city's taverns, listening as travelers and traders recounted their tales of the road. Of what waited beyond Vistu, he knew but little—only that the lands beyond were bleak, demon-haunted, and fraught with peril.

Thurmond heard Bombardo's voice booming from up ahead. The caravan master kept to the front of the long, winding column, sitting astride his huge horse, scanning the trees and ridges for signs of hidden threat. His bull's bellow warned the teamsters of potholes that might snap an axel or soft verges likely to give way beneath a dray's crushing weight. Gallopers were sent up and down the column to speed the sluggard or slow the reckless.

Thurmond instinctively liked the caravan master, admiring his consummate professionalism and good-humored blustering. Bombardo was a big man, as tall and broad as Roscoe but without the great round paunch. A prodigious beard covered most of his face and spread upon his chest like a fan. He was always loud, his voice seeming to have but one pitch—that of an enraged lion.

The position of caravan master carried grave responsibility, for the cargo in his charge could purchase a small earldom. The drays were filled with raw materials of the west bound for the legendary cities of the east. There were ingots of copper and tin, bales of flax, exotic furs, and iron-bound chests of unpolished amber. Barrels of raw pitch nestled against others holding beeswax. A gigantic weasel the size of a small bear snarled angrily from a massive hutch fronted by close-set bronze bars.

One dray carried a pile of untanned hides atop a large number of casks supposedly containing salted fish. In fact, these held the consignment of uisge that Roscoe and Scrymgeour had smuggled across the river. It had been sold and re-sold so that Roscoe had no inkling of its presence in the caravan. Nor did Bombardo have any idea of Roscoe's connection with his cargo.

The caravan was comprised of such a wide array of vehicles and personalities that Bombardo was hard put to keep them in an orderly line of march. Each coterie, it seemed, was determined to proceed at its own pace. The caravan's scouts cantered on quick-stepping palfreys, while its men-at-arms rode sturdy cobs. In addition to the drays, a multitude of light wagons and small carts carried the tools and materials of the many blacksmiths, wheelwrights, cooks, grooms, and hunters needed to keep things rolling.

Most of the teamsters and servants traveled afoot. Some brought their families along, so toddlers wandered amid the hooves and wheels. Drovers prodded a small herd of cattle. Shepherds with dogs drove a flock of sheep and goats. And every caravan included a designated soothsayer to cast the bones and read the entrails—these being the surest means of divining Lady Fortune's intentions, good or ill.

A motley assortment of wayfarers, pilgrims, minstrels, and itinerant craftsmen paid a fee to enjoy the security of the caravan. The wealthier were mounted or rode in private conveyances. Most trudged wearily beneath the weight of rucksacks and panniers.

A troupe of traveling players sat on a large pageant wagon, which doubled as their stage. Next came a group of Blue Friars on mules. Then a magician with a long gray beard and huge bulbous turban, riding in a covered wagonette pulled by four milk-white ponies.

A knight on a long-legged hunter wore a habergeon of rusty mail. A dented and equally rusted helm hung from the cantle of his saddle. His squire, a lean somewhat foppish youth, rode at his side. Behind them, a yeoman dressed in the green tunic of a forester led a packhorse.

It was imperative that this disparate and often contentious assembly be kept together. Anyone falling behind was isolated and vulnerable. Though the Royal Road Guards patrolled the Golden Road, gangs of highwaymen, goblins, and even ogres lurked in the adjacent hills and woodlands, ever eager for likely prey. The unwary or ill-prepared traveler could expect no mercy from such as these.

The Road Guards could be a source of menace as well. They were notorious for extorting exorbitant tolls, bullying travelers, stealing their goods, and violating their women. The caravan encountered several squadrons of guards. In each case Bombardo produced official documents to prove the appropriate road tolls had been paid. He was also careful to bribe the guards with coins and wine.

There were of course inevitable conflicts between disgruntled caravaneers. Two wagon-drivers lashed at each other—first with words, then with whips—when their wheels inadvertently locked together. A youngster was severely thrashed for theft but later found to be altogether innocent. A more serious fray ended in a stabbing after a traveling peddler discovered his wife in a strenuous physical engagement with a Blue Friar.

Less dramatic events provided a modicum of diversion. An old man was found dead in his blankets, but the cause of his demise could not be determined. Several oxen were struck by an inexplicable malady that caused their tongues to blacken and hang limply from their mouths. Three rambunctious boys were badly stung after disturbing a nest of hornets. Witchcraft was suspected in each these incidents.

Indeed, life in the caravan was not remarkably different than that in a typical village. People loved and hated, joked and squabbled, gossiped and boasted. They worked, played, fought, lied, laughed, ate, shat, and brooded just as they always did. Some groups struck up fast friendships and banded together for mutual support. Others remained aloof, avoiding unnecessary involvement in the affairs of their travel companions.

At night, secure in the laager, the caravaneers pursued a number of pastimes. The friars prayed ... well ... some of them did. The caravan's official soothsayer opened his tent for business, supplementing his regular salary by charging the travelers for palm readings. Young men regularly competed in wrestling and other feats of strength.

A family of itinerant tinkers hosted a lively gathering each evening. Their encampment resounded with the music of fiddles, flutes, and bagpipes. Ale could be had for a farthing a cup. That was a steep price, but there were no alehouses along the route, and a man had to drink. Ale, it was said, cleaned the blood of impurities, so it was consumed with good gusto.

As the evenings progressed and the ale continued to flow, the music grew louder and the dancing wilder. The pounding of drums lured friars from their devotions. And in the shadows, the tinker women sold their affections to the caravan's lonely men. Lars loved visiting the tinkers. Bodo, older and more sedate of temperament, held back from such diversions.

Sarah took little interest in the affairs of the other caravaneers. She was content that each day's journey brought her closer to the achievement of her most pressing task, the return of the medallion to Castle Sathas. She knew not why she must accomplish this task, only that she must. Every slight delay wrenched at her soul. Only when the caravan was actually making headway— slow going though it was—did she feel at ease.

For Thurmond, ablaze with youthful energy and hungry for adventure, the long dragging trek through eastern Poitiers was painfully tedious. The road wound through a seemingly endless expanse of grassy hills and hardwood forest. They came from time to time to remote towns, but these were drab, impoverished affairs that offered nothing to draw a young man's notice.

Small villages falling between the larger communities were even drearier. The bedraggled denizens would rush forth with desperate sincerity to offer for sale whatever sorry goods they chanced to possess—wilted vegetables, coarse homespun cloth, even their hard-favored daughters. Thurmond, born in such a village, ignored them with studied disinterest.

As they progressed toward Poitiers' eastern frontier, the villages grew even smaller, shabbier, and farther apart, the inhabitants dirtier, uglier, and, if possible, stupider. The landscape also changed, rolling hills and wide valleys gradually giving way to steep slopes and dense evergreen forests.

The scouts' behavior changed as well. Some ranged far ahead of the lumbering caravan, alert for indications of ambush, while flankers probed gullies and thickets for concealed attackers. A contingent of men-at-arms fell back to form a rearguard. Thurmond noted the increased vigilance and re-sharpened his sword, but this was scarcely necessary—he always kept it honed to a fine edge.

CHAPTER 18

BANDITTI, PART ONE

The monotony was broken when the trumpeter sounded the call to arms. The advance scouts had spotted a large party of armed riders approaching from the east and galloped back to give warning to the caravan. Thurmond quickly gathered his war-gear—shield, helmet, and spear. He was already wearing his mailshirt and carrying his sword. Lars and Bodo fetched their crossbows from their baggage. Torgul and Roscoe, veterans that they were, dressed for battle without rush or fuss.

Sarah pulled on a lightweight mailshirt and a small, round, open-faced helmet. She carried a bow, and a cut-and-thrust sword hung on her hip. Though she was much more valuable as a magic user than a fighter, she was prepared to draw steel if necessary.

The group joined Bombardo's men-at-arms. With them came the caravan's sole belted knight with his squire and yeoman. These experienced warriors would be the backbone of the defense.

The unknown horsemen assumed a wide crescent formation as they approached the head of the caravan. The caravan master led his soldiers forward, well ahead of the lead wagon, spreading his men across the road. His scouts produced bows and fanned out on either flank. It was imperative that they delay the attackers long enough for the drays to be drawn into a defensive square.

Behind the caravan master and his soldiers, the professional dray drivers were doing their best to haul their vehicles into position, but their efforts were hampered. The ground was uneven, and a state of confusion soon erupted amongst the inexperienced caravaneers. Although every man, woman, and child had been instructed what to do in case of attack, many, seized by panic, forgot all they had been told. A few tried to turn their wagons about and flee the way they had come. Others fled into the wilderness on foot. Most simply huddled together and got in the way. Women wailed, children cried, and priests prayed. Finally, after the drivers laid on with fists, whips, and cudgels, the wagon-square began to take shape.

Bombardo spurred over to Roscoe and pointed at the approaching raiders.

"They're hillmen. The bastards live by looting caravans. They swoop down, strike before anybody can get ready, and steal everything they can grab hold of. Then they run back into the bloody mountains, where nobody's ever been able to dig 'em out."

As the raiders grew closer, they slowed and finally came to a dead stop as if inviting their foe to come forward to meet them. The distance was too great to ascertain details, but they appeared to be short, stocky men mounted on shaggy ponies.

Bombardo continued.

"These little arseholes can be tricky. This group might be a distraction while a bigger bunch rides up from the flanks. Or maybe they're looking to lure us into chasing them so they can ambush us somewheres up the road. You never can tell."

Behind them the cursing teamsters were still frantically trying to position their wagons.

Roscoe looked thoughtful.

"Seems to me if these fellas were really lookin' to attack us, they would've done it straight away, before the wagons could get in position. So maybe they're just sizin' us up, not really intendin' to attack."

But these words were scarcely from his mouth when, with the blare of a brass horn, the raiders advanced.

In one fluid motion, Roscoe pulled the heavy crossbow from the back of his saddle, drew it with a cranequin, and loaded a bolt. He raised the weapon and took aim at an imposing figure in a tall pointed hat who appeared to be the leader.

The two groups were well outside normal archery range, even for a crossbow. None of the other archers had yet set arrow to string, but Roscoe's bow was exceptionally powerful and his aim true. His bolt carried the pointed hat from the leader's head.

The hillman screamed in astonishment and threw up his hands in a convulsive gesture that jerked hard on his reins. This drove the bit into his horse's sensitive mouth, causing it to rear, spin, and tumble the rider from its back. With their leader down, the other hillmen became confused and curbed their mounts. The attack stalled.

Bombardo's soldiers laughed loudly, adding to the leader's embarrassment as he fought to mount the skittish horse. Enraged and humiliated, he finally regained the saddle and immediately gathered his men to renew the attack.

A horn sounded from the direction of the wagons. That was the signal for Bombardo and his force to withdraw. The drays were finally in position, so it was time to fall back to their protection. Roscoe's good shot had disrupted the hillmen's initial attack, buying precious moments the wagon drivers needed to make vital preparations.

Bombardo led his group through a narrow opening between two drays. Once they were through, a smaller wagon was pulled across the opening. Had there been more time, the drays would have been pushed tightly together with the axels chained to form a solid wall. Given sufficient time, baggage could have been arranged like a parapet along the top of each dray. Boxes and bundles would have been unloaded and used to block the spaces beneath.

Unfortunately, the drivers could do no more than push the wagons into a rough rectangle with inviting gaps between the vehicles. The caravan's flocks and herds had been driven inside, along with the oxen and mules. Thus, the interior was a chaotic tangle of aimlessly milling men, women, children, and animals.

Bombardo immediately took charge, riding back and forth, shouting commands, buffeting laggards, and restoring confidence. There was a flurry of activity as men and women ran to find weapons.

Each of the caravan's groups—the troupe of players, the Blue Friars, the tinkers, the drovers and teamsters, the hunters, the merchants and craftsmen—were assigned a specific wagon to defend. The archer-scouts were sent to find suitable firing positions. Man, woman, and child stood by to defend the caravan with bows, slings, boar-spears, pitchforks, sickles, and clubs.

The guard group dismounted, since wagons were best defended on foot. They remained in the center, held in reserve until a decisive moment. The knight was given command of this contingent. An old warrior, he could be counted on to lead with skill and daring.

Thurmond was awestruck by Roscoe's skill with the crossbow.

"By God's hairy toes, you nearly won the battle single-handed. That was the greatest shot I've ever seen."

"Nay, wasn't that at all."

"Don't be so modest. You knocked that hat right off his head."

"I'm not so modest, Prospect. I was aiming between his eyes."

The hillmen whipped their mounts and charged the caravan at top speed. All carried bows. They rode low in the saddle, rising up only long enough to fire an arrow before ducking down again. Shielded by the wagons, the caravaneers were well protected against such sporadic fire.

As the raiders drew near, they were met by a barrage of arrows and sling-stones. Several were dumped from their mounts. The attack faltered and then veered off to the left, following the perimeter of the wagon-wall, seeking a weak spot.

Many defenders abandoned their assigned positions to run along the inside of the inside of the walls, keeping pace with the horsemen, shooting arrows and hurling sling stones. More saddles were dumped. The defenders' resistance was too intense, too determined. The hillmen could gain no entrance, but still they swept on, rounding the corner and coursing down the next line of wagons. Encouraged by their success, more caravaneers rushed to the threatened section, eager to add their missiles to those of their companions. But in so doing, they left their original positions unprotected.

This was exactly what the canny bandit leader had intended from the start. His trumpeter gave a signal, and a second body of riders, larger than the first, debouched from a hidden fold in the earth. They rode straight and hard for the now undefended section.

The knight recognized the danger at once and led the reserve to meet it. Roscoe and his group were sent to defend a dray stacked high with boxes and bales. It was directly in the path of the onrushing horde of bandits. Roscoe sent Bodo scurrying to the top of the load to hold off any raiders attempting to scale up the side. He ducked behind a bale of untanned hides and cocked his crossbow. Torgul and Lars took one end of the wagon, Thurmond and Roscoe the other.

Sarah was to stay behind with the wagon and to have a spell ready. From there, she could come to the aid of either end as the situation demanded. She could also guard against some sneaky little hillman trying to slither up from beneath the vehicle.

As serfs, Murd and Skrot were not expected to enter the fray. Utterly untrained in the use of weapons, they would have been slain in their first exchange with the warlike raiders. They would hold the horses while the others did the fighting.

The weakest points were definitely the gaps between the wagons. There had been no time to block them up with baggage, so the only barrier between the defenders and the galloping horde was a wagon tongue.

Roscoe placed himself on the left side of the gap. He held his large triangular shield before him, his heavy broadsword low at his side. Armed with a spear, Thurmond took his accustomed spot behind and slightly to the left of his companion-in-arms—something they had practiced many times. From this position, he could skewer anyone attempting to force his way between the wagons. Roscoe's shield would cover them both, while his sword would cut to pieces anyone foolish enough to press in close.

Then the banditti were upon them. One spirited rider, armed with a saber and round shield, sped ahead of his companions, his horse's neck stretched forward. He aimed straight for the gap where Roscoe and Thurmond stood ready, and reaching it, he did not pause. His horse jumped high, easily clearing the intervening wagon tongue. Upon landing, its shoulder struck the two defenders and bowled them over backward before they had a chance to swing a single blow.

The rider wheeled to finish them off while they were helpless on the ground. He would have done so had Bodo not shot him with his crossbow from atop the wagon. The stricken man toppled from the saddle, Bodo's bolt buried to its vanes in the back of his neck.

A second rider, armed like the first, followed close behind, again clearing the wagon tongue with ease. But his horse faltered upon landing, unwilling to tread upon the fallen body beneath its hooves. That awkward moment afforded Thurmond the chance to plunge his spear into the creature's flank. It whinnied and spun sharply away from the source of its pain.

This exposed the rider's unshielded side to Roscoe, who—once more on his feet—chopped down with all his might on the man's thigh. The raider wore no armor, so the blow sliced cleanly through the bone and nearly severed the limb. Without hesitation, the old Adventurer delivered an equally powerful blow just inches above the first. Simultaneously, Thurmond drove his spearpoint into the rider's armpit, knocking him from the saddle.

The third rider fared no better than the second. His mount, frightened by the carnage before it, hesitated as it made its leap over the wagon tongue, causing its rear hooves to strike that barrier. The beast tumbled forward and almost stood on its head. The rider was pitched off and landed face down on the ground, where he was instantly slain by the two stalwart defenders.

On the far end of the dray, Torgul and Lars battled with equal determination. The dwarf's two-handed axe was the perfect weapon for this situation. The first rider was stopped in his tracks when Torgul smashed his horse full in the mouth.

The unfortunate beast screamed and tried to back away, causing it to collide with the mount of the rider who followed close behind. Horses and riders went down in a flurry of flailing hooves and broken limbs. The defenders moved in quickly to finish off both man and steed.

No other riders dared to pass the gaps now blocked by the bodies of their comrades and held by such stout warriors. There were other, easier places where the dead were not piled so high.

CHAPTER 19

BANDITTI, PART TWO

The Blue Friars defended the three drays immediately to the left of Thurmond and Roscoe. These militant clerics were as eager to shed blood as to save souls. They were a large group of more than a score, and well disciplined, so they did not abandon their position to chase the mounted archers around the laager's perimeter. Formidable fighters, they proved quite able to hold their own against the hillmen's initial assaults.

When their mounted attacks failed to penetrate the wagon-walls, the raiders dismounted to assail the friars on foot. While some attempted to force their way through the gaps with spears and shields, others stood on the backs of their mounts to climb up and over the baggage piled atop the wagons. Still others crawled through the spaces between the wheels.

Outnumbered and in danger of being surrounded, the friars were forced to give ground. At their leader's command, they stepped away from the wagons and formed a battle line at a right angle to their former one. Fighting hard all the way, they retreated step by step in an attempt to link up with Roscoe's position behind them.

On the other end, Torgul wiped the perspiration from his brow. Fighting was always hot and thirsty work. He noticed the knight's party, holding the wagon to his right, was in dire trouble. Originally five men defended their wagon—the knight, his squire and yeoman, and two teamsters who he had impressed into his service. One of the teamsters had been slain in the first moments of the attack. Seeing his companion's blood, the other immediately took to his heels.

The remaining three did their utmost to hold their position, but they were simply too few. To avoid being overwhelmed, they too were forced away from their wagon. They were now struggling desperately for their lives as enemy riders poured around the gap at their wagon's far end where no defenders remained. These three stalwart defenders joined with Torgul and Lars.

Gradually the friars, the Adventurers, and the knight's group merged into a tight half-circle, their backs to a dray. Bodo, standing on its top, potted one raider but missed a second. Out of bolts, he dropped his crossbow and jumped down to join his companions.

There was little hope now. They were hemmed in from both sides, cut off and left with no room to maneuver. There was nothing for it but to stand and die.

Riders, couching their long spears under their arms, swarmed in from the right. Thurmond knew he was looking at death. They had no way to protect themselves against the power of charging horsemen.

All this happened so quickly—a matter of moments really—and the confusion was so complete that Sarah had had no chance to cast a spell. Now, at this most critical moment, she knew she must react quickly to stop the advance of the riders. But what spell could she put in their path? A horse, she knew, would be unaffected by illusion—only humans and their ilk could be made to see things that were not really there. Then she had an idea.

A trio of bandits led the charge. They came on eagerly, recognizing the helpless knot of defenders as easy prey. They would ride them down and finish off the survivors with their sabers. Just a few more minutes of fighting and it would all be over—then there would be booty and women and wine.

But of a sudden, out of some devilry, there grew a deadly peril. A line of stakes sprang up from the ground, angled directly at the chests of their mounts. The stakes were as long as a man is tall, the ends sharpened to deadly points. There was no time to think or shout—only to react. The bandits hauled back on their reins with all their strength, bringing their steeds to a crashing halt. Unprepared as they were, all three were hurled from their saddles.

The next rank of riders, unaffected by the spell, spurred forward and piled into the rearing, plunging mounts of the first. The rearmost horsemen, seeing the unhappy fate of their comrades, had time to slow and turn aside to avoid the churning madness looming before them.

The charge was broken. Yet Sarah's clever spell had done nothing more than delay the inevitable. Raiders on horse and foot continued to appear on both sides. There could be no escape.

The bandit leader—he who had lost his hat to Roscoe's lucky shot and then led the diversionary attack by the horse-archers—was now completing a circuit of the laager and was eager to rejoin the main assault group. He was a cunning man and an experienced raider who knew how to weigh the strength of a caravan before committing to an attack. He also possessed a wide array of witty stratagems to place his prey at a disadvantage.

He was quite pleased because his scheme was working to perfection. He and his mounted archers had easily drawn the defenders from their posted positions. Then, according to plan, his real assault force had cut through the wagon-wall like so much soft, white cake. They were now busily slaughtering those few defenders who had any value as fighting men.

The leader spurred his horse onward, lusting for the blood of the merchants and mule-drivers who huddled helplessly within the wagon-square. It would be glorious butchery. The pampered lowlanders and city-dwellers were not warriors, and therefore unworthy of life. He smiled. It was always his pleasure to put them to the sword. Afterward he would have his men make a pyramid of their heads.

But just as he and his riders were about to join the assault group, he sensed things had started to go bad. Some of his men, bloody, weaponless, and without mounts, came fleeing out through the gaps in the wagons. Riderless horses appeared among them, stirrups flying, eyes wide with panic, trampling any who got in their way. Then came a group of riders, swords flailing, striking their own companions as the fought to escape. Arrows and slingstones once again poured from the wagons, shooting down the remaining raiders as they scrambled away.

The bandit chief could not imagine what had gone wrong, but clearly the attack had failed, so there was nothing for it but to break away and head back to the safety of the hills. He was, of course, angry and frustrated—but not dismayed. There were always many young swordsmen and archers eager to join his band. His losses would be made good, and there would always be another caravan.

Inside the wagon-square, the hillmen had been on the verge of a resounding success. The defenses had been penetrated in multiple places. Roscoe's group, the knight, and the friars were penned against a wagon and facing immediate annihilation. More and more raiders were coming through the gaps.

Then, as from nowhere, came Bombardo, his voice booming over the clash of steel and the screams of the dying. With curses, threats, and blows, he had pulled the rest of the caravaneers from their fruitless pursuit around the inside of the wagon-wall. With the sheer force of his will, he had turned his people about and unleashed them on a more reachable foe.

Now they came, falling upon the attackers with the fury of a dragon defending its eggs. Taken by surprise, the hillmen were cut to pieces by a force that seemed to materialize out of thin air. One moment they could taste the victory that was about to be theirs, and the next their bellies were being slashed with bill-hooks, their skulls crushed by farriers' hammers. The raiders were encircled and slain, no prisoners were taken. When one fell wounded, the caravan's women moved in with knives and hatchets to finish the job.

When the last throat was cut, the teamsters and traders and craftsmen, blood-spattered and still aquiver with the thrill of battle, stood silent and unmoving as if holding their collective breath. Then, from somewhere in the back, a cry was raised, and in an instant, it came booming from the mouth of every surviving caravaneer.

"Bombardo! Bombardo! Bombardo! Bombardo! Bombardo!"

They shouted it out again and again and again in honor of the man who had saved them from their own folly and in so doing had given them life. They screamed his name until their voices were raw. Men and women wept openly. Strangers kissed and embraced with an intimacy otherwise unknown.

Those who had not participated in the caravan's defense, who had hidden themselves beneath piles of bedding or among the stacks of boxes and barrels, now came forth, shamefaced but equally happy to be alive. There was a minstrel with his lute, the turbaned magician with his servants, a trio of painted harlots bound for the seraglio of some eastern lord, and the soothsayer. All were overjoyed.

Thurmond joined the revelry as lustily as the rest, hardly believing he and his friends still lived. Sarah, at his side, screamed Bombardo's praises until her voice gave out. Both had fought hard. Thurmond had stood faithfully in his place behind Roscoe, lashing out with his spear until it lodged in a raider's shield and was torn from his grasp. He had then strapped on his shield and drawn his sword, but by the time he was again prepared to fight, the battle was over. Sarah had thrown sleep spells and illusions into the raiders' faces until her magical energies were exhausted. Then she, too, had gone to the sword.

Roscoe, Torgul, Bodo, Lars—all had survived, though every member of their party carried cuts and bruises. No one who fought with edged weapons escaped unbloodied. Bodo had the worst hurts—a long diagonal laceration across his cheek and a bloody contusion of the scalp where his helmet had been struck by something heavy and blunt.

The battle over, the caravaneers began to sort through the aftermath of war. The slain hillmen were thoroughly looted for valuables, but they found very little worth taking. Some of their shaggy horses were rounded up, but otherwise the pickings were slim. The bandits' weapons were crude, and they wore almost no armor. Those ragged scraps of mail and leather that they did possess were scarcely worth stripping from their bodies. Neither gold nor silver did they carry, only a few crude bronze coins. They were an altogether sorry lot.

The looting complete, the raiders' heads were removed and stuck on stakes along the trail as a warning to other would-be bandits. Their bodies were left in a great heap for the nourishment of whatever carrion creatures might come in the night. It was said with some authority that the region abounded in ghouls. And as everyone knew, when a dead man's flesh was consumed by a ghoul, his spirit must wander the earth as a lost and hungry ghost.

The caravaneers had suffered injury, but their losses were not appalling. A goodly number of the scouts and guards were dead, these being among the defenders who had tried to hold their positions against the main attack force. About half the friars were down as well. Losses were relatively light among the rest. A few had been struck by the arrows of the mounted archers, while others fell in the last frantic moments as they overwhelmed the trapped hillmen.

The caravan's dead were treated with as much reverence as time allowed. A long trench was dug, and they were laid out side by side. The grave was covered with a heavy layer of stones to discourage the scavenging claws of wolves and bears. Charonite symbols were placed at the four cardinal points to discourage ghouls. The surviving friars, battered and bandaged, sang a dirge traditionally reserved for those who fell in defense of the faith.

With their dead buried, their wounds bound, and their damaged wagons repaired, it was time to continue the journey. Sarah was relieved to see the oxen being placed in their yokes. The medallion had left her in peace during the battle, but its call returned as soon as the last enemy fell. Now it was filling her with a desperate yearning to be moving, as if it sensed its growing proximity to the desired destination.

CHAPTER 20

ON THE FAR SIDE
OF THE RIVER

The caravan arrived at Vistu without further incident. The city was situated on the western bank of the River Vash, which served as the border between Poitiers and the Kingdom of Bukovia. Vistu was much smaller and less prosperous than Gorgonholm, built more of wood than of stone. Nevertheless, it was of vital strategic importance since it defended the kingdom's eastern border and controlled traffic up and down the river.

For several days the caravan camped just outside the city walls, its wagons chained together in a stout defensive formation. Additional stores were purchased. Various travelers joined the caravan at this point, while several others left it.

One of those to depart was the serf Skrot, who absconded the first night with his horse, a large sack of food, a hatchet, and Murd's ragged cloak. His camp duties were assigned to Lars and Bodo, who grumbled a bit, believing their status as fighting men put them above such things. One stern look from Roscoe, however, corrected this misconception.

Murd remained, presumably because he lacked imagination enough to conceive of a life other than that of a serf. Roscoe bought him a new cloak, since the mountains of Carpat would be cold. He also purchased additional equipment for his men-at-arms.

The hutch containing the giant weasel was unloaded and carted into the city. Thurmond was glad to see it gone. It was a vile beast that exuded a foul, musky stench, which seemed to cling to his hair and clothes whenever he walked by its cage.

There were no bridges across the Vash. When the caravan resumed its journey, it was ferried over on large rafts. These were fixed to a heavy hawser that stretched across the river and passed through an immense block and tackle mounted in a stone tower on the far side. The line was carried back high over the water to an identical tower on the near side and then down to a huge revolving drum. Teams of gigantic oxen—the biggest Thurmond had ever seen—were yoked to an elaborate system of massive wooden gears. When they walked, they turned the drum that wound the line that drew the rafts back and forth across the river.

The caravan was large, so the ferrying was a slow, monotonous process. Sarah grew antsy. The medallion's call grew ever more persistent as she waited her turn to cross the river. It was especially bothersome at night, keeping her from sleep with its incessant demand that she recommence her journey east.

Once on the eastern shore, the caravan was met by a troop of officious Bukovian border guards who demanded a substantial fee before allowing them to proceed. Bombardo paid without complaint. As an experienced caravan master, he was well aware of local customs.

The wide Golden Road at once shrank to a winding track filled with potholes and jutting rocks that tested the skill of the teamsters. Fallen trees and sections of collapsed roadbed necessitated frequent stops. Under these conditions, the wagons began to break down, causing further delays.

Bukovia was a small, sparsely populated land ruled by a cruel and inbred aristocracy that had come up from the south many generations ago. These families kept the kingdom's limited wealth firmly within their own grasp, leaving the native population, the near-feral Slovags, to live or die as best they could manage. The nobility lived in small, foreboding castles perched on craggy outcroppings amid forests even more dark and primordial than those of eastern Poitiers. The caravan came upon no proper towns and only a few sad villages. Such cities and towns as existed in Bukovia were located in the less forested lands in the south.

From time to time, the travelers came upon bands of wandering Slovags. These were a short, muscular folk, dark of hair and eye, swarthy of skin. Their outer garb was comprised largely of sheepskins. All were ragged and filthy. The men rode shaggy ponies, while the women carried heavy burdens and went afoot. The Slovags carried no visible weapons and inevitably drew back into the trees to clear the road for the approaching caravan. They initiated no contact with the caravaneers, watching in silence as the long train passed them by. They looked more hungry than dangerous.

Thurmond had seen that same look in the eyes of serfs who suffered a lifetime of abuse and deprivation—blank faces and empty eyes. Deprived of their humanity, these unfortunate souls had lost the capacity to hate their oppressors or even hope for a better life.

Thurmond was fairly certain the raiders they encountered in Poitiers had been Slovags, though that bunch had been well armed and aggressive. So, he reasoned, not all the native folk had been broken by the oppressive nobles. The surrounding hills must still shelter wild tribes that continued to practice the old ways—stealing cattle, pillaging neighbors, and feuding among themselves.

Beyond Bukovia they crossed into Carpat, a shadowed realm of which men spoke only in guarded whispers. A land of doomed souls, foul blasphemy, and blood-hungry ghouls. A land where sane men seldom ventured. The caravan route followed the wide glacial valleys in the south, avoiding the northern mountains wherein the most hideous legends found their source. But that was the very place the Sisters of Sathas had their lair. Roscoe and company would soon have to strike out on their own along a twisting path leading into the mountains' cold heart.

On the fifth day, the caravan pitched camp for the evening. In the morning, the old Adventurer and his companions would leave it and head northeast on a lesser road. They were resting by a campfire when a man dressed in the livery of a servant approached Roscoe and bowed deeply.

"My master, Buyuk ve Korkunc Sihirbazi, sends his compliments and extends an invitation to take refreshment at his encampment. Is such a thing within the scope of possibility?"

Roscoe's curiosity was piqued. He knew Sihirbazi was the gray-bearded magician who rode in a cart pulled by white ponies, but they had never so much as exchanged greetings. What could he want? Just as important, what kind of refreshment might he offer?

"Am I the only one invited, or are my companions included?"

"As it pleases milord."

"Then you may inform your master that we will call on him as soon as we've attended to a few details here."

"Very well, milord."

As soon as the servant withdrew, the others erupted into a torrent of speculation. According to caravan gossip, Buyuk ve Korkunc Sihirbazi was a thaumaturgist of great accomplishment. Roscoe gestured for quiet.

"Now maybe this fella is just bein' neighborly or maybe he's up to somethin', but I can't see no harm in us havin' a wee chat with him. Maybe he's lookin' to hire a company of intrepid Adventurers, so keep your eyes and ears open while I do the talkin'. Try to get the gist of what he really wants.

"Sarah, do you think your truth spell would work on him?"

"Very unlikely. It's just a simple spell, and a magus like him must be quite able to protect himself. I'd probably just make him mad."

With nothing more to be said, it was time to pay their call.

The magician's encampment was concealed behind brocade screens. A different servant slid back a section that served as a gate, then bowed and gestured for them to enter. Inside, a small circular tent stood beside the magician's covered wagonette. The front of the tent was open, and their host sat cross-legged upon a thick, elaborately patterned carpet. He rose, beckoning them forward and inviting them to help themselves from a pile of plush cushions stacked on one side.

He was a tall man but stooped with age. His thick, gray beard grew nearly to his eyes and achieved such length as to fill Torgul with envy. A huge globose turban of blue silk covered his head. His dark eyes seemed weary and sad as he spoke.

"Ah, Captain Roscoe Franklin if I'm not mistaken. Please forgive my intrusion upon your privacy, but I have asked about you among our fellow caravaneers, and they speak of you in the highest terms. That crossbow shot was magnificent, truly the work of an expert. Welcome to my rather austere domicile. I am Buyuk ve Korkunc Sihirbazi. May I offer you refreshment?"

"Well, aye, refreshment would be nice, so it would."

The magician clapped his hands, and a servant appeared with a silver urn filled with tea, which he served in tiny glasses. Roscoe tried to hide his disappointment—he had hoped for uisge. Thurmond found the drink loathsome.

Buyuk ve Korkunc Sihirbazi continued.

"You must be curious as to why I have extended this rather abrupt invitation. Quite simply, I just learned that you will be leaving the caravan on the morrow and heading into the terrible mountains in the north. My business takes me in that direction as well. Would it be possible for our two parties to join forces and travel together until our paths diverge? I am not a wealthy man, but I could offer a modest remuneration."

The wizard made Thurmond uneasy. There was something in his voice he did not like. He scrutinized the encampment but could find nothing out of place. The tent, the cooking gear, the wagon—all appeared to be perfectly normal. The front flap of the wagonette's cover was tied back, affording him a look inside. An old woman sat wrapped in a shawl. A servant brought her a plate of food, which she broke into tiny bits and ate with her fingers.

Thurmond decided to try his trick, something he often did when a situation seemed amiss. He knew that certain illusion spells—Sarah called them glamours—could be broken by a statement of disbelief. He did this now, whispering behind his hand.

"Disbelieve, disbelieve, disbelieve."

Nothing changed. The magician, the servants, and the old woman remained exactly the same. This did not mean they could be trusted, only that they were not disguised by a glamour spell.

Roscoe was less distrustful than Thurmond, but he did not know what to make of Buyuk ve Korkunc Sihirbazi. What kind of a name was that? It sounded like someone trying to gargle a mouthful of piss. But the magician had been with the caravan since the beginning and had not, to Roscoe's knowledge, caused problems of any kind. His words were polite and his request reasonable.

The old Adventurer did not, however, particularly care for the wizard's three servants. Though they were attired in traditional livery, their scars and tattoos were, to his mind, those of hooligans rather than domestic servants. But perhaps that really did not signify. In their part of the world—wherever that might be—scars and tattoos might carry a very different connotation. Nonetheless, he decided to err on the side of caution.

"Master wizard, I must apologize but I fear my clumsy tongue cannot do justice to your illustrious name. I must confer with my comrades before rendering a decision about your joining us. I'm sure you understand."

"I respect your prudence, Captain Franklin, but I do hope your answer will be in the affirmative. May I also suggest that a man of my unique abilities might prove quite useful in the treacherous land for which you are bound? Please consider well."

Back at their own camp, the companions shared their various impressions. Roscoe was in favor of the alliance.

"I think I like him. He made his request but left it for us to decide—no threats, no boasting, no wheedling—just a straightforward proposal. His servants look a bit rough, but their deportment was above reproach. He'd be a good one to have on our side. I say we accept his offer."

Sarah, too, liked the idea.

"When no one was looking, I cast a small spell that detects the presence of evil. It would have told me if any demonic entities were hovering around him. You know—if he had a familiar lurking about. There was nothing. I think he's all right. Anyway, maybe I can learn something from him."

Torgul remained silent until Roscoe asked for his opinion. His response was, as usual, laconic.

"I could see nothing wrong with him. He has a worthy beard."

Thurmond, however, did not share their inclinations.

"I just don't like his looks. I don't know why, but I don't trust him. We've always been able to take care of ourselves. We don't need him."

In the end, Thurmond was overruled. It was decided that the advantages of traveling with a powerful magician was worth whatever risk it entailed.

ᚱ

Carpat proved even more desolate than Bukovia. The travelers encountered few wayfarers coming or going. The desolate track led through neither town nor village. No castles clung to the sides of the cliffs, and no ruins told of an earlier habitation. Only the broken remains of an ancient roadbed indicated any former human presence.

Progress was slower than ever. When the road became too bumpy, Buyuk ve Korkunc Sihirbazi had his servants unhitch and saddle one of the white ponies, leaving the others to pull the wagonette as best they could. He rode beside Roscoe and proved, rather surprisingly, to be a garrulous companion.

He was, he said, a native of Carpat, though his family had left that land many years ago. He was returning now because his mother, whose health was rapidly failing, had expressed her desire to spend her remaining years in Bok Cukuru, the city of her birth.

From time to time Thurmond caught glimpses of the old lady swaddled in blankets within the canvas covering of the wagonette. She was an ugly crone who seemed content to sit without moving or speaking day after day. A disquieting smell lingered about her, and the young man was glad to leave her acquaintance unmade.

Buyuk ve Korkunc Sihirbazi —Thurmond secretly shortened his name to Bazi—was especially concerned for the adventuring party's safety and questioned Roscoe closely about their route and destination. His soft brown eyes were clouded with apprehension.

"Your chosen path is most difficult, my friend. What business could be so important as to bring you to this remote and dangerous place?"

The old Adventurer was evasive.

"Well, it's like this, you see—we been hired by a great noble from County Avincraik to handle a bit of delicate business, somethin' I can't tell you about. Let's leave it at that."

The wizard was apologetic.

"A thousand pardons, my friend. I have no desire to thrust myself into your affairs. Let us never speak of the matter again."

Sarah, always eager for new magical knowledge, attempted to initiate a different conversation with their new companion, but he remained aloof, actually turning away and refusing to answer when she tried to speak to him. She finally gave up. Maybe he felt a cultural aversion to women. Or perhaps he had taken some sort of mystic vow to eschew the company of young females. Or maybe he just did not like her.

Thurmond and Torgul made no friendly overtures. The young man's opinion of the magician did not change, and the dwarf was never particularly outgoing.

As their second day of travel drew to a close, the magician announced this would be their last night together. Tomorrow the road would fork, and he would continue east toward Bok Cukuru. The Adventurers would take the northern fork into the mountains. Shortly before mid-day, the road diverged just as the magician had predicted. He thanked the companions for the protection and proffered three gold coins, which Roscoe graciously refused.

He nodded and gave the old Adventurer a penetrating look.

"I will be returning by this path after I have seen my mother settled with our relatives. The ways of destiny are strange, my friend. Mayhap we will meet again."

Then Buyuk ve Korkunc Sihirbazi and his people turned east, leaving our heroes to turn their faces north.

CHAPTER 21

SHAPESHIFTER

Though careful to show no outward sign, Ghleet was delighted. By the moon and stars, he was downright joyful! The faint scent of distant mountains was for him the smell of freedom, and that was enough to fill his soul with jubilation.

As he rejoiced, his mind slipped back to his childhood, to the pathetic cluster of tiny stone huts clinging to the sheer face of the cliff. The herds of scrawny goats devouring such sparse grasses and stunted brush as grew in the thin patches of soil. The short, swarthy men, as brutish as the goats they tended. The long, fearful nights huddled around a cold fire while the wolves proclaimed their mastery of the mountains.

He recalled the foul breath of his father, soured by fermented goat milk. His callused hands, so ready to strike. The empty eyes of his mother, who knew too well the hardness of her husband's hands. The snarling, weeping sisters and brothers whose names he had long since forgotten.

But mostly he remembered the greasy reek of the goats that shared their hut. The sharp tang of their piss on the dirt floor. The sickening sweetness of their droppings. Even as a child, Ghleet had been acutely sensitive to smells.

The mountains abounded with danger. The narrow paths frequently gave way, sending the most skilled mountaineers to their deaths. Avalanches carried away entire villages. Sudden ice storms swept down from the peaks to catch man and goat in exposed upland meadows, where their frozen remains would be found during the spring thaw.

Other perils came on two legs—raiders from neighboring villages in search of food or drink or women, stealthy snow goblins, and savage mountain trolls that could pull a man apart with the strength of their hands.

The worst threat, however, came on four legs—the wolves. The undisputed lords of the mountains, they descended in huge packs, gliding out of the mist as silent as ghosts. Driven as much by blood-lust as by hunger, they pulled down any and all who came within reach of their jaws.

Then one day, a stranger arrived. He went on two legs, but he inspired almost as much dread as the wolves. Seeing him, Ghleet's mother had grabbed as many of her children as she could and fled into their hut. Other panicked mothers screamed for their children to run and hide on the hillsides. Frightened fathers took up their bows and flint-tipped spears.

Such reactions were futile, silly even. Though the stranger had not appeared in Ghleet's village for over a lifetime, all had heard the tales of terrible power. None would dare raise a hand against him. No hiding place would escape his notice.

Inside the hut, young Ghleet pushed a younger sister away from the rickety door and peeked through a crack in the planks. A monster stood in the center of his village. It was small for a monster, no taller than his father, but ugly beyond the boy's imagination. The pointed snout of a wolf jutted from between large, round, yellow eyes. Head and body were covered by a thick pelt of gray fur. To Ghleet's great surprise, the creature lifted off its face to reveal a normal human visage. The hideous face was only a mask! Beneath the fur, the stranger was an old man.

The stranger stood for a few moments more, then raised his chin and sniffed the air through widely flaring nostrils. Three steps brought him to the very door through which Ghleet was peeking. He gave it push, causing the flimsy, unbolted barrier to swing open.

Ghleet's mother shrieked for her children to hide beneath her skirts, but as the boy tried to comply, his father seized him by the hair and hurled at the intruder's feet. Quaking in terror, Ghleet could do nothing but close his eyes and curl into a ball.

A hand grasped the neck of tunic and pulled him upright, but his eyes stayed screwed shut until they were opened by a sharp slap to the side of his head. He looked up into eyes lacking the barest trace of humanity. Ghleet would have screamed but fear had closed his throat.

The stranger took the boy's hand in his and examined each of the fingers in turn. He shoved back the sleeve of the heavy woolen tunic and looked at his arms, pinching them painfully as if testing the muscle. He forced open the boy's mouth and examined the teeth and tongue, paying special attention to the latter.

When the stranger stared into his eyes, the boy felt as if a hot knife had been thrust into his skull. The hut and his screeching mother faded, and he stood in a mountain valley where a great wolf held his throat in its jaws, staring at him with yellow eyes. With one swift movement, the stranger caught the petrified child under his arm and carried him off the way he had come. Ghleet never saw his village or his family again.

The boy was carried to a cave in a forbidden valley known to be haunted by malign spirits. He wailed until his voice gave out, but the stranger paid him no heed. Contrary to his expectations, Ghleet was neither eaten by wolves nor offered to some hateful mountain spirit. Instead, he was given a thick pile of skins to sleep and on fed gobbets of raw meat.

Never before had Ghleet slept in such comfort nor known such a full belly. Meat had been a particular rarity in his village. Most was consumed by the men and their dogs. Women and children received only their leavings.

Why, the boy wondered, had he been brought here? He could not ask, for he and the stranger shared no common language. Instead of words, the old man relied on smart blows from an alder switch to make his wishes known. Yet he demanded little of the boy, allowing him to eat his fill and spend most of his days hiding beneath the furs of his pallet.

During the dark of winter, huddled by a small fire in their cave, the boy slowly learned the old man's tongue. His new master, he discovered, was known as Xortai, a name that inspired fear in all the mountain villages, for he was a shaman of dreadful power. Ghleet had been selected as his pupil. He would learn the ancient lore—how to read the meaning of the stars and comprehend the sigh of the wind in the trees, to beat the drum to induce trance, to answer the calls of wild beasts.

When Xortai judged him ready, Ghleet was given challenges to gauge his physical endurance. He spent a night standing naked on a huge boulder while wolves howled in the mountaintops and a hard wind blew frozen rain against his shivering body. He scaled sheer, ice-coated cliffs and swam through freezing rivers. Long, lonely treks through dark woods in deep snow toughened his muscles and resolve.

When the snows melted in the spring, the boy learned the virtues of trees and plants. He was taught which berries eased a compacted bowel and which brought madness. He pulled bright red fungus from rotting logs, scraped lichen from stones, and gathered the leaves of henbane, bitter hemlock, and the notorious white hellebore.

In the short, cool summer, Ghleet learned of beast and bird. He shot the wary mountain sheep with small venom-tipped arrows and stole eggs from the eyries of great crested eagles. He trapped badgers for their bile, stoats and polecats for their musk, and blacksnakes for their deadly milk.

Except during lessons, the old man seldom spoke. Words, he said, were merely made up things that blocked the natural flow of the world. Better to remain silent and observe.

This cycle continued for many seasons. Ghleet's body grew in size and strength, and his mind was filled with knowledge. When hairs began to sprout on his chin, Xortai announced it was time to hunt wolves. Here the young man's courage nearly failed him, for the bravest hunters of his father's village would never willingly confront the gray death.

But the old shaman was wise to the ways of the pack. So advanced were his hunting skills, that their quarry never caught their scent or spied their movement. Master and pupil watched from hidden blinds as the shaggy killers slipped through the trees, bellies low, stalking their prey. They saw the roebuck taken by the throat, and the mighty auroch pulled down by its hanging guts. Ghleet marveled to see the monstrous cave-bear abandon its kill rather than face the fangs of the wolfpack.

Only one wolf did Ghleet slay, for his master allowed him but a single arrow. It was a magnificent male, lured from its pack Xortai's call, and taken with a masterful shot through its eye. The boy feasted on its raw flesh and wore its bloody skin draped around his shoulders as he trudged back to the shaman's lair.

One night by the fire, Xortai announced that Ghleet now ready for *the change*. Without warning, he seized the young man's wrist and placed a hot rock on the underside of his forearm. Ghleet gritted his teeth as the tender skin bubbled and peeled away. The old shaman used a flat stick to smear a paste over the burn.

The paste contained an array of powerful vision inducing substances, the most potent being slime scraped from backs of blue newts. It had been used for innumerable generations of Carpatan shamans to bring *the change* to their disciples. Ghleet's change was to be far more extreme than most.

Xortai had been aware Ghleet since the hour of his birth. The wind had brought his savage smell all the way to his cave in the haunted valley. The boy's father must have smelled it too, for he had been all to ready to relinquish his child when the shaman appeared at his hut.

The paste took effect quickly. Ghleet was certain he was dying as his muscles contracted, keeping him from drawing breath. Soon his whole body was as rigid as a corpse. His tongue felt like a length of wood. His soul seemed to detach from his corporal form and hover in the air so he could look down on what he had been. He felt no regret about being dead. Actually, he had no feelings about anything.

He was suddenly surrounded by a pack of men with the heads of wolves. Since he was now dead, they told him, the true meaning of his existence could now be revealed. Ghleet listened attentively. When he awoke again in the world of men, his body looked and functioned normally, but his old spirit had truly died during the change. In his heart and mind, Ghleet was no longer human.

Xortai had also elected to make a change. He lay dead on his pallet of skins, his arms crossed on his chest. Ghleet knew exactly what he had to do. He ate his master's body, meat and brain and marrow, and thus became the shaman of the haunted valley.

The change brought him power such as he had never imagined. His senses, particularly his nose, had acquired a keenness that altered the very texture of the world. Most importantly, he could now shift shape into a shaggy, rapacious man-beast that ran on four legs almost as easily as two.

Ghleet delighted in his new life and fell with savage abandon upon the herds and flocks of the human villages nearby. He killed long after his ravenous appetite was sated, killed until he was too exhausted to kill more.

Imagine Ghleet's immense distress when he was captured by villagers after falling into a covered pit dug specifically to trap the mad wolf that was ravaging their livestock.

In the morning, the villagers took one look at the enraged man-wolf snapping at them from the bottom of the pit, and immediately sent for their headman. They recognized a shapeshifter when they saw one. The headman consulted the local shaman, who was far less destructive in temperament than Ghleet. He suggested they wait until the wolf spirit ran its course and the captive returned to human form.

As soon as Ghleet lost his frightful claws and fangs, the villagers knocked him unconscious with a rock and bound him with an ensorcelled rope. Charms were hung around his neck to nullify his shapeshifting powers.

A captive man-wolf was certainly a unique and significant acquisition, though no one could quite conceive of a practical purpose to which he could be put. Thus, Ghleet was traded village to village, headman to headman—once for a bundle of iron-tipped spears, once for a comely young maiden—until he was sold to a westward bound caravan, where he was locked in a cage used for the transportation of slaves. In this way, the luckless shaman eventually arrived in Gorgonholm.

Gavin's call brought Ghleet back to the present. Ghleet had no reason to hate his new master, who had, after all, shown him much more kindness than he had known in the Patron's gaol. His sores were healed. He was well clothed and fed. And not once had he been struck with a whip or cudgel. The master's incessant boasting could be tiresome, but it was not insufferable.

He had resented the geas. It was supposed to ensure his unstinting allegiance, but any worthwhile shaman knew how to slip the bonds of such a spell. So Ghleet remained loyal because his master was providing the means for his homeward trek. He had been promised his freedom on completion of their quest. Could he trust the master to keep his word? Ghleet doubted it.

CHAPTER 22

SNOW BEAST

No cart or wagon could have fought its way up the switchbacks of that steep, perilous track. Sheer granite cliffs fell to incalculable depths. Boulders of all sizes tumbled from the crags far above. As the group climbed higher, the trees and bushes became stunted and grotesquely misshapen. Some stretches of trail grew so narrow they were forced to dismount and walk the horses and pack mules.

Fat black vipers coiled in the fissures of the cliffside, raising their heads and flicking red tongues as the companions trudged by. Thurmond had assumed the locality too cold for reptiles, but the hideous creatures seemed to be thriving.

Summer had long since given way to autumn, and winter would arrive early in that northern clime. It was essential they make every effort to complete their quest and return to the lowlands lest they be trapped in the frozen mountains until the spring thaw.

Nights were cold, and howling wolves made the horses restive. Thurmond found the dim-witted Murd, who was normally as dispassionate as a cow, drawn up in a ball and quivering in fear.

"What's the matter, Murd? Are you sick?"

"A werewolf—can't you hear it? Callin' to the others, gatherin' 'em. Be comin' for us soon."

The young man tried to sooth the frightened serf.

"Nay, Murd, that's only regular wolves. They won't attack us—not if we stick together."

But Murd was not to be reassured.

"Nuh—it's a werewolf. Different song—not sweet and nice like real wolfs."

Now it was Thurmond's turn to be frightened. Murd, after all, had an uncanny connection with animals. Maybe he really could recognize the call of a werewolf. He decided to consult Sarah. If anyone in the party knew about werewolves, she would.

Sarah was skeptical.

"I don't think so, Thurmond. Murd's just away from home and scared of the unknown. Who ever heard of werewolves calling to other wolves? They're solitary creatures—everybody knows that. I think you can relax."

Torgul joined them.

"I'm not so certain, missy. Werewolves might be loners, just as you say, but some old legends tell that they can summon and command normal wolves. Maybe that's what Murd's listenin' to."

Now they were all scared. Bodo and Lars, who usually kept a bit apart from the others, pulled in closer. Roscoe knew he must step in before their fears overcame their reason.

"Sarah, darlin', I've no doubt you're correct and that them are just regular wolves we hear singin'. But just for fun, what kind of weapons will kill a werewolf?"

"Well, not normal ones, I'm pretty sure. There's an enchantment on them that makes them proof against ordinary weapons. Silver is supposed to work if it's forged into a dagger or a spearpoint—maybe arrowheads."

The old Adventurer's voice tightened slightly.

"Do any of you possess such a thing—a weapon with a silver blade?"

Of course, no one did.

"Then do we have enough silver to fashion such a thing?"

A quick search of pouches and saddlebags revealed a handful of silver coins—enough perhaps for a small dagger blade or a half dozen arrowheads.

Roscoe continued.

"Torgul, my brother, what thinks ye? Can you use your dwarfish skills to turn these coins into a proper weapon to stop a werewolf?"

The dwarf squinted his eyes and let out a long breath.

"Certes I could, but it would take time. Time we don't have. I'd have to carve a mold somehow, and find something with a flat surface to use as an anvil. I'd probably need to make a bellows to heat the silver to its melting point. Then I'd have to—"

Thurmond interrupted, struck by a sudden idea.

"Wait! Maybe we don't need any of this! Sarah, what about Torgul's axe? It's got some kind of magic in it. Wouldn't it do for a werewolf?"

This was a beautifully decorated two-handed axe that Torgul had recovered from the goblin treasure room. Thurmond had once used it to dispatch a semi-corporeal shadow creature that non-magical weapons could not touch. Furthermore, its blade was inlaid with silver. The weapon's name was Bloodtroll.

Sarah paused and gave thought.

"Look, all of you, I'm no expert on were-beasts, but I do know a little bit about how lycanthropic sorcery works. It's really nasty black magic. I think Torgul's axe would probably work fine against a werewolf."

Roscoe placed an encouraging hand on her shoulder.

"I'm assured you're right, Sarah. Torgul's axe will keep us all safe and snug, so it will."

Thurmond wished he could share his friend's confidence.

The path shrank to a thin ledge no horse or mule could negotiate. Bodo and Murd must, therefore, stay behind with the animals to await the return of the rest of the group. All nonessential supplies and equipment would have to be left as well. Spears, shields, crossbows, and even helmets were forsaken. Roscoe considered them too awkward and heavy for the difficult trek ahead.

The companions debated leaving their mailshirts, but finally decided to retain them. Should they prove too burdensome, they could always be dropped along the trail and recovered on the return trip.

Sarah strapped on a wicker pannier with such magical implements as she deemed imperative. A leather wallet stuffed with food hung over her shoulder. Roscoe, Thurmond, and Torgul carried rucksacks holding food and gear. The dwarf contrived a baldric that allowed him to sling his axe across his back.

Thurmond felt terribly guilty about abandoning Bodo and Murd in this desolate, wolf-haunted wilderness. The two were plainly unhappy about being left alone. But the young man also knew their situation was certainly preferable to what he would be facing in the peaks ahead.

He also worried about his horse Millie, of which he had grown quite fond. Should the horses be lost, the party would face a long, long walk back to civilization.

Just before leaving, Roscoe handed Bodo their hoard of silver coins.

"Here, laddie, you'll have some time on your hands. See if you can't make these into somethin' to keep the wolves at bay."

With Torgul in the lead, the party headed up the mountain.

They inched sideways along a steep, uneven ledge scarcely a cubit in width. Every step had to be carefully negotiated. Their chests pressed against the cliffside, while the packs on their backs dangled over empty space. Their hands searched desperately for finger-holds in the cold surface of the rock. The peaks ahead were capped with snow, so the way would soon grow slick with ice.

Torgul, born and reared in the mountains, was a skilled and confident climber. Despite his shortness of limb, he scrambled over difficult obstacles with great aplomb. Again and again, he placed himself at great risk to help the others surmount dangerous passages.

Though a complete novice, Lars demonstrated a natural aptitude for mountaineering. He seemed completely at ease even in the most challenging places and apparently enjoyed this soaring adventure. Thurmond and Sarah crept fearfully along the mountainside, one tremulous step at a time, expecting each to be their last. Only sheer determination kept them moving.

Roscoe had it far worse. His huge paunch took up so much room on the ledge that his feet teetered on the very edge. In addition, his bad leg quickly became a source of agony. Tough as he was, the old Adventurer started to fall behind, forcing the rest of the party to hold in place while he caught up. This did not bode well.

They were forced to halt when their meager trail abruptly ended, having been buried beneath a scree of broken boulders brought down from the cliffs above. It would be necessary to scale this difficult obstacle before resuming their march on the other side.

Here, at least, they found a place to rest. The trail opened into a wide flat shelf, where they could drop their rucks and stretch out. Thurmond closed his eyes and fell asleep. The cold, hard stone felt as soft as a featherbed. Sarah sat as if stunned, her head sagging between her knees. Roscoe swigged from a silver flask containing a potion that eased the pain in his leg.

Lars, however, was curious about the path ahead. Wondering where it resumed, he climbed the scree, using the fallen boulders like stairs. At the top, he turned and waved to Torgul who was watching from below. He did not see the hulking white shape that rose from a projection behind him.

Horror-struck, the dwarf pointed wildly and shouted a warning. Lars turned about just as a massive paw smashed into the side of his head. The hooked talons ripped into his right eye, slashed through his nose, and continued on to take off most of his upper lip.

Lars raised his hand to his ruined face, but before he could complete this futile gesture, his attacker struck again, this time with a great circular blow to the back of the head. Lars was thrown forward, his face driven against the stones with crushing force. The thing—whatever it was—gave a terrible howl of triumph and bounded down the scree toward the others.

So quickly did the creature move that the companions had no time to prepare for its assault. They were barely able to draw weapons before it was upon them. Torgul had no chance to unsling Bloodtroll and stood with only his scramasax.

Thurmond had one quick glimpse of something big, white, and hairy—something vaguely in the shape of a man. It came straight at Torgul, who stood his ground, knees flexed, ready to fight. But the doughty dwarf stood no chance against this murderous juggernaut. It was too big, too fast, and too reckless.

The thing plucked Torgul from his feet with one of its powerful arms and carried him toward a gaping mouth filled with yellow fangs. The dwarf lashed out with his scramasax—once, twice, thrice—stabbing deep into the unprotected belly, but the creature, in its rage, seemed not to notice.

Roscoe leaped to his friend's aid, the pain of his leg forgotten. He circled two steps to the right and chopped savagely at the arm that held the dwarf. The creature roared and flung Torgul against the rocks as a child might throw a poppet. Roscoe's sword cut into the massive limb but did not disable it. The thing seemed in no way impaired by any of the wounds that stained its white coat with running blood. It turned on the old Adventurer, lashing out with savage claws.

Thurmond struck from the other side, guiding his blows straight into the monster's face. His position was precarious, for the edge of the cliff loomed threateningly behind him. One hard shove would send him spinning into the void. He pressed his attack heedless of the risk, battering the beast's face, head, and neck with the edge of his sword. Each stroke drew blood, but they did not seem to slow or even distract the horrible brute.

Sarah attacked with an illusion spell—the image of a fireball aimed directly at the creature's eyes. Her illusion spells were always the best, but this one drew no response from the target. Perhaps it lacked the intelligence to perceive illusions.

She tried her sleep spell, but this one was dicey. When it worked, the results were excellent, but unfortunately it often failed. Alas, there was no visible response from the creature. Was it immune to magic?

Desperate, she took a chance. There was a spell—a twining spell. It was difficult and uncertain, and would, exhausted as she was, seriously deplete her psychic energy. There could be no other spells until she had had a long rest afterward. If it failed, she must resort to the sword.

She cast the twining spell without another thought. Bands of ghostly mist swirled about the creature's shaggy legs and rose to envelop its upper body. Like a serpent stifling its prey, the bands contracted, binding the legs together, tying the arms to the trunk. The creature, aware of the sudden hindrance, thrashed in an effort to free itself. Its struggles were in vain. The more it struggled, the tighter the misty bands grew.

The brute continued to flail and scream, but even its abominable strength was insufficient to defeat the relentless power of the spell. Its ankles were inexorably drawn together, causing it to topple on its face. Roscoe and

Thurmond immediately redoubled their attack, striking without remorse at their fallen foe's back. Roscoe, breathing hard, called for a halt.

"Hold! Hold, I say! Leave off! I've got a better idea! Help me roll this beastie off the edge. The fall'll do for him better than our blades. Help me before the spell wears off!"

The creature gnashed its teeth, still trying to bite as they used their boots to shove it off the shelf. It gave one last blood-chilling shriek as it plummeted toward the rocks far, far below.

Their foe disposed of, they ran to Torgul, who lay in a pool of dark blood with his left leg bent at an unnatural angle. Roscoe carefully straightened the skewed leg and rolled him gently onto his back. He then lowered his ear to the dwarf's bearded lips.

"He breathes! He lives! Go see to Sarah. She's down!"

Thurmond wheeled in horror. Sarah was hurt?

She was face down, unmoving, her arms thrown wide as if she had attempted to catch her fall but failed. Her body looked weirdly small, almost like the corpse of a child. In a panic, Thurmond shook her shoulders and spoke her name sharply.

"Sarah! Sarah! What's the matter? Are you hurt?"

She groaned and opened her eyes. Her chin and front were speckled with vomit. A thin line of blood ran from one nostril.

"No, not hurt—just drained, sick. My last spell took the last of my strength. I just couldn't stand up anymore. Really, I'm all right. I just need to rest a little. Go help Torgul."

By this time, Roscoe had completed his examination of the injured dwarf.

"The blood don't matter, nothing serious there. Just some cuts from landin' on sharp stones. I think maybe his nose is broke and he's got a big knot on his head. The leg's more serious. Plumb broke, it is. This boyo won't be climbin' no more mountains for a while, that's a fact."

Thurmond was frightened, confused.

"What are we going to do, Roscoe?"

"What *you're* gonna do, Prospect, is go see about Lars. Did it occur to you he might be still alive up on them boulders and needin' your help? Go see what you can do for the lad."

CHAPTER 23

DARK PASSAGE

Thurmond clambered up the scree as fast as he was able, but he need not have hurried. Lars was very dead. He lay among the jagged fragments of stone, his body twisted at the waist in an uncomfortable pose. Half his face was torn away, and his forehead sported a deep, wedge-shaped depression from being hurled against the rocks by the force of the creature's reach-around blow.

Thurmond had confronted violent death on many occasions and had slain two men in hand-to-hand combat, but this was the first time one so close to him had fallen. Lars had been Roscoe's man-at-arms, so he had not been an intimate friend, but they shared desperate exploits in which Lars had proven himself wholly courageous and reliable. Thurmond would miss his venturesome spirit and ribald sense of humor.

Then Thurmond remembered where he was. This was not the time for such mopery. He climbed to the very top of the scree and examined the cliff beyond, hoping to locate the continuation of the trail. Unfortunately, it did not continue. The cliff face was entirely sheer, without so much as a toehold. They would not be proceeding in that direction. He did, however, discover another stone shelf, the one from which the creature had risen to strike down Lars. He stepped onto it and spied, around a slight bend in the cliff, what seemed to be the mouth of a cave. The creature's lair?

A noxious stench greeted him as he approached. Aye, it was the lair.

Could another such brute be skulking inside? Perhaps a vengeful mate? He doubted it. The first snow-thing had been filled with mindless rage. If there were another like it lurking about, it would have been on him long before this. Thurmond proceeded boldly into the opening, sword in hand. The place stank as bad as a troll den.

The cave floor was strewn with a plethora of bones. All were broken to expose the delicious marrow inside. An assortment of skulls, a few human, had been cracked open like eggs to allow the luscious brains to be scooped out and consumed. In one corner, a pile of untanned pelts served as a kind of nest.

Aware that even the most dim-witted of monsters instinctively hoarded riches, Thurmond poked about in the noisome skins with the point of his weapon. Sure enough, the snow creature's simple treasures were revealed—a gnawed shoe, a rusty dagger with a broken point, a scattering of bronze farthings, and the hooves from a small goat.

Then he spotted the casket, a small bronze box about the size of Roscoe's big fists put together. A stout iron lock secured its curved lid. The sides were dented and twisted out of plumb. The sturdy little box had obviously resisted the creature's efforts to tear it open. Thurmond tucked it inside his leather wallet.

An even more important discovery was yet to be made. Hidden in the shadows of the far end, Thurmond came upon an opening. It was low and crude but certainly a tunnel rather than a cave, the product of canny and determined excavation rather than natural phenomena. This would be the path on which they would proceed. He listened carefully, but no sound came to his ear. He took a dozen careful steps, and the creature's stench waned noticeably.

Returning to the others, Thurmond found Sarah much restored by a nip from Roscoe's silver flask. She was helping Roscoe tie a splint to Torgul's leg. The old Adventurer's visage was set and grim. He didn't look up from his task when speaking.

"How's Lars?"

"He's dead. His skull is crushed. What about Torgul?"

Roscoe's voice was very tense.

"He ain't good, not a'tall. He's still unconscious, and his leg is bad busted. He'll most like die if I don't get him back down the mountain. Most of the chirurgeon gear is down there with Bodo. If I can get him there, I'll dose him with a strong physic and give him a righteous bleeding. That should cool his blood and give him a chance to regain his strength. It's his only chance."

Thurmond was dismayed. Torgul was short, true enough, but extremely muscular and thick of bone, so he weighed as much as a good-size human. How were they to transport him back along the treacherous ledge they had just ascended? There was barely room to creep along without tumbling into the abyss. Both hands were required to clutch finger-holds in the cliff-face. Nay, lugging the dwarf in such conditions would be impossible.

"Roscoe, look, I care for Torgul as much as you do, but we could barely drag ourselves up that damned ledge. We sure as shit can't carry Torgul back down it."

"I never said, *we* were goin' to, Prospect. I said *I* would do it, and so I shall. You and Sarah are goin' to continue up the mountain and finish the adventure. That's the way real Adventurers do things—they don't give up till they're dead. So now, if you truly want to join up with the Brotherhood, you'll find the balls to keep goin'."

Thurmond was incredulous.

"Come on, Roscoe. How are you going to carry Torgul by yourself? You could barely make it this far as it was."

Roscoe, insulted by the young man's lack of tact, grew stern.

"I want to remind you that a Prospect's purpose is to take orders, not offer opinions. You will have problems enough, so you will, without frettin' about how this old man will see things through. Did you, by the way, locate the trail on the other side of the landslide?"

"There is no more trail—it ends here. But I found a tunnel that must lead up the mountain. It looks a lot easier than the trail. You ... we ... could walk it easy."

"Now I'm sure that's true, and temptin' it is, to be sure. But as I told you, I'll be takin' Torgul back down."

He pulled the silver flask from a pouch on his belt.

"I'll take one more big pull and then give Torgul the rest. I don't know what the dwarves put into this stuff, but it keeps a body goin' when all your natural strength is gone. You feel terrible after, but it's pure comfort at times like this. Now you two better get goin'."

Thurmond protested, but the old Adventurer was adamant.

"That wasn't a suggestion, Prospect. Hie thee hence!"

Reminded of his inferior position, Thurmond was silent, but he did not move, but Sarah spoke up.

"Roscoe's right, Thurmond. We've come so far. We can't just give up now. Don't you want to see what's up on the top of the mountains? Summon your courage."

This was surprising. Thurmond had assumed Sarah would want to go back. He was, in part, trying to protect her by suggesting a withdrawal. But with both she and Roscoe opposing the idea, he knew he had no choice.

Though the day was beginning to fade, Thurmond and Sarah took the time to pull Lars's body onto the upper shelf. There was no way to bury or burn it, no time even to cover it with a cairn of stones. They crossed his arms on his mailed breast and left his sword girded about his hips—a warrior in death as he had been in life. It was the best they could do.

From that position, they looked down on the lower shelf, where Roscoe was removing his mailshirt, obviously preparing for the descent. They shouted and waved good-bye. The old Adventurer gave them one quick wave and then returned to his business.

Thurmond took a bundle of torches from the bottom of his rucksack. Custom dictated that fledgling Adventurers were responsible for carrying this item. The torches were small, and there were only six of them. He could only hope they would emerge from the darkness of the tunnel before the last one burned away. With flint and steel, he struck sparks into a fragment of oily fleece wrapped about the end of one torch. When it was alight, he gestured toward the cave.

"Hold your breath going through—it's really rank in there. The air gets better once you're in the tunnel."

He took one last glance below. Roscoe was now pulling the mailshirt from the supine dwarf.

r

They had been walking for days. Well, maybe not days really, but it seemed like days, felt like days. There was no way to judge the passage of time in the lightless confines of the tunnel, no sun to mark the passing of the hours, no cooling and warming of the ambient air, only complete blackness. Thurmond waved a hand before his face. *Nothing.*

The torches had long since been consumed. They had tried burning whatever small combustibles they had in their packs, but that effort was unsuccessful.

There was nothing to do but trudge forward into the dark.

Thurmond was using his sword as a blind man uses a walking stick, searching the floor for unseen hazards. He was afraid. Who could guess what manner of cave-dwelling monster might be waiting just ahead? Or perhaps they were about to fall into a sudden drop-off. His nerves were badly frayed as he imagined all sorts of unseen hazards.

"Hey Sarah, isn't there such a thing as a glow spell, some way to light things up without a fire?"

Sarah's reply was guarded. She knew what was coming. Thurmond was tired and growing peevish.

"Certes, such a spell exists."

"Then please use it now. I don't think I can stand this dark much longer."

He knew, of course, that she could command no such spell, but he needed the sound of his own voice—or hers—to bolster his courage.

"By God's twin tails, Thurmond, if I knew how to cast such a spell, don't you think I'd have done so long before this?"

"Well, damn it, why didn't you learn it back in Grimsgard? You've got a whole sorcerer's workshop. Why didn't you teach yourself a light spell? It would be so valuable—especially right now."

Sarah, too, was frightened and in no mood to put up with his silly bickering.

"Because I hate you so much that I want you to die in the dark, even if I have to die too."

Her retort forced him to take stock.

"Sorry, Sarah. I didn't mean anything. I just got a little carried away."

"I know. It's all right. I didn't mean what I said. Listen, let's rest a bit. Roscoe's potion has worn off, and I feel just awful."

They sat against the tunnel's wall, their knees and shoulders touching. Both were worn out but somehow too tired to fall asleep. After a while, Thurmond spoke.

"Have you noticed anything odd about this tunnel?"

"Nay, but how should I have? It's absolutely dark in here."

"When we first entered, it sloped upward, right?"

"Aye, of course—the direction we wanted to go."

"But now, in fact, for a long time, it's been heading down. The slope is gentle, but it's definitely going down, not up."

Sarah's voice grew concerned.

"Then it's taking us away from our destination."

"Mayhap—but wherever it's taking us, that's where we'll end up. We don't have much choice other than turning back. Are you ready to do *that*?"

"Nay, not so long as you're willing to go forward."

"It's forward we go then. Hey, I forgot to tell you about this box I found back in the snow-thing's bed…"

Both were soon fast asleep.

The Carpatan air was chilly, but Gavin was snug in his bed and in the merriest of moods. He had so much to be happy about. He had understood since childhood that he was under the personal auspices of Lady Fortune. It could not be otherwise because her wheel always turned in his favor. If he waited patiently, she was certain to fulfill his every desire. It could not be otherwise.

And he knew that his father was not a mere man, that he had been sired by a being of divine origin, making him a demigod at the very least. Which deity could have lain with Mother, could have sired him? Certainly, it had been one given to intelligence and guile— and to sensual pleasure as well.

Mother had always laughed at such ideas. Far too many soldiers, she always told him, had spent their seed between her thighs for her to remember any one in particular. His father could be any of dozens, but none had been more than a simple soldier—not even an officer. None had been a god. She had been such a stupid woman, but even she had eventually learned what it meant to laugh at him, to doubt him, or to thwart his will.

As a demigod, he was far above the laws and customs of human society. He could do anything. He was immune to the debilitating effects of guilt, remorse, or love. When he wanted something from the lesser beings around him, he had only to reach out and take it. He was happy indeed. His plan was faultless and working wonderfully. He had at first intended to simply slay the slut along the trail and recover his stolen medallion, but now a better plan came to mind.

He would, as he often did, connive to have others do the fighting and take the risks. When the appropriate moment came, he would step forward to pluck the spoils from their grasp. That would certainly come as quite a shock to them! That would be the moment to take his revenge! He decided to celebrate himself with another glass of wine.

CHAPTER 24

AT THE NAVEL OF
THE WORLD

Thurmond and Sarah had entered the seemingly endless tunnel from a world of cheerless gray—a realm of bare granite cliffs, leaden skies, and dismal expectations. But after the stumbling, groping, faltering trek though suffocating darkness, they found themselves in a wide valley surrounded by high mountains. The sun shone down from a clear blue sky. Lush pasturage and well-tended farm fields filled the air with the rich aroma of vegetation.

A cluster of small rectangular structures, most likely houses, squatted in the distance, a light pall of smoke hanging above flat roofs. Workers tended crops in adjacent fields. A man drove a cart pulled by a great round-bellied buffalo.

Thurmond studied the scene and pondered the best course of action. Having grown up in a rural farming village, he knew the people here would no doubt harbor an instinctive hostility toward strangers. Yet the field workers did not appear dangerous, and he saw no sign of a castle or manor house that would suggest the presence of warriors. He glanced at Sarah, who read his thoughts, shrugged slightly, and nodded in the direction of the village. She, like him, did not anticipate danger. They headed across the field.

They had closed most of the distance before the workers saw them. The man with the cart threw his hands above his head and screamed as shrilly as a castrated goblin. He leaped from the cart and fled toward the settlement without a backward glance. The entire field crew dropped their tools and followed his example. There was nothing for it but to follow them.

The village was unimpressive—perhaps two dozen low, shabby houses with walls of rammed earth. Pigs and chickens wandered aimlessly, entirely disinterested in the intruders. The human inhabitants—four score or so from puling toddlers to toothless grandams—huddled before the greatest of the structures, which was only slightly larger than the rest. The wooden sun symbol above the door proclaimed it a Charonite church.

A shriveled little man pushed forward, insinuating himself between the villagers and the newcomers. The faded azure of his patched and ragged robe identified him as belonging to the fraternity of Blue Friars.

He was obviously not of the same ethnic stock as his congregation. The villagers were broad of brow, dark of hair, and swarthy of skin. The priest, though weather-beaten and wizened, displayed the ruddy complexion of the west. His graying hair yet bore traces of its original blond.

He extended his arm, palm out, an unmistakable demand that Thurmond and Sarah stop and come no closer. His blue eyes bored directly into theirs. When he spoke, his voice carried authority and self-assurance rather than trepidation.

"How now, strangers—why come you to our peaceful land armed as if for war?"

His words were clear and correct, delivered in the common language of trade. Surprisingly, his pronunciation carried the familiar lilt of Poitiers. The priest, like the two young wayfarers, was a long way from home.

Thurmond admired the man's courage. He bore no visible weapon, yet he stood before them, willing to confront two potentially lethal interlopers. The villagers exhibited no such spunk. A few looked sullen and angry, but most just appeared frightened.

The young man was unsure how to respond. Should he attempt to cultivate amicability by assuring the priest of their benign intentions? Or would a germ of fear better motivate cooperation?

Before he could decide, Sarah stepped forward.

"Good friar, we come here as friends, not foes. I am Sarah, daughter of Lord Percy Staynes, a great noble of the Kingdom of Poitiers. This is Thurmond of Grimsgard, a warrior of renown. We have traveled far to be of service to you and yours."

The friar's brows furrowed. He plainly disbelieved her.

"Why are we so deserving of such bother on our behalf?"

Sarah fumbled for a moment, and then had a flash of inspiration.

"We heard of your village in the city of Gorgonholm. Bishop Boniface, himself of your order, spoke of it in a sermon so inspirational that we vowed to come here and ease your burden."

The brow grew more furrowed, her brilliant lie was obviously a failure.

"And what is the nature of this terrible burden you would ease from our weary shoulders?'

"Why, by delivering you from the evil forces that oppress you."

Sarah was growing desperate. She knew she was taking a chance here. These villagers looked innocent, but for all she knew, they could be in league with the Sisters of Sathas.

The priest's countenance now registered open skepticism.

"What *evil forces* do you have in mind, *young lady*?"

She heard his ironic emphasis on the words *evil forces* and the condescension in *young lady*. She began to stammer, but at that moment Thurmond took up the conversation. He was very skilled with words when he needed to be.

"Holy friar, please forgive our intrusion. I will be entirely forthcoming with you. We do, as you must discern from our speech, indeed come from Poitiers, from the city of Gorgonholm. I suspect you know of that city, for I hear in your words the accents of our homeland. And my companion speaks in sooth when she says our purposes here are altogether benign. But mayhap she did lapse in courtesy a tad when she failed to inform you that we are hopelessly lost. We have no idea where the path through the mountain has led us."

The priest's brow seemed to unfurrow by the slightest increment.

"How came you here?"

"Through the tunnel in yonder hillside."

The furrow was back, deeper than ever.

"Liar! That tunnel is guarded on the far side by a fearsome *hyut*."

"I know nothing of a...a hyut. But we did slay a shaggy white monster near the tunnel's mouth. It came upon us just as—"

The friar's mouth drew down in a sneer.

"Your falsehood disgusts me. Had you truly met a hyut, you'd have both been slain. Their enchanted hide makes them nearly impervious to iron weapons."

"As we discovered to our great cost, holy friar! Please, allow me to continue uninterrupted."

Thurmond quickly related the tale of their encounter with the snow beast.

The priest, however, remained unsmiling.

"You are trying very hard to convince me of your sincerity. Perhaps you did manage to defeat the hyut. The truth of that can be determined in due time. Let us, for the nonce, proceed as if your story were true. Why exactly have you come here? What is your purpose?"

Thurmond drew a deep breath before proceeding. The friar was keeping him off balance and on the defensive. He needed to regain the initiative.

"We have given you our names, holy friar. Does not custom dictate we be told yours?"

"I am the son of my father—that is sufficient."

"Well, the name of this village at least. What is this place called?"

"In the common tongue, it would be known as the Navel of the World. Now I ask you again, why are you here?"

"As I have already stated, we journeyed here with only the best of intentions. We are sworn to destroy a coven of evil witches known as the Sisters of Sathas."

The priest stood blank-faced as if his hearing had failed him.

"You will please say that again."

"We have come here to destroy the Sisters of Sathas."

The priest clutched his stomach and bent slightly, like a man taken ill, then burst out in an enormous peal of laughter. He turned to the villagers and said something in an unknown tongue. They, too, erupted in mirth.

A surge of conflicting emotions gushed through Thurmond—rage, embarrassment, fear, frustration. He looked at Sarah and found her staring straight back at him, the same utter confusion plain on her face. He could not, however, afford to merely stand like an incompetent fool.

"May I inquire, holy friar, why my honest words meet with such derision? What is it about me you find so ridiculous that you must laugh in my face?"

The cleric at once stopped chuckling and paused for a moment to regain his breath.

"Nay, nay, brave warrior, I mean you no dishonor. You must pardon my discourtesy. Your words did but take me by surprise. Few strangers come here, and when they do, it can only bode ill for us. They want either to plunder our livestock or to escape some foe who, arriving here later, gleefully kill and torture my people in an effort to locate their quarry. We could not even imagine a purpose more unlikely than yours."

"Then we are in the wrong place? You know naught of the malevolent sisters?"

"On the contrary, we know all about them. See that mountain behind me? That's the Blue Fang. Now look closely. See their castle perched on the pinnacle like a tall hat?"

Thurmond could just make it out—a castle, high upon a sheer peak, mostly concealed by a swirl of mist.

"Are they not, as I have heard, murdersome instruments of evil? Do they not visit the most atrocious deprivations upon your village?"

The corners of the priest's lips twitched—he was obviously trying to repress a smile.

"Oh, aye, bad as could be, those witches. They sent nightgaunts to take the lambs, the calves, sometimes even the children to feed their demons. Unspeakable things came down from that mountain to plague this village. Life was hard then."

"You said life *was* hard *then*. They no longer do such things?"

"Son, those witches were wiped out decades ago. To my knowledge, there's only one left. She may be powerful, but she is very old, and her demands upon us are slight. We have no reason to love her, certainly, but neither do we live beneath her shadow."

The conversation was interrupted when a grimy child of perhaps five years ran from one of the houses and tugged mightily at the priest's robe. She whispered into his ear and scampered away.

The cleric relaxed slightly.

"I am informed that Mother Cirkin, our seeress, has successfully cast your auras and detects only slight deception in your words. She finds no sign of evil. You will now be treated as guests rather than invaders."

CHAPTER 25

THE PRIEST'S TALE

The meal was hearty, toothsome, and eminently satisfying—goat meat grilled on skewers, buttered rye cakes, and strong barley beer. They sat around an open fire pit in the church, which also served as the residence of Father Hieronymus, who was the village priest. The interior was dark and murky, lit only by small oil lamps. Smoke from the cooking fire meandered about the rafters before finding its way out through a hole in the ceiling.

The priest, now much more cordial, continued their previous conversation between bites of succulent goat.

"We must always be on guard. We try to live in peace, but have also gotten quite adept at protecting ourselves. You will recall those helpless villagers behind me, how vulnerable they seemed. Not so! All carried weapons, even the children—knives beneath skirts and up sleeves, cudgels tucked in belts behind their backs. One gesture from me, and they would have fallen upon you.

"Aye, and there's more—I had archers and slingers lying concealed on the roofs of the houses, ready to rise up on my command. I, of course, can cast a nasty spell or two, and have done so when forced to. I delayed you with talk while Mother Cirkin did her work. She is amazingly accurate in such matters."

Thurmond took another swig of beer. He found his host was boastful and arrogant but was careful to remain meticulously polite.

"Friar Hieronymus, I—"

"The correct form of address is *Father*. I am the spiritual leader of this village and the priest of this holy church. I am therefore *Father* Hieronymus."

"Please forgive me, *Father*. I meant no disrespect. Could you tell us more of—"

"Your transgression is forgiven, my son, but even in this desolate wilderness, it is important that decorum be maintained. By so honoring me, you express your devotion to our blessed faith."

Sarah was better able to steer the conversation. Hieronymus, she saw, loved to talk about himself above all things. She gave him her best girlish smile.

"Good Father, how did one such as yourself, a man of exceptional piety and erudition, come to this isolated place? I see you more as a mitered bishop in an opulent cathedral or perhaps a high-ranking assistant to the blessed Pontiff in the holy city of Ravenna."

Sometimes Sarah knew just what to say.

"Your eyes, then, are indeed as keen as your wits, dear Sarah."

Thurmond heard this flattery, especially the *dear Sarah*, and rankled. Charonite clerics were supposed to be celibate, but few were. Hieronymus's wife, a full-breasted girl much younger than the priest, sat passively in a far corner, excluded from the conversation, with two small children nestled at her feet.

Hieronymus told his story.

"I began life as a humble village boy, the son of simple peasants of no particular account. Our parish priest recognized my worth and brought me into the Church. I was taught my letters and set to work as a scribe. My acumen allowed me to rise quickly through the ranks, and I soon became—as you so astutely deduced, my dear—the personal clerk to a powerful prince of the Church. I shall not name his name.

"I was so young and naïve back then. I looked about me and was shocked by the flagrant luxury in which my master lived—the fine horses on which he rode to the hunt, the lavish banquets at which the most scandalous entertainments were held, the beautiful courtesans given private sessions of spiritual advisement. How could a man of such holiness not realize that his deeds were contrary to the teachings of Mother Church?

"I knew there must be some underlying answer that would explain all, some justification that would reconcile the seeming hypocrisy. I thought of myself as too young and stupid to understand. I composed a note and left it on his desk. In it, I asked how a prince of the Church could expend so much on personal pleasure while citizens of our own city, which I shall not identify, perished for want of sustenance. How could he routinely commit deeds for which he condemned others to the fires of Hell?

"Please understand, I truly believed he would provide an answer that would put my conscience at ease. Perhaps a man with his awesome responsibilities required such diversions to maintain stability of mind. I was ready to accept whatever explanation he offered.

"But no such response was forthcoming. Instead I found myself posted here and was made to understand I can never expect a change of circumstance. At first I was angry. I railed and ranted and cursed the unfairness of my fate—that I, a man of exceptional talents, had been thrown upon a dung heap, where my abilities were wasted. Cast out like a fallen angel—it was not to be borne.

"But growing older, I came to see that by sending me here, my superiors gave me that chance to escape the trap into which they have fallen. Here I have no choice but to live the simple, humble life Allfather Charon advocates. I have learned to love these people. I use my healing powers to ease the pain of childbirth and broken limbs. I bring joy when I join young couples in wedlock and give solace to the grieving widow when her husband of many years is laid in the earth. And as you have seen, I protect my village from intruders.

"I find such things are much more fulfilling than fine clothes or concubines, so perhaps my soul is saved. Now you have heard my story. What else would you like to know?"

Sarah was ready for this opportunity.

"Tell of the Sisters of Sathas, Father. What befell them? How were they wiped out?"

The old man stared dreamily into the fire.

"It was many years ago. A few of our oldest villagers were told the tale by their grandsires, who as children watched the mountain burn red as if engulfed in flame. The shriek of demonic voices was carried on the wind. The earth trembled. Pigs and goats fell dead, and their flesh was found putrefied and inedible. On the morrow, the sun refused to rise.

"But after that night, the calves and children were no longer taken. There were no more nightgaunts, no more foul things slithering into the village in the dark. That, at least, is the way they tell it. It was many years before my time."

Sarah needed more.

"What went on up there? What caused their destruction?"

"None can say. I would assume the witches loosed their unhallowed arts upon one another in some internecine feud, but that's only my guess."

"You said one witch still survives. What of her?"

"She's still up there, that's a certainty. She sends down dreams that tell the villagers of the things she needs. Always just simple items—cheeses, dried meats, sacks of flour—things we can provide without difficulty. In return, she allows us to live our lives without molestation."

"Has this foul hag a name?"

"If she does, it is unknown to us. The villagers simply call her Old One."

"There have been no other evil portents, no more shrieking in the night or hellish visitations?"

"On certain unholy nights, strange red lightning slashes the sky and strikes the castle, but it never seems to suffer damage."

Now that the old priest was being more cooperative, Thurmond re-entered the conversation.

"Do any of the villagers ever approach the castle?"

Hieronymus shook his head emphatically.

"God's guts, nay! An aura of terrible evil lingers about the place. No one here would even think of climbing that cliff."

"But there must be a way to do so—to climb up there if someone were so inclined."

"If you are considering such a feat, young man, I advise most strongly against it. You would likely experience the most unpleasant of deaths. You might well anger the witch and turn her against us."

"But such a way does exist?"

The friar was annoyed by the young man's persistence.

"Aye, it exists, but it is a far more difficult path than any you encountered getting here, and none of my villagers will show it to you. However well-intentioned you might be, your quest is foolish and best forgotten."

Sarah recognized it was time for her to step in again. Thurmond was not having very good luck with their cantankerous host.

"We thank you, good Father, for the many kindnesses you've shown us—the nourishing food and good fellowship. I see now that conditions here are not at all what we expected, and we will certainly be guided by your wisdom. But now the hour grows late. Thurmond and I must seek our rest."

"Certes, my dear. You are welcome to remain here in the church, but it would not be seemly for a young man and a young lady to sleep side by side in this sanctified place. A pallet has been prepared for your friend in the hut of our village elder."

Thurmond was on his feet in an instant, his hand groping for the hilt of his sword. They had once been betrayed by a village priest who invited them to sleep in the home of the local headman. His machinations had nearly cost them their lives, so he was not about to fall into such a trap a second time.

Sarah hopped to her feet as well. She laid a restraining hand on Thurmond's just as his fingers found the hilt. She smiled broadly in the hope of covering her companion's agitation.

"Nay, that will not be necessary, holy Father. We have become accustomed to fresh air and the sight of stars overhead. With your permission, we will take our ease out of doors. Keeping in close communion with the four elements helps stimulate my psychic energies. Again, I thank you for all your hospitality."

Hieronymus looked disappointed but said nothing.

The young couple left the church and sought privacy in a bean field far away from eavesdropping ears. Thurmond burst out.

"I don't like that priest! You do understand, don't you, why he was so eager for you to stay in the church—why he wanted to send me out?"

"I think I know what he had in mind."

"And he would have put me in the hut of the village headman. You do recall what happened in that village in the reeds?"

"I do. I made the connection as quickly as you did. I knew you would never accept such an offer."

"Then why are you so calm? We must get away from here. These people mean us ill. I believe they're the minions of the witch. You heard him say how they have made peace with her. And anyway, how can we know if he wasn't lying about everything? Maybe the whole batch of 'em is still alive up there and eager for the blood of some fresh young victims."

Sarah reached out and took both his hands in hers.

"Did you try disbelieving?"

"Certes! I kept repeating *disbelieve, disbelieve* the full time you were talking to him."

"And?"

"Nothing changed, but that doesn't mean anything. Did you try your truth spell?"

"Nay, he's nobody to fool with. I could feel the energy oozing from him. He's too powerful. Look, Thurmond, I agree that the priest is something of a lecher—and arrogant—but he is not an evil man. You heard him talk about how he loves the villagers."

"Just a clever masquerade. Do you remember how kind Father James appeared to be?"

This was the treacherous priest who had plotted to feed their blood to evil frog-people. They escaped only because Thurmond disbelieved at the right moment.

"This is different, Thurmond. I know it is."

The young man was frustrated by Sarah's refusal to take the matter seriously.

"How is it different? How do you know it is? Convince me!"

Sarah knew it was time to reveal something she had not intended to reveal.

"Listen, I have to tell you something. Something I don't think you're going to like. But here it is—remember that medallion we stole with the bones?"

"Of course I do. It's the reason we came here, isn't it? You said we could use it to steal the witches' treasure."

"Quite so, but that is only partially correct. Since we found it, the medallion has been guiding me. It wasn't my idea to come here. The medallion suggested it—demanded it really. It wants me to return it to its proper place, and if we do so, we are promised a sumptuous reward."

"What do you mean it was *guiding* you?"

"I mean it filled me with an irrefutable need to return it to the castle."

"It's controlling you?"

"Nay...well, only somewhat."

Thurmond was aghast. He pulled away and turned his back to her. His voice, when it came, was terse with anger.

"What have you done, Sarah? Think about what you have led us to. Lars is dead. Roscoe and Torgul probably are to. They must have fallen while trying to get back down the mountain. Mayhap Bodo and Murd are already eaten by wolves. We're at the mercy of this weird priest and his villagers, whatever their intentions are. And now you want to climb up to that castle and return your haunted medallion—all because you listened to the whispering of some dead witch? You could at least have made that part known. That was selfish and wrong."

Sarah was startled by the intensity of his response. Thurmond had never spoken so harshly to her before. He had always been so compliant. She did not expect his reaction to be so strong.

"Come on, Thurmond—I didn't make anyone do anything. You all came of your own volition. It seemed the most direct way to raise the money we needed—the solution to our problems."

Thurmond's voice remained low and glowering. It was the voice of a stranger.

"We might have decided otherwise had we known the real reason you wanted to come."

"I'm sorry—I truly am. I feel terrible about Lars, and I worry constantly about Torgul and Roscoe. But you heard Roscoe—Adventurers always carry on. That's why you kept going—not because of me."

Thurmond's voice was now a low growl.

"None of us would have come here except for you."

Sarah began to cry. Thurmond had never turned away from her like this. It frightened her.

"I didn't think it mattered. Coming here was just so important to me, something I had to do."

"Aye, you made it clear you would come alone if need be. What choice do you think that left me?"

Sarah felt like she was losing her mind. She had never considered the loss of Thurmond's love for her. That possibility made her feel completely confused and alone. She sobbed harder now, her voice breaking as she attempted to speak through the streaming tears.

"Thurmond, please...I'm sorry—really, really sorry. If you can forgive me, I'll never deceive you again, not ever. You decide what to do next. We'll leave right now—tonight if you want to, or in the morning when it's light and we've rested. Whatever you say."

Thurmond hated himself for making Sarah unhappy, for making her cry. She had a point—they had all agreed to come on the adventure. She had not forced him to accompany her. Torgul and Roscoe had agreed to the journey with scarcely a second thought. Adventurers, after all, undertook such risks as a matter of course. Even the serfs had been allowed to choose whether to come or stay home.

Yet she, his closest friend and ally, had misled him, and in so doing she had betrayed his trust, so he had every reason to be angry. He finally turned to face her.

"You'd really do that—leave here without going to the castle?"

She nodded.

"Then we leave in the morning."

But it was not to be.

CHAPTER 26

THE GIRL IN THE BEAN FIELD

Thurmond clawed his way into wakefulness just as the sun was struggling to hoist itself over the surrounding rim of mountains. He was at first disoriented, unable to recall where he was. Then his bitter words with Sarah came flooding back to him.

She was curled up on the ground, still asleep. Her cloak was damp with morning dew with her soft brown hair curled around her face. How could he stay mad at someone who looked like that? He felt terrible about hurting her. She had, as always, sound reasons for the decisions she made, but he had been too angry to listen to them.

Sarah gave a wiggle and then sat up, stretched, yawned, and rubbed her eyes. The moment was awkward, colored by the strife of the night before. Neither knew what to say, so they just looked at each other.

Happily, the tension was relieved when a figure came striding toward them from the direction of the village. It was a girl of perhaps twelve summers—thin and long of limb. Her dark hair fell over her shoulders. Her kirtle was hiked up, exposing her brown legs above the knee as she made her way through the dew-misted bean-vines. She carried a wooden bucket.

Her voice, when it came, was fraught with good humor.

"Good morrow! Father Hieronymus bade me to bring your morning meal. I've got baked eggs, lentil pottage, and fresh bread. Are you ready to break your fast?"

She struck a sassy pose and smiled, her dark eyes burning with intelligence. Sarah was first to respond.

"We would eat, gladly. How are you called, child?

This last was presumptuous—Sarah was no more than four or five years her senior.

"I am Pozzina, but call me Pozi. I like that better."

Sarah smiled.

"Then Pozi it shall be. You speak the trade tongue quite well for a village girl. How did you learn it?"

"Father Hieronymus taught me. He says I am quick of wit and might one day become his assistant. He even promised to teach me letters."

Sarah could well imagine the kind of duties the priest's assistant would be called on to perform.

"Is that why Father Hieronymus chose you to fetch our morning repast?"

Pozi's tone suddenly grew serious.

"Nay, I asked to be allowed to do so. I wanted the chance to speak to you out of his earshot—out of everyone's earshot. I have a scheme you might like."

Sarah was intensely interested but tried to restrain the eagerness in her voice.

"What do you mean by a *scheme*, Pozi?"

"I mean a plan to get you into the witches' castle. If you really want to go there, I know how it can be done. I've climbed up there many times. I'll show you the way, but you must agree to my terms."

Thurmond, true to form, was dubious.

"You would show us the way into the castle?"

"I will."

"And you would do so even if the good Father has forbidden it?"

"I would."

"You say you've been there many times before?"

"I have."

"That was a dangerous undertaking—why would you do such a thing?"

"For the same reason I'm willing to help you. I was looking for a way out of this village. Next summer I will become a woman. Then must I marry a great lummox named Samp, who bought me from my father for ten goats and an iron kettle."

Hearing this, Thurmond grew even more suspicious.

"I have always heard that most young girls are eager to wed. What makes you so different?"

"Samp is stupid and ugly and old—older than my father. He has hair growing from his nose and ears. He would treat me like a slave, and I would soon grow as gray and bitter as the other women of our village. I would rather die."

Her brave words immediately won Sarah's sympathy. They were kindred spirits. Pozi sensed this and stared straight into her eyes.

"Help me escape. Take me with you, and I will do everything I can to aid you in your quest."

Sarah was impressed by the girl's audacity and curious about her incursions into Castle Sathas.

"You said that you went into the castle looking for a way to escape your pending marriage. Why? What did you hope to find there?"

"I didn't know at first—anything. Maybe I could stay up there and learn to be a witch. Or maybe steal something valuable and buy my freedom. I didn't know, but I was ready to take any chance rather than marry that hog Samp."

"Well, you must have found something if you went back many times."

"Aye, old iron. Scraps of it were lying about the courtyard and in the broken buildings. Old tools, rusty hinges, things like that. I carry down as much as I can and sell it to the blacksmith.

"This is all very secret. My father would beat me if he found out and take the coins I got for the iron. The villagers would be furious if they learned their rakes and hoes were forged from witch-metal.

"Anyway, I planned to run away when my pouch was filled with coins, but now everything is changed. I'd rather go with you."

The arrival of Pozi in the bean field changed things for Thurmond as well. He was already reconsidering his rash decision to abandon the quest.

With Pozi as a guide, they might have a chance for success. He resumed his interrogation.

"Did you ever see the witch Father Hieronymus spoke of?"

"Nay, I did not."

"Then how do you know she exists? Should you not have seen her when you were creeping about in her halls and chambers?"

"I never ventured beyond the courtyard and outbuildings. I found plenty of old metal there and felt no need to go further."

"You don't know for certain if there really is a witch."

"Not so! She is very real. She sends the entire village the same troubling dreams when she requires victuals. We carry her things up the mountain as far as we can. She lowers a big basket from far above on a very long rope. We fill it, and she pulls it up again."

"But you admit you've never entered the main part of the castle and know of no way to do so."

"Actually, I might know a way. I discovered the entrance to what I think was once a secret tunnel. I think it leads inside."

The conversation lulled. Thurmond stepped back and hid his mouth with his hand. Sarah knew he was disbelieving to dispel a glamour. She decided to run a little test of her own.

"You have beautiful hair, Pozi. It's so shiny and dark. I wish mine were like yours. I think it would look even better if it was tucked back a little behind your ears. May I?"

She reached out as if to make the suggested change but then whispered her truth spell. The effect was immediate. Pozi stiffened and her eyes rolled back to white.

"Pozi, what is your real purpose in approaching us with your story?"

"I want to escape this village."

"Why?"

"So Samp won't have my body."

"Is the story you told us entirely true?"

"Aye, I just want to escape."

"Is Father Hieronymus a good man?"

"Aye."

"Can we trust him not to harm us?"

"Uuugggh ...."

The spell wore off before Pozi could respond. The girl's awareness returned to normal, leaving her no inkling of what just occurred.

Sarah smiled.

"You're quite right. Your hair looks better the way you already had it."

Pozi wrinkled her brow in momentary confusion but then smiled back.

"Gramercy, but I like yours better. It's so pale and clean-looking. None of us have hair the color of yours."

Thurmond was not eager to dwell on the subject of female grooming. He needed to get back to the important business at hand.

"Pozi, if we agree to your scheme, what exactly do you want in return?"

"To go with you when you leave. You must agree to protect me and take care of me until I can do so for myself, or until I want to go my own way. In exchange, I will work for you—mend your clothes, tend your sheep, gather your crops—just like I do for my father. And anything else you can think of, as long as it's not...well ... you know."

Thurmond glanced at Sarah, who responded with a slight nod.

"And when do you think we should storm Castle Sathas? Tonight perhaps?"

"If you want to do it tonight, we must go at once. The climb up the mountain is difficult and will take most of the day."

"How will Father Hieronymus feel about us doing this thing? Will he be angry?"

"Maybe a little, but the village can only gain if the witch is destroyed. That would certainly please him."

Thurmond's voice took on a slight edge.

"Pozi, did he send you here with this story?"

"Nay, I swear by Allfather Charon that I came on my own and without his knowledge."

Sarah gave Thurmond another subtle nod, and he returned it. The decision was made. They had come too far and suffered too much to give up with their goal so clearly in sight. They would ascend the Blue Fang.

Thurmond smiled as he often seen Roscoe do when making a difficult decision. "It's settled then. We will begin at once. What preparations are needed, Pozi?"

"I will run home and fetch a rope and more food—some bread and dried meat. Fill your water flasks. Leave your iron coats behind. The climb will be hard enough without extra weight. I'll show you a place to hide them till we return. Bring nothing you don't need."

With that, the girl took off for home, her skinny legs a blur as she sprinted across the bean field.

Pozi's heart was pounding like a blacksmith's hammer as she sprinted back to the village. She was about to abandon her parents, her myriad siblings, and the village that had been her home since birth. Never had she been so exuberant.

There was naturally some trepidation. Who were these strangers? They must be extravagantly wealthy to possess such fine swords and iron coats. Most likely they were royalty. The one called Thurmond, she guessed, was a famous prince who would someday inherit a kingdom. The other, the one called Sarah, was obviously his ladylove, but she could not be a princess. Princesses did not traipse about the country in search of witches to slay.

No matter. She had felt an instant affinity for them both, a stronger connection than she had ever felt with the folk of her own village. She would be more than glad to share the risks of their undertaking in order to flee the soul-slaying drudgery of being a village wife and to escape that great heap of turds named Samp.

Mama, she knew, would wail for a time as she always did when one of her offspring met with an unexpected demise. But the season of sorrow would pass quickly, for there would be many other children demanding her time and attention. Father would be glad to see her go—one less hungry mouth to feed.

Some trouble would come when Samp tried to reclaim his goats and kettle. Father would never give them up. But she could not concern herself with a feud between two selfish old men. Father Hieronymus might get grumpy, but he could always choose another assistant from among the village girls. His current wife had once been his assistant.

Arriving at her family's cottage, she was relieved to find it empty. Everyone was off at some task. She quickly gathered a large loaf, several strips of jerked goat, and her threadbare cloak. Her other pitiful possessions she would leave behind for her brothers and sisters. She took the small work knife from its wooden peg. Father would be furious, but she needed it more than he. Outside, she hung a coil of rope over one shoulder and pulled her pouch of small coins from its hiding place beneath a rock. Time to go.

That Pozi was quite a girl.

CHAPTER 27

UP THE BLUE FANG

The narrow path—quite similar to the one they had climbed with Roscoe and Torgul—ended abruptly in a sheer drop-off. There was simply no more path. From this point they would have to proceed by stepping along a series of iron pegs driven horizontally into the cliff-face. These were about a cubit in length and badly rusted, some were bent and looked loose. There were no corresponding pegs to serve as handholds. The climbers would have to cling to the cliff with their fingers.

Thurmond and Sarah were horrified, but Pozi remained unfazed.

"This is where we bring the witch her food, where she lowers the basket. I know the pegs look scary, but they're not too bad as long as you hang on tight. They get slippery when they're wet, so watch out."

She skipped out onto the first pegs, scampering across like a monkey. Thurmond followed, very glad he had left his mailshirt down below. He glanced back at Sarah. She was trembling but following close behind.

Some pegs were indeed loose, shifting when he stepped on them. Others were wet and slick from the rivulets of melted snow that trickled down from above. Some were missing altogether, leaving wide gaps he had to stretch across. Pozi hopped across these with the ease of a flying weasel.

They inched along, keeping their attention riveted on each new peg and on each tenuous handhold. Thurmond found in Pozi a source of inspiration.

If a stripling girl could climb this cliff so readily, an experienced almost-Adventurer like himself could certainly do so.

For a time, Pozi was far ahead of the other two, but she waited until they closed the distance. Drawing nigh, they saw that she stood on the final peg. Beyond her were only a series of holes from which the iron bars had been removed.

She laughed, entirely unfazed by this obstacle.

"Now the climb gets more difficult. Somebody pulled out the rest of the pegs to keep us from reaching the castle, but I found another way. See that crack in the rock?"

She pointed to a long cleft, the kind mountaineers call a chimney, that ran almost straight up the cliff face.

"Just copy what I do."

She inserted herself into the cleft, then bracing her back against one side and her feet on the other, and wormed her way vertically up the crack. The other two could only stare in disbelief. The girl called down to them.

"Come on, milord, milady! You must come now if you want to reach the top before it gets too dark. Use your feet to push yourself along."

This time Sarah went first. At Pozi's insistence, her pannier with most of her magical items had been left below with the mail. She carried only her leather wallet on a shoulder strap and a light cut-and-thrust sword on a waistbelt. These she pulled around to the front before slowly working her way up the chimney.

Thurmond carried his rucksack, which had been emptied of everything but the most essential gear. He had reversed it so it rode across his chest rather than his back and had pulled his sword to the front as Sarah had done. This would allow the long blade to dangle between his legs without interfering with his climbing.

The climb was miserable. Sharp rocks tore at his back, and his legs soon ached with exhaustion. His felt his toes going numb and worried his feet and legs would soon follow their example. Still he continued to shove himself upward, all the while trying to keep enough distance between himself and Sarah so the tip of her sword scabbard did not poke him in the eye.

Then he heard the strangest thing—the high-pitched voice of a girl singing a merry tune. It was Pozi, who sang while she climbed. What kind of a girl could find the heart to make music while ascending this treacherous mountain?

He again used her courage for stimulation, telling himself that if a child like Pozi could sing in the face of such danger, he must do so as well. But the mountain was too demanding, and no jaunty tune came to mind. With numb legs and aching back, Thurmond finally pushed himself to the top of the chimney and stood on a narrow ledge that led to the summit of the Blue Fang.

Sarah, who had arrived only moments before him, was stretched out on her back. Pozi sat on a boulder. Her knee was scratched—she had climbed the Blue Fang in a dress—and she wiped away the droplets of blood with her spit.

Castle Sathas loomed above them, silhouetted by the day's waning light. The sinister battlements rose from behind a curtain wall that extended edge to edge across a rocky outcropping. The gatehouse was stout and imposing. Its wooden gates, though gray with age, remained intact and were firmly shut.

The castle consisted of four connected parts. In its center, an immense roundtower, capped with a conical spire, rose to twenty times the height of a man. Of immense circumference and covered with lichen, it seemed to be the oldest part of the structure. Two square towers, of lesser girth but even taller, clasp the back of the round one. These stood at the very edge of the vertical cliff, which plunged hundreds of feet to the valley below. A large rectangular fore-tower projected from the roundtower's front. Only three stories tall, its parapet was just visible over the high curtain wall. All was stark and forbidding.

Thurmond studied the curtain wall. Pozi had spoken of various outbuildings behind it, but these remained out of sight. He marveled that such a quantity of stones, many of great size, could have been carried to such a difficult site. The builders, he decided, must have had supernatural assistance.

Neither Thurmond nor Sarah had been in a castle before and so had no idea what they would encounter inside. Their towerhouse at Grimsgard, nothing more than an old watchtower, was small and simple by comparison.

Thurmond could discern no way to gain entrance. He turned to Sarah.

"Would your knock spell work on the gates?"

"Nay, they are huge and would require far more psychic energy than I can muster."

He looked at Pozi.

"How did you get inside?"

"I found a spot in that wall where some of the dirt has washed out and left a hole underneath. I can squeeze through, but we might need to dig it out for you two."

Pozi's hole was situated at the end of the wall and right on the edge of the cliff, so it would be necessary to swing one's legs out into space in order to crawl through. Lady Fortune always enjoyed her little jokes. Thurmond sighed and set to work enlarging it with the tip of his sword. He hated to use his weapon in this fashion but saw no other way. After a while, Sarah took his place.

While Thurmond rested, he recalled the bent and twisted box he had recovered from the den of the dead hyut. He had brought it along on the off chance it might contain some item that would be useful against the witch. Maybe Pozi would recognize it—maybe it came from her village. He took it from his rucksack and handed it to her.

"Ever seen anything like this, girl? I took it from the hyut I slew."

"Nay, lord, but it must be well fashioned to withstand the fingers of such a beast. What's inside?"

"I know not. I was hoping you might have an answer."

She examined the lock then drew something from the cloth bag suspended around her neck—a length of wire pounded flat.

"Mayhap with this, milord, I may satisfy your curiosity."

Pozi applied herself to the lock while Thurmond continued expanding the hole. Just as he was finishing, he heard her squeal of delight.

"Got it! Look, look! I got it open. I did it!"

She handed the box to Thurmond. The lock was indeed unfastened. He was amazed—was there anything this girl could not do?

"How did you learn to do this, Pozi?"

"From the blacksmith. I watched him make a lock like this, so I know how it works. It isn't hard. You just have to push the wire into the right place."

Pozi continued to astonish him.

"You're not like the other village girls, are you?"

"Nay, Mama says I'm a changeling left by the faerie-folk, but my father says Mama must have mated with a snow goblin."

Sarah joined them.

"Are you two ever going to stop talking and open the damned box? I want to see what's in it."

Inside, wrapped in fleece and packed in straw, was a collection of tiny teeth—thin, curved, and extremely sharp—about enough to fill a hen's egg. Thurmond was mystified.

"What are these? Not from a warm-blooded creature surely—a snake mayhap? Or a fish?"

Pozi had no idea. Sarah stirred them with the tip of her finger.

"They're so small, and there's so many of them. There must be over a hundred."

Something caught Thurmond's eye.

"Hey, look here."

He pulled a folded square of parchment from inside the straw lining. It bore an inscription in an unfamiliar alphabet. Sarah grew very excited.

"Let me see that parchment—maybe I can read it. I think it's a spell."

Spells were often written in cipher to keep the uninitiated from stumbling across dangerous, often deadly, knowledge. Sarah had studied several such alphabets and was certain she could unravel this one.

"Look, I'm going to need a bit of time to work this out." Why don't you two rest? When it gets dark, we'll crawl through the hole into the courtyard."

When the sun finally got sleepy and crawled off over the horizon, the moon rose full and bright, drenching the summit in its ghastly silver light. Thurmond regarded it with mixed feelings. The moonlight would make it easier for them to find their way, but also much easier for the witch, who was perhaps looking down from the castle's battlements, to see them. He was growing impatient.

"We have to go. Can you read that note yet?"

"These are definitely enchanted teeth, but the parchment doesn't reveal what creature they came out of. It says, *cast on ye grund as ye wuld sow ye sedes of wheet.* Then there's an incantation. I guess you use it to control them. But

I still don't know what they do. Maybe they shoot like little darts—I'm just not sure."

Thurmond was disappointed. The tiny teeth did not seem very useful.

"They're too little to be effective darts unless maybe they're poisonous."

"I see no trace of venom, so I don't think so. What do you think they do?"

"I don't know, but bring 'em. Let's go."

Pozi was a scrawny child and slipped through the hole with ease. The swords and other gear went through next. Sarah made it without difficulty, but Thurmond got stuck. He was by no means of stocky build, but the opening was too narrow for him to wriggle through. With his feet hanging over the precipice, he could find nothing to push against. Finally Sarah took him beneath the arms and gave a mighty heave that yanked him the rest of the way in.

The castle's courtyard was just as Pozi had described it. The inner side of the wall was lined with the broken remains of buildings—stables, workshops, storehouses, dwellings. All were deserted, their doors standing open, their furnishings decayed and coated with dust. The rising moon provided an abundance of light. An overabundance.

As Thurmond had feared, the castle's iron-braced doors were tightly closed. He pushed on them first with his hands, then with his shoulders. He may as well have been trying to push through the thick stone wall.

Pozi led them to a dilapidated structure with a fallen roof. A brick forge proclaimed it to be the workshop of some long-dead smith. The girl spoke in a whisper.

"When I found this place, I could stop searching around for random scraps. There's lots of iron inside."

Entering, Thurmond saw billets of raw pig iron, corroded rivets, and roughly hammered plates scattered on the structure's dirt floor. He recognized some of the distinctive shapes. This had not been the workplace of a common blacksmith but of an armorer—a specialist in one of the most intricate forms of metalsmithing.

He was delighted, since all his armor had been left behind. Maybe there was something here he could use. He searched the ruins of the shop, pushing aside fragments of broken roof and sorting through piles of rusted plates.

He found nothing wearable, but his efforts were rewarded when he came upon a buckler—a small round shield forged from iron. It was scabby with rust but nonetheless still solid. He had often used such an item in practice bouts with Roscoe and Torgul. A larger shield would have been preferable, but the buckler was very welcome. He hung it on his belt.

It was time to find a way inside the castle. The rectangular fore-tower had massive doors even more formidable than those of the gatehouse, but Pozi knew of a partially collapsed tunnel that could possibly provide an entrance. She led them to it.

It was nothing more than a ragged hole illuminated by the moonlight. A section of a subterranean roof had fallen in, revealing a narrow passage lined with narrow bricks of the old Etrusian style. It was singularly uninviting.

Thurmond stretched out on his belly and leaned inside as far as he dared. He could not see very far in either direction, but the tunnel seemed intact and only partially blocked by debris from the collapsed roof.

"Did you ever go down there, Pozi?"

"Nay, I had no need to enter the castle, and I didn't want to meet the old witch."

And with that Thurmond tied one end of Pozi's rope to an iron ring set in a nearby wall and lowered himself into the hole.

PART 3

IN THE CASTLE OF THE WITCH CULT

CHAPTER 28

INTO CASTLE SATHAS

A barrage of bats, frightened by the violation of their lair, pelted Thurmond's cheeks like an angry woman's slap—*whap, whap, whap, whap, whap*! One after the other, without warning, coming out of the dark before he could raise his hands in defense or turn his back. There was nothing left to do but scream.

He heard Sarah and Pozi squealing in surprise as the panicked creatures surged out of the tunnel and into their faces. If the witch had not been alerted by their voices and footsteps, the column of bats billowing across the moonlit sky would certainly announce their presence.

The air in the tunnel was foul with bat dung, and the light from the moon was dim. Thurmond took a fragment of oily fleece from his rucksack and lashed it to a wooden stick from the ruined blacksmith shop. As his companions were climbing down the rope to join him, he used his flint and steel to ignite the makeshift torch.

The passage was short and straight. It ended at a solid wooden door to what they assumed was the entrance to the castle's undercroft. Their searching fingers could discover no trace of a concealed keyhole or latch.

"Sarah …?"

Thurmond left the rest of his question unspoken—there was no need to say more.

"Aye, this one's small. Shouldn't be too difficult."

She took her wand from her shoulder bag, a length of hazel wood about as long as her forearm and big around as her thumb. Its ends were capped with iron and occult runes were carved along its length.

Spells drew on the store of psychic energy residing in the magician's physical body. Each new casting reduced the available supply. Spells that manipulated the material world or controlled malevolent spirits were by far the costliest and therefore the prerogative of master magicians whose reservoir of energy was far greater than that of a novice. When the supply of energy was depleted, there could be no more spells until it was renewed through rest and meditation. An over-expenditure of psychic energy typically left a magician sick and exhausted.

This was why the wand was a vital component of any magician's equipage. It held a supply of reserve energy to augment that residing within the magician. There were many different kinds of wands. Some, like Sarah's, were relatively small. Others were as large as a yeoman's quarter-staff. Different woods were used in the creation of wands, and the cutting and carving was carried out on specific days and at certain hours in accord with the positions of the stars and planets.

Sarah held her wand in both hands, feeling its energy course through her body. Then she cast her knock spell, the same one that had so readily opened the door to the Blue Friar's courtyard. But this time it failed, as spells were prone to do. She tried again, but the door remained stubbornly shut. She tried a third time, fearing the attempt would be a foolish waste of energy, but she was too stubborn to give up.

There was an audible click as the bolts on the inside drew back, and the door swung slightly ajar. Sarah was relieved but also concerned. As a novice, her reserve of psychic energy, even when supplemented by a wand, was quite limited. The knock spell was expensive, involving as it did the moving of physical matter. Three tries left her energy level noticeably reduced.

The trio entered a large room with a high groin-vaulted ceiling supported by massive stone columns—a crypt. The torchlight revealed a score or more stone sarcophagi. Many were adorned with effigies of knights in armor. Others bore the figures of what must have once been the beautiful ladies whose moldy bones now lay within. The chamber was damp and long forgotten. Not so much as a rat crept within its shadows.

Along one wall, a long stone stair led into the gloom far above. The trio ascended as quietly as possible, their ears and eyes straining for any sound or movement that could indicate danger. They arrived at an ancient door, its wood grey and splintered, it hinges rusted and sagging. Thurmond gave it a gentle nudge. It moved! It was unlocked!

Peeking through a narrow crack, he saw wide stone corridor. They were above ground level now, and moonlight drifted in through slit windows in the right-hand wall. There was just enough illumination not to need the torch. The witch of Castle Sathas did not confront them, so perhaps she had not witnessed the flight of the bats or heard them screaming in her courtyard.

The corridor ended in another large chamber. Moonlight streamed in from windows set high in the soaring ceiling. Large doors, presumably the ones they had seen from outside, were set in the wall to the left. Straight ahead was a fireplace large enough to accommodate the roasting of an ox. Moth-chewed tapestries and faded banners hung from the walls. The floor was strewn with broken benches and overturned tables, as if a battle had once been waged therein.

This room was obviously the castle's great hall, where perhaps—well before the coming of the witch-queen Sathas or the evil cult that later took her name—some long- forgotten noble and his retainers had gathered to feast and make merry. But the room had been abandoned many years ago, and the once-fine furnishings were decayed and covered with dust.

Thurmond whispered to the others.

"Before we go any farther, let us go unbar the big doors. It'll give us another way out."

They quickly removed the heavy wooden bar and drew the thick iron bolts that secured the door against intruders. This was accomplished with very little noise, so odds were good that the castle's inhabitant was still unaware of their presence.

But then Lady Fortune gave her wheel an evil turn.

"EEEEEEEEE! EEEEEEEEE!"

The voice was shrill and deafeningly loud. They spun about, hands groping for weapons, and beheld the strangest creature any of them had ever seen. It looked to be a lizard about half as long as a man is tall, its back covered in a hideous layer of knobs, plates, and scales. But instead of the pointed snout of a reptile, it bore a human face—that of an aged female.

It spoke in a quavering human voice.

"You—intruders! I command you to go! Get ye gone! At once!"

Thurmond advanced, intending to slay the abomination before it could attack or summon aid, but the lizard-thing was too fast. It gave another ear-splitting scream, spat something brown, and scuttled across the room on its short reptilian legs. It then ran straight up the far wall and disappeared into the minstrel's gallery above.

The creature's noxious brown spittle emitted a stench so horrific that Thurmond thought he must vomit. Sarah and Pozi fared no better, gagging uncontrollably until able to push open the great doors and let in some fresh air.

Only with a supreme effort did Thurmond recover his composure.

"Well, I'd say the witch knows we're here."

Sarah nodded.

"Undoubtedly—but I don't think that was her. That thing was more frightened of us than we were of it. I don't think the witch would react like that. And it wasn't a demon either, in spite of what it looked like. A demon would have no reason to fear us. I think it's just some disgusting freak created by magic."

"We had better move—better to find the witch before she finds us. I see a staircase through that door in the corner."

The trio headed toward the stairway, pausing while Thurmond selected a spear from what had once been a gleaming stand of arms, most likely trophies from some bygone victory. The point was deeply pitted with rust, and the shaft was dry and undoubtedly brittle. Still, it could be effective in the confines of the castle's corridors.

Suddenly a black cloud engulfed the room and smothered the moonlight. It settled on their bodies, causing every bit of exposed skin to burn as if consumed by fire. The darkness entered their eyes, bringing blindness, and poured down their throats, choking off their breath. It seeped inside their armor, carrying its agony to their chests, bellies, and backs.

They beat at this insidious foe with their hands, as if they could somehow scrape off or extinguish the burning, but this did no good. Once again, they could only scream—scream and go mad. Scream and pray for the deliverance of death.

Then it was gone, as if it had never been. Sight returned to blinded eyes and breath to constricted throat. The terrible burn subsided from hands and face, from beneath the arms and between the legs. The moonlight returned.

Thurmond looked to his companions. Sarah was on her knees, her palms pressed to her face. She was alone.

"Sarah—where's Pozi?"

As yet unable to speak, Sarah could do no more than wave a limp hand toward the hall's open doors.

"She ran out? Got away?"

Sarah nodded. Thurmond was relieved. He did not like having a youngster on such a dangerous quest. They had needed her to show them the way in, but it was much better that she was now gone.

A peal of insane, cackling laughter boomed across the hall. An appalling laugh, high-pitched and reedy, yet unfathomably commanding and infused with such deep and appalling evil that Thurmond and Sarah felt pushed nearly to the brink of madness.

An ancient woman was looking down at them from the minstrel's gallery, her long tangled hair so white, her skin so pale, that she seemed almost translucent. She wore what appeared to be a long, white shroud. Here was the witch of Castle Sathas—the last witch—the entity known as Old One. The lizard-thing crouched at her feet, peeking through the gallery's railing.

She laughed again, once more filling their souls with dread. Then she spoke.

"Welcome, honored guests, to Castle Sathas. Had you sent word ahead, I could have made your stay a bit more…diverting."

She sniggered as if this remark were somehow darkly humorous.

"I cannot imagine why two such as yourselves would care to visit an old recluse like me. I'd think you'd be more interested in rutting behind your father's barn. You must want something. Mmmmm?"

Again the malevolent giggle.

Sarah straightened and looked up at her host. She did not like what she saw. The witch's face was so thin as to resemble a skull. Her eyes—if eyes she had—were invisible in their dark, blank sockets. A faint red glow bathed her head and shoulders like an unholy halo.

Sarah was very careful to keep her voice firm.

"Good mother, we ask nothing from you. Rather, we are come to return a precious item that belongs here."

The young witch drew the medallion from her shoulder bag and held it up for the other to see. The crone, for a brief moment, looked startled, but she quickly regained her attitude of confident superiority.

"So—you've returned. And after all these years. I should have recognized you from the first, but who could guess you'd keep your looks for so long. Isn't that curious. I'd have thought you would be smarter than to come back here. You were lucky to escape the first time, were you not? Well, since you're back, we might as well have a little fun!"

She gave another laugh and disappeared. Even after her departure, her unwholesome red aura hung in the air, as did the reverberations of her fearsome cackling. Sarah was wide-eyed with terror.

"What did she mean, Thurmond? Why did she talk like that to me? She seems to think she knows me from long ago."

"She's completely deranged, out of her mind. Come on, we've got to find her and kill her before she can summon that black cloud again, or maybe something worse. Keep the medallion handy. Did you see the look on her face when you pulled it out? I think she fears it."

They headed up the winding stairs to the tower's upper floors. Fortunately, the moon remained bright, so the light was adequate. They came to a heavy bronze door. Thurmond pushed it open with one foot and advanced with the spear's rusty point thrust out before him. Sarah followed, clutching her wand in one hand and the medallion in the other.

Down below, the great hall was a dust-filled ruin, but the decayed banners and broken tables suggested that normalcy had once prevailed within these walls. The castle's overlord might have been kind or cruel, clever or foolish, but he had lived as his fellow nobles had lived—hunting, fighting, feasting. The hall's forlorn relics testified to that.

The room in which they now stood testified to a very different reality. It was huge, round, and devoid of furnishings. The tiled floor was set with a mosaic of the same interlaced serpent design as on the medallion. Nine bronze doors, spaced evenly along the circular wall, were embellished with occult symbols and mystic writing. On the floor between the doors, nine magic circles carried words of power and protection.

Glass globes suspended from a ceiling far overhead emitted a sour yellow light. Noxious smoke wafted from brazen censers. The air was noticeably cooler, unnaturally so. Thurmond was immediately struck with queasiness in his stomach and a strong disinclination to remain in the chamber.

Sarah was fascinated.

"Do you know what this is, Thurmond? It's called an invocatory—at least I think that's what this is. It's a special chamber dedicated to the summoning of spirits. This is a place of tremendous power. Can't you feel its psychic emanations?"

"I can—and I don't like them. This is an evil place. Let us leave it."

"Aye, evil it is. Nothing benign could be called forth here. Still, I am in awe. The women who used this room possessed marvelous abilities, even if they were misguided. I…"

Thurmond was well aware of Sarah's susceptibility to the seductive voice of power, and took her by the arm.

"Let us leave this room before you start calling up an arch-fiend. We have a witch to kill."

He pulled her through the closest door. Its bronze panels held bas-relief depictions of tortured, twisted faces with staring eyes and slack mouths— perhaps countenances of those who looked too deeply into the mysteries of the spectral realm.

CHAPTER 29

WITCHY GAMES

They entered a long interior corridor bereft of windows, the only light coming from more glass spheres suspended above. With nowhere to go but straight ahead, they went until the passage ended at a locked door. Again came the hateful laughter, behind them this time. They spun about, and Old One was there, enwrapped in her crimson aura. She grinned broadly and waved a long wooden staff.

There suddenly appeared a crawling horror—a green, slouching, pulpy mass resembling the segmented caterpillars that are the bane of fields and gardens. Those worms, however, were but harmless pests. This one was large enough to fill the corridor and armed with a set of mandibles strong enough to cut a man in twain.

Thurmond hesitated. He, as a boy, always found such worms loathsome. The witch had obviously reached into his mind and found this childhood fear. Well—no matter! He thrust with his spear at what he thought might be an eye, but the worm was far more agile than expected. It twisted and caught the spear shaft in its mandibles, wrenched it from his hands and snapped off the head.

Thurmond fell back, vaguely aware that Sarah was casting some sort of spell. Something sizzled past his shoulder and struck the monstrous creature in the center of what passed for its face. The energy bolt—for that is what it was—left a charred and gaping wound in the worm-thing's quaggy flesh, but the vile creature did not seem to notice. It came on, its mandibles opening and closing in an unrelenting rhythm.

That spell was one of Sarah's most powerful, and casting it left her reeling and dizzy. Thurmond saw this and grabbed her arm. They must run—run and hide—but there was no place to run to. They desperately pushed and pulled at the door, but to no avail. It remained firmly locked. The worm was upon them much more quickly than seemed possible. Sarah, too drained to throw another spell, held up the medallion.

"Be gone!"

This simple command had worked admirably against the angry ghost that attacked them at the tomb of the dead witch, but it failed utterly against this huge wallowing monster. Its mandibles snapped open and closed, open and closed like a pair of huge steel shears. Thurmond expected to die, but he would make a fight of it. He grabbed Sarah by the arm and thrust her behind him. Then he drew his sword and unhooked the rusty buckler from his belt. The blade and shield would, he knew, be of little use against such a colossus, but it was the best he could do.

Suddenly an inspiration struck him, and he shouted as loudly as he could. "Disbelieve! Disbelieve! Disbelieve!"

The worm dissolved into a green mist that swirled for a moment into the likeness of the witch. She gave a single obscene snigger and disappeared.

They were at the end of their strength. Sarah was bent forward, hands on knees, in a posture of exhaustion. Thurmond lowered his sword and sagged back against the door, which swung inward. The heavy portal that had, only seconds before, been barred against their entry now stood ajar. They stepped through and shut it behind them, the locking mechanism engaging with a metallic *snap*.

The chamber was unlike any they had yet encountered in Castle Sathas. A cheery fire burned in a grate, and the yellow globes cast a warm pleasant glow. Twin couches were heaped with furs, cushions, and coverlets. A long trestle table offered platters of meats, cheeses, breads, and soups. A large decanter was filled with wine, a stone pitcher with beer.

Thurmond's distrust was immediately aroused.

"Don't touch any of this stuff. I'll bet it's poisoned—or enchanted. That witch wants to kill us, not feed us."

Sarah was less certain.

"Maybe not. If she wanted to kill us, she could have used her black cloud back in the great hall. And I'm pretty sure that worm was intended only to scare us. A witch that powerful wouldn't have to use a simple illusion spell that can be broken by disbelief. She's playing with us. Like she said, she was having a little fun at our expense."

"You don't think she really means us ill?"

"Oh, she means us ill all right, no doubt about that, but she doesn't want her game to end just yet. She knows we're exhausted, so she's giving us food and a chance to rest in order to keep us going, to keep the game going. Look, we're about done in anyway, so I don't see that we have much to lose. Do what you want, but I'm going to eat and lie down."

The aroma of roasted meats was even more persuasive than Sarah's logic. They ate their fill, drained the decanters of wine and beer, and fell into a sound slumber on the wonderfully soft couches. Their sleep was undisturbed by troubling dreams, and they awoke refreshed and invigorated.

As they dined on the remnants of their previous repast, Thurmond spoke up, his mouth half-filled with a fragment of bread.

"Something is amiss here. How long were we asleep—an hour or two? I don't think it was more than that, but I feel well rested, like I slept a whole night through."

"I know. I feel the same way, and my psychic energy is replenished as if I'd meditated for a couple of days."

"How long do you think we slept?"

"Can't say—there's no way to judge the passage of hours here. The chamber has no windows, so there's no moonlight or sunlight coming in. There are only those globes up by the ceiling."

Thurmond jumped to his feet.

"The fire! It was burning when we came in here, and it still is. If we were asleep for hours, the wood would be burned up. It looks exactly like it did when we came in here. It's putting out heat, but the flames aren't really burning the logs."

Sarah could only shake her head.

"This place is deeply weird, Thurmond. It's like time doesn't exist here. And if time isn't real, I'm not sure anything else is either."

Then Thurmond saw something that made such metaphysical questions less compelling.

"Hey, looky there!"

A table on the room's far side was laden with weapons and armor—two mailshirts, two open-faced helmets, and a short spear. All appeared to be of excellent quality and closely resembled the very items they had been forced to leave behind at various stages of their journey.

"Sarah, was this gear here all along or was it delivered while we slept?"

She could not answer his question. She had not seen it, but maybe she had just overlooked it in her eagerness for food and rest. They agreed they should accept the war gear as they had the food and drink, on the assumption it was not harmful and had been provided to prolong the witchy game.

Thurmond dropped a mail shirt over his head and strapped his swordbelt round his waist. He hooked the buckler in an easily accessible position slightly behind his left hip. Then he donned the helmet and buckled the chinstrap.

Sarah gave a little gasp.

"Here's something else! I just picked up my wand, and guess what—it's fully charged. I didn't do it. The old witch must have recharged it."

Of a sudden the air was rent by a tremendous crash of a gong, a big one from the depth of its pitch. Startled, the pair jumped as if stung by a serpent. Thurmond allowed himself a slight smile.

"I'd say the witch wants us to wake up now. What say we get going and try to get the jump on her?"

Sarah was agreeable. She wiggled into her mail while Thurmond explored the chamber. The bronze door was again locked, so their only option was a stairway leading to the floors above. Thurmond led the way, spearpoint first. He expected the climb to be long and arduous, but they emerged into another corridor after climbing no more than thirty steps. The overhead globes dimmed to a sickly yellow, making it difficult to see. They moved along, the light fading with each step. Soon they could not see their own feet, and their movement felt like they were swimming rather than walking through the dark.

The corridor twisted erratically to the right, and dropped down a staircase of at least a hundred steps. At the bottom, the corridor again twisted right to left, but then turned left to right, and finally right to left again. Spiral stairs took them up and down, down and up. Passages and stairways in many castles were specifically constructed to confuse invaders, but there was neither logic nor sanity in this random, contradictory design.

The light continued to dim until only the faintest of gleams was visible on the point of Thurmond's spear. They walked and walked, their only measure of time or distance being the fatigue in their legs. The way became even more irrational, at one point winding in upon itself in an impossibly constricted spiral. At another point, the passage seemed to double back under itself, giving them the sensation of walking on the ceiling. There were no doors or side openings, so their only option was to continue down that mad corridor.

Sarah finally called a halt to their aimless wandering.

"We're getting nowhere. We're in a maze, and it's all part of the witch's game. She's somewhere laughing at us while we stumble along in the dark."

Thurmond was equally frustrated.

"You're right—it's some kind of illusion. This is a big castle but not big enough to hold all these crazy corridors. It can't be real. I've been disbelieving all along, but it doesn't help."

"That only works for simple illusions. The witch's magic is too strong. But I'm tired of this."

Sarah screamed at the ceiling.

"Hey, you poxy old hag! Show yourself now, or leave this castle forever. Face us if you're not afraid! Stop hiding in the darkness like some cringing scullery maid! Come on! Fight us if you've got the stomach for it!"

Sarah should have perhaps been more thoughtful before issuing such a challenge. The lights suddenly burned bright, and Old One stood before them.

"Lady Agnes, your years away have made you abrupt—rude even. You've never spoken to me like that before. But I suppose my sport has made you peevish. There's no need to apologize, for I'm not offended.

"In sooth, I'm quite delighted to see you again. How many years has it been? Fifty? Sixty? More than a hundred? I've quite lost track of the years. You've preserved your looks wonderfully. Welcome home."

Sarah was baffled. The witch spoke as if she were an old acquaintance, called her by the name of Agnes. What could this mean? Before she could formulate a response, the crone spoke again.

"I'm sure you want to say hello to Leticia. You two were ever so close. Leticia, come greet your old friend."

The human-faced lizard-thing slithered out from behind the witch's skirts. It gazed at Sarah, who—to her dismay—saw recognition in its eyes. Did this living atrocity know her? How could this be? And why did the witch keep calling her Agnes?

The hag chortled evilly.

"Leticia is rather changed from the last time you saw her, but I think enough remains for you to mark the visage of your most intimate friend. 'Tis pity she didn't join you in your flight. Life here has been...challenging for her."

The lizard creature gave a mournful twitter and disappeared behind witch.

Sarah finally found her voice.

"Why do you call me Agnes? My name is Sarah."

"Not Agnes? Well, you certainly bear her features. But Sarah or Agnes, it makes no difference, for her blood runs in your veins of a certain. And you could have but one purpose in coming—vengeance."

"Nay, nay, we came only to return this medal...."

Old One erupted in a torrent of insane mirth.

"Hee-hee! Hee-hee! Hee-hee! If you want to overthrow me, Agnes, then by all means, let us proceed. Perchance you remember my girls—no illusion this time! Girls, come say hello to Agnes!"

Three gigantic amazon warriors stepped from the shadows behind the witch. They were dressed in mail and carried large iron-bound shields. Their long, curved swords glimmered in the dim light. Sarah took one look at their slack lips and blank eyes and was certain she looked upon the undead dead. The trio advanced, swords raised.

Thurmond screamed out.

"Sarah, the teeth! The teeth! Try the teeth!"

They had, until that moment, forgotten the box of tiny curved teeth. Sarah was quick. She cast a handful as if sowing a plot of wheat and spoke the incantation of command prescribed on the parchment. With that, the small curved teeth began to twitch, jump, and spin. They inched along the floor like worms and then started to change shape.

As the trio of amazons bore down on them, Thurmond stepped ahead of his companion, aimed his spear at the woman-thing in the middle. He feinted slightly and then drove it at the one on his left with all his body weight behind it. Her reaction was slow. The spear cleared the top edge of her shield and struck her smack in the middle of the chest. Its point burst through the riveted links of her mail and lodged in her breastbone. As she toppled backward, Thurmond was forced to relinquish the weapon to avoid being pulled down on top of her.

Sarah did not know if her spells would work on the living dead, but she opened with an illusion spell. She was good with them, and they took but a modest toll on her energy. She summoned the first thing that came to mind—a vision of a ferocious bear standing directly before the two remaining amazons. It worked! The amazons attacked it with their ponderous swords as if it were real.

The bear, infuriated, struck back with its claws. But then the hellish laughter of the witch rose to a maddening pitch, and the bear disappeared—the spell was broken. The illusion only slowed the attackers for a moment, but that was enough. It gave Thurmond time to draw his sword.

He swept in from the left side just as the bear faded from view. Distracted, the middle amazon was not aware of him until his weapon sliced through the tendons behind her knee—a move he had learned from Torgul. She dropped in a clumsy heap.

The third amazon stepped through the dissolving image of the bear and aimed a great roundhouse at Sarah's head. Had it landed square, it would have split her helmet and cloven her skull. But the amazon's aim was poor, so the sword's point scraped across the stone wall, greatly reducing its force. Even so, its impact was sufficient to send Sarah reeling to the floor.

Their transformation complete, the teeth commenced their attack. Each had morphed into a tiny skeletal serpent about as long as a peapod. They possessed no skin, flesh, or organs of any kind—only vertebrae, ribs, and skulls with fangs. With uncanny speed, these swarmed over the feet of the third amazon and squirmed up her legs, striking with their fangs all the while.

The amazon kicked, sending serpents flying against the wall, and stamped down, crushing the bones of others to white powder. But some managed to surge up under her mail to strike the sensitive places beneath. Confused, she dropped her sword and shield and began to flail wildly with her hands. Taking advantage of her distraction, Thurmond sent the edge of his blade slicing through her neck, half-removing her head from her shoulders.

He spun, expecting an attack by her lamed sister, but she was also fully engaged with the bone-snakes, which squirmed up her arms and onto her shoulders as she attempted to pull herself to a sitting position. Thurmond delivered a hard shot to the side of the head, cutting away a section of her skull.

But when is an undead creature truly dead? Can it live with only half a neck or part of a brain? These apparently could not, for they slumped to the floor and moved no more. The first, however—the one Thurmond had stabbed—obviously did not require a beating heart, for she rose up, brandishing the very spear that had struck her down. Occupied with killing the second amazon, Thurmond failed to see her as she came from behind.

The young man would have surely been slain with his own spear had not Sarah, emerging from her stupor, shot an energy bolt straight into the amazon's eye. The white-hot missile caused the eyeball to burst, and the brain to sizzle and fry.

The amazon fell, but in falling managed to plunge her spear into Thurmond's left arm just below the shoulder. With her inordinate strength behind it, the point sheared through the iron rings of his armor as easily as a sharp knife cuts through burlap. Yet the mail saved him from grievous hurt, for the spearhead was turned so that the deadly point did not enter his flesh. He received instead a deep cut as the weapon's sharp edge sliced across his bicep.

The amazon still refused to die. She lay sprawled on her stomach, legs and arms flopping spastically. Thurmond pushed the tip of his sword into the base of the skull and ended her grotesque dance.

Sarah regained her feet but clung to the wall for support. Her helmet was deeply dented, and blood trickled down the side of her face. The tooth-spell had run its course. The bone-snakes had ceased to move and quickly crumbled to a dusting of white powder. Thurmond stood ready to meet the next attack.

Old One was gone, but her voice resonated out of the empty air.

"I see you've got some serpent teeth. I used to have a box of those, but I can't seem to find it. Fun little things, aren't they? Hee-hee! Hee-hee!"

And then the voice was gone as well.

CHAPTER 30

STRANGE TRUTHS

Sarah removed her helmet. Thurmond carefully wiped the blood from her face and examined her wound. The amazon's heavy sword had delivered a hefty blow that raised a large lump and broke the skin of her forehead, but its edge had not penetrated the helmet, so the wound, while painful, was not serious.

Thurmond was loath to remove his mailshirt, but finally did so because his arm required binding to stanch the flow of blood. Sarah wrapped it with a bandage from her shoulder bag. As soon as she finished, he slipped the armor back over his head.

His injury forced him to abandon the spear. It required two hands, and his left arm was too weak and sore. He found that he could, with difficulty, still grip the buckler. Sarah had to discard her helmet. Her broken brow made it too painful to wear.

They gave the dead amazons a quick inspection but found nothing valuable or useful. Their swords and shields were far too heavy for anyone of mortal strength.

Thurmond mused.

"Too bad the witch didn't give us a bow with the other gear. Maybe one of us could have picked her off, and we wouldn't have had to fight these things."

Sarah shook her head.

"Nay, that wasn't the real witch—only her fetch, a spirit double. Did you notice that red glow around her and how you could almost see through her? Not an ordinary physical body, I'm positive. An arrow would have passed right through and done nothing."

"Where's the real witch?"

"In some private sanctuary in a trance state. If we can find her, we could probably kill her before she comes out of it."

Sarah felt increasingly uneasy.

"Why does that mad old woman keep calling me Agnes? Who the hell is Agnes? Why does she keep talking as if she knows me?"

Thurmond was pretty sure he knew the answer, but he was hesitant to tell her.

"Like you said, she's mad. That's all."

Sarah could tell by his face he was holding back.

"Tell me what you know."

He had to tell her.

"First, I don't *know* anything. I just have a suspicion. Do you remember the name on that tomb back in Gorgonholm, the one where we stole the medallion?"

Sarah's eyes grew wide with dread.

"Nay, that's impossible."

"Aye, it's quite possible. She was Agnes de Roache. The witch said you look just like someone named Agnes. I think it was your grandam or your great-grandam, who fled from this castle many years ago."

"That's absurd. The tomb said she was *Lady* Agnes—she was a lady of rank."

"All the nobility intermarry, so why couldn't she have wed one of the Staynes?"

Sarah grew angry.

"Nay, by God's fingers, I don't want to be descended from some evil member of an insidious cult."

"Well, mayhap she wasn't so evil. She apparently left here on no good terms with the present resident. Perchance she didn't approve of the goings-on."

"The witch said I…*she*…Agnes…would only come back for vengeance, so there must have been a bitter falling out. The witch must have done something horrible to her."

"That seems pretty likely. She obviously did something to her friend Leticia—the one who's now mostly a lizard."

Disturbing questions took shape in Sarah's mind. The medallion's incessant call, that haunting relentless enjoinder that forced her hither—had that been the voice of her own deceased grandam? Or perhaps great-grandam? Had she been tasked by some long dead ancestor to bring a sharp reckoning to the witch of Castle Sathas?

Was she here against her will, or had she, in some hidden way, always been eager to visit this haunted place? She suspected the latter.

Had Agnes been a naïve young woman who had escaped to Gorgonholm when the witch's profound malevolence became known to her? Sarah had no real reason to think so, yet she chose to believe that this had been the case.

Suddenly, she knew why she had been charged with returning the medallion to the castle and what she must do. It was not her job to destroy the witch. Her task was to fetch the medallion so Lady Agnes might seek revenge in her own fashion. There was but one more deed she must perform.

"Thurmond, I finally understand why I…we…were sent here. Only one thing remains to be done."

"That damned medallion been talking to you again?"

"I don't know … I guess so. Something spoke to me. All we have to do is find the invocatory."

"The invocatory—what would that be?"

"The big round room with the snakes on the floor, the place you didn't like."

"I did indeed dislike that place. Why go there? Shouldn't we be looking for the witch's private sanctuary so we can kill her?"

"If we can find the invocatory, I don't think we'll need to kill her. That will be taken care of for us."

Thurmond was by no means convinced.

"I'd like that well enough, but that room is infused with such evil it made me ill just to pass through. That ball of snakes is a cursed symbol. Why do you want to go there?"

"You are mistaken—this talisman isn't evil. It's just a useful tool for focusing the will and holding psychic energy. Items of this nature are used by lots of witches for many purposes. This probably won't make a lot of sense to you, but the nine serpents are symbols of creation. They can represent the nine states of astral existence or the nine cardinal directions or the nine elements."

"I thought there were only four elements—fire, water, earth, and air."

"Those are the natural *physical* elements. There are five more on the spiritual level. The interlaced serpents remind us how things that seem far apart are really connected. They all come together in a non-ending circle, so it's a perfect symbol to use for invocations, for summonings. It becomes a powerful portal. That's what the big round room is for."

"If that room isn't evil, why did I get such a horrible feeling when I went in there. You said it was an evil place."

"You're right about that room. It's been used for malign purposes, so it absorbed a great deal of negative energy. I felt it, too."

"It's not just in the room—that medallion gives me a bad feeling as well. Roscoe and Torgul, too. Remember?"

"I tried to explain that back in Grimsgard. That wasn't negative energy you were feeling. The talisman doesn't feel evil to me at all. You men don't understand woman magic, so you fear it. You can call up things besides spirits with a talisman like this. A witch can use to it invoke and channel emotional energy—feelings so complex, so strong that men can never understand them."

Thurmond made a gesture of resignation.

"You're right, Sarah. I'm not understanding much of this. I guess I'll just have to trust you. What do we need to do?"

"I need to place the talisman in the center of the snake circle and invoke the spirit of Agnes. That's what she wanted since the start. When we robbed her tomb, it was her chance to return to this castle and seek revenge."

Thurmond was liking this less and less.

"If she was so eager for us to bring her here, why did her ghost try to kill us? It almost did, I hope you will recall."

"That wasn't her ghost. That was some other malignant spirit. Maybe someone placed it there to keep her in her tomb—I don't know. Maybe it just wandered by and found us."

"By God's splayed feet, I don't like getting involved in some witch-war."

"I understand your feelings entirely."

"Are you really certain you want to summon the shade of Agnes?"

"I am, but I promised to always be honest with you, so I have to tell you this. I think she'll be far more powerful and deadly than anything we've yet faced. I don't know what we'll be setting loose. She might be the very essence of evil. Things might go bad."

"I don't see how they can get much worse than they already are, Sarah. This whole adventure went bad a long time ago."

They proceeded down the winding corridors in search of the invocatory. The enchanted maze of passages had disappeared, but they were nonetheless lost in the dimly lighted bowels of a labyrinthine structure. They went up stairs, down stairs, and through myriad chambers. Some were bare, others had rank, dust-drenched furnishings.

And there, in one such chamber, they were again greeted by Old One.

"I still can't find my box of teeth. I thought we might have a little game—your teeth against mine. But you mustn't fret because I've still got one tooth left. A big one! Tooth—come greet our guests!"

A gigantic figure lumbered out of a shadowed alcove. It was a man, completely hairless and utterly naked. His blank face bore no trace of intelligence or emotion. He was armed with a huge club studded with iron.

Sarah gasped, intimidated by the sight of so much raw masculinity.

"I know what that is. It's a homunculus, a person grown in a vat in the witch's workshop. He's got no soul, never had one. Even she can't give him that."

Sarah was correct. Though she had never actually created a homunculus, she was familiar with the process. She had a recipe for such a creature in her workshop back in Grimsgard. This homunculus, however, was far from typical. Most were small, no more than a cubit in stature. This one stood half again as tall as Thurmond.

The muscles of his arms and legs were of Herculean proportion, but seemingly soft and flabby as if never toughened by hard work. His skin was as soft and pink as a baby's, and his head was strangely fleshy, as if not fully formed.

At the witch's command, the Tooth advanced with its club raised. The legs were bowed, causing the creature to waddle like a toddler. Thurmond and Sarah knew they had no chance against such an immense mass of lurching tissue. Once again, there was nothing to do but run, the screaming laughter of Old One ringing in their ears.

They fled down a random corridor, gaining slightly on the ungainly Tooth. The flagstones shook beneath the impact of his bare feet. Thurmond saw an open door at the end of the passage. It was of bronze and perhaps stout enough to baffle their pursuer. They dashed through it, slammed it shut, and shot the heavy bolt.

Almost immediately, the door buckled beneath the terrible weight of the Tooth as he smashed into it again and again. The bolt began to give way as the rivets holding it stretched and bent. Large bulges appeared in the bronze plates when the monster battered the other side with his club. The door was robust, but it would soon give way under such devastating force.

The pair turned to continue their flight, only to discover, quite to their surprise, that they now stood in the invocatory—the very room they were seeking. Sarah acted immediately.

"Get one of those other doors open, and whatever happens, be ready to run. I've never done a summoning like this before, but I know a conjuring spell that might work. Just be ready to run."

She threw the talisman into the center of the design on the floor. Then, taking a position in one of the magic circles, she recited the formula of invocation. An intense red glow began to emanate from the talisman, and Sarah felt an unknown force take command of her body. She began to recite a new spell—one she did not know and in a language she did not understand. The words rolled from her mouth without hesitation or mistake as if someone were whispering them in her ear.

Her surroundings and circumstances faded from her mind. She could no longer hear the pounding of the club against the door. She forgot the witch and the Tooth, forgot the castle, forgot Thurmond. Only the spell remained. The red glow became a mist, which grew and grew. It was of a brighter red than that of Old One. Hers was the deep crimson of old blood. This one was bright scarlet.

Thurmond shook Sarah's shoulders and screamed her name, but she did not notice. He took her arm and attempted to drag her from the room, but he was unable to shift her from the circle in which she stood. Finally, he tried to lift her bodily, but she seemed to have grown as heavy as a granite boulder. And so the spell continued.

The mist condensed to an opaque sphere with long vaporous tendrils, which whipped and writhed as if in torment. Then it shot skyward and disappeared through the ceiling high overhead.

CHAPTER 31

BATTLE ROYALE

"Sarah, come out of it! Now! We must flee! The door is giving way! Come at once!"

She was dimly aware of someone shouting her name but could summon no recollection of where she was or why anyone would want to yell at her. She was being pulled along by the arm—more dragged than pulled actually, for her feet seemed incapable of movement. And then it all came back—the red mist, the castle, and…oh shit!…the homunculus. There was a tremendous clang as the bronze door was at last heaved from its hinges and struck the flagstone floor. The giant pink man-thing strode through the open doorway.

"Sarah, come out of it! Run!"

Clarity returned and Sarah turned to run. As she did, she hurled the last handful of teeth and said the words of command. What the tiny bone-snakes might do against this behemoth, she could not guess, but it was the best she could think of. As before, the bone snakes twitched, transformed, and dutifully moved to the attack.

The Tooth remained unaware of the snakes' existence until his bare foot came down directly in the middle of their swarm, smashing them to bits. His feet were as tender as a newborn's, so the bony fragments dug into the soft white flesh like a clump of thorns. The Tooth howled in shock and pain, raised his injured foot and jumped backward. Off balance, he tottered for a moment, sat down on his butt, and began picking bone splinters from his offended skin.

Thurmond and Sarah fled from the invocatory and dashed down the stairs toward the great hall. They prayed the castle's main doors, their only chance to escape, remained open. But Old One was again ahead of them. She stood at the foot of the stairs, waving her arms as if conducting musicians and chanting in some unknown tongue.

Answering her unholy call, a host of hollow-eyed liches, ripped from the sanctity of their tombs, came shambling up from the castle's crypt—the decayed remains of long- dead knights and highborn ladies clad in the rotting cerements of the grave. Eye sockets empty, skin stretched dry and taut over bones green with mold, mouths agape, brown teeth hanging from fleshless gums. Driven forward by the witch, the staggering, groping dead ascended the stairs.

Thurmond and Sarah turned to flee back to the upper floor, but they had taken no more than two or three steps before the Tooth appeared above them. The stairway was narrow and its ceiling was low, so he had to hunch down awkwardly to squeeze inside. His great bulk completely blocked the passage, trapping Thurmond and Sarah inside.

There was no choice but to descend and face the foul, shuffling contingent of animated dead. Sarah planted a single brief kiss on Thurmond's lips and drew her sword—they would go down together, go down fighting. Seeing this, Old One giggled insanely. She pronounced a single, incomprehensible word, and the armor she had provided earlier vanished into nothingness, leaving their bodies unprotected.

Then several things happened at once.

Standing in the great hall, Old One spun round and round like a mad dervish, laughing so hard the drool flew from her mouth. So absorbed was she in her reverie that she failed to notice the scarlet mist above her head until a single wispy tendril wrapped itself around her neck.

With that, the grotesque laughter finally ceased. Old One gave a single shriek and dissolved into a cloud of crimson mist. The two red clouds, scarlet and crimson, began to battle—roiling through the air, spinning, tumbling, and engulfing each other like human wrestlers striving to gain an inexorable grip.

At that same moment, Father Hieronymus and a party of armed men strode through the hall's main doors, which had fortunately remained open. The priest carried a cudgel in one hand and the sacred sun-sign of the Charonite church in the other. Seeing the ghoulish array of corpses climbing the stairs, he held force the sacred symbol and uttered a stern command.

"I enjoin you—go! Return to your graves and find the peace of death. Depart!"

Roughly half the walking dead did as instructed, shuffling off in the direction of the crypt. The others stood for a moment before turning on Hieronymus and his party as if instinctively recognizing the priest as a mortal foe. The men did not hesitate. They surged forward to meet the attack.

Hieronymus's followers were not armored soldiers with swords and halberds. They were the simple men of his village, dressed in homespun tunics and armed with nothing more than work knives and farm tools. Yet they displayed a degree of valor of which the most chivalrous knight could be proud.

They went in swinging against foes that could not be slain because they were already dead. The only way to stop the vile crypt-things was to smash them to pieces. The desiccated bodies were awkward and jerky in their movement, but what they lacked in speed and skill, they made up for in tenacity. They continued to gouge and bite and throttle until hairless skulls were smashed and mummified arms were pulled from their sockets.

They also possessed preternatural strength. Savo the woodcutter fought well, his heavy broadax shearing through chalky bones and dried gristle. But then he was seized by the neck, and blackened fingernails tore through his throat as easily as one scoops seeds from a melon. Another lich clenched its hands together into a single fist and crushed the skull of Borto the blacksmith—he who had purchased Pozi's iron scrap—with a single terrible buffet.

The battle was not going well. Skeletal fingers ripped at eyes and cheeks, or sought purchase in stomachs and groins. The men bled and died, but those who remained fought on undaunted. Father Hieronymus was always in the fore, holding his sun-sign like a shield and smiting with his cudgel. Yet for all their courage, they were gradually forced back to the doors.

Thurmond and Sarah charged down the stairs and struck the hell-swarm from behind. Seeing the need for a weightier weapon, the young man picked up Savo's broadax, a tool used in the shaping of logs. It would be an unwieldy weapon, but its sheer mass was far more effective than his sword against the nearly unkillable crypt creatures.

He struck again and again, delivering savage blows that smashed the ancient bones like rotten sticks. Previously, the pain of his wounded arm would not have permitted such strenuous activity, but so great was the young warrior's battle-lust that it now went unheeded. Taken from behind, the liches faltered, and in faltering they were destroyed.

Heartened by Thurmond's fury, the village men attacked with renewed vigor—chopping, battering, rending. Bits of bone, grave cloth, and mummified skin flew through the air. Soon the remaining creatures were hacked to harmless fragments.

Sarah was struck by a sharp pain in her right leg and nearly pulled from her feet. Leticia the lizard-woman was digging into Sarah's ankle with her saurian claws. Her eyes were glazed over in madness and despair, and her tongue protruded, forked and bright blue.

Sarah thrust her sword into the reptile body just behind the base of the neck. The repulsive creature thrashed and twisted but did not relinquish its grip. Sarah stabbed again and then a third time. Leticia finally died, but her claws and teeth refused to let go. With the greatest loathing, Sarah pulled the carcass away from her leg with her fingers.

While the living and the dead fought among chairs and tables of the great hall, the two red clouds continued their war along the ceiling. They plunged, careened, and then darted apart only to rush forward into headlong collisions like rams in the rut. At other times they twined together like mating snakes.

Ever so gradually, the darker, crimson cloud faded and shrank. Then it recoiled from its scarlet counterpart as if trying to escape. With a speed that defied human sight, it leaped from the ceiling and disappeared up the stairs to the invocatory. Its foe kept pace barely a handbreadth behind.

But even now the battle was not concluded, for at that moment the homunculus entered the room. He had been worming his way down the stairs while the fighting raged. Once in the spacious great hall, he again had ample room to stand erect and swing its club.

The baby-pink monstrosity went straight for Thurmond, who dodged back as the ponderous club came down. It struck the top of a dust-covered table, shattering the ancient wood, flinging shards in all directions, and knocking Thurmond over backward.

The Tooth turned its attention to Hieronymus, who stood protectively in front of the surviving villagers. Confused, the creature remained still, club held low, as if trying to determine whether the friar was friend or foe. Then he saw Sarah and waddled toward her. When a villager got in the way, and the homunculus spattered his brains against the wall.

Thurmond rose from behind. He planted his feet firmly, adjusted his grip on the haft of the broadax, and delivered a hard blow straight across the monster's bare foot. Toes scattered like mice from a hungry cat.

The Tooth squealed, his voice remarkably high-pitched for a creature of such size, and slumped to the ground, his face stamped with fear and misery. He flopped and rolled, struggling to raise himself on his hands, as Thurmond continued to rain blows along its back and head. The villagers piled on with sickles, hatchets, and knives. Sarah pushed her sword between two ribs. The flesh was flabby and amazingly easy to penetrate.

So died the Tooth.

Father Hieronymus moved among his men, examining their injuries. Of the twelve who had followed him up the mountain, three were dead, one was unconscious, one was in agony from a smashed shoulder, one had lost an eye, and all were bloodied. The priest bore a long, nasty gash down the side of his face, and two of his fingers were broken.

Now that the thrill of battle had waned, the ache in Thurmond's wounded arm was excruciating. His exertions had opened the gash and set it to bleeding again. Sarah sat nearby, nursing her chewed leg. She could only hope that Leticia's bite would not prove venomous. Hieronymus gave their hurts a cursory look.

"These mere scratches are not deserving of my healing powers while others suffer from grievous injury."

The spiritual power of clerics, like the psychic energy of magicians, was limited. The more powerful the healing spell, the more energy it drew from them. The knitting of broken bones was difficult and demanded a large expenditure of holy power, and the repair of internal organs was even more costly. Spiritual energy could be restored only through a period of rest and prayer, so Hieronymus wisely chose to conserve his.

Thurmond did not view his torn arm as a *mere scratch*, but he said nothing. He had long since given up trying to engage Hieronymus in pleasant conversation. Sarah, however, was tingling with the exaltation of victory, and this made her talkative. She explained to Hieronymus the invocation of Lady Agnes and the battling clouds of red mist.

When the wounds were bound, it was time to explore the castle, though all were apprehensive about what they might find. The four most badly injured remained in the great hall. A pair of able-bodied villagers was assigned to accompany Thurmond and Sarah. The other three men would remain with the cleric. The two search parties went off in separate directions to find and slay the witch. Each group carried a horn that could be blown to summon the other.

Thurmond led his group into the upper floors of the fore-tower. The great hall comprised the entire ground level. Those above contained what appeared to have been various storerooms, an armory, and quarters for the castle's soldiers and servants. The furnishings, like those of the great hall, were in advanced states of decay and were buried beneath a thick coat of dust. They had obviously not been disturbed for many decades—perhaps hundreds of years.

When the fore-tower had been thoroughly searched, they moved into the massive central tower. It was a warren of winding passages and secluded chambers blanketed in layers of cobwebs, rot, and grime. They passed through bowers, apartments, and wardrobes with once-elegant furnishings now gray and crumbling with age. They passed through a chapel with a desecrated alter, and empty solariums where highborn ladies, now long dead, once gossiped and intrigued.

There was nothing in these rooms to suggest the terrible evil that had come to reside in the castle. Though much decayed, the furnishings were those that might be found in any noble residence. Only the obscene invocatory spoke of black magic.

Thurmond recalled the story of the castle's original owner, the Countess Sathas. She might have been a powerful witch, but the broken remnants of household furnishings suggested her life had not greatly differed from that of most wealthy nobles. She had enjoyed a life of ease and pleasure, surrounded by a host of servants and minions.

The two tall clasping towers told a different story. It was in them that the Sisters of Sathas had established themselves after the overthrow of their namesake, while the rest of the castle was allowed to disintegrate under the weight of the years.

These towers were perched on the very edge of the cliff on which the castle stood. They were smaller in girth than the huge central tower, containing only a few chambers per floor. There were, however, many steps and many floors. Here the Sisters had worked their evil magic.

The searchers found a library filled with mildewed tomes and crumbling parchments. A parlor of divination held torn astrological charts and a shattered crystal ball. Several occult workrooms had long counters filled with stoppered flasks and crockery jars, many of which lay shattered on the stone floor.

In one room, an iron cauldron was suspended in a large fireplace. It still held the powdery residue of a long-forgotten brew. An alchemist's laboratory contained an assortment of beakers and flasks, a large kiln, and a huge alembic of blown glass.

They found Old One on the topmost floor. She was lying beneath a ragged quilt on a simple wooden bed. She looked as any ancient woman might appear in death—white hair thin and lank, a tuft of hairs on the point of her chin, yellow teeth projecting from puckered lips. Her skin was still warm to the touch—she had not been dead many minutes. Sarah pulled back the quilt to reveal the naked corpse beneath. The emaciated body was dotted with sores, its spindly legs streaked with purple veins.

Thurmond was appalled.

"This could be somebody's grandam. Are you sure it's her?"

Sarah replaced the cover.

"It's her all right. The thing we saw was her fetch—her spirit double.

She fought us without ever leaving her bed. I don't think she really needed her physical body anymore, but it doesn't matter. She's dead now—Agnes saw to that. We need to burn this corpse. Witch's bones, as you know, hold powerful magic."

No trace of Lady Agnes, neither in spirit nor body, did they find.

CHAPTER 32

A BARGAIN STRUCK

Sarah wrapped the corpse of the dead witch in a quilt. Thurmond gestured for the village men to carry it downstairs for burning, but they adamantly refused to touch it. With no other option, Thurmond took the shoulders while Sarah held the feet. It was surprisingly light.

Hieronymus awaited them in the great hall. His findings in the second tower mirrored their own. The Sisters had obviously inhabited the two tall towers, leaving the rest of the castle and its furnishings to rot away. The only exception was the room of invocation, where a palpable shroud of evil still lingered.

The priest agreed that the witch's body must be burned at once. He ordered his men to build a pyre in the courtyard, using the great hall's broken tables and benches as fuel. The fragments of undead would be added to the flames.

The castle's great doors were now thrown wide, allowing wholesome sunlight to stream inside. And through these doors came Pozi, wide-eyed and breathless. She ran to the priest and clasped him around the waist with both arms. He took her by the shoulders and gently forced her back. His voice was calm and kind but also firm.

"I told you to wait outside, girl. It's not yet safe in here."

"I know, but I couldn't wait any longer. I was so scared for you."

"That matters not. You must learn to obey. I am very busy at the moment."

Hieronymus stepped away from the child to see to one of the injured men—a farmer named Fulvar, who had been struck on the head and remained unconscious. Pozi turned to Sarah.

"I'm so glad you're alive! I thought I'd never see you again. Please believe me, I didn't mean to run out on you, but I knew of nothing else to do. That black cloud… I just couldn't…"

Thurmond placed a reassuring hand on the crown of her head.

"Pozi, you did nothing wrong. We were glad you got away. We didn't want to see you hurt."

She started to cry. Her words came in gasps between her sobs.

"I could think of…nothing else "I…went back down the mountain…to fetch Father Hieronymus. I knew…he wouldn't let you die. He brought the village men…to help you."

Sarah spoke in a comforting tone.

"You saved us from a horrid death, Pozi. Maybe even saved our souls from the old witch, who would have trapped them in some blasphemous form. We would have certainly perished here, if not for your good sense to bring help. I am very grateful."

The sobs subsided.

"I thought you'd be mad because I ran away."

"Nay, not mad. Exceedingly glad, both of us."

Thurmond nodded in agreement.

"Aye, Pozi, both of us are exceedingly glad. I, too, thank you."

Finishing with the unfortunate Fulvar—there was little hope he would recover—Hieronymus joined Sarah and Thurmond as Pozi was completing her story.

"I knew I could do you no good against the witch. I don't know how to use weapons or cast magic spells, but I had to stick with you because of our bargain we'd made. You know, so I can go with you when you leave."

The priest frowned when he heard this. His concern deepened as he listened to the rest of Pozi's story.

"When that black cloud went down my throat, I couldn't breathe. I went outside where there was air. I didn't mean to run away, but I just couldn't stop. My feet just kept going, so I climbed back down the mountain as fast as I could, and I guess I didn't stop running till I found Father Hieronymus."

The girl looked to the priest for support, and he took up the story.

"When Pozi brought the news, I was of course angry because I had forbidden you to interfere with the witch. I really did not expect to be obeyed, and I expected you to reap the full reward of your foolishness. But this girl swore that you are good and true, and she begged me to save you. My resolve weakened, and I called for my best mountaineers to arm themselves and follow me up the mountain. She led us up here in the black of the night."

Then the friar's face darkened.

"But she did not tell me of your plot to take her away with you. I learned of it only now. Are her parents to have no say? Are my wishes as her spiritual father to be disregarded? She is perhaps to be my next assistant. I begin to regret not leaving you to your fate."

Pozi flew into a panic.

"Nay, nay, I beg you, Father. Please don't say such things! Leaving was all my idea. I begged to go with them. I'll die before I marry Samp, so I must be away. As you said to the others, having the castle will make our village rich and powerful. My family can live in luxury, and so can Samp. Nobody will miss me. I have always been ugly and discontented and ill-mannered. You must let me go."

Hieronymus had not intended to reveal that the rescue was motivated more by self-interest than altruism. Pozi always had an awkward knack of blurting out details best left unsaid. Truth be told, the priest and his men had come to seize the castle for themselves, not to save two reckless young foreigners.

Hieronymus had long harbored a grand design, a plan for what could be done if the castle were to come under his control. It had always seemed an impossibility, but when Pozi brought news that the two fools had actually gained entrance, he saw his moment. If the pair kept the witch sufficiently occupied, he and his men might have a chance.

He was dismayed that Thurmond and Sarah now knew of his real intentions. He wanted them grateful, satisfied with merely being alive, indebted rather than demanding. But that addle-pated Pozi had opened her mouth, so now they might try to assert themselves.

They had brought the medallion that disposed of the witch, so they might feel entitled to the castle. He could not allow that. What, then, could he offer them? Having lost the moral high ground, he tried another tack.

"I will speak to your father, Pozi, and see if we can reach some accord. Perhaps he will be agreeable to your departure."

He turned to Thurmond.

"I acknowledge that possession of this castle will offer the villagers a chance to raise their children without fear. We will now be able to protect ourselves from the marauders who routinely come to take what is ours. I am prepared to be quite generous in recognition of your efforts on our behalf. Ask what you will."

Pozi's slip of the tongue was not lost on Thurmond. He understood that the priest had come not to rescue but to conquer. It was clear Hieronymus already viewed the castle and its furnishings as his personal property and was most likely ready to kill in order to keep what he assumed to be his own. This one-time ally could quickly become an enemy. He knew from listening to the stories of Roscoe and Torgul that the division of spoils was always a tricky.

Sarah, equally wary, gave her companion a quick glance that expressed her understanding. Thurmond decided to try the rule-of-three ploy. He had fallen for it, Sarah had, too. The old priest had spent most of his life in this isolated village, so maybe he had never heard it. He kept his voice solemn and deliberate.

"Sir Priest, you are well aware, I am sure, that important things often come in threes. Legends provide many such examples. A condemned man might be afforded three chances to answer the riddle that will save his neck, or…"

Hieronymus was clearly unimpressed with such adolescent oratory.

"You will please come to the point."

Thurmond continued.

"I ask for three things as our rightful share. The first is a small thing. In fact, you have already agreed to it—that Pozi be allowed to come with us when we leave. Next, I ask that we may have our choice of the many items of treasure the castle is certain to hold, and that we be permitted to depart with as much of it as our small party can carry away on our backs. My third and final request is that when your men have been attended to and your holy powers restored, you perform a ceremony of healing. Are these terms agreeable?"

Hieronymus was surprised the young warrior should ask for so little. He was certain the castle contained a wagonload of treasure. Even if the pair were to carry off a hundredweight of gold, it would not matter. The castle was, to the friar, worth far more than its contents. The girl Pozi mattered not at all. As for the healing—their minor wounds would cost him nothing. Hieronymus smiled.

"Of course, young man, I am agreed."

Now Thurmond smiled.

"Then you will be pleased to clasp hands upon our bargain."

Thurmond spat in his hand and extended it toward the priest.

Hieronymus hesitated. The handclasp was serious business, for it wove an unbreakable bond between those who shared in it. An agreement so sealed became a sacred vow. To renege on a handclasped promise was to invite the worst possible luck at the hands of Lady Fortune. Only a madman would choose to inspire her ill will.

The friar hesitated. Could this young adventure-seeker be up to something? Laying a subtle trap? Hieronymus doubted it. He was just a whippersnapper with more brawn than brain. The girl Sarah was different, she was smart enough to be guileful. But he could see no danger in the boy's proposal.

These foreign intruders could have no inkling as to his true intentions, of the marvelous plan that he had developed slowly over the many years. It was impossible that a man such as himself could live out his life as a humble village priest. There was most certainly a larger purpose in his being sent to this valley, for it was his destiny to do great things. That opportunity lay before him, so he must act.

Hieronymus spat in his hand and gripped Thurmond's palm to palm. Then Sarah did likewise, laying hers atop the other two. This was surprising to the priest. Females were not customarily included in handclasps. A gentle tingling rippled through their palms and fingers. Lady Fortune was listening.

It was time to scour the castle for its treasure, to throw open the chests and cupboards, to tap the walls for secret niches, to spill the insides of pillows and featherbeds. To look up the chimney flue and down the well. To check the privies and dig through the cold ashes of the kitchen hearth. To peel back the rugs in search of trapdoors and shift the cabinets to reveal hidden passageways.

The treasure trove was discovered in a concealed pit beneath a false floor in what had once been the Countess Sathas' sitting room. It had apparently remained undiscovered by the angry villagers that had long ago stormed the castle with pitchforks and pruning bills. The Sisters, it seemed, had missed it as well, or perhaps they were disinterested in items as material as silver and gold.

The wooden chests had fallen to ruin, spilling a torrent of wealth into the pit. Here was the coinage of the known world, from realms near and far, present and past. Golden *sovereigns* of Poitiers and silver *krona* from Carpat. Big *angels-of-gold* from doomed Zarkas, still bright in spite of their antiquity. Thin Bukovian *florins*. *Ducati* and *manci* from Tiberia far to the south. *Rials* from the island city of Ibez, and massive Rhenntish *scutti*.

So vast was this hoard that Hieronymus's men used shovels to scoop it onto the chamber's flagstone floor. Thurmond was delighted with the gold, but when he struck his bargain, he had been hoping for things worth far more than their weight in gold. Things like gems or fine jewelry. Perhaps charms of powerful magic or other valuable ensorcelled items. He kept his eyes skinned for such treasure. He and Sarah faced a long and difficult journey, so the lighter their load the better.

The shoveling continued, revealing a pile of heavy silver bars and a strongbox of gold ingots. One wooden chest held gold and silver brooches, arm rings, and torques—the work of master Vanarian craftsmen from centuries before. Next a dozen swords with fantastically embellished hilts and blades pitted by corrosion. Then jars filled with silver buttons, now dark with tarnish. Beneath these came an assortment of gold and silver bowls, plates, and spoons, along with a goblet carved from a single block of quartz.

The pit was deeper than anticipated, and the pile of treasure grew as the workers delved. They shoveled up old Etrusian *dinari* and *soldi*, along with the tiny golden *sequins* of the Forbidden Empire, and even crude bronze squares known as *yarmag* with which the Hunnic nomads bartered among themselves. Further down, a wealth of unfamiliar coins from realms long forgotten.

Finally, from the treasure pit's very bottom, came the very things that Thurmond had been hoping for. A decayed velvet bag held a gold coronet studded with amethysts and opals, and a small golden casket, wonderfully worked with garnet cloisonné, contained an assortment of rings, necklaces, and bracelets set with the most precious of gemstones—rubies, sapphires, emeralds, and diamonds.

Sarah, meanwhile, stayed busy ransacking the rooms and workshops in the clasping towers, in search of valuable occult paraphernalia. She began in the library, quickly perusing the shelves of leather-bound grimoires and crumbling parchment codices. It nearly broke her heart to pass them by, but books were too heavy and bulky. In the end, she selected but one slim volume of spells, many of which seemed simple enough for a witch of her ability.

She continued her hunt, systematically moving from floor to floor, chamber to chamber. She rummaged through chests and wardrobes, sniffed the contents of jars and flasks. Her efforts were rewarded with a plethora of magical trinkets—amulets, talismans, fetishes, pentangles. She found philters to inspire love and potions to restore manhood. There were deadly curse tablets, periapts of good fortune, and elixirs to bring exotic visions. Most of the pieces, however, remained unidentifiable.

No matter—she scooped them into her shoulder bag. The most important thing at the moment was to carry away as much as she could. Magical items were valuable, and Hieronymus had ordered his men to burn whatever she left behind. They were already kindling a blaze in one of the large fireplaces.

Sarah came across a number of spell scrolls—these were indeed worth saving. These were spells stored in written form on parchment scrolls, where they remained inactive until read. This allowed a magic user to conserve psychic energy, because the scroll spells cost nothing to read. Trouble was, no one but the magician who wrote them could know beforehand the nature of such spells since reading them automatically put them into effect. This was dangerous because anything could happen. The spell might well summon a monster that would eat the magician as well as the intended target. Nonetheless, she rolled them together tightly and stuck them in her shoulder bag.

Finally, there was a leathern box, neatly divided into six square compartments. Each was padded with fleece and held a clear glass globe about the size of an egg. A colored mist swirled endlessly inside each globe. There was one each of red, black, yellow, blue, green, and purple. The globes were obviously magical, but Sarah had no idea what purpose they might serve. She took them anyway. Her bag was filled to overflowing as she headed back downstairs to find Thurmond.

Father Hieronymus had no time for the treasure hunt. Money was naturally essential to his design, but he had other concerns that were far more important than silver or gold. He must put the castle in order, and to do so, he must first exorcise the malignant entity inhabiting the room of invocation. This could only be the disembodied spirit of the Contessa Sathas, who, had been walled-up alive until her spirit entered the stones of the castle. That, at least, was the tale old grandams told the village children.

He could now believe it true, for the invocatory was permeated with a tangible evil. Merely to enter it was to suffer a sickening of the body and withering of the soul. For his design to go forward, the chamber must be cleansed. He would start with an exorcism. If that proved insufficient, he would have his men dismantle the invocatory stone by stone, find the witch's bones, and burn them as he had the others.

The plundering complete, Thurmond and Sarah retired to the courtyard to see the remains of Old One consumed by flames. The fire was immense and intensely hot, for the old furniture that fed it was dry and eager to burn. The remains of the crypt-creatures were quickly reduced to ash. With great difficulty, the village men dragged forth the slain homunculus and heaved it into the roaring mass of flame. The slain amazons were burned last.

After watching the bonfire, Sarah suggested they explore the courtyard, which they had not yet seen in daylight. They discovered, to their surprise, an ancient road leading from the castle to a valley on the far side of the mountain. It was in extreme disrepair, choked by landslides in some places and washed away in others, but at one time this road would have provided reasonably easy access to the castle.

They continued their exploration, climbing to the top of the curtain wall and taking in the view. A massive wooden crane extended a long arm outward from wall and cliff. Its huge barrel windlass carried a very long rope. This was how the witch retrieved her foodstuffs from the villagers. Thurmond wondered who in the castle would have been strong enough to wind such an engine—not Old One certainly—then he remembered the phenomenal strength of the amazons.

A container of woven willow branches lay nearby, obviously the witch's food-basket. It gave Thurmond and idea, and he ran to speak to the men tending the pyre. He soon had them scouting for salvageable lumber and rusty nails among the abandoned workshops that lined the inside of the curtain wall.

In short order, the villagers constructed a box robust enough to carry the weight of two men to their village far below. This would make comings and goings between the two locations much quicker and easier than scaling the cliff.

Thurmond intended to test the device with a load of stones, but Pozi appeared suddenly and demanded the first ride. Both he and Sarah objected strenuously, but she remained insistent, and the workmen rose in her defense. She was, they informed Thurmond, a child of their village and would not be ordered about by outsiders.

There was nothing for it but to acquiesce, and Pozi disappeared down the cliff with a smile and a wave, entirely unconcerned about the frightful abyss beneath her feet. Soon more workers and their tools were hauled up from below. Then came supplies of food and drink, for hours had passed and bellies were empty. After the wounded were lowered, Thurmond and Sarah gathered their treasure and took their own ride down the Blue Fang.

CHAPTER 33

THURMOND'S GAMBIT

At the priest's command, the villagers prepared a feast of celebration and thanksgiving. They would soon, he promised them, be living the lives of great ladies and noble gentlemen. There would be no more thieving bandits or hungry winters, only ease and comfort and plenty. They should, he proclaimed, be thankful and joyful. Allfather Charon had ordained that he, Hieronymus, would lead them to a new way of living and thinking.

They must not hold not back, but must embrace their destiny with open hearts! So, broach the casks of ale, and slaughter lambs for the feast! Accept this bounty as their god-given right! Let the people revel!

The simple villagers were more than willing to take their spiritual leader at his word. A sumptuous feast was prepared, and the entire population seemed on the verge of religious ecstasy. Thurmond found such fervor unsettling. Despite Sarah's assurances, he had never fully trusted the villagers. But, he reasoned, he might as well eat and drink his fill, since he and Sarah would be leaving in the morning.

When the feasting was done, the two young stalwarts prepared for their departure. Their mailshirts and other kit were fetched from the hiding place, and they sorted through what they would and would not take. Treasure was a top priority. Comfort items like cloaks or gloves must be abandoned. They would carry only enough food to sustain their lives. Weapons were deemed necessary to survival, but the armor would be left behind.

The selected items of treasure were carefully shown to Hieronymus for inspection and approval. These included the gem-encrusted jewelry and gold coronet as well as the many magical items gathered by Sarah. Thurmond's rucksack and Sarah's pannier were topped off with as many gold coins as they could reasonably carry.

Thurmond expected a dispute over the gems, but the priest made no complaint and remained cordial and cooperative throughout the discussion. The young man somewhat regretted that such good spirits were about to come to a crashing halt. He was about to do something he knew would most definitely sour their host's fine humor.

"Holy Father, do you recall that the final stipulation of our agreement called for you to perform a healing?"

Father Hieronymus beamed with compassion.

"Certes, my boy, and I stand ready to carry it out whenever you ask for it. I have by now rested and prayed, so my holy powers are fully restored. Your injuries are minor, the young lady's even less serious. It will be easily accomplished. You have only to say the word and I will lay on hands."

Thurmond now assumed a most grave and formal demeanor.

"I'm afraid you misapprehend, Father. It was neither for Sarah nor myself that the agreement was made."

The priest's eyes narrowed in suspicion.

"Who exactly was it made for then? Pozi perhaps? Is she ill?"

"Nay, not Pozi. I require healing for my boon companion, who now lies with an injured leg far down the mountain. You must go with us to heal him there."

Hieronymus's suspicion turned to anger.

"I will do no such thing. I agreed to heal you or Sarah, perhaps the both of you, and I am prepared to do so here and now—that is all."

Thurmond almost laughed in the man's face.

"Nay, good Father, the recipient of the healing was not specified, nor was the place. You only assumed otherwise, and that assumption was your error. You must accompany us or break your handclasped oath."

The priest's anger grew to rage.

"You young whelp, I serve God's holy church. You cannot deceive me or bend me to your will. Beware! You may well bargain yourself to your own destruction."

Thurmond heard the threat but remained adamant.

"Mayhap, Father, but I will have to take that chance, for my friend is in sore need. You will now please equip yourself for the journey. You will require a large rucksack. Our agreement assured us as much treasure as our party could carry away on our backs. You are now a member of that party, so you will be helping us carry a heavy load of gold."

Rage became stony silence. The priest glared, then spun about and stalked away.

In spite of his bitterness, Father Hieronymus dutifully appeared before dawn with a large pack strapped to his back. This was filled with as much gold as he was able to bear. Pozi was also there with her own travel kit, a ragtag assortment assembled from whatever she could lay her hands on. She, too, would carry a load of gold. Her mother and several siblings came to see her off. There were tears, to be sure, but no real grief at her departure. The father was not present. He was, Pozi explained, still in a stupor from the previous evening's revels.

It was time to find Roscoe and Torgul.

The journey through the long lightless tunnel was far less frightening than before. They came well stocked with torches, so they were never at the mercy of the dark. And this time they could be certain of returning to a world of open sky. They came at last to the lair of the hyut. Though the stench lingered, it was noticeably diminished. This boded well, suggesting that the creature had not shared its abode with a vengeful mate.

Lars's body remained surprisingly untouched by scavenging animals. Perhaps the abiding smell of the hyut discouraged carrion eaters. Thurmond would have liked to cover Lars with stones, but there was no time. Torgul was possibly alive, and if so, he needed the friar's healing as soon as possible.

They picked their way across the scree, arriving at the flat shelf where they had fought the hyut. There were the mailshirts and rucksacks Roscoe and Torgul had carried up the mountain but had been forced to leave behind. Thurmond cast about for the doughty dwarf's axe. He hoped to return his friend's treasured possession, but it was not to be found.

As he picked his way along the treacherous path, Thurmond kept thinking of his two lost friends. How could a fat old cripple ever hope to carry a heavily muscled dwarf along such a perilous track? Clearly it was impossible. They must have inevitably fallen to their deaths somewhere along the way. Whenever he dared, he stole a furtive glance toward the valley floor, but no shattered bodies did he spy.

The way eventually widened and became less dangerous, opening into a narrow gorge. The air was a bit warmer now, and the stony ground boasted patches of greenery. The trip down the mountain had been exhausting. Their legs felt rubbery, and their shoulders ached with the weight of their gold-laden packs.

Then there came, from somewhere up ahead, the braying of a mule. Soon after, on the far side of a turn, Thurmond spotted Murd, gently stroking the nose of a pack animal. Its ears were pinned back, and its eyes were rolling in fright. Murd looked up, as placid and slow-witted as ever, speaking to Thurmond as if he had never been away.

"Night comin'. Mule gettin' scared 'cause pretty soon wolfs start to howl."

Sarah exploded in relief, at that moment realizing that they had finally arrived at their destination.

"Murd! Oooh, you're alive. I'm so glad. And Bodo, is he still alive?"

Murd seemed at first confused by the question but then gave an awkward grin.

"Aye, Bodo's at camp with the others."

He pointed down the trail with his thumb. Thurmond jumped at Murd's words.

"What others? Murd, what others? Did Roscoe make it back? How about Torgul?"

The vehemence of his questioning frightened the docile serf, who drew back without answering. Thurmond pressed relentlessly.

"Is Roscoe here, Murd? Roscoe and Torgul?"

Without waiting for a reply, Thurmond jumped past Murd and ran down the path. He rounded a curve and emerged into a small clearing. The sun was just setting, sending its last brave rays slantwise through the darkening sky.

A pair of small tents stood next to a tiny stream. Millie was second from left in a picket line of a half dozen horses. Smoke curled up from a campfire, where Bodo was preparing the evening meal. Then Roscoe emerged from a tent and emptied a bowl of something red into the stream.

Thurmond charged down the trail, unmindful of the wobbliness of his legs and ache in his shoulders, calling out this friend's name with all the voice he could muster.

"Roscoe! Roscoe! Roscoe!"

The old Adventurer looked up, startled, and then smiled broadly as his protégé caught him in a bear hug.

"Well, now, if it ain't my Prospect come home from the mountains all safe and sound—and about time, too."

Thurmond was out of breath from his run and so overcome with relief that he could scarcely get words out.

"I thought I'd…never…see you again. I thought…"

Roscoe interrupted.

"Never see me again? What tomfoolery is this now?"

Sarah now ran up and embraced Roscoe with equal enthusiasm.

"You made it, Roscoe! You got back! Oh, by God's bony knees, Thurmond didn't think you'd make it, but I never gave up."

Roscoe pushed her back.

"What are you two jabberin' about? Did you think I was too old and fat and lame to get back down the mountain without fallin' off it? Is that it?"

Both were silent, shamefaced, their expressions revealing their guilt. Then Sarah spoke.

"What of Torgul? Is he here? Does he yet live?"

Her voice trailed off when Roscoe shot her a steely look.

"If you're askin' if I left my brother Adventurer to die alone and be eaten by buzzards, nay, I did not. He's in the tent behind me."

Both young people shouted at once.

"Alive?"

"Aye, of course alive. There'd be precious little need to have him in the tent if he was dead."

Thurmond was incredulous.

"But that path is so steep and narrow. How did you ever bring him down alone?"

"Aye, steep and narrow it is. I fashioned a harness out of our swordbelts and the straps from our rucksacks. Made kind of a sling for him to sit in and wore him on my back. Wasn't exactly comfortable, but it worked. I went real slow, so I did."

Sarah then asked the most important question.

"How fares Torgul?"

Roscoe sighed.

"Not good, lass, not good at all. Bodo and me was able to set his broken leg and splint it nice and proper, but he's got a fever in his blood that makes him rave terrible. I've bled him good and regular, but the fever won't break. Unless it does, I think he's like to die."

Pozi and Hieronymus finally arrived and were introduced. Sarah started to recount their exploits at Castle Sathas, but Thurmond stopped her. He was intent on helping Torgul.

"This priest is a great healer, Roscoe. He is here under handclasp for this purpose. Let us take him to the tent at once."

Roscoe's face broke into a great gleaming grin.

"Now that's a right worthy idea, so it is. You've done well, the two of you, bringin' this man down the hill."

CHAPTER 34

THE PRICE OF GUILE

Roscoe lit a candle and led them into the tent. The dwarf lay unconscious and unmoving on a pile of saddle pads, his beard spread atop a cloak that covered him to the chin. Beads of sweat stood upon his brow. Roscoe spoke in a hushed tone.

"He's quiet at the moment, but he's been swearin' somethin' frightful. I never knew my brother Adventurer was so given to strong oaths."

Thurmond turned to Hieronymus.

"You agreed to come here and heal my friend's leg. Are you prepared to fulfill your promise here and now?"

"I am. But I must ask you to acknowledge that in so doing, I will have fulfilled my part of our bargain to the letter. You have brought away your pick of the treasure, as much as you could carry. Indeed, I helped you do so. The girl Pozi was allowed to come with you and now waits outside this tent. When your companion's leg has been healed, our agreement will have been completed. Do you agree?"

Thurmond felt himself growing impatient with the priest's needless prattle.

"Of course, that was what we clasped hands upon. Will you please now cast your spell of healing? My friend suffers while we talk."

Hieronymus said not a word, only gestured imperiously for the others to stand back. He closed his eyes, lifted his palms in a gesture of supplication, and started to chant in a low, soft voice. A current of powerful energy coursed through Thurmond's body, and a buzzing filled his ears. As the chanting increased in volume, his hands and then his arms trembled as if cold. The hair rose from the back of his neck. He could no longer focus his eyes.

The priest turned his hands inward so the palms faced each other. A ball of white light formed between them, hanging suspended in the air by the force of his holy power. It grew brighter and brighter until it hurt the eyes to look upon it.

Hieronymus abruptly pulled his hands away. The light-ball hovered for a moment, then darted across the tent to strike Roscoe directly on his injured hip. The light flared brightly and then disappeared, leaving everyone temporarily blind in the dim candlelight.

Their eyes adjusted and their vision returned. Something remarkable had occurred, and their faces revealed a great variety of expressions and emotions. Roscoe appeared confused but not displeased, as if he had just received an unexpected gift. Sarah looked distrustful, worried, unsure of what was about to follow. The priest's mouth was twisted into an ugly, self-satisfied smirk.

Thurmond's face was dark with rage.

"Incompetent fool! Your spell missed its mark. You must repeat it and guide it correctly. It is Torgul who requires your healing, not Roscoe."

Hieronymus was quick to respond, his voice cold and controlled.

"It is you who are the fool, young man. My spell went precisely where I directed it."

"Is this some jest? You will attend Torgul at once, as we agreed."

"Nay, boy, I have fulfilled my obligation to you. I promised to perform a healing, and so I have. I owe you nothing more, just as you admitted a few moments ago."

Thurmond sensed what was coming and was beside himself with frustration.

"You were directed to heal the dwarf. You have violated our handclasp. Woe unto you, oath breaker!"

"I have broken no oath. You never specified who I was to help. You told me only to heal the leg of *your friend*, and I have done so. How was I to know you meant this…creature? I assumed you meant this man here. His hip was grossly deformed from an old injury causing him to walk with a bad limp, so I repaired it."

Thurmond thought about plunging his dagger into the priest's heart, but common sense held his hand. His voice rose.

"You knew exactly who I was speaking of! It's obvious that it's Torgul who requires your healing! Do so at once!"

"Nay, I will not. And I would think that you of all people, who used a similar twisting of words to force me here against my will, should see the justice in my point of view. Besides, it is impossible because my holy powers are quite exhausted. A major healing is very demanding. I won't be able to perform another like it until after I return to my church for a prayer vigil."

Thurmond was now bursting with rage.

"You'll just leave Torgul to die? To lie there consumed by fever because you're angry at me for tricking you? What kind of a holy man are you that would do such a thing?"

Hieronymus smiled sourly.

"I'm the kind of holy man who doesn't like to be made a fool of. The kind who has many important affairs to attend to at the moment, things more important than the life of this dwarf."

Sarah knew it was time for her to intervene.

"Please, good Father, the trick Thurmond played on you was inexcusable, but don't make poor Torgul suffer for it. The dwarf is our true and loyal friend. Please, you must help him. There must be something you can do."

Roscoe also stepped forward.

"Sir Priest, that's my boon companion layin' there. We've a closer bond than what I ever had with my own brothers. What can I offer you to change your mind? Just name it, and it's yours."

Some of the maliciousness now left the cleric's face.

"I am not a heartless man, and I hear the sincerity in your voices. As a priest, it is my sworn duty to extend compassion even, I suppose, to a dwarf. Still…"

Thurmond saw what he must do. Putting aside his anger and pride, he knelt at the friar's feet.

"Holy Father, I am truly sorry for offending you in such an underhanded way. I am ready to make any amends you require, to endure punishment if that is your will. Please, I implore you, help my friend Torgul."

Hieronymus stared down at Thurmond with a satisfied smile.

"As I said, my holy powers are drained for the nonce. But I have with me an item of especial power, a holy relic—the jawbone of the blessed martyr Prunella de Krok. With it I can save your friend, but there must first be atonement for your base actions."

"What must I do?"

"You have already confessed your transgression and tendered a sincere apology, that was a good start. Next you must return to me the items of jewelry and the golden coronet in your rucksacks. The magical items and gold you may keep.

"I should, I suppose, require you to carry it all back up the mountain, but I am not a vindictive man. Anyway, I have an abundance of gold, and the occult implements are repugnant to me.

"Lastly, Pozi must return to her village. It is her rightful place. She cannot go cavorting off with ruffians such as yourselves."

Sarah strenuously objected to the final condition, but she was silenced when Pozi ran into the tent. She had been standing just outside the opening, listening to all that was said.

"Nay, Lady Sarah, I will gladly go with Father Hieronymus. He is correct. My village is my proper home, and I miss it already. I thought a life of travel and adventure would be to my liking, but I find it frightening and confusing. Please, I just want to go home."

Sarah was shocked by her change of attitude but did not dispute the issue. Pozi then turned to the priest.

"Will you grant me a request, Father, for my part in ridding us of that terrible witch? Can I ask but one thing of you?"

Hieronymus nodded benignly, obviously pleased by her willing acquiescence.

"You can certainly ask, and I will grant it if it is reasonable and within my power."

"I ask that my father's agreement with Samp be broken, for I will not marry that awful man. Give him but a single piece of gold, and he will be happy to find himself another wife. Will you promise to do this for me, Father?"

"Aye, child, that is a thing easily done. Life in our village is about to change in many, many ways. The old ways and old agreements will be best forgotten."

"And Father, one more small thing—might I, perhaps in a year, be chosen to serve as your assistant?"

The priest's eyes gleamed.

"Pozi, you have proven yourself as sharp of wit as you are agile of limb. Aye, in a year when you become a woman, I will appoint you as my assistant."

"Oh, thank you, Father Hieronymus. That is the honor to which I have always aspired. You have made my happiness complete."

These words filled Sarah with horror. Was the girl so innocent that she was unaware of the bargain she had just struck? Or did she really want to deliver herself body and soul into the hands of the lecherous priest? She decided to keep silent. Pozi seemed entirely capable of making her own decisions.

Roscoe spoke again.

"Holy father, can you see to our friend now?

"I can and will, but first the young man must seal it with a handclasp."

He spat in his palm and extended it toward Thurmond, who was still kneeling at his feet.

When they left the tent, the second healing done, night was dark and cold. A full moon was struggling to penetrate that cover of clouds. Hieronymus explained that the relic's effects were more gradual than those of his healing spell. By morning the fever would be gone, and by the next evening, the dwarf would be able to stand. One day more, and he would be able to walk about with the aid of a crutch. In a week, his leg would be fully healed.

The restoration of Torgul was not the only cause of rejoicing that evening. The priest's initial spell completely repaired the grievous damage to Roscoe's hip. The painful limp that had plagued him for many a year was entirely gone.

The old Adventurer was ecstatic. He had sought out any number of magic users and clerics in the hope of such a cure. Many had taken his gold and proclaimed their great healing powers, but all had failed. Now this unpleasant priest had fixed him without being asked. Roscoe simply could not dislike Hieronymus, whatever his faults might be. He felt young again!

Thurmond and Sarah had their own reasons to be glad. The painful wounds they had sustained in combat with the minions of Old One were also healed, presumably due to their proximity to the priest's powerful healing spell. Even old scars had disappeared.

The comrades took places around the campfire. Pozi joined them, but Hieronymus chose to keep apart. Sarah and Thurmond took turns describing their adventure in Castle Sathas. Roscoe listened intently, demanding details and asking questions.

Even without the gems and jewelry, they now possessed a fortune in gold. The value of the many charms and amulets was as yet incalculable, but might well be of even greater worth. The two young treasure seekers had performed brilliantly. They had helped rid the world of an evil witch and, in so doing, enriched themselves. That was what being an Adventurer was all about.

As it grew darker, the howling of the wolves resonated from the surrounding mountainsides, waxing louder as more and more voices joined in. This had been a nightly occurrence since Bodo and Murd established the camp, but lately the creatures had gotten bolder. Two nights ago, they had dragged off a mule from the picket line. The next night they took the horse Lars had ridden. Now the wolves' evil yellow eyes could be seen gleaming in the reflected light of the fire that was kept burning all night. Murd swore he had seen the pack leader jumping from boulder to boulder on two legs, running upright as a man runs. *The werewolf.*

The cold mountain air was sweet on Ghleet's tongue. Much had changed since his return to his beloved homeland. The years of captivity had taken a terrible toll on Ghleet's powers. Trapped in a city, cut off from the natural world, his energies had dwindled until he could no longer shift shape. He could neither call the winds nor summon the rain. Only the least worthy animals answered his call.

But as he traveled among the snowy peaks, his strength had flooded back with the force of a mountain torrent. The power of the mountains swelled in his soul, and he found himself growing stronger and stronger. The years of solitude and deprivation had, in some unforeseen manner, honed his will to the sharpness of a spearpoint. The spirit of the wolf now burned within his body with an energy so ferocious as to be unfathomable to a common man. Only a gifted shaman could withstand such a force without falling into madness.

Ghleet leaped to a slab of granite the size of a small house and looked down on the camp below. He eyed the picket line that so tempted his grey kindred and the fire that struck their hearts with fear. He heard the squawking voices of the man-things and smelled the sickness rising from one of the tents. He hated them. They brought filth and corruption to his beautiful, pristine wilderness.

His call had summoned a savage race of merciless killers that slew for the joy of slaying. The wolves, his wolves, would soon taste the blood of the hairless man-things below. He raised his voice in a cry to bring more of his siblings down from their dens in the higher peaks.

CHAPTER 35

AN UNEXPECTED ENCOUNTER

At first light Hieronymus and Pozi set off for home. The priest was courteous but remained, as always, cold and aloof. It broke Sarah's heart to see the girl returning to the life she had so recently professed to hate. She could not help but believe that Pozi had feigned homesickness only to save Torgul. What could she say about a girl who would so willingly sacrifice her own happiness for the life of a stranger? Sarah did not have an answer.

The night had been long and frightful. The wolves had kept up an incessant chorus until dawn. The horses had been restive in spite of Murd's efforts to calm them down. Nobody had gotten much sleep.

The sun rose higher in the sky, banishing the sinister shadows from the rocks and trees, and from the tent came the throaty roar of an angry dwarf. The others ran to attend him and were shocked by what they found. Still unable to rise, Torgul had pulled himself onto his elbows and was casting his gaze about the interior of the tent.

"Where's Bloodtroll? Where's my axe? Roscoe, you better not have left it up on the trail. If you did, you'll trot right back up there and fetch it!"

"Nay, nay, my brother, it's right here beside the bed, it's been there all along. I knew better than to leave it behind, so I did. I hung it off your back on the way down, along with my own sword. Don't you remember?"

The dwarf seemed greatly relieved.

"Nay, I don't recall much of anything about that time. I was layin' there on the ground while you were still fightin' that snow-beast. Everything started gettin' dreamy, and I figured I was dyin'…then nothin' much more."

Roscoe told his companion how he carried him down the mountain, emphasizing with great histrionics the terrible suffering he had endured on his behalf. Even the stoic dwarf was forced to chuckle at his performance.

Sarah and Thurmond told him of their exploits, of their reception at the mountain village, of their entry into the castle, of the witch and her minions. When they revealed the treasure they had won, Torgul's eyes gleamed with pleasure.

"You've done right well, the two of you."

They knew this to be effusive praise when uttered by a dwarf.

The fever, as Hieronymus had predicted, was altogether gone from his eyes. By tomorrow he would walk, so they would wait until then before starting the journey home. A cold wind was blowing. Snow would follow soon enough. They needed to move out as soon as possible

Roscoe was so thrilled with his new mobility that he no longer just walked around the camp—he strutted and gamboled, marched and cavorted. At times he could be said to stroll. For the first time in many years, it did not hurt him to walk. He looked and acted younger, expressing uncharacteristic thoughts and opinions.

He might, he said, shave off his beard. It was going too gray and made him look like someone's gaffer. And perhaps he should take more exercise and reduce his intake of beer to shrink the size of his belly. He would need some new clothes. His current wardrobe was simply out of fashion. He needed a shorter tunic to emphasize his muscular legs, and a longer belt—one that hung down past his knees. And some new hose. Perhaps bright yellow and cross-gartered.

All this was very unlike the bluff bear-of-a-man the others had always known and loved. The old Roscoe had always taken great pride in his paunch and had given little thought to his apparel. They could only hope that the spell would soon pass and that the old Adventurer would return to his former self.

While Bodo and Murd napped, having kept watch throughout the night,

Roscoe was bursting with energy and pranced about camp, packing up gear for their anticipated departure. Worn out from his exploits, Thurmond was content to sit by the fire and sharpen his sword. Sarah inventoried the contents of her shoulder bag.

She came across the leather box with its half dozen glass globes. Perhaps, she mused, each contained a spell, its type designated by its color. But what could the colors mean? Red for anger? Green for envy? Purple for lust? Were these the philters of the deadly sins? She doubted it.

Perhaps they held small demons that would be released when the glass shattered. If so, the globes were supremely dangerous. She knew well that freeing imprisoned hell-spawn could be deadly to anyone in the vicinity. She carefully packed the leather box in her pannier.

In the late afternoon, Torgul emerged from the tent, using a spear as a walking staff. His leg still hurt, but it was, as Hieronymus promised, clearly on the mend.

That night camping was as rough, if not rougher, than the one before. The howling was louder, as the wolf pack continued to swell in numbers. Their gleaming yellow eyes were more numerous and crept ever closer. Murd struggled to calm the stamping, snorting horses, while Bodo kept the bonfire well fed. The others, Torgul included, sat with weapons in hand, awaiting the inevitable attack. Yet it did not come. The strident chorus suddenly ceased when the first gray streaks of dawn appeared in the sky. The companions were cold, tired, and stiff of limb, but all were grateful to have survived another night. It was time to head for home.

They packed their remaining gear and set out as soon as it was light enough to see the path. A light snow started to fall, a harbinger of the deep winter cold that followed close behind. The trip down the mountain was far less difficult than their climb up it. Their mounts were as eager as their riders to leave behind the wolf-haunted peaks, so they maintained a steady pace in spite of the narrowness of the trail. Thurmond was glad to see that the fat black snakes, so prevalent during their ascent, had retreated to their winter burrows.

All were in high spirits. Though they had not yet tallied their coins, Sarah, who had a good head for figures, estimated that their saddlebags held five or six thousand gold sovereigns. This was an astounding pile of wealth, far more than what was required to settle their debts and set Grimsgard in good order. The value of the occult items—the scrolls, spells, and amulets crammed in Sarah's pannier—remained unknown. She would, she said, have to learn an advanced divination spell to discover the function of each piece and thus determine its worth. Any item she wished to retain would be credited toward her share. The remainder would be sold.

Sarah placed their gold under a glamour spell, which made the heavy bags appear to be filled with books. It was a simple spell that did not tax her psychic energy, but it was short-lived and required renewal at the dawn of every day. The companions would, if questioned, claim to be agents of Sarah's father, a wealthy collector of ancient books. The facade would be easy to maintain.

All was going well. Torgul was mending nicely, Roscoe's bad leg had been set right, and they had more coin than they had ever anticipated. Now they had only to bring themselves and their loot through hundreds of miles of savage wilderness.

The daylight was taking its last gasping breaths when the wagonette of Buyuk ve Korkunc Sihirbazi hove into view. It stood in a small clearing near the fork in the road, where they had previously bidden him farewell. The wizard had predicted they might encounter him at some future time, and here he was, but something did not look right. No one was about, and his milk-white ponies were missing. The wagonette's canvas covering was slashed from top to bottom. A rear wheel had been removed, causing the vehicle to cant down awkwardly on one corner.

As they rode closer, the bearded face of Buyuk ve Korkunc Sihirbazi peered out through the rent in the canvas. The wizard's hitherto calm expression was haggard and streaked with dirt. The bulbous turban that he had kept so meticulously arranged was gone, revealing a heavy thatch of gray hair.

Things were clearly amiss. Roscoe nudged his horse forward, wary but eager to help the amicable wizard. Buyuk ve Korkunc Sihirbazi, however, did not respond as anticipated. Rather, he threw aside the torn canvas cover, thrust the nose of a crossbow through the opening, and fired it directly at Roscoe's face.

At such short range, he could scarcely miss, so it must have been the hand of Lady Fortune that saved the old Adventurer from death. The sudden flapping of canvas so close to its nose caused Roscoe's horse to rear slightly and toss its head, thus protecting the rider's face with its own. The crossbow bolt struck it just below the left eye.

The stricken creature whinnied in outrage and rose on its back legs. Roscoe, unprepared for such antics, was flung from the saddle. He hit the ground hard, flat on his back, with a loud hollow thump. At the same moment, three shrouded figures emerged from concealed positions behind a pile of boulders and let fly with their crossbows. The first fired at Torgul but missed. The dwarf was too fast, rolling immediately from the saddle and taking cover amongst the milling horses.

The second shooter hit Thurmond, whose reflexes were not as honed as Torgul's. He was just swinging his leg over his mount's back when the bolt struck his head. Fortunately, it glanced from the curved side of his iron helmet.

The third crossbowman made a fatal mistake. He had been instructed to dispatch Sarah, but he saw no point in wasting his first shot on a mere girl when a giant of a man rode directly behind her. His bolt took Murd square in the chest, knocking him backward over his horse's rump.

The archers immediately loaded their bows for the next volley.

Hidden in the cliff high above, Ghleet salivated. This was the moment. Now would come the vengeance—and the feasting—for which he had lusted so long. He slipped out to a large flat ledge from where he could observe the scene below. The riders were approaching the wagon. Master would soon be springing the ambush.

All around, the wolves emerged from behind rocks and bushes, from between trees and out of the shadows, crawling on their bellies, silent and stealthy, massing just behind Master's servants.

Ghleet was well apprised of Master's plan—a sudden barrage of crossbow bolts to kill the riders, and then Master would claim their gold for himself. It was a goodly plan, except Master was no longer Master. But he did not know that yet.

The shaman felt the change begin—the painful lengthening of the jaw, the intense sharpening of sight and sound, the itchy growth of the shaggy coat. He rose on hind legs that were no longer those of a man, then raised his snout to the sky and howled. The cry was long, hungry, and filled with doom. The pack, released at last, surged forward in a gray wave.

Sarah groped frantically in her shoulder bag in search of her wand. She did not fully understand what was happening around her, but she knew they were under attack. Something had knocked Roscoe from his horse and men with crossbows were firing from the flank. She needed the damned wand, but in the panic of the moment, she could not find it. She grasped instead the box containing the colored glass spheres.

This was not the moment to hesitate. It was time to discover, for better or worse, just what the globes would do. She fumbled with the catch, trying desperately to open the box before the next crossbow volley knocked her from the saddle. But then a strange thing occurred. Instead of deadly bolts, there came screams—the death screams of men in mortal agony. Then came the wolves—low, fast, tails out, snarling.

Sarah grabbed a globe at random, a yellow one, and flung it at the front of the pack. It burst with a loud *whoosh* into a ball of fire that set the foremost wolves ablaze and sent them rolling, yipping, and spinning in panicked circles. The rest of the pack, frightened and confused, hesitated as their leaders burned.

Pleased with the results, Sarah threw the red globe into the midst of the gray swarm. It exploded like a crash of thunder and shook the earth beneath their feet. Canine forms were cast high in the air to fall back limp and lifeless. The remaining wolves, deafened, broken, and disheartened, turned tail and fled from this terrible source of fire and pain.

In spite of his still healing leg, Torgul stormed through the wall of flame, Bodo close behind him. No living foemen, however, did they find—only their mangled remains. The crossbowmen had been pulled down and savaged by the wolves.

Thurmond charged the wagon, intent on killing the treacherous wizard who, as far as he could tell, had slain his friend. Sword in hand, he tore down the wagonette's rear curtain and prepared to leap inside. The vehicle was empty, its occupant having escaped through a slit in the cover's opposite side. The young man heard footsteps behind him and spun about, sword raised. It was Roscoe, not dead after all. He had been stunned by the fall, but now he was up and eager for the blood of his assailant. The wizard was not to be found.

Thurmond climbed into the wagon's bed and kicked through the items therein, but no one crouched behind the various chests nor lay hidden beneath the rolls of tenting. He did find the wizard's bulbous turban, a gray wig, and his long, embroidered robe—also his beard, its inner surfaces smeared with a gummy substance that had held it in place.

Ghleet stared at the smoldering remains of the wolf pack, anger and dismay swelling in his throat. He seethed with hatred for humankind, but there was little he could do. The girl's magic was much stronger than expected. Worst of all, Master had escaped, galloping away on one of the white ponies that had pulled his wagon.

At least he would not go hungry. The remains of Master's servants and a dying horse waited below, and three more ponies were hidden nearby.

CHAPTER 36

THE LONG ROAD WEST

Gavin believed he must be going mad. He could feel insects crawling across the surface of his brain, maggots tunneling deep within its core. His eyes were bleary, and he could not focus his thoughts. His mind floundered in an irrepressible whirlpool of emotion—rage, frustration, fear, and confusion. Miseries piled one upon the other until he thought his skull must burst.

And his arse ached. He had no saddle, so the pony's spine dug unmercifully into his tailbone. There were no stirrups, so his long legs dangled nearly to the ground. He was hungry and cold. The narrow escape from the wagonette had allowed him no chance to gather supplies, not even his cloak. Luckily, he had the pony, though it was ridiculously small for a man of his stature.

Worst of all, Gavin was consumed by a feeling with which he had scant experience—uncertainty. His plan had been perfect, every detail carefully considered and revised until there was could be no possibility of failure. Ghleet had kept him well informed, so Gavin had known almost to the minute when the fat lout Roscoe and his party would arrive at the site of the ambush. He knew the order in which they rode and that they carried treasure. He knew they had lost a man in the mountains and that the dwarf had been injured.

It should have been easy. His archers had been perfectly positioned—completely concealed and yet close enough to almost touch their targets. At such range, it was nearly impossible to miss. But miss they had, all three of them. Even his own shot had gone awry, thought that was scarcely his fault. Who could anticipate the thrashings of an ill-trained horse?

None of that, however, was the real cause of the disaster. It had been the wolves—the wolves Ghleet had sworn he could control. The wolves that had run amok, pulling down his archers instead of the riders.

Gavin was suddenly struck by the most hideous of thoughts. Ghleet, that filthy, scabby, lump of dung, had betrayed him. He had deliberately thwarted his plan. Had intentionally turned his wolves against the archers. Then another even worse realization piled onto the first. God's holy bones! Ghleet had intended to murder him as well!

Gavin had trusted Ghleet. Believed in him, rescued him from captivity, fed him, brought him home to his mountains. That is what made this treachery so excruciating. Gavin had thought of Ghleet as his loyal hound, never suspecting the duplicity that coiled like a viper within his louse-ridden carcass. But Ghleet was not a faithful dog. He was a lone wolf—vicious, cunning, and infinitely self-serving.

Gavin had, of course, never intended to keep the shaman alive once he had fulfilled his purpose, but Ghleet had no way of knowing that. His perfidy had not been inspired by a primitive desire to survive. It had sprung from the innate foulness of his black bestial heart.

Gavin was never personally constrained by feelings of loyalty or commitment. Not bloody likely! One such as himself need not be bothered by the desires of inferiors. That would be a thing unnatural. Loyalty was for lesser men. Men like Ghleet. It was only fitting that minions be devoted to their masters. Creatures like Ghleet existed to serve, so his disloyalty was profoundly sordid, disgusting. Unnatural even.

Then Gavin remembered Sarah, and wrath consumed him like an infernal fire. This was the third time she had forestalled his plans. First she had nearly emasculated him in that accursed circle of stones. Then she had stabbed his buttock and caused him to fall just as he was about to dispatch her paramour. He fingered the scar at the base of his neck. That incident had almost cost him his life.

The third time she threw fireballs. One could, he supposed, argue that she had actually saved his life by driving off the wolf pack. But that was not the point. The little bitch had no right to fireballs because her skills as a magic user had not reached that level. By refusing to act properly, she had disrupted his perfect plan. Her refusal to behave according to form was every bit as brazen and deviant as Ghleet's bad faith. Thus, she had to die—not just slowly and painfully, but exquisitely.

Yet surrendering to ire was always foolish. As much as she deserved a hideous death, perhaps she could serve a more useful purpose. As Gavin's mind cleared, a new plan took shape. He considered the many small castles that clung to the hillsides of Bukovia. He tried to envision the kind of men who inhabited such castles.

Gavin dug his heels mercilessly into the pony's flanks. He knew the animal might die if he kept driving her at such a frantic pace, but he had need of haste. He had to put distance between himself and the fat lout's party. He needed time to get acquainted with some congenial Bukovian noble.

With luck—and he always had luck—he might yet gain great wealth from this adventure. He would certainly enjoy an exquisite revenge. There were, after all, certain things a young girl would find more distressing than mere death. Far more.

Murd was dead. The big, simpleminded lover of animals lay with the vanes of a crossbow bolt protruding from his breastbone. Roscoe's horse was also down, thrashing its legs in agony until Torgul stilled it with a blow from his axe. Bodo searched the torn bodies of the archers but found little of value— weapons of middling quality and not worth taking, purses holding only small coins. Roscoe pulled his saddle from his fallen mount and cinched it on Murd's big-boned roan. Sarah dismounted and stood by his side, frightened and watchful.

Thurmond approached, the false beard in one hand and the bulbous turban in the other. He shook them under the old Adventurer's nose.

"I knew there was something wrong with your wizard friend, but nobody would listen. Look at these. He left his stupid robe behind as well. I don't think he was even a real wizard."

Roscoe took the items from his hands and examined them thoughtfully.

"It appears, laddie, that you have the right of it, sure enough. I began to entertain my own doubts just at the moment that crossbow was thrust in my face. Well, my wizard friend certainly wasn't a real friend, and maybe not even a wizard. Who do you suppose he was? Why was he so intent on our destruction?"

No one knew. They stood silent for a moment, searching for an answer. When Sarah spoke, she struggled to control a tremor in her voice. The sudden attack had left her badly shaken.

"He was with the caravan all the way from Gorgonholm. Could he have joined it just to get close to us? Did the Brethren perhaps send him?"

Roscoe shook his head.

"That don't seem likely. They might want us dead after what you did to their thief, but I don't think they'd wait so long. If he was their assassin, we'd have been dead long ago, so we would."

Thurmond tried to picture the wizard in his mind, struggled to recall specific physical details. He was, though stooped, a tall man, and of robust build for his age. Was there not something familiar in cadence of his voice, the arrogant cast of his gaze? Had he not encountered such mannerisms before? He tried to recall where that might have been.

They buried Murd beneath a pile of heavy stones—perhaps it would deter the wolves for a while. The wagonette held a small store of foodstuffs, but fearing poison, they declined to touch it. Though still puzzled by the identity and purpose of their mysterious adversary, they turned their horses west and headed for home.

The high, bare crags of the north were left behind. The terrain, though still mountainous, was not nearly so steep and precarious, nor so cold. They moved through forests of tall, swaying evergreens. The road was badly eroded and pockmarked with holes, but much wider and smoother than the winding mountain paths.

They were still in the Kingdom of Carpat. The countryside was rugged but certainly habitable. Yet as before, they met no other party coming or going. There were no cities or towns. No castles, villages, or farms. What circumstance had prevented human civilization from pushing into this region?

The party wended steadily south and west. The evergreens were now intermixed with immense broadleaf trees that spread their limbs over the road so the travelers often rode in a tunnel. Their leaves had long since fallen, and the bare black boughs reminded Thurmond of the bony arms of the lich-things he had fought in Castle Sathas. The trees stretched their limbs above his head like long, skeletal fingers lusting to pluck him from the saddle.

It rained most days, a constant drizzle that soaked their cloaks and gear. The downed branches they gathered for firewood were sodden and hard to ignite. Once burning, such wood produced little heat, so the nights were cold and miserable.

Provisions ran low. Although the surrounding forest abounded in game, they were loath to enter it to hunt. Something disquieting lurked in that dark expanse, something that kept ambitious settlers from clearing the trees for homes and farms. Something that left a sour flavor on the back of one's tongue.

They came at last to the Golden Road, that vast trade route they had traveled with Bombardo and his caravan. Here they would rejoin human society, find an occasional farmstead or village. This part of Carpat was a bleak and dreary land, but such comforts as it held could be found along the Golden Road.

The identity of the false wizard was a subject of endless debate. Thurmond and Sarah tried to recall even the most trivial details about him, anything that might provide a clue. What color were his eyes? Did he wear rings of other jewelry that might have a symbolic meaning? His servants had tattoos—what were they? Did they show affiliation with the Brethren or some other criminal cult?

And who was the crone who rode in the back of the wagon? The wizard claimed she was his mother, but Thurmond dismissed this as an obvious lie. He had found a woman's gown and bonnet when he searched the vehicle, but none of the comforts or accessories an older woman would require. This clothing, like the wizard's robe, was just another disguise. What had become of this unknown person?

If nothing else, this discussion and contemplation helped while away tedious hours as they made their way toward home. There was little else to divert them. The tiny hamlets they encountered consisted of little more than a handful of squat log shanties. There were no proper markets or inns, only squinting, lumpish people eager to exchange their wretched goods for coin. All wore small bull's-eye amulets to guard against the evil eye.

A stone plinth bearing a crude rendition of the royal arms delineated the Bukovian frontier. There were more people on the road now—messengers, merchants, drovers with herds, a high-ranking churchman and his entourage.

On the verdant hillsides, castles and watchtowers sprouted like misshapen fungi. These were the strongholds of border lords—ruthless, grasping robber-knights who preyed upon anyone unfortunate enough to fall within their power. As members of the caravan on the outward trip, the companions had been safe enough. Caravans were shielded by royal decree, a protection for which caravan owners paid in gold. But four shabby travelers on the road alone were a different story. They had returned to civilization, but the road was no less dangerous than the one through the haunted mountains of Carpat.

PART 4

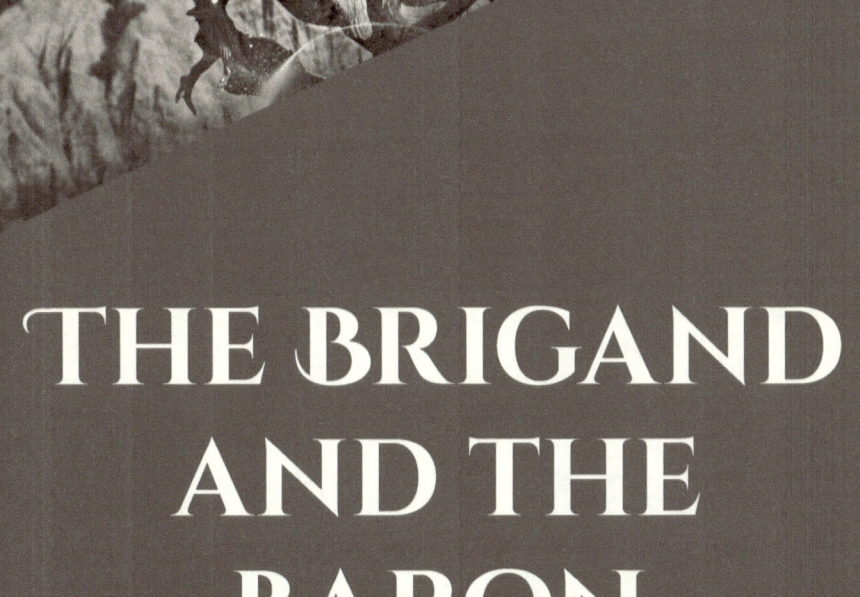

THE BRIGAND AND THE BARON

CHAPTER 37

ONE LOST AND
ONE REGAINED

Gavin was smugly satisfied with himself, not that there was anything unusual about that. His latest plan was coming together perfectly. His previous frustrations no longer troubled him because he knew Lady Fortune was always on his side. If past schemes had gone awry, they did so only through the incompetence of others. But now, his true path of destiny lay before him.

Gone was the milk-white pony. He rode instead a swift palfrey with an excellent saddle and bridle. His attire was that of a young gentleman, and a sword hung by his side. His hair was neatly trimmed after the fashion of Bukovian nobility. A thick mustache covered his upper lip.

The original owner of these fine things had been a foolish young man who tarried too long at a tavern before heading home to his father's estate. Gavin had swooped on him out of the dark like an owl seizing a mouse. One savage twist, and the neck was broken. Then the remains were concealed beneath a pile of old leaves. After that, Gavin rode many leagues before stopping. This made it less likely that the horse and garb would be recognized. It also gave him a chance to concoct a new person to be.

As the sun rose, he had spied a small castle atop a knob of rock on the side of a steep ravine. The lord's banner, flying over the battlements, unfurled in the breeze to reveal its gruesome charge—on a blood red field, a black raven with wide-spread wings. Unlike the eagle or falcon, ravens were seldom found in heraldry. Still more odd—this one hung upside down, its neck kinked and broken.

Perfect. Gavin had known at once that the lord who flew such a banner would respond readily to his story, and he had been correct. Now he rode with a purse of that lord's gold tucked inside his tunic. Four of the lord's men-at-arms rode behind him, ready to assist him and ensure his safety on this dangerous road.

"Wake up! Roscoe, do you hear me? Wake up! God's curse, Roscoe, wake up now!"

The old Adventurer opened sleep-encrusted eyes.

"Whaaa...?"

"Sarah's gone! Come on, get up! You've got to help me."

It was still quite dark, though a faint glow in the eastern sky meant the sun was not far below the horizon. Roscoe climbed groggily to his feet. Behind him, Torgul and Bodo were likewise rising.

"What do you mean by she's *gone*?"

"I mean Sarah is gone! Not in her bedding, not in camp, not anywhere about. She's just gone."

The others all started talking at once. Where did she go? Did somebody take her? Did anyone see anything? Hear anything? Why would she leave?

They examined her empty blankets, called her name, and searched around the camp. They fetched torches and looked for footprints in the muddy ground. Her horse and all her possessions, even her pannier of occult items, were untouched. She would never have left that behind. Something bad had befallen Sarah.

Roscoe took Thurmond by the shoulders.

"Tell me exactly what you know, Prospect."

He knew very little. It was their custom to rise shortly before dawn and be ready to ride as soon as it was light enough to do so. Thurmond had taken the last watch, so it had fallen to him to rouse the others at the appropriate time. That was when he had found her gone.

Bodo spoke up.

"I might know something. I had the second watch. I saw Sarah get up and walk into the bushes. I just thought she was goin' for a squat, you know? Nothin' special about that, so I didn't pay it no mind—let a lady have her privacy. I think maybe she never came back, but I don't think somebody grabbed her. There would have been a tussle, and I would've heard."

When it was lighter, they re-examined the bushes were Bodo had seen her go. They found nothing—no broken branches suggesting a struggle, no scraps of torn clothing, not so much as a footprint. She had, for all appearances, simply disappeared into the night.

Roscoe's voice had the deep, authoritative tone it took on when he assumed his official role of Adventure Captain.

"Now this is grave indeed, so it is. Sarah seems to have walked off and left us, and that's a thing most strange. She's just not the kind of girl to do such a thing on her own, so somthin' musta got her. Even if she was walkin' on her own legs, somethin' took her.

"So now we've got to get her back. I don't care what it takes or what it costs us, I'm not willin' ride off and leave her. If any of you feel otherwise, we can divide the gold right now so you can be on your way, and good luck to you. Anyone?"

Thurmond said nothing. He just drew his sword and stuck its point in the ground at Roscoe's feet. He rested his right hand on its pommel. Torgul was also silent as he rested his hand upon Thurmond's. Bodo did the same. Roscoe smiled and covered the hands of his companions with his own big paw. This was their silent pledge to rescue Sarah or die in the trying.

Their courage and resolve were extremely gallant, but such fine feelings were meaningless without a course of action, and that was exactly what they did not have. They packed their gear, saddled their horses, and then stood and stared at each other. They had no idea how to proceed. Should they continue west or backtrack east? They might continue to scour the surrounding area for sign, but that would be a tedious, time-consuming, and most likely fruitless endeavor. Meanwhile Sarah might be enduring a captivity of unspeakable horror. What, then, should they do?

The sun came up. Without Sarah to renew the illusion spell, the sacks of gold resumed their rightful appearance. This could be a serious problem. Should a greedy noble or thieving highwayman discover the hoard, the adventuring party would most assuredly be murdered to guarantee their silence. They hid the gold in a dense thicket of thorn and covered it with fallen leaves. Sarah's pannier and shoulder bag were hung on a nearby branch.

They continued to debate their options until interrupted by the *clop-clop* of hoofbeats approaching from the east—a light quick canter rather than the heavy pounding of a warhorse or the fleet drumming of a palfrey. A single rider. This did not bode well. The road was too remote, too dangerous for solitary wayfarers. Something felt wrong.

Roscoe loaded his heavy crossbow. Its square-headed bolts could punch through the stoutest armor. Thurmond strung his bow and hid behind a holly bush, watching the road through its branches. Torgul crouched behind a rock, axe in both hands, eyes alert. Roscoe and Bodo stepped behind trees.

The hoofbeats got louder as the rider drew near. Thurmond saw the approaching figure, or at least his mount—a white pony. Holly leaves blocked a full view of the rider. He nocked an arrow and drew his bow to his chin, waiting for Roscoe's signal.

But that signal never came. Instead, Roscoe's voice boomed out in surprise.

"Lower your bow, laddie! Don't shoot!"

Thurmond's view was still obscured. By the time he stepped around the holly bush, Roscoe was already in the road, holding the pony by its makeshift bridle. A young girl sat on its back, perhaps the last person anyone expected to see—Pozi!

She smiled broadly and hopped from her mount's back.

"Well, here you are at last. I've been riding hard for days, trying to catch up. I rather thought you might wait for me, but I'm glad I finally found you. Where's Sarah?"

She was clad in the same ragged dress they last saw her in, her shoulders draped with a thin, equally ragged blanket. A cloth bag hung from the cord that girded her narrow waist.

The pony had no saddle, not even a pad. Its bridle was a length of rope fashioned into a hackamore. The old Adventurer handed the animal to Bodo, who led it behind a screen of bushes where the other horses were tethered. Roscoe returned Pozi's smile but with trepidation.

"Well now, lassie, this is a surprise, so it is. Who'd of thought to see you comin' along? I'm glad to see you, to be sure ... but what are you doin' here?"

"What? I'm here because Lord Thurmond and Lady Sarah said I could come with you."

Her brow furrowed and her voice grew shaky.

"You're not trying to back out of the deal, are you? Where's Sarah? Ask her—she'll tell you."

Roscoe laid a comforting hand on her shoulder.

"Nay, girl, that's not it at all ... not at all. We thought you wanted to go back to your village and help the priest. We didn't look to see you again."

Pozi rolled her eyes.

"You believed me when I said that? After all the things I told you, you really believed me?"

"We thought..."

She interrupted.

"I would do anything...well, almost anything...to escape from that sad place. I used the same kind of tricky words Thurmond and Father Hieronymus used to fool each other. I promised to return to the village, and I did, but I never promised to stay. As soon as we got back there, I ran off again.

"I thought you'd wait for me, but you left. I got worried, but I knew Sarah would never break her promise to me. So here I am. Where *is* Sarah? I want to see her."

Roscoe hesitated, uncertain of what to say. Thurmond stepped in.

"It's all right, Pozi. Sarah isn't here right now, but she'll...she'll be back soon. We're just surprised to see you. We really thought you were going back home for good. You'd make a wonderful play-actor because you fooled us entirely."

Pozi was obviously disappointed by the dim-wittedness of her friends.

"That's silly. I wanted Father Hieronymus to heal your friend the dwarf lord. I never meant what I told him. I thought you knew that."

It was Torgul's turn to join the conversation. He doffed his hat and bowed so low most of his beard swept the ground.

"Lord Torgul Bonelip, twenty-third of that name, at your service, Miss Pozi. I am exceedingly grateful for the trouble you went through on my behalf. Thank you, and may good fortune shower forever upon you and yours. You must be hungry. Can I offer you provender?"

"I am very hungry, milord. I was in such a hurry to catch up with you that I scarcely stopped to eat. But what is *prov…*?"

She paused, unsure of the word. Torgul smiled.

"Provender—foodstuffs, missy. We have only rough trail fare—stale bread, hard cheese, dried meat—but it will fill an empty belly."

The dwarf went to fetch the proffered items. Thurmond resumed the conversation.

"You really had no intention of staying home and becoming the old priest's assistant? You asked him for the job."

"God's holy molars, nay! I would be most happy to learn sums and letters from him, but I know Father would expect certain other things of me when I get a little older. That would be better than being wife to Samp, but it's not a life I hanker for.

"Anyways, I only asked him to *choose* me for his assistant. I never promised to accept. Just more tricky words."

Torgul returned with the victuals, which Pozi consumed in large, rapid bites. After a dozen mouthfuls, she paused as if remembering something and began to untie the bag at her belt.

"I forgot—I wanted to steal back all that jewelry that Father took from you. I couldn't get it without being caught, but I snagged this."

She produced the gem-studded coronet from Castle Sathas.

"Father Hieronymus is usually very kind. He just got mean because you fooled him. But you also killed Old One, so you deserve the reward. Here—take it."

She handed the piece to Thurmond, who stared at it in amazement. Pozi was always full of surprises. He looked at her pony. It was obviously one of the four that once pulled the false wizard's wagonette. Pozi seemed to read Thurmond's thoughts.

"I found him by the side of the road. I think he was as glad to see me as I was him. Something bad happened on the road back there. Did you see the wrecked wagon and the dead horse with an arrow in its eye? There was a bunch of stuff scattered about. I wanted to stop and have a look—maybe find a cloak or a hat or something. But that dead horse was all chewed by wolves, so I was afraid. Anyways, I was in a hurry to catch up with you."

She suddenly stopped eating and looked Thurmond straight in the eye.

"I've told you my story, Lord Thurmond, and now you must tell me where Sarah is. I know you didn't speak the truth before."

Thurmond quickly related the unfortunate events of the night before. Pozi burst into tears.

CHAPTER 38

SUCH JOLLY COMPANY

Lady Fortune demands balance in all things. The adventuring companions had experienced, to this point, a remarkable run of good luck. They had survived a devastating bandit attack and destroyed a close-to-indestructible hyut. Thurmond and Sarah had overcome the witch of Castle Sathas and her evil minions, both real and illusionary, winning a great wealth of treasure. And now they had escaped the false wizard's deadly trap.

Such fine fortune must be paid for. He who rides to the top of the Lady's wheel must inevitably take his turn at the bottom. Thus, Sarah's disappearance was only the first payment of this reckoning. A second payment was about to be made, and when it came, it was, as such things often are, a complete surprise.

After much debate, they decided the false wizard was somehow behind Sarah's disappearance, though they had no idea how she had been carried off or where he had taken her. The area was so dark and wild that she could be anywhere. They needed help. They would, therefore, ride west until they came to a town or village or castle and hire local hunters or woodsmen to track her down. It was a reasonable plan that, and it might have proven successful had Lady Fortune been smiling. But on that day, her face wore a frown.

Though they rode for the best part of the morning, they came to no towns, villages, or castles. Nor did they pass any other travelers. The road was so desolate it seemed as if the world might have ended, as if all humanity had been stricken down by some dread pestilence that they alone had survived. Such were Thurmond's thoughts when a lasso suddenly fell around his shoulders, and he was yanked sideways from his saddle. He landed hard, his upper arms pinioned to his sides by the rope. An ugly bearded man appeared over him and held the point of a dagger under his chin.

The others fared in similar fashion, all either lassoed or entangled in large nets. The attack came so suddenly and took them so utterly unaware, that the four experienced warriors were captured before they could draw their weapons. Even Pozi, quick as a snake and slippery as a trout, was caught and thrown to the ground.

Torgul, trapped in a net, managed to draw his scramasax and was cutting himself free when he was struck senseless by the heavy blow of a cudgel. Bodo, on the other hand, prudently did not struggle but remained where he had fallen. Roscoe fought to tear from a net of woven vines, but to no avail. He was seized by four strong, wild-looking men, one for each arm and leg.

Rough hands held the captives down while their wrists were bound with leather thongs. Their assailants bestowed kicks and buffets aplenty to the helpless victims, laughing mightily as they did. They spoke a thick, guttural language heavily spiced with glottal stops and velar fricatives.

Thurmond guessed they must be Slovags, but these men were not the downtrodden, sad-eyed creatures they had passed on their eastbound journey. They were fierce, belligerent, and heavily armed. One placed a heavy boot in the middle of Thurmond's back, pinning him to the ground. He pricked menacingly at the nape of the young man's neck with the point of his spear. From where he lay, Thurmond could see Pozi. She was similarly trussed, lying on her stomach in the road. Several Slovags stood around her, all speaking at once.

They quieted when a swarthy man in a pointy sheepskin hat approached. He was taller and leaner than most of the others, who tended to be stocky and short-legged. Their deferential attitudes left no doubt that he was their leader. Pointy-Hat flipped Pozi over onto her back. He looked closely at her hair, her eyes, and her teeth. He inspected her skinned and scabby knees, and even her fingernails. What he saw obviously did not please him. He turned to his men and said something that left them visibly afraid. He next walked to Roscoe, who lay nearby, seized him by the hair, lifted his head, and stared straight into his face. This displeased him even more than the sight of Pozi's scrawny body. He roared and delivered a series of hard kicks to the old Adventurer's ribs.

Thurmond struggled against his bonds, expecting at any moment to feel the spear plunged into his back. Instead, a strangely familiar voice spoke to him in his own language, and in the familiar accent of Poitiers.

"Take it easy, Thurmond. Baidan is mighty pissed off right now. You keep squirmin' around, and you'll draw his eye. That ain't what you want, believe me."

His guard had called him by name! In his own tongue! Who could it be? Thurmond tried to turn over for a look but received a slight jab from the spear.

"Damn it, I said hold still. There might be a way out for you, but not if you keep makin' a ruckus. I'm gonna try to talk to Baidan before he kicks Roscoe to death, but if you keep fidgetin', one of the other guys is sure to slip his knife twixt your ribs. You gotta calm down."

Thurmond watched the man's back as he walked toward the leader. Who could he be? Nothings distinguished him from any of the others. Like them, he wore dark homespun trews and tunic with a ragged sheepskin vest. His hair was long and greasy. A small axe was tucked diagonally through the back of his belt. Yet he recognized Thurmond and even knew his name.

The man's conversation with the leader was animated and volatile—much waving of arms and stamping of feet. Within a few minutes, he returned and bent close. Thurmond finally got a good look at his bearded face and recognized him at once. Thurmond suddenly recognized the face and voice. He also remembered the stolen axe.

"Skrot? You're Skrot, our runaway serf."

"Aye, Skrot I am, but your serf I am not. I now serve Baidan, King of the *Kopce*—the Hills. I bear you no grudge, Thurmond, but I must do as he commands, and he ordered me to cut your throats, all of you except for Roscoe. He wants to pull him apart between four horses. Sorry, I tried. Prepare yourself."

"Wait! Wait! Don't kill me yet, I pray thee! Not until I can talk to King Baidan. I beg you, let me plead for my life—for all our lives."

"Look Thurmond, it's not for me to question a command from my king.

I know he's not a real king, but he's a big man around these parts. If I don't cut your throat, he'll cut mine—understand?"

"Tell him if he kills me, he'll be throwing away his chance to become a real king—with a crown and everything. Tell him we can help him claim the throne he's always wanted, the one that's rightfully his. Please, tell him."

Thurmond, of course, had no idea if Baidan had even a remote claim to any throne, but he guessed that a man so vain as to name himself a king must enjoy such pretensions.

Skrot seemed to fear another encounter with his overlord but finally approached him with Thurmond's proposal. Baidan turned on Skrot with a filthy look, but hesitated as he listened to his minion's words. Baidan then walked to his captive and kicked him in the face. Bending low, he spoke the common tongue with the slow, barbarous drawl of the hills.

"Make Baidan a real king, you? Baidan already king! Don't need pretty boy for that."

Thurmond took his courage in both hands.

"Do you have a crown? A real crown? Made of gold and studded with precious gems? A real king must have a real crown. All I see is a pointed sheepskin hat. No real king would wear such an ugly hat."

This made Baidan reveal his rotted teeth in what might have been a smile. He knelt down so close his mouth touched Thurmond's ear. His voice was an evil whisper.

"Maybe Baidan wear you guts on head for hat. How like that, you?"

"I wouldn't like it at all. Neither would you, because if you kill me, you'll never get the crown I can get for you. That's the only thing you need to be a real king. Your people will see it and show you proper respect. Warriors will flock to your banner."

The bandits were now rifling their victims' baggage. Baidan raised his eyes and watched them briefly, then turned back to Thurmond.

"I don't see no crown, you. I think a liar, you."

"Nay, not so! It would be foolish to gad about with such a precious thing, but it is nearby—someplace safe. Let us live, and you shall have it."

This was not untrue. The coronet Pozi had brought them was hanging on a branch in the thorn thicket beside Sarah's shoulder bag. Baidan remained unconvinced. He drew a short, curved knife and held the edge against the side of the young man's face. It felt extremely sharp.

"Baidan don't like liars, you. Maybe I slice off a few pieces, then tell me true, you. Maybe start with a thumb or maybe you prick. What say?"

Thurmond had no idea what to say. All his words had fled in a panic. Then Roscoe bellowed.

"Hey, boyo! You want to be king? Then start actin' like one! Real kings don't behave like this, not a'tall! They don't kill and rob innocent wayfarers!"

This was, of course, a preposterous argument. Anointed kings routinely committed the most wanton of acts. Thurmond, however, was supremely grateful for the interruption.

Roscoe continued to berate Baidan.

"I'm a landed gentleman, and I know my rights. Custom says I get to have trial-by-combat, and I demand it! Fight me yourself if you're not too scared. Or if you are, have your best fighter do it. Come on, damn your eyes—untie me and fight me!"

As a franklin, Roscoe was indeed a landholder, but he was not a noble and therefore not entitled to the ancient rite of trial-by-combat. But this made no real difference because Baidan had never heard of such a thing anyway. Fights to the death were common enough among his followers, but the old Adventurer's words implied this trial-by-combat was somehow different. It sounded like something a real king would know about and value. And Baidan was very eager to be recognized as a real king.

Skrot understood Roscoe's stratagem and immediately jumped in.

"He's correct, Your…uh…Majesty. Out in the western kingdoms, noble knights like Roscoe always get trial-by-combat. It happens all the time. Let him fight Ouichi."

He pointed toward a huge, lumbering lummox with squinty porcine eyes. This was Baidan's personal enforcer. He was well regarded for his ferocity and heartlessness, though not necessarily his intelligence.

"Nay, foreign dog use some devil magic on Ouichi. Baidan need Ouichi."

But then Baidan had a thought.

The King of the Hills said something unintelligible to the men looting Roscoe's saddlebags. They most obviously liked what they heard, for they laughed excitedly and bounced up and down, chanting in their rough language—*hra! hra! hra!* The rest of the bandits heard this and took up the phrase, bouncing in their enthusiasm.

Skrot hooked a hand beneath Thurmond's arm and hauled him to his feet.

"What's happening, Skrot? What are they cheering about?"

"Baidan told them we would play the Game."

Thurmond did not like the sound of it.

"What exactly is the nature of this game?"

Skrot grimaced, obviously reluctant to explain.

"Think of it as the local version of trial-by-combat. If Roscoe wins, Baidan might let him go. Hell, he might let all of you go. Hard to say. It's Baidan's method of settling disputes."

"What does Roscoe have to do?"

Their conversation was interrupted as an explosion of laughter erupted from the bandits. They had raised Pozi to her feet and were dragging her by her bound arms. Thurmond asked again.

"What does Roscoe have to do?"

"It's complicated—the story I heard was that years ago Baidan tried to shoot a goblet of wine off the head of his favorite wife. I guess he liked to do that kind of thing when he got drunk. But this time he missed and put an arrow right through her eye."

"So now ....?"

"Now Roscoe's gonna have to shoot one off that girl's head."

A pair of bandits came running with a gigantic longbow and a fistful of arrows.

"These boys take the Game serious. They always use a certain bow and special arrows."

This scared Thurmond. Roscoe was a crack shot with his crossbow but no great shakes with a longbow. Still, he had a lot experience as an archer, so maybe ... just maybe ....

But then Skrot added some unwelcome details.

"Problem is, the Game ain't fun if it's just a straight archery shoot, so they do some things to make it more interestin'.

"What kind of things?"

"Well, the bow is very stiff. Much too stout for most men to draw, so even a strong man's arm gets shaky. Also, all them arrows are a little curved, so they don't fly in a straight line. And they cut the feathers crooked to make it even worse. And…"

He paused.

"And? And?"

"Look for yourself."

Three bandits had Roscoe on his back. One pinch was pinching his nose while another forced his mouth open by pulling his beard and prying at his lips with the point of a knife. A third poured a skin of wine down his throat. The old Adventurer choked and sputtered, but a copious amount of the liquid found its way into his stomach.

"The rules say he's got to be as shit-faced as Baidan was when he killed his wife. And he's got to keep shootin' until he knocks the goblet from her head. The boys wanna see the target get stuck full of arrows. That's what makes it fun."

The first wineskin empty, the bandits started on another. Thurmond knew his friend had a wonderful capacity for strong drink, but the bandits were not stinting on the quantity. One of them had a third wineskin hanging from his shoulder.

Meanwhile others tied Pozi to a tree and were attempting to balance various drinking vessels atop her head. The bandits carried a large assortment of such implements so as to always be ready for the Game. They began with an immense pewter flagon. This one won Thurmond's immediate approval, but it was summarily rejected by the bandits. A large leather jack followed, then a slightly smaller crockery mug, a two-handled copper chalice, and a brass goblet. They settled on a diminutive wooden cannikin only slightly larger than a troll's eyeball.

This was not going at all well. Roscoe, now reeling drunk, was prodded into position perhaps twenty paces from where Pozi was tied to the tree. Torgul and Bodo were dragged over to enjoy the day's entertainment. They lay on their stomachs, hands and feet hog-tied behind their backs.

Several bandits drew their bows and took dead aim at Roscoe as his hands were untied, and the ceremonial bow and arrows were placed before him. No instructions were proffered, but the expectation was quite obvious. He must shoot the small wooden cup from the girl's head, or they would all be slain.

Baidan stood by himself, hands on hips, smiling hugely. There was, Thurmond thought, something familiar about him. Where have I seen him before? And then it struck him! The raiders who had attacked the caravan on the trek east—their leader had worn a tall pointed hat just like Baidan's. Could he be the same man?

Thurmond twisted his head slightly to speak to Skrot, who still held a knife to his neck.

"Are these the same bandits from before? The ones who attacked the caravan?"

Skrot cleared his throat as if answering made him uncomfortable.

"Aye, they would be the same."

"Baidan was their leader then as well?"

"Aye, that he was."

Thurmond saw a chance, a slim one to be sure, but a chance nonetheless.

"Tell him to stop this stupid game. It is unworthy of a hero like Roscoe and demeaning of a king such as himself. Tell him I know a far superior game, one that cannot fail to bring him the honor and respect he deserves. Or call him over here so I can talk to him."

Skrot squirmed. Baidan would not appreciate having his good time disrupted.

"I dunno, Thurmond. There ain't nothin' you can say that's gonna change his mind. He—"

"God rot you, Skrot! You said you want to help us, so do it. This is our last chance. Roscoe won't shoot Pozi. He'll shoot Baidan. And then we all die!"

CHAPTER 39

KING BAIDAN'S GAME

Skrot did as he was bidden, though his words to Baidan were apologetic, tentative, fearful. The bandit king stopped smiling, removed his hands from his hips, and strode toward Thurmond, who braced himself for pain—maybe a blow, a kick, or the thrust of knife.

"What want, you? You want wear cup on head, you? Maybe next, you?"

This, above all things, was exactly what Thurmond hoped to hear.

"Certainly, I'll wear the cup—a smaller one if you've got it since that great bowl on the girl's head hardly seems like a proper target for a man to shoot at. And the distance—what is it? One score paces? No worthy warrior would lower himself to shoot at such a distance. This is a game for beardless boys! Make it worth our effort or release us on the instant. These antics are tiring."

Baidan was puzzled. No one had ever despised the Game as unworthy. Thurmond read his face and pressed his accusation.

"This bow you offer is less than contemptible. Better to break it up and use it as kindling for the evening fire. If you want to see a real exhibition of a warrior's skill, let Roscoe shoot his own bow from a proper distance at a laudable mark. I demand nothing less."

These words again gave Baidan pause. These foreigners seemed to know how things were done in the world of knights and nobles and kings—the proper way of things. This was a world the bandit chief always dreamed of joining but in which he had no practical experience. He was loath to relinquish his authority over these captives, yet he was eager to acquire the expected behaviors of the nobility.

Thurmond again read the hesitancy in Baidan's face and pushed his luck another step.

"When Roscoe succeeds, as I know he will, you will agree to release us unharmed."

Baidan only smirked.

"Why Baidan do that?"

Thurmond knew he must take his greatest gamble.

"Because it was Roscoe who shot the hat off your head and stopped your charge when you attacked our caravan. But for him, you might have killed us all and captured great treasure. Beyond doubt, he is a greater warrior than you. Because of that, you owe him this chance to prove his worth instead of dishonoring him with your silly game. And if he succeeds, you owe him—all of us—our lives."

This was taking a big chance. Did this savage bandit have the slightest concept of honor? Probably not. But Thurmond could think of no other argument, no other angle. There was an awkward moment of silence while Baidan chewed his lower lip.

In sooth, Baidan had no concept of honor, not at least as Thurmond conceived of it. His first thought was to kill this troublesome piss-ant so he could get on with the Game. The old man—he would die more slowly for embarrassing him during the caravan raid.

But the bandit chief was by no means a stupid man. He could divvy up loot so cleverly that his men never suspected they had been cheated, and he was quite adept at devising the most cunning ambuscades. At times, what might even be called a flicker of wisdom sparked in the back of his brain. Perhaps this is what preserved the lives of his captives.

Baidan was fairly new to his leadership role, having come into it shortly before the abortive caravan raid. That had been the first major test of his leadership, and he knew he was indeed fortunate to have retained his rank and his life after its failure. He was also aware that he now needed some grand success if he expected to hold the position for long.

He needed prestige. Something beyond the reputation for utter ruthlessness he had cultivated to this point. He must gain the genuine respect of his men so they would continue to follow him in spite of setbacks. That was why he had declared himself *Kral Kopce*, the King of the Hills—to foster the idea that he was more than a grubby bandit from the wildwood.

His followers dutifully addressed him by his royal title—they were afraid not to—but Baidan knew his kingdom was naught but a shadow play. Or so he had believed until these strangers came along. They were from lands beyond his forest and hills. They knew of things he did not. They spoke of things a king should know about. As badly as he wanted to see their blood, he also wanted to learn from them.

"All right, boy, wear the cup, you. We find one right size."

Thurmond pressed his luck again.

"And Roscoe will be allowed to use his own bow, the same crossbow he used to shoot the hat from your head. That miserable tree branch you call a bow is beneath his notice. After he shoots the cup from my head, I'll fetch your crown—a real king's crown. Do you pledge your word on this?"

The concept of pledging his word meant nothing to Baidan. He was well aware that there were people who put stock in such things. People who would actually inconvenience themselves rather than break a pledge. He was not such a person, nor did he believe this whelp of a boy could provide a king's crown. But he chose to play along.

"Baidan pledge."

Thurmond spat in his palm and extended it Baidan.

"Handclasp then?"

This ancient custom was familiar to the bandit. He knew great evil would befall anyone who violated an agreement so sealed. This need not worry him, however, for the whelp was about to be killed by his own companion. Abruptly he spat in his hand and took Thurmond's in a bone-crushing grip.

Baidan called out to his men. Pozi was cut loose from the tree, and Thurmond took her place, brushing away their attempts to bind him. A tiny cordial glass with a long, narrow stem was placed on his head. The bandits chortled in evil glee.

Thurmond cast a nervous glance at Roscoe. His mentor was so drunk he had to be braced up to keep from falling. His knees buckled, and his head drooped to one side. He vomited violently on the bandit who supported his left arm.

Baidan barked an order, and the bandits fell silent. Roscoe was pulled back an additional twenty paces, his feet stumbling with each step. His crossbow and a single bolt were put in his hands. Bandit archers stood by with arrows aimed at his heart lest he be tempted to select an alternate target. The old Adventurer caught his breath and straightened up. He wound the cranequin, cocked the bow, and loaded the bolt. Then in one fluid motion, Roscoe raised the weapon, sighted briefly, and fired.

A great many factors affect the flight of a crossbow bolt— the quality and condition of the missile, the tautness of the string, the degree and angle of the wind. But mostly it depends on the keen eye and steady hand of the shooter. Thurmond could not recall ever being so scared. He could hardly draw breath as he stood, his eyes screwed tightly shut. He heard the *snap* of the bow and almost instantly his scalp was sprinkled with shards of crystal as the cordial glass shattered.

The Game had been played.

"So why does Baidan hate us?"

Thurmond was riding on his own horse but had been stripped of his weapons and armor. He tried to turn his head to look at Skrot while he spoke, but the noose around his neck made movement uncomfortable. Ouichi, riding directly behind him, had the other end of the rope wrapped around his hand. Every time Thurmond tried to shift position, Ouichi gave it a painful tug.

Skrot rode closer so Thurmond could see him more easily.

"Well you can hardly blame him. Roscoe cheated by pretending to be drunk."

"That's not what I mean. He hated us right from the start, even before we beat him at his stupid game."

"Hey! The Game's not stupid. The guys take it real serious. But you're right about Baidan havin' a down on you even before. It's because he thought that wench ridin' with you was a princess, only she wasn't. He was pretty disappointed."

Thurmond was astounded.

"Why would he think Pozi was a princess? She's just a skinny village girl."

"He got word that Melgwyn—he's the baron of these parts—was lookin' to capture a princess and hold her for ransom. She was supposed to be in disguise and ridin' with three men and a dwarf. When we saw you, Baidan was certain it was her. Everything fit."

Thurmond was suspicious. How many young girls kept company with three men and a dwarf? Skrot continued the story.

"Baidan wanted to catch this princess and collect the ransom for himself. Things have been tough for him lately. He lost a lot of men attacking the caravan, and a lot more drifted off after. I guess they figured he was kind of a loser. He needs to pull off somethin' really special, or he ain't gonna last long."

"How did you come to join him, Skrot?"

"After I took off from the caravan, I didn't have no plan, except I wasn't never gonna be nobody's serf again. Roscoe—he treated us good, but I always figured to skip out first chance I got.

"I headed east, hopin' to find some way to live, you know? Well, I ran *spang* into Baidan's boys. They were gonna kill me at first, but since I spoke their language, they let me join up. Baidan likes that I can speak the Common Tongue so good."

"How did you learn their language?"

"My ma—she was from Bukovia. She taught me when I was a little boy. Pretty lucky, huh?"

A new plan took form in Thurmond's brain, rather like a turtle poking its head from its shell.

"You say Melgwyn is in charge around here?"

"Aye, this valley and all the forests hereabout are his demesne."

"Tell me about him."

"He's mean as an ogre's arse. Him and Baidan hate each other like poison."

"Why doesn't Melgwyn just track Baidan down and hang him?"

"Oh, he's tried. But the bandits' got a stronghold way back in the hills.

Every time Melgwyn sends men up there, they roll rocks down on 'em, then shoot the survivors full of arrows—always the same thing."

"What's Baidan doing in these parts? Why isn't he up in the hills?"

"We come down to steal horses—just a couple score of us. The rest stayed at the fort. We got a temporary camp back in the woods."

"Does Baidan know you know us, Skrot?"

"Nay, and please don't tell him. He'd be pissed I kept it quiet. You don't think Roscoe or the dwarf will say anything, do you? Or that other guy—Bodo?"

"Worry not. They're smarter than that."

"Hey! Where's Murd? And your ladylove Sarah? And Lars? They all get killed off?"

"Aye, Lars and Murd are dead, sorry to say. Listen, about Sarah, something strange has happened, and we need your help."

"Whoa! Wait a minute! I already risked my neck for you, speakin' up to Baidan like I did. If you got some mad plan to escape, best put it from your mind. We've been tasked with fetchin' back this crown you say you got, and that's all we're gonna do. I wish you no ill, Thurmond, but I'll not be carved up for your sake."

"Not an escape, Skrot—nothing like that. Just hear me out, please. I really have got a crown, and we're going to bring it back to Baidan. And then he'll be obligated by the handclasp to set us free…."

Skrot interrupted.

"You don't know him! He's like to set you all free without heads on your shoulders."

"I know we can't trust him. The only thing we can count on is that he'll do whatever he thinks suits his own purposes—correct?"

Skrot did not like the sound of this. He knew that Thurmond was leading him around to some point where he would be compelled to take chances he did not care to take. That, of course, was exactly what Thurmond had in mind.

"Skrot, how often does a girl come riding through with three men and a dwarf?"

The young bandit became evasive.

"I wouldn't know. I don't wanna know."

"This Melgwyn is obviously looking for Sarah, me, and the others. For some reason he thinks Sarah is a princess, though she's no more royalty than you are."

When Skrot remained silent, Thurmond continued.

"But what your friend Baidan doesn't know is that somebody—maybe Melgwyn—has already got Sarah. At least that's the way it looks. That's why he thought Pozi was the princess—he thought she was Sarah."

Skrot had been doing his best to ignore Thurmond, but this got his attention. He listened carefully as Thurmond told of Sarah's disappearance.

"Now I'm thinking, Skrot, that if anybody would be able to find out where she's being held, Baidan could. And he has enough men to help us get her back."

Skrot held his breath. He could feel himself about to be drawn into Thurmond's plan.

"I need you to help me convince Baidan to rescue her. What does he want so badly that he'd be willing make a deal like that? We don't have any money, so we can't just offer to pay him."

Thurmond was lying. They had a fortune in gold hidden nearby, but if Baidan learned of it, he would not hesitate to kill them and seize it.

Skrot's response was disappointing.

"I can't think of nothin' he'd want more'n gold unless it was a castle to go along with that crown. You got one of them? And you better be careful with Baidan. When he gets mad, he gets real mean. I seen him lots worse than he was this mornin'. And you better understand somthin'—I don't want no part of your plan. If Baidan even suspects I've been makin' plots with you, he'll kill me certain."

Thurmond cleared his throat.

"I'm sorry, Skrot, but you're already part of this. You think Ouichi back there hasn't been listening all the time we've been talking? He may not understand our words, but he knows we're up to something, and he's sure to tell Baidan. Your best chance is to help us find a way to win him over."

Skrot slumped down in his saddle, visibly distraught. Thurmond played his final card.

"Besides, this is all for the good. How long do you think you'd last with these guys? If you aren't killed in some ill-conceived raid, you'll end up with a wine glass on your head. You'll be lucky to live six more months. Help us. Come back with us, and Roscoe will make you a man-at-arms. You'll eat good food, wear warm clothes, and sleep in a soft bed. We'll train you to use weapons. It'll be a much better life, and you'll live longer."

CHAPTER 40

BARON MELGWYN'S GUEST

Sarah woke up in darkness—well, near darkness. A weak shaft of sunlight had somehow managed to ooze in from a tiny opening in one wall. She was, she realized, lying on a stone floor. It was cold and damp. So was the air—and it stank. Where the hell was she?

She could vaguely recall getting up in the night. Someone had called to her. Had it been Thurmond? Roscoe? Fragments of memory slipped away from her like the ephemeral bits of a broken dream. She had gotten up … but then there was nothing.

She groped about. The room seemed to be hewn from solid rock and was entirely devoid of furnishings. It was small, perhaps twice her height in length and width. An opening in one wall was sealed by a heavy iron gate of thick, flat, riveted bars. *Locked.* She could just make out a small room and a narrow passage on the other side. There was nothing else.

Since no one seemed to be about, this was a perfect occasion for her knock spell. But, alas, she could not summon the requisite energy to cast it. It was as if all her psychic vigor had been drained away.

It must have been a magician that called her. A powerful magician had entered her dream and somehow brought her to this place. Sarah had never before heard of such a spell, but it would be a good one to have on hand. And now that same someone was blocking her from casting her own spells.

She knew she should be afraid, but her situation seemed more odd than frightening. If her captors wanted to kill or ravage her, they could have already done it. What then was the point of this horrid little cell? There were no prisoner essentials—no jug of tepid water or crust of moldy bread. Neither a ragged blanket nor a pile of vermin-ridden straw. Nothing. It made no sense—why would they capture her then just throw her in a hole to die?

She would not, she reasoned, be kept down here for an extended time. Most likely, this was intended to frighten her into submission. Unfortunately, their scheme was working. As the reality of her situation set in, she felt her stomach clench in a spasm of panic. She looked about the cell for some way to occupy her thoughts with something other than the likelihood of suffering and death—no easy task with such austere surroundings.

As a young girl, she had read many ancient stories—tales of stalwart heroes and knightly derring-do. She was well aware that innocent young maidens routinely found themselves in foul lockups, but they were at least given things to look at—skeletons chained to walls, crumbling instruments of torture, or maybe a menagerie of spiders, rats, and snakes. She had nothing, not even a slop bucket. Oooh! Until that moment she had not realized how badly she needed to relieve herself. What to do? Without a bucket, there was only the stone floor—a most distasteful option. But as the moments ticked by and her bladder continued to swell, this choice became inevitable.

She lowered the leather breeks she always wore on adventures and squatted in one corner, determined to complete this necessary task with as little fuss as possible. She was nearly done when a harsh voice boomed out through the gloom.

"Well look here now, the little girly is havin' a pee-pee. Ain't that just too cute? Maybe she'd like me to wipe her little fanny for her. What you say, girly. Want me to lend a hand?"

There was the sound of a key turning in a lock and a loud *creak* as the iron grate opened. Sarah struggled to her feet, but before she completely raised and laced her breeks, a large round man entered the cell and seized her by the wrist.

"C'mon, the Baron is wantin' to see you. Ain't no use strugglin'. There ain't no place for you to run to, so just come along nice-like. Make it easier on yourself, all righty?"

Sarah was dragged from the cell, one hand helpless in the gaoler's grip, the other struggling to keep her unlaced breeks from slipping to her knees. Now was the moment for panic if ever there was one.

They passed through a short passageway, climbed a flight of steps, then continued along a wider corridor pierced with slits for archers. Doors were set at random intervals along its length. At the far end were more steps and a door, which stood slightly ajar. The rotund gaoler thrust it open and pulled her inside.

Sarah stumbled into what appeared to be the great hall of a castle. A serving boy stood by an immense fireplace, turning a spit. The fat of a dead beast spluttered and flared as it dripped into the banked coals beneath. The warmth felt wonderful after the chill of the damp cell.

A commanding voice called out.

"Dollop, you great oaf, don't stand there being stupid. Bring her over. Fetch her here, you fat toad."

Dollop—for that was the round fellow's name—gave Sarah's wrist a hard yank. The voice came again, sharper.

"Easy, you stupid shitpile. That's a royal princess you're manhandling. May God blast your balls! Show proper courtesy, or I'll have that kitchen boy shove his spit up your arse."

Dollop, clearly frightened, released his prisoner's wrist and took a step backward. Attempting to regain her dignity, Sarah straightened her back before striding toward a long trestle table where a dozen men sat drinking. Above them, a red banner displaying a black bird was suspended from iron stanchions.

The speaker rose to his feet as she approached. He was of medium height, but big of bone and well-muscled. His gown was quartered, black and red. The white belt of a knight rode low on his hips. He had large brown eyes— rather gentle eyes, actually—and a round face. His dark beard and hair were neatly trimmed. Sarah guessed his age to be somewhere around thirty.

His men were of a different breed. All were big, shaggy, and uncouth. Three wore the belts of knights. They positively leered at her as she stood before them, struggling to maintain her dignity. As she gathered her thoughts, the man spoke again.

"Welcome, Your Highness, to Castle Skynslip. It is a humble abode, certainly, but we will make every effort to make your stay agreeable. I am Baron Sir Melgwyn de Pudni, your dutiful host. My men and I are entirely at your service."

Sarah was tempted to try a charm spell, but she was too closely watched. They had called her a princess, not once but several times now. Is that what they believed her to be? If so, she would do her best to present herself as one. It would probably be the decisive factor in keeping her alive.

Before she could reply, Baron Melgwyn spoke again.

"Never before has Castle Skynslip had the honor of a royal guest. I've never before seen a real princess. This is indeed a special occasion."

Melgwyn was obviously a backwoods knight from a poor and isolated realm, so it was unlikely he would possess detailed knowledge of who was who in the reigning dynasties. Her own knowledge of such things was practically nil. But he had admitted he had never met a princess, so his expectations would almost certainly stem from the same tales of chivalry that Sarah had read as a child.

She would play that role to the hilt.

"Baron Sir Melgwyn, I thank you for your courtesy. Since my guise as a humble wayfarer has failed, allow me to reveal my true identity. I am Grand Ducal Highness Sarafina, second daughter of Grand Duchess Renata, third sister of Tancred, King of Poitiers.

"I am, because of my youth, sometimes styled Princess, but that is strictly a title of courtesy. You may address me as Your Grand Ducal Highness."

This was all nonsense, of course. Sarah knew nothing of King Tancred's sisters or their offspring, but it sounded good, and she was betting this Melgwyn character was equally ignorant.

She kept at it.

"Furthermore, I cannot imagine how you will explain to my father Grand Duke Thurmond or my uncle King Tancred why you have brought me here against my will and kept me confined in a vile prison cell."

Melgwyn threw up his hands in dismay.

"Milady…Your Grand Ducal Highness…please understand. My foresters found you walking in the woods, out of your senses, unable to account for yourself. They thought you mad and brought you to me as an act of compassion. You were confined to keep you from doing yourself an injury. It is only in the last few minutes that word has come of your true identity. I had my servant bring you at once."

"Then I will take my leave at once. You will be pleased to have your porter open the gates."

She turned as if to stalk off. Melgwyn spoke to her back.

"Nay, Your Grand Ducal Highness, that I cannot do. The woods around here abound with cutthroats and savage beasts. You must remain as our guest until your royal parent can send a suitable retinue to escort you on your way."

Sarah spun about and stared straight into his eyes.

"Then I was correct in my assumption that I am a prisoner here."

"Not at all! Not at all! You are my guest—a very *valuable* guest."

His minions smirked openly at this remark. The baron shot them a scathing glance.

"You must forgive my men, milady. They are rough soldiers, not the smooth-tongued courtiers I'm sure you're used to. But they fight like maddened bears when need be.

"Let us mince no more words. You will remain my guest until I receive adequate compensation for rescuing you from the dangers of the wildwood. The transaction might take several months to complete, so let us not quarrel. Please regard me as your protector."

This was no less than Sarah anticipated, yet she was careful to portray the shock and outrage of a spoiled teenager accustomed to getting her own way.

"I will not be kept here! I demand that you open the gates immediately! I disdain your protection and will find my own way out of this miserable wilderness. Fail to do this, sirrah, and my father will offer you a very different form of compensation."

The mask of courtesy was now removed from Melgwyn's countenance.

"Get this straight, girl. This isn't the Kingdom of Poitiers, and your father is a long, long way off. You'll be here until I say you can go. If you behave, you'll eat well, and I'll keep my men off you. Cause me trouble, and you'll go back into your hole with Dollop for company. Understand?"

Staying in character, Sarah burst into tears.

"I hate you! I hate you! You're no true knight—you're nothing but a filthy brigand. Why are you treating me like this? It's not fair!"

Out of patience, Melgwyn signaled to his gaoler.

"Dollop! Back to the hole."

Sarah shrieked as if stabbed, stamped her foot furiously, and stormed off toward her cell—a commendable portrayal of a princess in a pique of rage. She kept up a rapid pace, hoping to discover an avenue of escape. Unfortunately, the gaoler followed closely behind her. As she proceeded through the long corridor, she could hear his heavy breathing as he struggled to keep pace with her.

"Just a moment...Your Princess-ship...wait here. I have to get... something."

Dollop left her standing alone in the deserted passage as he disappeared through a side door. Sarah wasted no time. She immediately tried her invisibility spell—naught! Three other doors opened onto the corridor. She tried them all and found them locked. Ahead lay nothing more than her dismal cell. Behind were Melgwyn and his ill-mannered warriors.

Her musings were interrupted by the return of Dollop with a thick wool blanket over his arm. He seemed entirely unconcerned that she was frantically yanking on a door handle.

"Here, take this. You're gonna need it. That cell gets mighty cold at night. I told the kitchen boy to bring us some of that boar he's got turnin' on that spit. The Baron's wine is kinda sour, but you won't find nothin' better."

As they descended the second flight of steps and moved through the lower passage, Dollop made no move to touch her, offered no more lewd remarks. Rather he was distinctly amiable.

"I didn't wanna be so mean before, but the Baron said I hadda scare you so you'd do as he says. I didn't know you was a princess until he said so just now. I was told you was a runaway wife...well...almost a wife. Then the Baron, he called you *Your Highness*, and I heard how you talked, and I knew straight off you really was a princess.

"Real princesses ain't like other folks, I know that. I won't be mean to you no more. Just tell me if you're wantin' somethin', and I'll try an' bring it."

Just before locking her in, he produced a slop bucket from an alcove and placed it in her cell.

"Here—you'll be wantin' this later for when...well..."

Dollop seemed terribly embarrassed.

"... you know. And one more thing—you gotta be more careful of the Baron. He ain't nobody to mess with. Mighty cruel he can be. Man or woman, don't make no matter."

Sarah wrapped herself in the blanket and slumped down in a corner, as far from the pee puddle as she could get. Dollop sat on a three-legged stool on the other side of the bars. He kept his back turned to her and left her alone. For that, she was grateful.

After a time, the kitchen boy arrived with two flat rounds of bread heaped with meat. Behind him, an even younger girl carried mugs of wine. Dollop spoke to them briefly, then unlocked the cell. The boy delivered a loaf and a mug to Sarah. The girl, producing a rag, bent and cleaned the mess from the corner. Sarah thanked them both. They nodded and left without saying a word.

Dollop chuckled as he relocked the grate.

"Don't expect much talk outta those two, Your Princess-ship. The Baron don't like his servants gettin' friendly with his prisoners. The talky ones gets their tongues cut off."

Dollop, however, appeared most eager to chat. This was good. Maybe he would reveal something useful. If nothing else, maybe conversation would win his sympathy. Sarah moved closer to the door. The gaoler sat just on the other side, consuming his dinner in huge bites, chewing loudly with his mouth open.

"Master Dollop, is it permitted that I address you as such?"

"Aye, I'm Dollop. And I be the master of the Baron's lockup, though I never been called by such a fancy title afore."

"Master Dollop it is. And you must call me Lady Sarah. Your Princess-ship is nice, but it's so hard to say. And Your Grand Ducal Highness just takes too long. It seems we are destined to spend much time together, so let us make our association as pleasant as possible. Is that agreeable to you, Master Dollop?"

Dollop was dumbstruck. He was quite accustomed to the scorn of the baron and his men, to the occasional kick or buffet. He was, he knew, ugly and soft-gutted, so he was equally used to the contempt of highborn women. No noble had ever before addressed him in such kindly tones or in such a respectful manner. He did not know what to say.

"Master Dollop, you look upset. Did my words offend you? If I have done so, I beg you to forgive me. I swear I had no such intention."

Thoughts and feelings became so muddled in Dollop's mind that he nearly swooned. *Such divine graciousness!* Princesses must truly stem from some heavenly realm. He almost threw himself on his knees in adoration. Instead he bobbed his head and mumbled.

"Aye, milady. I mean nay. Uh…as you will."

Sarah smiled.

"Excellent well! That's settled then. Now, tell me how I came to be here."

CHAPTER 41

THE KINGMAKER

"Ouch! Watch it, Thurmond. That hit me right in the eye. It hurts."
Thurmond replied without looking back.

"Sorry, Skrot. Didn't mean to."

In fact, he did mean to. He had carefully selected a thorn branch at eye level, bent it back, and released it as soon as Skrot came into range. While the bandit was occupied with rubbing his offended countenance, Thurmond took a quick step deeper into the thicket.

Not too fast, though. He still wore the noose around his neck, and Ouichi stood no more than six feet behind him, holding the other end. The large bandit remained on the thicket's edge, while Skrot followed Thurmond inside.

There was the golden coronet, hanging from a branch exactly as he had left it. Next to it hung Sarah's pannier and shoulder bag. He reached inside and found, as he hoped, the leather box of glass globes. He stuck it inside his doublet, then lifted the coronet from its branch.

"Got it, Skrot! Let's get back! I don't want to aggravate Baidan by making him wait."

He was eager to leave the thicket before Skrot spotted Sarah's gear hanging just a few feet in front of him. He need not have worried. The bandit was entirely occupied with a long shallow scratch under his left eye.

"God's bollocks, Thurmond. Look at this! I'm bleeding. Can't you be a bit more careful? Let's get out of this accursed thicket before it happens again."

Thurmond presented the coronet to Skrot, who gave it to Ouichi. They mounted their horses and started back. He felt the box inside his doublet. Luckily, it was a thick, quilted garment that he had worn beneath his armor, and it was now quite baggy as he had lost considerable weight during the course of the adventure. He hoped the bulge of the box would go unnoticed.

Thurmond was aware of the contents of the box. Following the encounter with the wolves, he and Sarah had discussed the globes at length. There had been six, one each of red, black, yellow, blue, green, and purple. The yellow, now expended, produced a wall of fire. The red caused a stupendous thunderclap that had hurled wolves high into the air and left a stench of burning brimstone—clearly infernal magic.

They had speculated as to the nature of the others. Black for death? Blue for cold? Green and purple remained mysteries. But they were powerful weapons, whatever they turned out to be.

Thurmond resumed his former conversation with Skrot.

"What do you think Baidan will do when I give him the crown? You think he'll let us go like he promised?"

"Hard to say with Baidan. He'll be happy with the crown, all right. He'll probably let you go on account of that handclasp. But after that, I dunno. Could go either way."

"Then you've got to help me convince him. C'mon, Skrot, you know it's the right thing…and the best thing for you, too. You gotta talk him into rescuing Sarah."

Ouichi did not speak the language of Poitiers, but he must have guessed from Thurmond's tone that something unseemly was afoot. He gave the rope a hard tug, effectively ending the conversation.

Arriving at Baidan's hidden camp, Thurmond was surprised to find his comrades no longer bound nor even under close guard. Roscoe sat on a log in the shade of an oak tree, Baidan beside him. Torgul and Bodo lounged on a grassy patch, passing a wineskin. Pozi sat off by herself, eating a piece of bread. Something had changed.

Seeing Thurmond, Roscoe jumped to his feet.

"They found Sarah! They just brought word to Baidan. She's being held by some noble name of Melgwyn—he's the lord hereabouts. She's at his castle."

Thurmond was so delighted to hear this that he gave a little whoop. That not being quite enough, he gave another one. Before he could begin a third, Roscoe cut in.

"If you'll leave off yowlin', Prospect, I'd like to discuss how this has changed things."

The young man calmed down, got serious.

"Certes, forgive me. You have my entire attention."

"Well and good, for this is a matter most delicate, so it is. Baidan ain't made up his mind about us yet. He's smarter than the rest of his bunch and a tad more thoughtful than I expected. I been workin' on him, tryin' to make him see we'd be much more helpful alive than dead."

"What did you say to him?"

"At first he only wanted to talk about what kings is like, about how royalty is. I don't really know nothin' about such things, you know, so I filled his head with some of the old stories—tales of courtly love, chivalry, knightly quests, that kind of thing."

"Did he believe you?"

"Seemed to. He kept interruptin' to tell me how stupid I am to hold with such things. For some reason, he seems to think I'm a knight. I thought it best not to tell him otherwise.

"But then a fella arrived with the news about Sarah bein' captured. It has to be her, except they all think she's a princess, and this Melgwyn is holdin' her for ransom. Where did they ever get such an idea?"

Thurmond shook his head.

"I dunno, but Skrot mentioned something about that, too."

"Well, now, I'm right pleased that Sarah's been took by a noble, even a bad 'un like Melgwyn. Nobles love money above all else, so they're more likely to be patient and wait for a ransom. A bunch like Baidan's—they'd have their way with her for a while, then kill her when they got bored. Gentlemen are dreadful enough, but not so bad as bandits."

Thurmond shrugged.

"I dunno, Roscoe. These bandits haven't hurt us much."

"You might think different if you'd been here, boyo. Turns out, this Lord Melgwyn is Baidan's bitterest of foes. Always interferin' with his thievery or interruptin' his murderin'. Swore an oath to track him and his bandits down and set their heads on his castle wall.

"Baidan wants the princess somethin' bad—wants her for himself. When he heard about Melgwyn havin' Sarah, it set him in a fury. He was runnin' all about, wavin' his sword, and screamin' how he won't be puttin' up with such trouble much longer. Wantin' blood so bad I thought he might kill us then and there just for spite. 'Twas a grim sight to behold, so it was."

"What did you do, Roscoe? You must have said something to settle him down."

"That I did, boyo, and that's a fact. It struck me that him and me—we have a common cause. Melgwyn is our mutual enemy. When he was calm enough to talk, I pointed that out and suggested maybe we should join forces against the cruel Lord Melgwyn. He liked the idea. That's what we was discussin' when you come back."

Thurmond was eager to tell what he had learned.

"I was talking to Skrot. He says Baidan's had a run of bad luck, and his men are losing trust in him. He needs a victory to win 'em back. Otherwise one of 'em will knife him and take over. That's why he calls himself King Baidan and why he's so keen on the crown. He's trying to make himself more impressive."

Baidan was in, in fact, doing so at that very moment. Skrot had given him the coronet as soon as he arrived back in camp. The outlaw chief was performed an impromptu ceremony of self-coronation. That done, he paraded among his men in an outlandish display of royal pomposity. Roscoe shook his head.

"Baidan's puttin' on quite a show, but surely the men ain't so stupid as to believe that crown makes him a real king."

"Nay, not so stupid as that. But Skrot said something that gave me an idea."

He quickly told his friend what he had in mind.

"Oh, by the way, I promised Skrot you'd make him a man-at-arms for helping us."

"What? That runaway serf? He stole one of my horses and a perfectly good hatchet. And I had to buy Murd a new cloak 'cause he took his old one. I'll do no such thing!"

"Show a little gratitude! He already risked his life by pleading with Baidan on our behalf. He was the one who told Baidan you were a knight. But we can this discuss later. Right now, we've got to work on Baidan. Are we allowed to walk around free? Can we go talk to Torgul and the others?"

"Don't know. I reckon we can find out easy enough."

The big man got to his feet and walked casually toward his companions with Thurmond a wary step behind. Seeing this, Pozi rose to join them. The bandits glanced in their direction, but they were too interested in their king's new crown to pay them much mind.

After a brief huddle, the group assumed a compact formation—Roscoe, Torgul, and Thurmond standing three abreast, the dwarf in the center, Pozi and Bodo close formed a second rank. They strode purposefully toward Baidan, chins held high, eyes straight ahead, unspeaking.

This caught the attention of the bandits, who grabbed their weapons and sought to intervene, but not before the advancing group stood directly before the new-crowned king. At Roscoe's signal, the group dropped to one knee and bowed their heads.

After a respectful pause, Roscoe spoke.

"Your Majesty, my comrades and me crave the honor of payin' our respects on this, the day of your coronation. We are joyous we were able to bring you this necessary symbol of kingliness, so we are. But this was only a minor service compared to what we are prepared to do on your behalf."

These words piqued Baidan's interest. These foreign dogs had already surprised him by actually having a crown. What else might they be capable of? He motioned his men away, though they remained ready and eager to plunge spears into the kneeling supplicants.

"Baidan will hear! Speak! What do for Baidan, you?"

Roscoe made a grand gesture toward Torgul.

"Your Majesty, with your permission, I would like to introduce our noble comrade, Torgul Bonelip, twenty-third of that name. His is a most esteemed lineage—being descended from Torgul the Great, first of the name. He is also, by right of birth, a great lord of the Spear Mountain dwarves."

Roscoe assumed Baidan had little or no experience with dwarves. If he had, he would know they almost all bore illustrious-sounding titles, which were largely honorific.

Roscoe was on a roll.

"In addition, he enjoys a touch of the second-sight, a gift from his mother, the daughter of that renowned dwarf prince, Borik the Bold."

Thurmond saw Torgul open his mouth to protest and quickly placed his hand on his shoulder. Roscoe had made a mistake in his lineage. Torgul's second-sight came from his great-grandmother, not his mother. And while he was truly descended from Borik, that renowned dwarf was only a distant ancestor. Dwarves were very particular about such details. Fortunately, Torgul understood Thurmond's warning and kept silent.

Roscoe went on.

"Last night, as Lord Torgul slept, he dreamed a most prophetic dream. Its true import remained hidden until this very moment. For he saw himself—nay, he saw himself and his companions—holding a huge iron key that he—we—presented to a most powerful king.

"Just now, as he saw you wearin' your kingly crown, it came to him—the great king in the dream was you, Baidan the First, King of the Hills and Forests. It had to be. But a king must have more than a crown. And that's the important part of the dream. Your Majesty, Lady Fortune has sent us to your land for a most wonderful purpose. We have come here to bring you such a key—the key to your very own castle.

"We will unlock for you the gates to Lord Melgwyn's castle, throw them wide so you and your men can enter and claim that which is rightfully yours—a crown *and* a castle. That will make you a real king. It's destiny, so it is. Lord Torgul's dream makes it all very clear."

Baidan's first royal proclamation was that they all had to get drunk.

CHAPTER 42

A CHAT WITH
MASTER DOLLOP

Nothing was going right. Sarah had tried every spell she could think of—knock, truth, charm, invisibility, sleep. The last should have worked readily on the well-fed Dollop, but all had failed. Something was clearly drawing off her psychic energy.

Fortunately, her gaoler had been so smitten by the thought of her being a real princess that he had charmed himself without her assistance. The baron might not like talkative servants, but Dollop was proving to be a congenial companion who responded readily to her questions.

"Well…uh…Your Princess-ship…uh…Your Highness-ship…you was brang in by some of the Baron's foresters. Walkin' on your own feet, you was, but eyes just starin' straight ahead and not seein' nothin'."

"Do you think I was under a spell?"

"Aye, most likely. Now I'm a god-fearin' man, I am, and don't hold with black magic and such like. What I seen there warn't natural. I'm thinkin' it's gotta be magic. Plus, I seen the baron talkin' with old Babs One-Eye the other day. They was plainly cookin' up some nuisance."

"Who might Babs One-Eye be?"

"Only the most powerful witchy-woman in these parts, that's who, and a bad lot she is, too. You can look for nothin' but troubles when old Babs comes around."

Sarah knew old Babs must indeed be a formidable witch. The ability to control a person through their dreams—it had to have been some form of possession spell—required a magician of advanced ability. Babs must now be blocking Sarah from using her own powers, another remarkable feat.

"Master Dollop, tell me about Baron Melgwyn. What is he like?"

"Oh…well…Your Highness-ship…the Baron—he's a de Pudni."

Dollop ceased to stammer, as if the mere mention of that name was a definitive answer.

Sarah cleared her throat.

"I see."

Of course, she did not see. Reading the confusion in her face, Dollop did his best to clarify.

"De Pudni means somethin' to people 'round here. It's an old name, and them what carries it decides who lives and who dies, and they ain't shy about choosin' the latter. They're a hard bunch, the de Pudnis.

"The Baron—he ain't so bad as his father, the Old Baron. Now there was a man with a right cruel temper. Why, take that cell your settin' in right at this moment. It was just there that he kept young Waldryn—that was his oldest boy—chained up for seven long years till he died."

"Seven years? His own son? God's golden britches! Why?"

"You see, Waldryn warn't much of a warrior. He was more of the talky type, don't you know, always wantin' to settle things with words instead o' steel. Well now, the Old Baron warn't wantin' a milksop for an heir, so he threw him down here. But Waldryn was a lot tougher than anybody thought. I guess he was a real de Pudni after all. He just refused to die."

Sarah was both horrified and intrigued.

"But you said he eventually died. What happened?"

"Aye, die he did, and a terrible death he had. 'Twas the doin' of his brother Methryn. Him, bein' next in line, was eager to see poor Waldryn pass over. Much more like the father, he was, with a mean streak as wide as a castle gate. Used to come down here and taunt his brother somethin' terrible.

"See that iron ring set in the wall behind you? That's where Waldryn was kept chained, only his chain was left long so he could move around a little. One day when Methryn got a little too close, Waldryn jumped up and grabbed him and threw him down on the floor. He took up a loop of his chain and started beatin' him and beatin' him as hard as he could.

"There was a turnkey standin' close by, so he run in and pulled Methryn free, but it was too late. His ribs was all stove in. Took him two weeks to die, but die he did."

By now Sarah was far more horrified than intrigued.

"What of Waldryn?"

"The Old Baron got mad, told the servants to give him all the salt meat he wanted but not a drop of water. There were always guards down here to make sure nobody slipped none in. I guess Waldryn's brain musta dried out after a fashion, 'cause he started to rave and thrash about like a man possessed of demons. Like I said, a bad death."

Sarah was ready for a change of subject.

"Melgwyn was the third son?"

"Nay, Your Highness-ship, the fifth. Fredryk came next, but he was gutted by a boar durin' a hunt. Warn't anybody's fault—just one of them things that happen sometimes. The Old Baron knew it, but he had all his huntsmen gutted and hung from trees along the highway. Wanted to make a point, I reckon.

"Then there was Franco. Oh, he was a wild one, he was, always after the ladies. Didn't matter who. The wife of a servant or the daughter of a noble—'twas all the same to him. Fiery tempered young buck, always ready to fight. Got hisself killed in a duel."

"And that left Melgwyn as the only heir?"

"Aye, the last son. He took over when the Old Baron passed on, must be 'bout ten year ago or so."

"You said he wasn't as cruel as his father, did you not?"

"That's right, not so bad as that. Maybe he's got a bit of the talkin' side like his brother Waldryn, but he's a real de Pudni, Your Highness-ship, never doubt it."

Sarah had another thought.

"Some of his men are knights. I saw their white belts. Would they help a princess in distress?"

Dollop shook his head regretfully.

"They're a bad lot, they are. The young one, Sir Terlan—he's mean as a snake. Always playing with his knife and talkin' to himself. You don't want any dealin's with him. And the big blonde one—that's Sir Ragarn. Stronger than a bear, he is. I seen him squeeze a man to death. He picked him up and squoze him until all his ribs busted and he died.

"But the worstest one is Sir Rothbert. He's the old one. Last year the king called out the army for most the summer. The Baron left Sir Rothbert in charge while he was gone. Well, when Rothbert hears the Baron is due to arrive home, he quick rounds up fifty Slovags, cuts off their heads, and puts them on the castle wall.

"They was just folk that happened to be old or sick or poor, but he called 'em miscreants. He wanted to show the Baron he was takin' proper care of his affairs in his absence. That's the way things go in these parts, Your Princess-ship."

Sarah felt the worm of despair gnawing at her heart. She was completely helpless and at the mercy of a despicable, heartless brute.

"How did the Baron learn I am a Princess?"

"Oh that—your young fella come through here a couple days past, told him all about you."

"My young fella?"

"The one you was pledged to marry afore you run off with some other fella. It was a sad tale, and he seemed like he was plain brokenhearted. That's why I warn't too nice at first, 'cause no real princess would act such a way. But when I heard you talk, I knowed you was gentle and goodly. You wouldn't of done what he said you done."

Sarah was now more confused than ever.

"Master Dollop, I swear to you I have never been engaged to anyone. Nor can I imagine why anyone would tell such a tale about me. Please believe me—I have no idea who this young man could be."

"Well, Your Highness-ship, he knew all about you. Described you to a tee, he did. Said you'd be comin' along with three men and a dwarf, and so you did."

"Can you describe this young man?"

"Tall, he was, and broad of shoulder. Good lookin' fella with a big bushy mustache. Nice clothes. Hair cut short like all the nobles 'round here, 'cept he warn't from 'round here. We knows all the young nobles from these parts. He come in ridin' a fine black courser. Seemed a nice young man, he did—well-mannered and sincere."

None of this meant anything to Sarah.

"And what story did he tell the Baron?"

"I don't know all of it, only what the servin' girls heard when they was fetchin' food and wine to 'em. Even the baron can't stop kitchen gossip. Anyways, this young man said you and him were gonna get married until you up and run off with someone else. Told the Baron that if he could find you and hold you here, your father the king would pay a handsome price to get you back. And once you was home, he could come and claim your hand like he was supposed to."

"Where is he now?"

"Set off with some of the Baron's men."

Sarah was completely befuddled. Who would make up such lies about her? To what end? Then an even more terrible question came to her.

"Master Dollop, my companions—what of them? Are they prisoners here as well?"

"Nay, Your Highness-ship, and that's somthin' what caused a terrible row. The young man was dead set on them bein' killed, and the Baron, he was naturally agreeable, so he sent out a band of foresters to take care of things. But them foresters got scared when they saw they was up against real fightin' men, and they slipped away and let 'em be.

"I wouldn't wanna be one of them foresters now. The Baron was mighty angry over bein' disobeyed. I reckon them foresters are likely hangin' from trees with their guts drippin' out."

"My companions are safe, then?"

"I don't rightly know. The Baron sent out riders, but they couldn't find hide nor hair of 'em. No one knows where they got to."

This was encouraging news. The disappearance of her friends meant that they were probably alive and safe. And if so, they would be planning a rescue. But how would they ever find her? And if they did, how could three men and a dwarf storm a castle? Her situation seemed hopeless.

And who was her mysterious fiancé? Dollop described him as young, attractive, and tall—not much to go on. Then a thought struck her. The false magician had been tall. True, he had been old and stooped, but could this not have been part of an elaborate disguise? His long gray beard had been a sham. Could he have been a young man made up to appear old?

Why was he plotting against her? If the false fiancé was in sooth the same as the false magician, he knew she was no princess. What could he hope to gain by having her seized and held? There would be no royal ransom. Perhaps her father would pay a modest sum but nothing large enough to pique the greed of a robber-knight like Melgwyn. Nay, she was not worth that much, and her father was too far away.

Worse yet, Babs One-Eye must know she was a magic user. Highborn ladies did not routinely soil their hands by dabbling with the occult, so she must assume that Babs was undeceived by her act. Had she revealed this information to Melgwyn?

Her mind overflowed with more questions. Who was the young man? What did he want from her? Where were her friends? And most importantly, what would Melgwyn do when he learned she was not the Grand Ducal Highness Sarafina? Would her head end up on the castle gate? Or would she be bound to a tree and disemboweled?

She saw only one possible chance, and it was a long shot—Dollop. He seemed to adore the idea of her being a princess. If she could persuade him…

"Master Dollop, I can see you are a good man with a true heart. I beg you to take pity on me. I am but a helpless girl undone by the lies of a scheming, deceiving blackguard. Won't you help me?"

"Certes! But what can I do for you, Your Highness-ship? I already brang you food and a blanket and a clean slop bucket. What else?"

"Help me escape from this filthy cell, from Baron Melgwyn and his horrible castle. Help me find my friends, and you will be well rewarded."

Dollop's mouth fell open. He raised his fat hands as if to ward off a blow. His voice was shrill with the intensity of his reaction.

"Your Princess-ness! God forfend—ask me anything, but *that* I cannot do!"

"But you must, Dollop. You simply must. I have no other friend to call upon, so it has to be you. I'm begging you…please, please, please."

Dollop shook his head emphatically, as if it were being pulled back and forth by the ears.

"I cannot, milady. Please, do not ask it of me. The Baron would most certain pluck out my eyes for just discussin' it. You can't imagine how cruel he can be."

Sarah was getting nowhere—her gaoler was simply too frightened of his master. But maybe she could wear him down a little at a time. Time was something she seemed to have in abundance.

She finished the last of the wine that had come with her dinner. *Damn!* She had to pee again.

"I understand, Master Dollop. But could I ask one small courtesy— something entirely different?"

'Anythin', Your Princess-ness—anythin' 'cept that one thing. You must not even speak it."

"Could I trouble you to turn your back for a moment or two?"

CHAPTER 43

A VIEW OF CASTLE SKYNSLIP

Thurmond's eye opened—eye—not *eyes*—for only the right one seemed to be functioning. Actually, the left one was pressed down in the dirt with the entire left side of his face, but he was as yet unaware of this particular detail. The cheery morning sun sent a lance of agony through his dehydrated brain.

From where he lay, he could see Roscoe, flopped on his belly, unmoving, arms and legs splayed wide. His mouth hung open, and his protruding tongue seemed to be covered with gray fuzz. Beyond him, Torgul was on hands and knees, creeping slowly toward a clump of bushes. Bodo was nowhere to be seen. Pozi was on her side, curled up with her knees against her chest.

It had all started out so well, a rollicking good time with huge flagons of nut-brown ale. Then the bandits, now designated as Baidan's royal guardsmen, had rolled out a barrel of their special homebrew, a drink they called *crackskull*. Its recipe was supposedly a closely kept secret, but after the first dram, they all boasted of its esoteric ingredients. It was a decoction of mildewed rye, fortified with an exotic assortment of toxic berries, baneful roots, and mushrooms—all known for their mind-bending properties. Also the poison glands of sundry malefic reptiles and the venom sacs of select insects.

Like good fortune, good times have to be paid for, and Thurmond was paying for his now. As his blood began again to circulate, he grew all too aware of the true depth of his misery. His stomach was in open rebellion, as if trying to tear itself free and escape from his body. He thought perhaps his skull was being ground between two millstones. Were his teeth loose in their sockets?

He risked a whisper.

"Roscoe, are you alive?"

Those three short words sent a hot shot of anguish spiraling through his brain.

"Roscoe!"

The young man was gratified to see the old Adventurer's finger begin to twitch. His friend was still among the living, though he might be suffering permanent brain damage. With the greatest effort, Thurmond dragged himself to his feet. He heard Torgul retching in the weeds and decided to join him. After a few moments, Roscoe did the same.

After a great emptying of stomachs and copious amounts of cool water, their senses started to clear. Thurmond remembered Bodo and cast his eyes into the branches of a nearby tree. Sure enough, there he was, still asleep, drooping over a limb high overhead. It was the bandits' beloved local custom to place their besotted comrades in awkward or embarrassing situations. He dimly recalled helping the royal guardsmen haul the unfortunate Bodo up there with a rope, laughing all the while.

Pozi continued to slumber. She had passed out after a single small cup of crackskull, consumed from the same wooden cannikin the bandits had previously placed upon her head as a target. Thurmond was seriously considering a nap when Roscoe laid a heavy hand on his shoulder.

"Laddie, I'm havin' a bit o' difficulty with my memory at the moment. Did we really do some of the nefarious deeds I seem to recollect?"

"Aye, most likely we did."

"I was afraid of that. Did I truly make knights of Baidan and his boyos?"

"Aye, with great flourish and formality, though I think it was the first time the words *rub-a-dub-dub* were ever used in such a ceremony."

"Oooohhh, this is grim indeed, so it is. I'll never drink again."

Then Baidan appeared, bustling with energy, taking huge steps, his voice booming, apparently unfazed by his men's vile potion. His smile was an evil grimace that was somehow more frightening than his frown.

"Ha! Not lookin' too good, you. Can't drink like a man, you? Time a-go now!"

The old Adventurer was at a loss.

"Go where…uh…Your Majesty?"

"Go lookit my castle. Gonna open the door pretty soon, you."

The bandit king strode over to Skrot, who lay asleep with his head on a saddle, and gave him a resounding kick in the ribs.

"Up! Time a-go, you."

Thurmond peeked over the edge of a rocky rim at Castle Skynslip far below. It was not, as castles go, a large structure—a single rectangular tower with a steeply pitched roof. It was, however, extremely well situated for defense, rising straight up from a sheer granite knob that jutted from the side of a vertical cliff face. A deep moat was cut into the rocky cliffside, isolating the tower from the landward side. The opposite side needed no moat, for the ravine plunged straight down for more than a hundred feet.

An intricate maze of curtain walls encircled the tower. These were unusually low, often no higher than the chest height of a man, but that was enough, for the steep sides of the moat and the cliff served as the castle's real guardians. The low walls were simply parapets atop walls of living granite.

A road wound torturously along the side of the gorge, leading to a drawbridge and a gatehouse. The structure was topped by a crenellated battlement on which decaying human skulls grinned down from between its merlons. The bridge and gates stood open, defended by two men-at-arms in long quilted coats and armed with spears. They were not particularly attentive to their duty as they loafed in the afternoon sunshine and apparently finding great amusement in throwing large chunks of stone into the moat.

Roscoe turned to Skrot who was serving as Baidan's translator. The bandit-king's command of the common tongue was not sufficient for the specific details the old Adventurer needed to find out.

"At night, do they keep the gates closed and the drawbridge raised?"

Skrot nodded.

"That's what Baidan said. *Shut as tight as Blue Friar's butt*—that's what he said."

"And is there a portcullis they can drop down behind them gates?"

There was a heated exchange as Skrot strove to make himself understood. He turned once more to Roscoe.

"Nay."

"Nay? All that palaver, and all I get is *nay*? What else did he say?"

"He got mad 'cause he don't know what a portcullis is, said he was gonna pull off one of my ears. He got even madder when I tried to explain."

"But he understands now?"

"I think so. He says there ain't nothin' else behind the gates. They're the last barrier."

Torgul piped up, entirely recovered from the hijinks of the night before. His eyes gleamed. He was in his element—dwarves were typically fond of siege-craft.

"Give me a hundred of my people, and we'd carve you a tunnel straight into the heart of that pile. Or we could level off the top of this ridge and set up a line of stone-casters. That'd keep their heads down while we threw an assault bridge across the moat."

Roscoe offered his friend a benign smile.

"Now those be right fine ideas, so they are. But we ain't got time for tunnels nor stone-casters nor assault bridges, even if we had a thousand dwarves. We must find a quicker way to rescue Sarah. Any ideas?"

Torgul grumbled and shook his head.

"Thurmond? Bodo? Can you boyos think of somethin'?"

Neither did.

Pozi who broke the silence.

"Will it help if I climb up there and open the gates?"

The men's heads swiveled in her direction. Roscoe proffered the same smile he had given Torgul.

"Lassie, take a look at those walls, how smooth they are. There's nary a handhold to be had. Nobody could climb up there. And looky there how the sides o' the moat is almost as bad."

But the girl was emphatic.

"I'm a mountain girl. I could climb the sides of that moat. You're right about those walls—smooth as ice from the look of 'em—but I think I see a place."

She pointed at a cluster of arrow slits on the left side of the tower. At that point, there was no curtain wall, for that section of tower was well beyond the limit of the moat and stood at the very edge of the long, long drop to the rocks at the bottom of the gorge.

"Look just to the left of the third little skinny window, then look down a bit. See that little hole? I bet I could climb up and squeeze through there."

Thurmond followed her pointing finger until he found the spot in question. A small square opening did indeed penetrate the side of the tower. He didn't like what he saw.

"Pozi, in case you haven't noticed, you can't climb to that place from the moat. It's out too far. You'd have to crawl sideways along the cliff—out over open space. If you fell off … well … that'd be the end of you."

Roscoe found her idea amusing.

"You know what that little hole is, girl? That's a shite-chute for sure. See them stains underneath it? That ain't honey."

This was an unusual feature. The typical castle garderobe projected straight out from a wall so waste dropped directly into a moat or cesspit. This one was nothing more than a narrow opening with a slight lip, presumably connected by a sloping channel to the privy above. The waste, therefore, dripped down the tower's wall.

Pozi was unconcerned.

"Aye, I see the stains. Look how those vines are growing up the wall just there. They must like the shite. If I can make it along the cliff until I'm under the hole, I can use them to pull myself up to it. There'll be almost a half moon tonight, so I'll have plenty of light."

Thurmond grew agitated. He had an ominous sense of where this talk might lead. He tried to discourage her.

"You can't go crawling through that hole. That's a stinking privy. You'll get covered in dung."

"Shite washes off. I've helped Mama clean my baby brothers and sisters many times. And I helped Papa manure his turnip fields. The only thing—I don't want to ruin my dress. Mama made it special for me."

Roscoe's eyes twinkled as the always did when he was planning some desperate deed. He was in complete awe of the girl's utter lack of fear.

"If you can really do this thing, Pozi, I'll buy you the prettiest dress you ever saw, with shoes to match!"

Pozi smiled, then paused.

"A store-bought dress? With shoes? I'll do it! Which one of you is coming with me? I might not be strong enough to open the gates by myself."

All eyes turned on Thurmond, and Roscoe beamed.

"Looks like you're elected, Prospect. You're the only one lean enough to fit through that hole, so you are. If it's a bit of a tight fit…well then…a slatherin' of shite might help you slip through a mite easier."

This was precisely what Thurmond feared, exactly what he anticipated. He was prepared to risk his life by scaling up and down the sides of the moat and scrambling along that terrible cliffside. He was willing to trust the vines to hold his weight, and he was even eager to face Sarah's abductors in close combat. But the thought of inching up the shite-chute filled him with overpowering revulsion.

He had no choice. Roscoe had called him *Prospect*, a not-so-subtle reminder that he was sworn to obey his Adventurer mentor.

And Lady Fortune was not quite done with him yet. Skrot was engaged in a murmured conversation with Baidan. Then he sidled over and spoke to Roscoe.

"Baidan wants you to know there's three or four savage bears down in the moat. Melgwyn keeps 'em real hungry and real mean. That's why the gate guards are throwin' rocks down there—keepin' 'em mean."

Dollop brought Sarah her evening meal and sat down for their accustomed chat. She could see something was agitating him, something that he was trying, not very successfully, to conceal.

"What is it, Master Dollop? You've got news for me. What is it? Does it concern my friends? Please, do tell."

His eyes looked off to his left.

"Ain't nothin', Your Princess-ness. Just one of the kitchen girls thinks she might be with child. Nothin' unusual 'bout that."

He was obviously lying.

"Master Dollop, I beg you. Tell me the truth, even if it's something dreadful. It's most obvious you really want to share it with me."

He hesitated, uncertain, then his resolve weakened.

"First off, Maggie really does think she's carryin', so I warn't lyin' to you, Your Highness-ness. But I just don't know quite how to tell you about a thing I just heard."

"Just say it, Dollop. Don't hold back."

"I was in the great hall fetchin' your supper, see, gettin' some slices of that venison you're eatin', and the Baron, he was talkin' to his men. They was drinkin' and was laughin' real loud. Then the Baron says ransom or no ransom, he's keepin' you for hisself."

Panic seized Sarah's stomach like the hairy hand of ogre. Her mouth opened, but she remained speechless.

Dollop continued.

"He says you bein' so highborn an' all, he'll marry you, so it won't be like you was really stolen. After the ransom is paid, he'll send word to your father that you was so grateful for bein' saved from bandits that you fell in love—that's what he said—then he can keep the ransom as dowry."

The ogre hand squeezed so hard Sarah thought she might throw up. The rest of the story, the worst part, spilled from Dollop in a torrent.

"This is bad, Your Highness-ship, 'cause I knows what always happens to the Baron's wives. He's had three in the past five years, and ain't one of 'em lasted more than a few months afore he grew tired of 'em. When that happens, it gets bad, milady, bad and sad."

Sarah struggled to gain control of her fear. Panic would serve no purpose. Only cold reason could help her now.

"Please explain, Master Dollop. What happened?"

"Well, the first two was real nice girls, pretty just like you, and they was brought up to be proper wives to a man like the Baron. But even that couldn't save 'em. Right off, he starts beatin' 'em, so they'd come to table with bruises and cuts on their faces. Then after a while, he didn't let 'em come down no more but kept 'em locked up in their chambers like prisoners in a cell. Then he..."

His voice trailed off.

"Please go on, Dollop. What did he do?"

"It got worse. First he gives 'em to his men to do as they pleased with 'em. Right out in the great hall. Right on the table where they eat their dinners. In front of the servants and everybody. In front of me!"

Dollop's voice grew strident as anger and fear rose in his throat.

"And then they died. Milady Delores, she bein' the first wife, she was found on the rocks way down in the bottom of the gorge. They say she slipped and fell off the wall, but I knows different. She was either flung there or jumped off in her misery. They threw Milady Trista, she were the next one, off the drawbridge into the moat. There was people seen 'em do it. The bears got her."

Sarah was now trembling. She struggled to control the quaver in her voice.

"You said the Baron had three wives. What of the third?"

"His last baroness, Milady Dulcie—that's the most heartbreakin' tale of 'em all. She was a lovely young thing, even younger than you. Nothin' more than a child really, but sweet and happy. Fond of cherries, she was. I brang her some once, and they made her clap her hands and giggle for joy. Them cherries were her undoin'.

"The Baron—he didn't like that giggle. One night at table, after they served up a compote of sweet cherries, poor milady forgot herself and giggled anyway. Well, the Baron, he stands up and says somethin' quiet to his men, and she didn't giggle no more...never again."

CHAPTER 44

The Whelming of Castle Skynslip, Part One

"God's guts, Roscoe, it's too dark. I can't see what I'm doing."

"All to the good, boyo, all to the good. The moon'll be up soon enough, so it will. But the dark is our friend while Baidan gets his men set. This will only work if we can catch 'em with their drawers down."

Pozi had already scurried down the rope to the bottom of the moat. There was no sound of her being ripped apart, so it seemed the bears were fast asleep. Hours earlier they had been fed haunches of meat heavily laced with the vision-inducing concoction used to fortify crackskull. After an extended period of frantic bellowing, the ferocious creatures had settled down in the shadows and were heard from no more. The bandits had complained mightily that this was the last of their special mixture, that it would take months of gathering to procure the essential ingredients for a fresh batch, but Roscoe had been adamant, and Baidan had at last relented.

With a sigh, Thurmond eased over the edge and went down the rope as quickly as he could. He wore no armor; his mail having been left behind in Pozi's village. His helmet and shield were deemed too cumbersome for climbing and sneaking. Even the box of glass globes was left with Torgul for fear a fall might activate the enclosed magic at an awkward moment.

At the moat's bottom, there was still no sign of Pozi.

Then the first pale beam of moonlight crept over the battlements of Castle Skynslip and illuminated the spot on which he stood. There, no more than three paces away, was the black mass of a sleeping bear.

No human foe had ever filled Thurmond with such dread. Perhaps it was some dim ancestral memory of when his cave-dwelling forefathers had fought such creatures for possession of a berry patch. Whatever it was, Thurmond froze. He did not draw his sword, did not even think to do so. His brain seemed to have shut down, leaving only a crushing fear.

Pozi's whisper came out of the darkness, breaking the paralysis.

"Come on, Thurmond. You gonna stand there all night? We have to get going."

The bear snored gently, no doubt enjoying weird visions of bruin ecstasy. It would be distinctly ill-tempered in the morning, however.

"Thurmond, are you coming?"

The girl stood at the far end of the moat. Intent on its inner wall, she did not seem to notice she was balanced on the very edge of the precipice. There was no barrier there as the moat simply dropped off into open space. Nothing but their own good sense kept the bears from plummeting to their doom.

Pozi began to climb, a long rope wound around her hips. Thurmond could see her readily in the emerging moonlight, but both of them, positioned as they were, would be invisible to anyone in the castle. True to her word, she scaled the moat's inner wall without difficulty, pausing only to brush the hair from her eyes.

A length of rope suddenly landed at Thurmond's feet. That was the signal—it was time to go up. Pozi had tied the other end to something solid—a root or a stone. He gave it several hard yanks, testing the purchase, and shinnied up, hand over hand.

At the top, Pozi clung to the wall as effortlessly as a lizard. The rope, Thurmond was dismayed to find, was looped around a knob of rock no bigger than his thumb. The young man seized the projection in a death grip.

With one hand, Pozi drew up the rope's other end and wrapped it over her shoulder. She set out across the face of the cliff, paying out the rope as she went along. When directly below the shite-chute, she used the vines to clamber up to the hole. In an instant, she disappeared inside.

The rope went taut. This meant Pozi was within the privy and had tied it off at that end. It was now Thurmond's lifeline into the castle. He buckled himself to it with a stout leather strap and set out over the void. Twice, his feet slid from the tiny stone ledges on which he stood, and frequently his fingers slipped from the nubbins of rock to which he sought to cling. If not for the lifeline, he must have been hurled to the rocks below.

The shite-chute was every bit as disgusting as he expected, but after the soul-numbing encounter with a drugged bear and nerve-shattering creep over a bottomless gorge, mere human waste had lost most of its horror. When he at last stood in the privy—his clothes, face, and hands thoroughly smeared with filth—there was again no sign of Pozi. The privy door began to creak open. He drew his dagger, fearing discovery, but it was only his lost companion, equally covered in dung. God's holy breath—did he reek as bad as she did?

Pozi raised a finger to her lips, winked, and beckoned for him to follow. As he drew nigh, she leaned close to whisper.

"This passage leads to the great hall. There's a big set of steps leading down to it. Nobody's about."

They made their way as silently as they could, though the scrape of their soft boots on the floorboards sounded in their ears like a charge of heavy cavalry. The great hall was not as deserted as Pozi had thought. Several bodies lay sprawled by the enormous hearth, its once furious blaze now reduced to a bed of red-hot embers. Discarded flagons and empty wine jugs suggested that these men were heavily in their cups.

Thurmond and Pozi glided through the room as quickly as they dared and crept down the spiral staircase at the far end. As in many towers, this great hall was located one floor up from ground level. Somewhere below, they would find an exit. The lower room was large and served as a storeroom. The huge door was high enough for a man on a horse to pass through without ducking and sufficiently wide for a large farm wagon to be drawn inside. Luckily, a small door was inset in the larger one. Thurmond threw the bolts and stepped into the moonlit courtyard.

He saw no one. No lookout stood atop the gate, and no sentries paced the battlements. A small hut, presumably a guardroom, stood just inside the gate. Neither light nor sound came from within. Baron Melgwyn's soldiers were not especially vigilant.

All was proceeding according to plan. Pozi kept watch while Thurmond moved across the courtyard to the gates. These were secured by a thick oaken bar and four heavy iron bolts. The first three drew easily, but the last was rust-covered and emitted a complaining *skreet*. That *skreet* was not especially loud, but 'twas enough, for it loosed a swarm of hell-fiends from a shadowy corner of the courtyard. They came in a horrific torrent, squawking and flapping, their bodies obscenely white in the moonlight. Necks outstretched as they moved to attack. *Geese!*

The furious geese immediately set upon Pozi. She shrieked and ran for her life, the flock hot behind her. They disappeared into the darkness, the girl screaming, the birds honking. Occupied with the gates, Thurmond could spare no time for Pozi. He pulled the bar from the massive brackets, but before he could open the gates, he had to drop the drawbridge. This was raised and lowered by a heavy hawser wound around a large windlass. There must be, he knew, a catch that would release it, but he had no time to look for it.

Sheathing his sword, he pulled a hatchet from the back of his belt. Skrot had given it to him just before he climbed into the moat, the same one he stole when he deserted the adventure party. *One...two...three*—Thurmond gave the rope a series of hard blows, but still it held.

"Hey, you! Stop that!"

A man emerged from the guard hut. He was barefoot and wore no armor, but he carried an evil-looking polearm—some kind of axe with a long spike on top and a hook on the back. Thurmond hurled the hatchet at the guard's face and drew his sword as the man dodged out of its way. Without a shield, Thurmond knew he stood little chance. His sword would not deflect the heavy blade of the polearm, and penned as he was against the drawbridge, he had no room to maneuver. His only chance was to close, to get inside the range of the longer weapon.

The man came on, keeping the point aimed at Thurmond's face, weaving, feinting—he was obviously an experienced fighter. He dropped the point as if going for a groin shot, and then spun it up for a slash to the face. Thurmond ducked, and the axe blade bit a chunk from the wood of the gate.

Rising up, Thurmond flicked out the tip of his sword and nipped off the man's left thumb. He sprang forward and seized the polearm's haft, wrenching it from his foe's weakened grasp. The man flung himself backward and threw up his hands in a doomed effort to ward off Thurmond's sword. Too late! Thurmond's first blow took him in the forehead, sending him to his knees. The second opened the base of his neck. That did for him.

Another man appeared in the doorway of the guard hut, but he held back, unwilling to face the unknown intruder who had slain his comrade. A horn blew from somewhere, and confused voices called out in the night. The castle was rousing. There was no more time. Thurmond lashed savagely at the stubborn hawser with this sword. The sharp blade sent fragments of hemp spraying through the air. At last the great line parted, and the bridge fell with a great wooden *wham.*

When Thurmond pushed opened the gates, the bandits gave a throaty war cry and sprang from their concealed positions on the far side of the moat. They surged onto the bridge, Baidan at their head with Roscoe, Torgul, and Bodo close behind. Thurmond turned and sprinted for the tower. He had to get there before someone bolted the outer door. It was vital to hold it open to give the bandits a point of entry. Arrows and crossbow bolts began to fly from slits in the structure's upper floors. One went by his ear with the hiss of an adder.

As the first bandits entered the courtyard, two were cut down by the ever-increasing hail of archery, forcing their comrades to seek shelter behind the barrels, carts, and benches strewn about the yard. Three entered the guard hut where they slaughtered the cowardly porter who had refused to engage Thurmond at the gate.

Thankfully, the small, man-size door still stood ajar. Thurmond darted inside and was struggling to open the large door, when the first man-at-arms came down the stairs from the great hall. He was dressed in mail and helmet, armed with sword and shield. Their eyes locked in silent acknowledgment that they were for each other.

Out in the courtyard, Torgul saw Thurmond enter the small door and understood his purpose. Defying the storm of arrows, he charged forth, a dwarven war-chant on his lips. Arrows buzzed around him like a hive of enraged wasps. On he went, bursting into the tower with Bloodtroll at high port.

Suddenly beset by two foes, the man-at-arms paused and took a step back as a very tall soldier emerged from the stairs and stood by his side. Shouts from above suggested any number of others were coming down.

Coming abreast of Thurmond, Torgul dug into a leather pouch hanging from his neck and thrust something into his comrade's hands.

"Here, boy, use these things. I'll hold 'em."

It was the box of colored spheres.

The two men-at-arms advanced, close together, shields held high, and swords raised. The dwarf ran to meet them, leaned slightly left, but then pivoted right and lashed out with his axe. Splinters of wood flew from his opponent's shield. The tall soldier tried to come in from the side, but Torgul kept shifting right, skillfully keeping out of reach while raining blows on the shorter one.

Thurmond was fumbling with the box lid when he noticed that the two men-at-arms, with their attention focused on Torgul, had apparently forgotten about him. The tall soldier was no more than three feet away, offering an easy shot at his unguarded back. He was, however, protected by a thigh-length habergeon and coif of mail.

Thurmond wasted no time. He dragged the edge of his blade across the backs of the man's knees, severing his hamstrings. The tall soldier dropped in a heap. But even as he did, three more soldiers emerged from the stairs and formed up to join the fray.

Torgul broke away from the fight to stand with his companion. His opponent, winded, seemed relieved for the respite. Spittle flew from the dwarf's lips as he shouted at Thurmond.

"Damn it, boy, the magic! Hurry it!"

With no time to think about it, Thurmond grabbed the purple globe and threw it at the knot of enemies now moving to the attack. There was no flash of light, no thunderclap, not even a cloud of purple mist. No dazzling wonderment to be seen or heard.

But the men started to dance…sort of. At least they started to move in a fashion that might be called dancing. They stomped with jerky, broken rhythm. Weapons dropped from nerveless fingers as arms waved and flapped as if possessed by evil spirits. Tongues hung slack from gaping mouths. Eyes drooped, void of reason or volition.

Thurmond looked at Torgul.

"Should we kill 'em?"

"No time. I'm gonna open the big door for Baidan's boys. You make sure nobody locks the door up above. Go!"

This conversation was nearly Thurmond's undoing, for the hamstrung soldier, crawling on his knees, had inched up behind him unseen and was about to bury a sword in his exposed back. Torgul, however, caught the movement from the corner of his eye. Bloodtroll's enchanted blade flashed red as it sheared through the man's mailshirt and into his lungs.

Thurmond paused long enough to take the dead soldier's shield. Then he bolted for the stairs. He heard the scrape of the large door being dragged open, and Torgul's deep, guttural voice called to the bandits to come join them. Then the dwarf was beside him again.

"Let's go, Prospect. We don't want the boys gettin' bottled up on these stairs."

Torgul was entirely correct. They needed to secure the great hall, so up they went—Thurmond first, crouching behind his shield.

No foeman opposed them, for the great hall was deserted. Melgwyn and his remaining men were apparently content to shoot arrows from the upper floors. They apparently had no idea that their enemies had entered the tower.

Shouts came from below as Baidan's men charged into the tower's ground floor and butchered the dancing soldiers. They would be up the stairs in a trice.

Torgul grabbed Thurmond's arm.

"We gotta find Sarah and get her the hell out of here. While you was down in the moat, Skrot told us somethin' bad. Seems Baidan's decided that havin' a crown and castle ain't enough. He's been sayin' a king's gotta have a queen. He's plannin' to keep Sarah for himself."

Thurmond was not surprised. Since their first meeting, he had anticipated bad trouble with the volatile bandit chief. At that moment, Ouichi led a dozen men into the great hall. Thurmond pointed up the broad stairs with the point of his sword.

"That way! The treasure room is on the top floor! Gold! Gold!"

It was unlikely any of the bandits understood his words, but they had come to conquer and needed no encouragement. They started up the steps, but their way was unexpectedly blocked by the sudden appearance of Melgwyn and his knights at the top. The bandits, eager for a fight, kept right on climbing.

Although outnumbered, the baron's men had a distinct advantage. They were better armored and more skilled with weapons. The stairs, though broad, allowed no more than three or four bandits to ascend abreast, so their weight of numbers could not be brought to bear. And from their higher position, the knights could strike down over the tops of their opponents' shields.

The clash of steel and screams of agony reverberated from the stone walls of the great hall. Two crossbowmen appeared behind the knights and fired whenever a target presented itself. One of their bolts passed clean through the throat of a tall bandit in a bearskin tunic.

Thurmond and Torgul ducked into an alcove. The companions had agreed to allow the bandits to do the fighting whenever possible. Baidan was welcome to the castle and whatever riches it held. Thurmond just wanted to find Sarah and get out.

CHAPTER 45

THE WHELMING OF CASTLE SKYNSLIP, PART TWO

Thurmond noticed a flicker of movement in a passageway on the far side of the great hall. Was a foeman lurking there, waiting to take them unawares? He nudged Torgul, and the pair darted across the room, zigzagging to frustrate the aim of the crossbowmen on the stairs. The dwarf ducked behind a pillar and gestured for his companion to go on. He would stay behind to keep the way open.

Thurmond entered the passage, just as a man disappeared down a flight of stairs. He raced after him. At the bottom, the man turned. He was very large, but soft and shaped like a gourd. In one hand he gripped a kitchen cleaver, in the other a three-legged stool that he held like a shield. It was obvious that this round fellow was no warrior. He looked more like the castle cook. Thurmond sneered as he spoke to the man, hoping to scare him.

"Put down the cleaver! I have no reason to kill you, so don't give me one."

The man said nothing but did not drop the weapon. He just stood there.

Thurmond had no time for such nonsense.

"I'll give you one more second. Put it down, or I'll carve your guts just as sure as you're standin' there."

In truth, he had no desire to hurt the gourd-shaped man, but he needed to frighten him. In this he succeeded. When the man at last spoke, his voice was high-pitched with terror.

"Then you'll have to kill me. Princess Sarafina is in my charge. I'll defend her as long as I be breathin'."

What? This was not what Thurmond expected to hear. Was the man speaking about Sarah? If so, he might be useful.

"Put down the cleaver and take me to her. Do that, and you'll live."

"I'll not! I'll die afore I give her over to a stinkin' brigand like you!"

Thurmond was insulted.

"I'm no brigand, you great oaf! I'm her closest friend."

"Then why'd you come here with them Slovag savages, huh? They ain't here for nothin' but blood and gold."

Thurmond had to admit that the guy had a point. He had not only come in the company of Slovag bandits, he also looked like one of them. He had no armor, and his clothing was foul with privy filth. His hair had grown long and matted from the many weeks of their journey. He lowered his sword.

"Look you, I'm not at my best right now, all right? I'm here to save Sarah from this Melgwyn, but I don't have much time. Either you help me, or, by God's great belly, I will carve you up. Anyway, do I sound like a Slovag?"

"Nay, you does not. You claims you and the princess are friends, so she'd know your face if she set eyes on it?"

"Certes! Take me to her, you'll see."

"Follow me, but keep back a pace. I'm tellin' you, though, this cleaver is terrible sharp. You're like to kill me, but I'll get me somethin' of yours afore you do."

With that, the round man walked backward down the passageway, his eyes never leaving Thurmond's. When he came to another flight of steps, he backed down them without faltering. Thurmond followed as instructed, alert for a sudden attack. He risked one quick glance over his shoulder and followed down the stairs.

The lower corridor was narrower, shorter. When the big man disappeared around a bend, Thurmond tensed, expecting trouble, but then the man reappeared and beckoned.

"Come on. She's right here."

Still suspicious, Thurmond stepped around the corner. The man stood in a small stone chamber, behind him was a cell door comprised of flat iron bars. Sarah stood on the other side, just visible in the dim light.

She squealed in delight.

"Thurmond! You came! Ohhh, I was losing hope. Dollop, this is my friend Thurmond. Please, you can let me out now."

Thurmond shot Dollop a smug look.

"Satisfied?"

The gaoler did not reply but busied himself unlocking the cell with a massive key from a peg on the wall. Sarah shot from the cell as if launched from a catapult and threw her arms around Thurmond's neck. She planted her lips on his and then just as abruptly pushed him away.

"Argh, you stink! What have you gotten into?"

"Long story—tell you later. We've gotta get out of here. Here, take these."

He handed her the leather box with the three remaining glass globes. She turned to Dollop.

"The Baron will crucify you when he discovers I'm gone. You must come with us."

The round man shook his head.

"Nay, Your Princess-ness. There's a battle bein' fought upstairs. Whoever wins is gonna blame the losers for you bein' gone, so that don't worry me none. I got the kitchen girls hidin' in my chamber. I gotta get them into a hidey-hole so don't nobody hurt 'em."

"Bring them with us! We'll keep you all safe."

"Nay, bad as it be sometimes, this is our home. They'd be too scared to leave it. I reckon I would be, too."

Sarah placed her hands on the gaoler's shoulders and kissed him lightly on the lips.

"Master Dollop, you are a very good man—far more a true gentleman than that evil baron you serve. You've been most kind to me, and I thank you for it. I will always remember you."

"Goodbye, Your Princess-ness."

Thurmond took Sarah's hand and led her up the steps to the long passage, then up the second flight to the great hall. They peeked into the room. The battle for the stairs still raged. Half the outlaws lay dead, slumped in grotesque postures on the uneven surface of the steps. Ouichi still lived, bellowing like a gored buffalo as his axe rose and fell.

Melgwyn, too, remained on his feet, though several of his men were down, and the fighting seemed to be tipping against him. His crossbowmen, out of bolts, had abandoned their bows and drawn their swords.

Torgul stepped from his hiding place and beckoned toward the stairs that led to the entrance hall. Thurmond and Sarah remained unnoticed as they crossed the room. They were about to descend when Baidan and another dozen bandits came charging up the stairs from below. Seeing Sarah, his eyes gleamed with sordid desire. He opened his mouth to speak, but before he could, Sarah threw a glass globe, the green one. It burst square on his chest.

As one, Baidan and his men gagged, sneezed, and clawed at their bodies as if they would tear themselves loose from their skins. Great slobbers of mucus ran from their noses and eyes. As their bodies erupted with angry red bumps, they threw off their clothes and dug at themselves with dirty fingernails.

Thurmond, Sarah, and Torgul went down the stairs as fast as their feet could fly. The lower floor had been transformed into a slaughterhouse, the hacked bodies of the dancing soldiers were lying in a bloody heap. The bandits had even taken the time to remove their heads and stack them in a neat pile.

Thurmond guessed that these were the men sleeping by the hearth when he and Pozi had crossed the great hall. *Pozi!* What had become of her? And Roscoe, where was he? Had he been hit by one of Melgwyn's archers? Thurmond clutched at the sleeve of the dwarf's mailshirt.

"Torgul, where's Roscoe?"

"When we came across the drawbridge, he heard Pozi screamin' and went to save her. Skrot stayed at the gates to make sure nobody tried to close 'em. We're gonna meet up there. We gotta get out quick. Bodo has the horses on the other side of the moat."

Sarah was of course entirely ignorant of recent events, confused by the events unfolding around her.

"Pozi? What about Pozi? What happened to her?"

Thurmond did not know how to reply. This was not the time for a lengthy explanation.

"She's joined us again. Don't worry—Roscoe's with her."

They stepped through the large entrance hall door into the castle's courtyard, now dotted with the arrow-pierced bodies of fallen bandits. The trio had hardly started to cross it when Roscoe's voice boomed out of the dark and echoed off the surrounding stone walls.

"Over here, Prospect! We're gathered by the gate!"

The shout was scarcely necessary, as the old Adventurer was quite visible in the lingering moonlight, but he was never one to restrain his enthusiasm. Thurmond was relieved to see Pozi with him. She was filthy and tattered, but seemed otherwise intact. Skrot, too, was there, dressed now in mail and helmet looted from the guard hut. A sword was strapped around his hips, and he again carried the hatchet Thurmond had thrown at the man at the gate.

Roscoe started to say more, but Torgul brushed right by him and bounded across the drawbridge. His message was clear—this was no time for a chat. The others ran after him, their footfalls thumping hollowly on the wooden planks. Bodo was on the other side, holding the horses. It was imperative that nothing interfere with a speedy getaway. Roscoe pulled Pozi up behind him. Her milk-white pony could not keep up with the long-legged horses and was cut loose. The moon was finally setting as they galloped off into the night.

Gavin was so excited that he thought he might have to stop riding and calm down. Everything was perfect. He could feel the hand of Lady Fortune guiding his every move. By now Roscoe and his lackeys would be naught but a pile of rotting corpses, slain by the command of that vicious baron. And the stupid little whore would be under lock and key, awaiting a ransom that would never come.

The baron reminded him of a quarrelsome dog, a yapping, ill-tempered fyce—always eager to nip the hand of the weak, but fawning and docile when confronted with real strength. That strutting, puffed-up creature had certainly put on airs at first, but his manner changed before they finished their first cup of wine. What would the baron do when he realized that the slut was no princess and no ransom would be forthcoming? Why, he would vent his spleen on her, naturally, as if it were her fault. And that was entirely right. It was her fault, her fault entirely. If she had shown the good sense to act properly from the beginning, such ill fortune need not have fallen to her. Let her reap the bitter consequences of her willfulness.

Yet Sarah's suffering at the hands of the querulous dog was of no real import. There were far greater issues to consider, for he was now on the way to claim his rightful place in the world. He had to keep his mind on that. Gavin was by now safely back in Poitiers, riding at top speed along the Royal Highway. His four men-at-arms had turned back at the Bukovian frontier. Better that way—he made faster time when he traveled alone. He would, sooner or later, have had to dispose of them in any case.

Gone was the garb and bristling mustache of a young Bukovian lordling. Gone, too, was the guise of the heartbroken swain. Gone the courser he had ridden into that baron's dreadful little castle. Now he wore the livery of a Royal Courier. A badge of office hung around his neck, and the official dispatch pouch bore the kingdom's royal arms. Having encountered the royal messenger was a great stroke of luck. His moldering remains were now concealed in a creek just west of the city of Vistu. The pouch contained but a single missive, which Gavin had opened and flawlessly resealed at the first opportunity. Its contents were uninteresting—only a report about an unsuccessful raid by Slovag bandits several weeks earlier on an eastward bound caravan.

The livery and the badge were a great boon. They entitled him to meals, lodging, and fresh horses at all wayside inns and villages. Royal Couriers always enjoyed right-of-way, so overloaded farm wains and even great caravans had to pull aside to let him pass. At the pace he was traveling, he would soon be back in Gorgonholm. There would be no major obstacle to him finally realizing his great ambition—an estate of his own. He would have serfs to till his fields and servants to prepare his meals, stables for his horses and kennels for his hounds, mews for his hawks, and a forest in which he could hunt.

There would be a marriage, of course, with the bride ever so carefully selected. With her would come the title. And after that, who could say? With his extraordinary powers, he was sure to rise quickly through the ranks of the nobility. With some deft maneuvering and a dash of treachery, could he not expect to ascend to a barony or even an earldom?

At his current pace, he would arrive in Grimsgard, the freehold of the fat, crippled lout, within two days. It was a grubby little place, but it was the key to everything.

CHAPTER 46

THURMOND'S EPIPHANY

It seemed unlikely that either the bandit or the baron would mount a hot pursuit. Both might well be dead. Baidan's boys had definitely been winning the battle, so Melgwyn might now be lying with his throat cut on the floor of his own great hall. On the other hand, the outlaw chief could have succumbed to the strangling gas from Sarah's green glass orb.

But if either of their adversaries survived, there could be trouble ahead. Both had expressed a desire to possess Sarah, and both were crazy enough to try to steal her back. Knowing they must put many leagues between themselves and Castle Skynslip, the companions turned their horses and rode west as quickly as the black Bukovian night would permit.

They stopped briefly at their former campsite to recover their buried gold and Sarah's magical paraphernalia. Once free of Skynslip's baleful influence, her psychic energy surged back, allowing her to renew the illusion spell that again made the sacks of coins appear as nothing more valuable than crumbling books.

Thurmond and Pozi quickly changed out of their filth-encrusted clothes. The girl at first balked at the breeches and tunic offered to her by Sarah, on the grounds they were boy's garments. But no proper feminine attire was available, so she eventually acquiesced. Back on the road, they shared their stories from the last couple days. Sarah told of her imprisonment, her encounter with Melgwyn, and the kindness of Dollop. She then learned of the coming of Pozi and of her friends' adventures with the bandits. Roscoe related how he saved Pozi from the geese.

"There I was, chargin' across the drawbridge, arrows flyin' by me like bolts of lightnin'. All I could think of was gettin' into that castle and helpin' Thurmond find you, but then, whadda ya know, I hear Pozi screamin' like some goblin had her by the petticoat. So off I goes in that direction.

"And what do you think I found? There she was, sittin' atop the dovecote, surrounded by a gaggle of honkin', hissin', flappin' geese. Well, I just bust out laughin', couldn't help myself. But I could tell Pozi wasn't seein' the humor of the moment, so I lopped off two or three of their little heads—*snick, snick, snick*—and that made the rest of 'em see the error of their ways. They took off scurryin' and squawkin' to places a tad bit safer."

Torgul's voice came from somewhere behind him.

"The way you was runnin', I'd say you were more interested in tryin' out your new leg than rescuin' Pozi."

"Not a'tall, not a'tall. My thoughts were entirely for the girl, so they were."

The sun came up, shining over their shoulders like a beacon pointing the way home. They spurred their mounts, riding hard and fast, the Golden Road unspooling beneath the drumming hooves.

But even the most valiant of heroes must eventually rest, and so it was with this intrepid band. Overcome by exhaustion, they were at last forced to cease their flight and seek repose in a secluded glade. Roscoe and the other men flung themselves beneath an ancient oak. The old Adventurer immediately began to snore.

Thurmond lay back and closed his eyes, but tired as he was, sleep would not come. The night's adventure continued to race through his brain—climbing the wall, the fight at the drawbridge, Sarah locked in a cell.

Torgul, also unable to sleep, spoke to him.

"Funny how it is, how you always think of what you shoulda done after a fight is over, things you never think of while it's goin' on."

This piqued Thurmond's interest. He was always eager to learn new stratagems.

What should we have done different?

"After we was back across, we shoulda knocked down the drawbridge somehow or set the gates on fire. That woulda trapped Baidan and Melgwyn in the castle together. Nobody coulda gotten out, so they woulda had to fight it out to the last man. That's what we shoulda done."

Bodo, also still awake, joined in.

"That would've taken too much time. Better to scatter the bandits' horses."

Thurmond assumed Skrot was fast asleep, but he now rolled over with his eyes wide open.

"Maybe, but what if Melgwyn's men won the battle? We'd be screwed 'cause we wasted time with the wrong horses. Better to just get ridin'."

Sarah and Pozi took no part in this conversation. They sat a little apart, preferring a mossy patch beside a barberry bush. Thurmond had often seen Sarah draw away slightly when he and the other men gathered, but he had never given it much thought. Girls, he assumed, must prefer their own company. But he was puzzled. Why did she take such scant interest in the tricks and dodges of adventuring? Was she not as much a part of the group as any of them?

And then it struck him like an ogre's club. She was not one of them— not really. They all liked and respected Sarah, admired her cool nerve, fierce tenacity, and occult skills. But she was not fully accepted. She was a girl.

So why would she want to sit with the group and engage in their banter? Could it be anything other than a painful reminder that she would always be an outsider? Adventurers were men, plain and simple. She was welcome to tag along with them, but she could never wear the black campaign hat or sport the wyvern tattoo. No wonder she kept herself back.

Thurmond recalled what she had told him before their journey—about her uncertain childhood. How she always felt alone, apart. How deeply she needed to feel connected with something established and legitimate. An idea came to him, and he sat up abruptly.

"Hey, Torgul, why can't girls be Adventurers?"

The dwarf was getting droopy-eyed as his need for sleep crept upon him.

"Uhhh? I dunno, it's just the way it is."

"Nay, I mean it. Why not? Why not Sarah? She's done everything we've done. Why can't she join the Brotherhood?"

Torgul was only halfway paying attention.

"You just said it, Prospect, it's a *brother*hood. That's why."

But the young man was not to be silenced.

"Because of the name? You could change the name. How about the *Society of Underworld Adventurers?*"

Torgul was tired and disinclined to continue the discussion.

"Talk to Roscoe. Maybe he can make you see sense."

With that, the doughty dwarf curled up and went to sleep.

Sarah gave Thurmond a penetrating look. Had she heard what he had said? He could not be certain. Without saying a word, she wrapped herself in her cloak and lay down in the moss to sleep.

Thurmond was unrelenting. As soon as they were in the saddle, he nudged his horse next to Roscoe's.

"If Sarah has endured all the hardships and faced all the dangers same as us, why can't she be an Adventurer?"

His friend, unfortunately, refused to take him seriously.

"Well, that would be a most fearsome sight, wouldn't it now, an Adventurer in a dress. Why goblins and trolls would fall to the ground in fits of mirth, maybe outright die of laughter. That would be a fine thing, so it would."

Thurmond was not amused by his jesting.

"Come on, Roscoe, Sarah wasn't wearing a dress when she faced off with the monsters in Castle Sathas. And even if she had been, none of 'em would've laughed. She's as brave as any of us. What does it matter if she's a girl?"

Roscoe sighed. His young Prospect was forcing him to give a real answer.

"All right then, it matters because it's against custom. Adventurers have always been men."

This was a strong argument. Deviation from custom was a most risky business certain to awaken the ire of Lady Fortune. Custom carried more authority than the decrees of a king.

The young man was undaunted.

"I know that, Roscoe, and I give custom its due respect. But aren't there times when exceptions must be made, when special people or situations make change necessary? Isn't Sarah like that?"

Roscoe shook his head as if in disbelief.

"Laddie, Sarah's a wonderful young lady. She's marvelous brave, and smarter than any of us. I was willin' to die tryin' to save her last night. If it was just up to me, she could be an Adventurer and wear a big black hat. But it ain't that simple, not at all. The other Adventurers would never accept her, and that's a fact. Nothin's gonna change that."

"Why does that matter so much? Let 'em accept her or not. Why should we care?"

"Cuz, laddie, we're a brotherhood. There's rules we gotta follow."

Thurmond interrupted.

"Is there a specific rule saying girls can't be Adventurers?"

"Not as far as I ever heard, but …"

The young man jumped in again.

"If there's no real rule, then we wouldn't be …."

Now it was Roscoe's turn to interrupt.

"If you'll just calm down and listen to me, Prospect, I'm tryin' my best to explain. As I was sayin', we're a brotherhood. You may recall that our line of work is a tad dangerous, so we gotta stick together. You don't wanna be doin' nothin' that causes grumblin' in the ranks. Such a thing wouldn't do at all."

Thurmond was angry, but tried not to show it.

"You're telling me Sarah will never be welcome just because she's a girl, no matter how brave or loyal she is. No matter how many times she saves our lives."

Roscoe shrugged.

"I don't make the rules, boyo."

"Then why would she want to stay with us? What's the point if we always shut her out?"

The old Adventurer at last grew stern.

"Looky here, Prospect, I love Sarah like she was my...my...my little sister. But her stayin' or goin' is her own decision. Understand?"

Thurmond understood all too well. He allowed his horse to drop back until he was alone. Then Sarah was beside him, close, so they rode knee to knee. She shot him the same knowing look she had given him earlier.

"You want to know the real reason I'm not allowed to join your club?"

Thurmond could only nod.

"Girls don't pee the right way."

Then she kicked her horse forward, leaving him alone once again.

Gavin used the toe of his boot to shove the priest's naked body into the hole. The livery, pouch, and badge of the Royal Courier followed. Then he pulled the dead man's voluminous robe, the distinctive vestment of the Black Friars, over his own head and shoulders. That garment alone would ensure that no one hampered his progress, since it was most unwise of anyone to risk the displeasure of the Black Friars.

A clergyman could not ride a steed bearing the brand of the Royal Couriers, so he removed its saddle and bridle and gave the beast a slap on the rump, sending it off to wander as it would. The dead friar had ridden a fine black courser, a much more fitting steed for a man of authority. He kept the messenger's spurs though. They were long and sharp and added a touch of swagger to his appearance.

First the messenger and now a Black Friar—both had been given to him at exactly the right moment. Lady Fortune was certainly smiling, so the rest of his design must proceed smoothly and easily.

Gavin felt the weight of Baron Melgwyn's gold in the purse on his belt. There was plenty to hire three or four rough boys in case the lout's servants were too stupid to cooperate. He doubted that would really be necessary. The friar's robe and his own commanding presence should guarantee his admittance to the tower, and once inside, he would have everything his own way. But it was always better to be prepared for unexpected adversity. Better to have and not need than to need and not have.

He swung into the saddle of his new mount. It tossed its head and reared slightly, as if testing its new master's control. A spirited beast—Gavin liked that. He jerked the reins and touched his spurs to its flanks. It spun in a tight half circle and set off down the road toward Gorgonholm.

And then, as Gavin rode, a great white light seemed to burst in his brain. Why had he never realized this before? The implications were staggering! He had always assumed his divinity had been bestowed by his father—that a god had chosen Mother as the instrument of his birth. Now he saw his mistake so clearly. His father, the seed donor, could indeed have been anybody. His father's identity was no longer of concern because he realized he had focused on the wrong parent.

Lady Fortune was his real mother!

The woman he had always called Mother had been no more than a wet nurse, a nanny, a surrogate. Good Lady Fortune had, in some godly fashion, taken possession of the whore's body to give human birth to a son with preternatural powers. There could be no other reason for his blessed existence. That was the only way to explain his extraordinarily good luck— how everything always went his way.

CHAPTER 47

TWEEDLE'S CARAVAN

The companions' homeward journey was undisturbed by vengeful bandits or rampaging robber-knights. Had either Melgwyn or Baidan even survive their battle? No one knew. Thurmond relished the idea of both dying with their fingers locked around each other's throats. Nonetheless, the Adventurers took no chances, speeding through the hills and forests of western Bukovia, stopping only when overtaken by exhaustion.

Bukovia was a smallish kingdom, so it took but three more days of determined riding to arrive at the River Vash. Though the kingdom of Poitiers and the city of Vistu lay just on the other side, they were forced to stop for the night, for it was evening, and the ferry had ceased to run. This was the borough of Estwark, a less than respectable collection of workshops, docks, and houses clustered along the riverbank. The main industry here was the smoking of fish, carried out in a multitude of large drying kilns whose emissions made everything in Estwark greasy and fishy. The Estwarkers were in fact subjects of Titus, King of Bukovia, but they spoke, thought, and behaved like proper natives of Poitiers. This meant they quarreled, cheated, and dissembled whenever the opportunity arose.

A large inn—The Brinded Cat—promised hot food and warm beds, welcome luxuries after so many nights of sleeping rough. It was a two-story, half-timbered affair built around a central courtyard. One wide wing was given over to stables. The food was plentiful and the ale was strong, but the sleeping accommodations were less than lavish. The Cat was nearly full up, so Sarah and Pozi had to share a chamber with a group of young nuns and their prioress. The men bedded down with a group of flatulent merchants in a communal sleeping loft. Skrot was sent to guard the horses. He grumbled a bit about being treated like a serf, but then changed his mind, smiled, and complied.

In spite of the bedbugs, the mildewed ticking, and the noisome emanations of the merchants, Thurmond slept soundly until awakened by Roscoe's great thundering bellow.

"God's liver and lungs! He's done it again, so he has!"

Still mostly asleep, Thurmond sat up too quickly and bumped his head on a joist—the loft had a low ceiling.

"Ouch! Aggh! What's the matter, Roscoe?"

The old Adventurer stood on the lower rungs of the loft's ladder so only his head was visible to Thurmond.

"It's Skrot! That's what the matter! He's skipped again, just like before!"

"Skipped? You mean taken off? Run away?'

"Aye, that's exactly what I mean. Cut and run durin' the night when he was supposed to be guardin' our horses."

"Our horses! Are they all right? Are they still there?"

"Aye, all but Skrot's. His gear's gone, too. He's skedaddled all righty, and it's your fault, Prospect."

"My fault? How do you figure that?"

"You vouched for him, told me I had to take him back when I didn't want to. Your fault entirely, so it is."

Thurmond was unwilling to challenge the old Adventurer's illogic. He tried to turn the discussion in a different direction.

"Maybe something happened to him. Or maybe he had some valid reason for taking off. Could be he'll come back."

"He ain't comin' back, Prospect. He made that entirely clear."

"What do you mean?"

"He took my camp hatchet, same as before. That's like a message, see. It's his way of tellin' me he's run off again, just like the first time."

"I think he might he telling you he didn't like being ordered to sleep in the stable. It made him feel like a serf again."

Thurmond's retort provoked Roscoe's already substantial ire.

"Serf or man-at-arms—makes no difference! He was sworn to my service! He's a damnable oath-breaker, and blast his eyes! You should never have made me take him back."

Thurmond was getting testy. He was a little hungover and his head hurt from its encounter with the joist.

"God's warty toes, Roscoe! I didn't *make* you do anything. I told you what I thought, and you made your own choice. At least he had his own cloak this time. He took Murd's before."

Weary of all the bickering, Torgul abruptly sat up. He was short enough that his head was safe from the treacherous joists.

"Prospect, if you plan to have any future as an Adventurer, you'll be sayin' nothin' more to Captain Roscoe. If he says you're to blame, you gotta thank him for pointin' it out and then shut up so a hardworkin' dwarf can get a decent bit o' sleep. Understand?"

Thurmond immediately calmed himself down.

"Sorry, Roscoe. I didn't mean to argue. Sorry."

The old Adventurer gave a loud *harrumph* and disappeared into the room below. A few moments later, he again erupted into a new fit of passion.

"God's bloody fangs! My cloak is gone!"

Roscoe could get grumpy, but his sour moods were never of long duration. After a quick bite to eat and a mug of morning ale, he felt much better. He stopped grousing and was even able to see the humor in the theft of his cloak. Skrot's disappearance, he was forced to concede, was probably for the best— the lad had serious problems when it came to fulfilling his commitments.

With the bonhomie of the Adventurers restored, the traveling merchants finally dared to descend from the loft and seek their breakfast in the common room. They were an amiable bunch and were delighted to learn that a party of seasoned warriors would be traveling in the same direction as themselves.

An arrangement was discussed, some coins changed hands, and another mug of ale was quaffed. Thus, Roscoe and company joined a small train of wagons bound for Gorgonholm.

This caravan was by no means as formidable as that commanded by Bombardo. There were no more than a dozen medium-size wains pulled by mules. These were much smaller and lighter than the massive ox-drawn drays of their previous trip. The cargo was less valuable as well—mostly iron cooking pots, bronze tureens, pewter ewers, trays of embossed brass, and urns of hammered copper. The wagons were being loaded in Vistu and would be ready to depart in a few days.

The caravan's complement consisted of two score assorted teamsters and grooms, a pair of scouts who doubled as hunters, a cook, and a tongueless mute who functioned as both blacksmith and wheelwright. The adventuring companions would serve as the guard contingent. The Golden Road had been quiet since the defeat of the Bukovian bandits earlier in the season, so no serious threats were anticipated.

Sarah and Pozi appeared from their sleeping chamber, stretching, yawning, and hungry. They were followed by a bevy of eight very young nuns, who sat silently with downcast eyes as they ate a simple meal of milk and porridge. The sisters, it turned out, were also bound for Gorgonholm, where they would tend to the needs of Bishop Boniface.

Their prioress, an elegant and dainty woman of perhaps five-and-twenty, seemed rather too young to have ascended to such a position of responsibility. Her name was Mother Eglantina. Following a brief conversation with the merchant leader, a sharp-eyed little man named Tweedle, she and her charges also joined the caravan.

After so many days of hard riding, the delay in Estwark was welcome. The companions ate, rested, and then ate some more. No matter how much or how often he ate, Thurmond could not seem to stay full. To Pozi, who had never before stayed in an inn, the seedy Brinded Cat seemed like a royal palace. She found the food so exotic she could barely bring herself to consume it.

On the second day, Tweedle sent the companions into Vistu to supervise the final loading of the wagons. The appearance of trained warriors, he said, would perhaps inspire the freight handlers to greater honesty. While in the city, they took the opportunity to replace the mailshirts and other gear they had abandoned in the mountains. Roscoe bought himself a new cloak to replace the one stolen by Skrot.

Pozi, who had never before seen a proper town, let alone a city, was left awestruck by Vistu's twisting byways and ramshackle buildings. She was even more delighted when Roscoe made good on his promise of a new dress complete with matching shoes and hat.

The caravan continued to expand. A company of religious pilgrims arrived the second evening and signed on. There was also the usual unsavory crew of vagabonds and vagrants, rovers and ramblers, dodgers and drifters, migrants and mendicants, wastrels and wanderers, and even a few honest travelers.

By the evening of the third day, all necessary preparations had been made. The caravan would depart at first light on the morrow.

Thurmond found the journey surprisingly pleasant. The pace was comfortable, neither mind-numbingly slow like the journey east nor frantically hurried like the flight from Castle Skynslip. The weather was unusually warm for the season, with only an occasional rain shower to remind them that winter had now officially arrived. All in all, it was an easy, agreeable passage.

The Adventurers found their fellow wayfarers affable and cooperative. Necessary tasks were attended to without undue complaint. At night the travelers sat around a fire and sang long, mournful songs about doomed love affairs and tragic deaths.

Mother Eglantina was rather worldly for a nun. She traveled with two small terriers on which she lavished a disturbing degree of affection. In speech, she affected a fashionable lisp. Her eyes, large and round, conveyed an expression of perpetual surprise. Roscoe was smitten and spent as much time as possible in her company.

Fulfilling his earlier resolution, he set about to create himself anew. He shaved most of his beard away in an attempt to alleviate the gray. Then out came the new garb, secretly purchased in Vistu and kept hidden in a saddlebag—a velvet tunic embroidered with flowers and cut so short as to barely cover his hips, a wide belt that when tied in a sword-knot reached past his knees, and bright yellow hose, wonderfully cross-gartered, of course. At night Roscoe avoided the campfire singsong as he accompanied the Mother Eglantina on long strolls. Thurmond never imagined a dwarf could roll his eyes in dismay, but that is exactly what Torgul did.

Such problems that did arise during the journey were minor. A wandering minstrel burned his hand while trying to snatch a fallen rutabaga from the smoldering coals of a campfire. A pair of hotheaded young teamsters came to blows over who had the best team of mules. One received a bloody lip.

A near tragic incident arose when a vagabond woman gave birth to a son with a large facial birthmark. This was taken as an omen of ill fortune and inspired a rabble of vagrants and wastrels to demand that the infant be left out to die. The unfortunate creature was saved after Tweedle stood them down. The merchant leader was a small man, but his courage was large. Backed by Roscoe and his companions, he stormed into the assembled riffraff, sword in hand, and promised to slay the first one to take a single step toward the newborn. The throng took a long look at Tweedle's sword, at the massive size of the old Adventurer, and at Bloodtroll's gleaming edge. They then turned away and no more was said of the matter.

The arrival of the Royal Road Guards was a more serious matter. These minor officials were typically bullying and avaricious, but they could usually be bought off for a few small coins and some drinks. This time they came with more determined purpose. They questioned the caravaneers regarding the murder of a Royal Courier, whose remains had been found in a creek a few leagues west of Vistu. Though the Road Guards threatened and stormed, the investigation came to naught, for there was nothing to connect any of the travelers to the crime. The unfortunate messenger had been dead at least a week, a time when the caravan members had still been in the city.

Sundry groups and individuals left the caravan at towns and villages along the route. The pilgrims headed south at Farthing Street—most of the teamsters called it Farting Street—bound for the shrine of Saint Gisela von Glopp, the first stop in a circuit of the kingdom's shrines and holy sites.

Tweedle and the merchants elected to deviate from their original purpose. Hearing of a large market-faire in a nearby town, they decided to sojourn thither before proceeding on to Gorgonholm. The adventuring companions were thereby released from their duty as guards. There now remained only the nuns and a handful of miscellaneous wayfarers to accompany them. The holy sisters also made a change of course when a messenger arrived from Bishop Boniface. His Most Reverend Excellency was no longer in residence at Gorgonholm's cathedral. The sisters were instructed to veer north and attend him at his hunting lodge.

After their departure, Sarah drew Thurmond aside.

"I have to tell you something."

The young man was always uneasy when Sarah said things like this.

"Something like what?"

"Something like none of those nuns were really nuns."

This was entirely unexpected.

"None of 'em?"

"None."

"Who were they then?"

"Concubines—specially trained concubines from some fancy brothel in the east."

Thurmond tilted his head and squinted one eye.

"Whaaaat? Nay …."

"Aye, it's true. Those girls like to chat. They told me all about it. Bishop Boniface sent for them."

"The prioress, too?"

Sarah nodded.

"She came along to keep the others in line and to make the necessary arrangements."

"What kind of arrangements?"

"Arrangements like…it didn't cost them any coin to join the caravan."

"You mean all this time …?"

"That's right. The girls kept Tweedle happy. Didn't you notice how tired he's looking?"

"Roscoe and the prioress—were they …?"

Sarah nodded again.

"I'm pretty sure."

"Damn it! Why didn't you tell me about this before?"

"I think you can figure that out."

PART 5

THE SIEGE OF GRIMSGARD

CHAPTER 48

FLORIO RECEIVES A GUEST

Grimsgard's previous owner, Lady Renata de la Pole, had enjoyed a profound taste for the grotesque and embellished her door with a great bronze knocker in the shape of a leering satyr's face. When employed, this device sent a sharp report echoing through the structure's passages and chambers.

Florio was at his writing table, seeking a way to stretch the freehold's available funds, when the pounding began. It was the loud, incessant boom of someone slamming the knocker as hard as he could. An imperious pounding that expressed the monumental egoism of the pounder. Florio shuffled his papers one last time and headed downstairs to see what all the fuss was about. He also tucked a dagger into the back of his belt, just in case the pounder was especially disagreeable.

A Black Friar stood at the door. He held a rolled parchment in one hand, which he flourished like a weapon.

"I am Monsignor Thaddeus de Gui, *Minister Terroris* of the Holy Inquisition. We have received disturbing reports concerning blasphemous activities on these premises. I have come to make an inspection. Stand aside."

Something about the priest did not seem right to Florio. His arrogant bearing? Nay, that was in keeping with his office. His garb? His sword? Again nay, his accouterments were entirely in order. Yet some innate quality did not bespeak a man of the church, even that of a sect as arrogant and greedy as the Black Friars. Certainly, there was the same assumption of entitlement and self-righteousness he so often saw in human clerics, but their pomposity and self-assurance stemmed from the might of the church. This fellow's vanity seemed to flow from some indefinable inner source.

Florio did not like this man.

Humans, he knew, were generally trained from childhood to fear the awesome power of the church. The authority of high-ranking priests rivaled that of the most powerful nobles. So, it was often in a man's second nature to yield to a cleric's commands without question. But as an elf, Florio had been raised outside of such traditions. Refusing this strange priest's demand for entry to the tower was not particularly difficult. Elves were accomplished dissemblers, a skill Florio now made use of.

"I am frightfully sorry, Sir Priest, but Captain Roscoe, he's the freeholder here, left strict instructions. No one unknown to me is to enter the premises."

He watched carefully to assess the priest's reaction to this lie. He saw for the briefest of moments a telling glimmer in the man's otherwise impassive eyes—the obsidian gleam of a reptile. Florio looked at the trio of armed men who sat on horses behind the priest. Common gutter trash. The Black Friars were an armed and militant sect, they had no need of such uncouth, ill-disciplined scum.

Florio again examined the man standing before him. All appeared in order except he spurs! He wore the long, iron prick spurs of a Royal Courier. The elf knew these to be a traditional accessory of that office. Black Friars did not wear such spurs. Without another word, Florio stepped back and slammed the door in the self-proclaimed friar's face. He quickly slid the heavy iron bolts and dropped the thick wooden bars into their brackets.

Gavin was speechless with rage. Never in his life had he been treated with such blatant disrespect, with such bald regard for common courtesy, and by a pointy-eared little twerp who was little more than a dressed-up goblin! How dare he treat a man of the church in such an offhand manner. He would live to regret it!

He seized the knocker and beat a furious tattoo upon the door. There was no response—the door remained implacable. He pounded even more violently, determined to do so until his demands were met. He would continue all night if need be, but he would not submit to such humiliation, especially at the hands of a mincing, green-blooded elf.

A heavy torrent of water suddenly struck the flagstones behind him, splashing upward to soak his boots and legs. Then a voice called from above.

"Be warned, Sir Priest, or whatever you are! If you do not depart at once, I will send down something far worse than water."

Gavin craned his neck upward. The elf was peering down from one of the machicolations that projected from the top of the tower. Gavin ignored him and continued to belabor the door. A rock the size of a man's fist bounced next to him. Dropped from such a height, it struck with enough force to smash a skull.

Again the voice came from above.

"That was your last warning. My next stone shall not miss. Begone! Or you shall be slain."

This was too much! Simply too much! First, he had been denied entry, then his knocking had been ignored, and now he was being ordered away like some poxy beggar! Gavin turned toward his men. They were just sitting there on their horses, safely out of range while their leader was being assailed. Their expressions were grim, but he knew they must be secretly laughing at his humiliation. The woman he had always called Mother—she had learned not to laugh, indeed she had. These slack-jawed ruffians would also learn.

With nothing else to do, Gavin abandoned the door knocker and retreated to the tower's grassy yard. He pointed a finger and screamed up at the elf.

"You'll rue the day that …."

An arrow landed between his spread feet, burying itself to the fletching in the soft sod. Gavin jumped back, then ran to his horse, vaulted into the saddle, and rode off as fast as he could. He could now hear the subdued laughter of his minions as they followed. For that they would pay. And as for the elf—he would flense the flesh from his bones.

The ride back to Gorgonholm calmed Gavin. He recalled that everything happened for his ultimate benefit. Lady Fortune would never subject him to such trying circumstances unless it ultimately led to his success. He must always bear that in mind. He considered his next move. How did one capture a castle? The question had never occurred to him before. But the elf, he was certain, would be even less informed about defending one.

The fat oaf Roscoe, Grimsgard's freeholder, was most certainly lying dead in the mountains of Bukovia, slain by the greedy little baron, but that fact was still unknown to anyone in these parts. He would have to work quickly and establish himself as the new owner before a rapacious noble heard of Roscoe's death and seized the estate for himself. There was no time for anything other than direct assault, so he would need more men—a dozen archers to keep the battlements free of whatever of rock-droppers and arrow-shooters the elf might muster. A half dozen big boys would be needed to beat down the door with a ram. Gavin paused in his musing. Where did one obtain a battering ram?

There had been no suggestion of any real soldiers about the place, so once the door was breached, resistance would be minimal. His men would simply slaughter everyone inside—all except the elf. He was for cutting up slow.

Gavin continued to search his mind for an easier way. He considered various methods for effecting a surreptitious entry. Could a servant be bribed to open the door? Or maybe the elf could be bluffed. A new scheme began to evolve. Maybe there was a way. It would be expensive, requiring more money than he carried in his purse, but money was never a problem. There was always someone he could take it from.

Florio immediately set to work. The priest—or whatever he was—would be back. The tower must be made ready to withstand an assault. There was precious little available in the way of weapons. Roscoe and his friends had taken the entire store of arms and armor on their adventure—well, almost. The elf did find a rusted mail coif, a couple heavy boar spears, and a short, choppy hunting sword. There was also a single bow but no great supply of arrows. Not much to work with.

He would have to sacrifice the village. There was no way to defend the cluster of barns, cottages, and workshops. The villagers would be brought into the tower and enlisted into its defense. None had any experience with weapons or fighting, but they would have to learn quickly if they hoped to preserve their lives.

Food—there was no immediate problem there. The stock of provender was good for at least two weeks. The cistern in the tower's basement held a more than adequate stock of water. He doubted the attackers could mount a siege, but it was best to prepare.

So how did one go about defending a castle? Florio had never considered such a question before. He could only pray the false priest was equally uninformed. The parapet of the towerhouse was circled by openings that allowed heavy stones to be dropped straight down on attackers gathered anywhere along its base. There were, however, very few stones piled on the roof. Florio would send the village children to fetch more.

In addition, Torgul had devised an ingenious method to dump scalding water on anyone assaulting the door. A large cauldron—he called it his siege-kettle—was mounted on a set of horizontal iron rails. In its normal position, it sat well back from the parapet, out of sight of attackers on the ground below. A fire could be kindled beneath it to bring the water to boil. The vessel could then be pushed forward along the rails until it was over the parapet's edge, directly above the door. Special handles allowed it to be pivoted forward to empty its contents on the unfortunates below.

Florio had already used this contraption to deliver the deluge of unheated water to his uninvited guest. The container would need to be refilled and an additional supply of water brought up. He would need wood, too, to keep a fire blazing beneath it.

Roscoe had long ago established an emergency signal to summon his tenants to the tower. A huge brass-bound warhorn hung on the wall of the great hall. Its throaty roar could be heard over the length and breadth of the fief—at least when the barrel-chested Adventurer was doing the blowing. The spindly elf doubted his blast would be so mighty, yet he strode into the village common, raised the instrument to his lips, and blew with all his might.

Heads immediately peeked from doors and windows. Workers laid down their tools and turned their attention in Florio's direction. One after another, the villagers shuffled toward him. Dull-eyed field workers, mothers with babes in arms, skinny children, a smattering of gaffers and grandams. They stood before Florio, expectant yet patient, fearful yet trusting. There was no time to be wasted in lengthy explanations. The elf got right to the point, striving to keep his voice calm and confident.

"We are going to be attacked. We can expect the village to be burned, so any goods you wish to preserve must be brought into the tower at once. Any tools that will serve as weapons are especially needed—pruning bills, sickles, mauls, pitchforks, anything.

"Some of you are skilled poachers. Nay, deny it not. Bring your slings and bows, as we have especial need of them. Also bring all pails and large pots that can be used for carrying water.

"Livestock and poultry must be brought inside, along with any food you have. Leave nothing that will benefit the enemy. We need firewood, a great pile of it, and big heaps of stones to drop upon their heads. We must see to these things at once. Do as I tell you, and you will live. Fail me, and you must surely die."

Florio organized labor parties to carry out each specific task. The villagers, quite used to obeying his dictates, plodded off to their assignments without question. They had much more faith in him than he had in himself. He stood alone, trying to prioritize the myriad jobs that he must attend to. His eyes fell upon the shaft of the arrow protruding from the ground where it had struck between the priest's feet. He seized it below its fletching and pulled it free. He would need every arrow he could find.

Work went on throughout the night. A disfigured poacher named Old Gripe—his ears had been sliced off many years ago—was also a fletcher. Indeed, it was he who made the arrows with which the village men routinely pillaged Roscoe's rabbits and partridges. He was set to work producing shafts. The village blacksmith and his son were tasked with the production of arrowheads.

Sharp-eyed boys were placed on the battlements to keep watch. Others were sent to gather stones from the surrounding pastures and fields. Women and girls hauled water, gathered firewood, collected more stones. The village cows were slaughtered and their meat carried to the larder. Pigs, goats, and sheep were penned together at one end of the great hall. Scythes, broadaxes, flails, and spades were stacked at the other end. A dim-eyed gaffer was set to sharpen their nicked and blunted edges.

Everyone was busy, busy, busy. Florio stood in the center of this great flurry, directing, correcting, assisting. A wide leather belt circled his narrow hips, the hunting sword hanging on one side and his dagger on the other. The rusty mail coif covered his head, and the warhorn hung over his shoulder on a baldric. He did not, in sooth, feel like a valiant warrior, but he was doing his best to convey that image to his followers.

Dawn broke, gray, rainy, and cold. When no attackers arrived, the work continued. Baskets of stones and kettles of water were carried up the long, twisting stairs to the battlements. Glass was removed from the arrow-slit windows. Chickens, geese, and ducks were brought inside and released to wander where they would. Makeshift shields were constructed from random boards and the green hides of the slaughtered cows. No one in the village knew how to make a proper shield, so there was much heated argument. Worse, no one knew the correct way to use a shield.

Arrow production was woefully slow. Old Gripe was a perfectionist and would not be hurried. Florio pointed out that the arrows need not be of the highest quality, for they would be used against targets much larger and slower than darting rabbits, but his protests went unheard. When men were sent to assist the choleric fletcher, he got mad, stopped work, and refused to resume until they were withdrawn.

Florio had, like all young elves, grown up listening to tales of valorous deeds of great heroes slaying of monstrous foes and facing bloodcurdling perils with unflinching courage. The tone of elven legends somewhat differed somewhat from those of men and dwarves. Elves favored cunning and trickery, at times even treachery, over blind courage and brute strength, yet the tales of all races had one thing in common—they lionized the warrior.

Elf, dwarf, or human—young male children were taught from birth that they should love the roar of battle. That war was the great test that divided the worthy from the wanting. That only a coward would balk at the opportunity to slay an enemy in honorable combat. Florio had never shared this sentiment, not as a child and certainly not now. The impending battle was for him tedious rather than glorious, an inconvenient necessity rather than a chance to win honor. The best he could hope for was simple survival. If he failed, the entire population of Grimsgard might be slain. He saw no glory in any of this.

Florio was exhausted and hungry, having neither slept during the previous night nor supped since yesterday's breakfast. Yet the commotion, the planning, and the impending danger kept him from feeling the effects of the hunger and exhaustion that wore inexorably at his body. At that moment, what he needed above all other things was more time.

Noon came and went—still no attack. The short winter day slipped away quickly, but no hostile force hove into view. The frantic pace of preparation slowed as the villagers tired. Bodo's wife Bess took charge in the kitchen, where she and a crew of women produced a huge communal meal. The villagers were to be well fed for their labors.

The sun went down. Florio wanted no surprise visitors in the night and sent the poachers to keep close watch on the surrounding woods and pastures. These men were used to navigating in the dark. They were intimately acquainted with every hidden path and secret game trail, with every stump or boulder behind which an illicit hunter might conceal himself.

The elf could only hope that these humans were up to the task. He knew how to motivate them to work, but he had never before had to inspire anyone to fight. He tried his trick of reaching into their memories, hoping to dredge up ancient resentments that could be directed at attackers. He found nothing. The will to fight seemed to have been beaten out of the downtrodden serfs.

At the Goddess Spring, Whisper the woodsprite tasted trouble in the air. Something was wrong at the tower—very wrong. There was a time when he could have journeyed there in semi-physical form to spy out the problem. But that was before, when his tree was a mammoth oak, mighty of limb and thick of trunk. Alas, it had, as all things must, eventually withered and died.

He, too, would have died had that young witch Sarah not found a way to shift his essence from the main trunk to a fledgling root-sprout that she had then transplanted at this sacred spring. In this way, his life was saved.

But with his rebirth had come a waning of his power, so he was now as weak as the willowy sapling in which he lived. His strength would return only as it grew into a brawny tree.

Yet there had to be some way to warn the witch.

CHAPTER 49

WHISPER'S WARNING

The Scorpion Inn was not named for the nasty, biting insect. Its signboard, creaking in the gentle breeze, featured a dart-flinging siege machine of the same name. It was an average inn, with lumpy, bug-ridden beds no better or worse than any of the others to be found along the Golden Road. And the food was acceptable, much more tasty than rough trail fare.

The soft *screaking* of the sign awakened Roscoe, who had slept well and long. He was hungry and needed to pee. Taking care not to wake the others, he made his way downstairs to the privy. In the common room he cadged a quick breakfast from the potboy—cold meat, bread, and beer—and went outside to enjoy the brisk morning air. There would be time for a proper feed later when his friends were up and about. Right now, he looked forward to a bit of quiet time.

The old Adventurer was in fine fettle. He had been distinctly grouchy after the departure of Eglantina—what a woman!—but it was too fine a morning to let the memory of her cloud his mood. The breeze was chilly, but the sky was unusually bright and blue for this time of year—a good sign, surely.

Another day and a half of easy riding, and he would be home, sleeping in his own featherbed, gorging on Florio's excellent cookery, and swilling Torgul's mead. They had won sacks of gold that would end their financial woes. Best of all, his bad leg was good as new. There was no pain, no stiffness, no limp. He felt like a young man again. What could possibly dampen his spirits?

Sarah suddenly stood before him, hands on hips, a look in her eye that could only mean trouble.

"Roscoe, there's a problem. We have to talk."

This was exactly what he did not need at the moment.

"Oohh, Sarah, darlin', why would you want to go and spoil such a beautiful mornin' with all this fussin'?"

She ignored his complaint, thrusting directly into her concerns.

"We've got to get back as quickly as we can. Something's wrong at the keep. Something's very wrong."

This was definitely not was he wanted to hear. They had had a thrilling and profitable adventure, their wounds were healed, and the roads were as safe and smooth as one could hope for. Now was the time for a leisurely ride in the crisp early winter air. For the singing of songs and the swapping of merry jests.

Nay, there could be nothing all that wrong at home. He had left his affairs in the elf's very competent hands, which were much more capable than his own. The girl was just nervous, nothing more than that.

"Now Sarah, tell me what could be so wrong as to get you in such a state?"

"I don't exactly know. But something very bad is happening or is about to happen, and we need to get back."

"And how is it that you came by this dire knowledge? Did you cast some kind of spell?"

"Not a spell, nay, nothing like that ...."

Roscoe noted her hesitation, her indecision.

"Go on, lassie, tell me what's disturbin' your pretty little head."

"All right, damn it, I'll tell you. I had a dream last night. I dreamed..."

She paused again, uncertain.

"What was it you dreamed, girl? Go on,"

"I don't know. That's why it's hard to tell you. There was nothing definite, just kind of a voice whispering that something bad is happening and we need to get back at once."

"What exactly did this voice say?"

"It wasn't like that. It didn't say words exactly. I just got this feeling. Look,

I know how this must sound to you. It doesn't make a lot of sense to me either. But I know it's real. The feeling is too strong not to be real."

Roscoe raised a hand to his mouth to conceal his smile. Sarah had got herself all worked up over a dream. It was rather charming when you thought about it—smart as Sarah was, she was still an excitable young girl.

"Sarah, darlin', you know how much we all love and respect you. I hold your ideas in the highest regard, so I do. But everyone knows there ain't no truth in dreams. The philosophers knew it in the olden days, and the churchmen still say so today. Dreams ain't nothin' more than wild fancies that float into us somehow from somewheres."

Frustrated, Sarah stamped her foot in frustration and stared hard into her friend's eyes.

"I knew you would say that, but you've got to listen to me. This dream was different. It…"

Roscoe cut her off, his voice assuming the edge of authority he used in his role of Adventure Captain.

"Sarah, I'll not be discussin' this further. I won't distress the others with this nonsense or come near to killin' our horses on a mad ride just because you had a bad dream. Now, little lady, I'll have you put such ridiculum out of your mind."

Getting nowhere with the hardheaded old Adventurer, Sarah stormed off in a pique of anger. Roscoe hated to upset her, but damn it, a man had a right to a peaceful morning beer did he not? Especially on such a lovely morning. He had but one sip of the thick yeasty brew before Thurmond took the girl's place and again began harping about making her a Prospect. *Damn!*

Again, no attack came—not that night nor the following day nor the next night. The villagers grumbled about the disruption of their daily affairs. They were creatures of habit, and any variance from normal routine was upsetting, unnatural, and sinful.

The tower had been designed, decades ago, to house a small contingent of frontier warders who guarded the southern approaches of Gorgonholm against sneak attacks from their Keltin neighbors. The ground floor was their stable, while the upper chambers offered sleeping quarters and living space for a garrison of about a dozen men. The structure had been modified over the years as new tenants took up residence. Lady Renata had built a large stone stable separate from the tower, so the reek of her horses would not offend her sense of smell. She also added many expensive adornments—window glass, a massive fireplace, and decorative gargoyles.

Roscoe had most of the ground floor partitioned as a storeroom, where his supply of food and drink—especially his precious ale and mead—was kept under lock and key. The next story held the huge fireplace and served as his great hall. Higher levels contained the companions' sleeping chambers, the armory, and Sarah's laboratorium.

More than two score villagers and their livestock were now crammed cheek to jowl within its narrow confines. The close quarters did not particularly irritate these people. An entire extended family traditionally shared a small hut, so they were quite used to sleeping with other people's feet shoved in their faces. They routinely dressed, fornicated, and evacuated their bowels within one another's sight.

But they were not used to spending much time indoors. Peasant farmworkers spent almost all their waking hours under an open sky. They sought refuge in their lice-ridden hovels only when compelled by the cold, the wet, or the terrors of the night. The sparse furnishings and dark, smoky interior of a typical peasant hut did not lend itself to comfortable social interaction. Thus, the stone walls of the tower filled the villagers with unease. Though they could, at this point, come and go about their business, the likelihood of a long internment made them nervous, hesitant, and at times even surly. The situation could only worsen when the fight started, and they were all sealed within.

When Gavin finally arrived, he came, like most unwelcome guests, at an inopportune time—just before dawn. An hour traditionally favored for surprise invasions and sudden assaults. A time when all honest folk were snuggled deep in their dreams, when even bedbugs had ceased to bite and were sleeping tight, when sentries were bleary-eyed and least vigilant.

Florio's poachers were all fast asleep in their scattered hides when a double column of riders came down the cart-road that connected Grimsgard with the Royal Highway. Forty grim-faced men in ragged mail, worn leather, and random bits of rusty plate. Axes, swords, and bows were lashed to their saddles or slung over their shoulders. Mercenaries. Gavin rode at the head of this troop, exuding the confidence and determination of an experienced battle leader. His hair was cut very short, and a new beard was beginning to cover his jaw and chin. He looked a proper warrior.

His Black Friar's robe had been discarded in favor of a long-sleeve hauberk reinforced with an iron breastplate. On his head, a graceful *celata* was trimmed with burnished bronze edging. Scaled gauntlets covered his hands, and a long, narrow-bladed war sword rode at his hip. A crossbow was tied to his saddle.

The riders made no attempt at stealth or concealment, coming on at a steady pace. The *clop-clop* of hooves and clatter of gear awakened the drowsing poachers, but instead of sounding their horns to alert their comrades in the tower, they huddled silently, too frightened to respond.

Florio remained unaware of the intruders until they were hewing at his door with axes. The elf's eyes flew open. He knew instantly that his misgivings about his sentries had been well founded. They had failed to give warning. He leaped, fully clothed, from his sleeping pallet and sprinted up the spiral stairs to the roof. He had not so much as removed his boots since the appearance of the friar.

The ringing of the axes continued, filling him with dismay. The two men on the roof should have dumped a basket of stones on the attackers, disrupting their assault on the door, but he heard nothing—no pause in the hewing, no screams. Were the people up there still asleep. Dead?

Fortunately, Lady Renata had liked her privacy, so the tower's main door was comprised of three layers of oaken planks. Iron sheeting covered the outside, and stout iron bars, lent additional strength. The door was a formidable barrier that would not soon be penetrated.

Florio knew he still had a few minutes.

Reaching the rooftop, the elf found his men alive and awake, hiding in the shadows as far back from the parapet as they could get. They were useless with terror, eyes white and round in the ragged darkness. The baskets of stones sat untouched. Without pause, Florio dragged on to machicolation directly over the door and dumped its contents over the edge. The axe blows stopped, and a great roar of pain and outrage rose from below. The stones had found their mark.

The attackers had come prepared for such bombardment. They wore heavy helmets and armor, and sturdy shields were strapped across their backs. Even so, they were driven from their work at the door. One man, struck square on his flat-topped pothelm, had to be dragged off by his fellows. But such hardened soldiers were not to be deterred for long. They gathered out of range, conferred briefly, and returned to their task. A larger group this time, with some of the men holding interlocking shields overhead so that they moved forward like a great multi-legged tortoise.

Florio was ready. He selected a much larger stone, a jagged chunk of shale bigger than his head. Falling from the top of a five-story tower, it would lay low anyone it struck, shielded or not. But before he could send it down, arrows began to pelt the rooftop all around him. He dropped, rolled, and flattened his back against the inside of the parapet. The two peasants, panicking, darted through the arrow storm toward the stairway door. Somehow they made it and disappeared into the safety of the lower floors.

Iron-tipped shafts continued to drop. The archers knew their business, aiming their bows at an extremely high angle so their missiles plummeted almost straight down. There was no real cover. Sooner or later, Florio knew, he would learn the feel of an arrow tearing through his flesh. But he must not simply cower in fear. Tensing against anticipated pain, he pushed the piece of shale through the machicolation. A terrible *crunch* and a long, gasping scream signaled an end to the assault on the door. The axemen withdrew under the cover of their shields until safely out of range of falling rocks. The archers released one final volley and then ceased fire. The attack was over.

Florio risked a quick peek between two of the merlons. A line of a dozen archers stood in the grassy common below, arrows nocked, bows at the ready. He ducked at once, expecting another deadly rain of shafts. Afraid to show himself from the same position, he scuttled like a spider until he came to the square corner where the broad wings of a gargoyle afforded a bit of concealment. One fast glimpse revealed a contingent of men drawn up in the village. Two figures, presumably leaders, stood a little apart from the others.

Keeping low, the elf scurried to where the siege-kettle, now filled with water, hung on its iron rails. With flint and steel, he ignited the tinder already laid beneath it, then added larger wood from a nearby pile. When the water was brought to a boil, it would do much to discourage anyone trying to force the door.

Still crawling on his belly, he gathered the spent arrows that littered the rooftop. They would be most useful. He knew he should be delighted, having successfully beaten off a sneak attack without loss or injury. But he was instead filled with great trepidation. His villagers had shown no aptitude for war. He would have to amend this if they were to have any hope of survival.

CHAPTER 50

THE WAR SOW

Gavin kept well back from the assault on the tower. He had no intention of dying during this enterprise. He might look like a warrior, but he did not feel like one. He hated the heavy, constricting armor. No reasonable person, he thought bitterly, would willingly wear a shell. His helmet was making his neck ache, and the long blade of his sword, projected behind him like a stupid steel tail.

His shield was the worst. He very much wanted its protection, but it was too heavy and cumbersome. As a trained knife-fighter, he had exceptional speed and agility. Such skills, he believed, served him better than some dreadful wooden board.

Gavin surveyed his mercenaries as they gathered about awaiting instructions. They were hard, capable-looking men, but they had failed him. He had patiently endured their stupid swaggering and posturing, listened without complaint to their childish boasting, all in the belief that they could carry out the job he hired them to do. Now they had been routed by an elf with a handful of rocks. He was furious.

Still, giving into his ire would accomplish nothing. He turned questioning eyes to the mercenary leader, a lean, leathery man named Vilnos—a foreigner of some sort who spoke the common tongue with a thick, barbaric accent.

"Damn door too strong."

Gavin was about to reply that this was patently obvious, since the axes had done little more than dent the portal's iron sheeting, but he restrained himself. Antagonizing the mercenaries would serve no purpose. Thus, he was careful to keep all traces of irritation from his voice.

"What then, Vilnos, do you recommend we do next?"

"Must make war sow."

"What exactly might that be?

"Like roof on wheels with big tree inside for knock down door."

"Do you mean a battering ram?"

"Like I say—war sow."

Gavin had no idea if that last remark was an *aye* or a *nay*. He could only hope that this greasy outlander knew what he was doing. What he had seen so far did not fill him with confidence. He had been certain that if they arrived at dawn, his men could be through the door before the tower's sleepy defenders could rouse themselves. This had not happened.

Instead, the defenders were now fully awake, and two of Vilnos's men were down. One had been knocked cold by the first barrage of rocks. He was now recovering and would soon rejoin his fellows. The other was alive but unable to move or feel his legs. He would have to be quietly dispatched.

"Well then, let us see about building a war sow—whatever that might be."

Vilnos barked commands, and the men rifled the huts and sheds of the nearby village. They found little of interest, as anything edible or valuable had been carried into the tower. They did, however, roust out four unlucky villagers—three men and a girl—who had chosen the comfort of their own beds over the security of the tower's crowded chambers. These were dragged to Vilnos and thrown to the ground at his feet.

The pillaging done, the mercenaries disassembled the huts for building materials. They pulled down beams and joists, planking and rafters. Doors were heaved from their frames, shutters from their windows. Beds and benches were knocked down for their posts and boards.

They lashed these random parts into a narrow structure resembling the framework of a shed. The construction was extremely robust with layers of thick timbers forming a flat roof. The open sides were heavily cross-braced to prevent buckling under the weight of the massive roof. The work proceeded, smoothly and efficiently. Three men were sent to find a long, straight tree for the ram. Others carried hut doors into the tower's yard and erected mantelets as shelter for the archers. They kept a careful eye on the tower's top, eager for a target.

Gavin was impressed. Vilnos's men had obviously done this sort of thing before. Perhaps they would serve their purpose after all. They were hard men and much more capable than the first sorry minions he had brought here. Those three had laughed at him. Well, they would not be doing that again—they had lost their sense of humor entirely.

Gavin was rather surprised that an old soldier like Vilnos could be so readily deceived by his ludicrous tale of a cache of elf jewels hidden in the tower. But then, people were always so eager to believe his tales, no matter how preposterous. That was part of his gift—he could make people trust him. Yet he knew he had better be wary of the mercenary captain. The weather-beaten campaigner had not survived in his perilous trade by being foolish. He was undoubtedly as treacherous as Gavin was himself and would undoubtedly turn on his employer as soon as he saw reason to do so.

Vilnos needed Gavin alive, believing he alone knew the location of the hidden gems. But when no gems were forthcoming, he would be merciless. Gavin could afford to take no chances—Vilnos would have to die. Then, after a bit of fast talking, the surviving mercenaries would become his personal retinue.

Gavin's reverie was interrupted when Vilnos thrust his seamy face into his.

"Talk to elf. Tell him, he don't come out, I cut throats of his friends."

The man was serious. He had the four captives lined up where they could be readily seen through the tower's narrow windows. Knives were held to their throats, ready for a quick slash. This was a good idea. If the elf was softhearted, he might relent rather than cause the death of these miserable peasants.

"I'll do it, but I want two of your men to cover me with shields. That elf is good with a bow. Have your archers ready just in case he shows himself. Maybe they can pick him off."

The captain's reply was gruff—he was not one to mince words.

"I do my job, you go do yours. Talk good. Make 'em believe. Then everything easy."

Gavin found himself trembling as he approached the tower. The elf was a skilled archer. The arrow he had placed between his feet had made that clear. Even with shieldmen guarding him on both sides, he felt woefully unprotected against the lethal kiss of an arrow. Did elves poison their arrowpoints?

Drawing within voice range, he summoned the tower.

"Hallo! Hallo the tower! We would parley. Speak up if you would spare your own life and those of your friends! Show yourself."

He hoped the elf would be careless, so one of Vilnos's archers could kill him with a lucky shot. Then a voice—Gavin recognized it as that of the elf—called down from one of the narrow windows.

"I hear you. Speak your mind."

Gavin kept all hint of fear out of his voice.

"My soldiers are, at this moment, constructing a ram. With it, we will smash your door, enter the tower, and slay everyone inside. I come with royal authority and will not hesitate to carry out my mission. You have one choice—to live or to die. If you open the door and leave the tower, your lives will be spared. But once the ram has touched the door, nothing can save you."

There was a brief pause before the elf spoke again.

"Who are you? Why do you attack us in this way—we who have never harmed you?"

Gavin allowed an angry snarl to creep into his response.

"Who I am matters naught. Concern yourself with the more important question of living or dying. Yourself and your friends."

Gavin gave a signal, and the four captives were pushed forward so the elf could get a good look.

"What's your answer, elf?"

The pause was longer this time.

"I must consider …."

Gavin interrupted.

"Well, consider *this* while you're considering!"

He raised a finger, and the razor edge of a knife was drawn across the throat of a captive—an old man.

Florio watched through a window as the gaffer's throat was cut. His name was Wod. He was so old, his mind was so feeble, that he could scarcely recognize the face of the daughter with whom he lived. He fell forward in a great gush of blood, his legs slowly squirming until he died.

Gavin screamed from the yard.

"Still considering, elf? Need some more convincing?"

Florio was frozen with horror. He could not open the door. That would mean death for them all. Yet he could not stand meekly by while they butchered his villagers. He had to act—but how?

"Wait! Wait! I need more time—just a moment to make arrangements!"

He knew this answer was meager, but it was the only thing he could think of to say. Gavin was similarly unimpressed. He held up two fingers, and another knife opened another throat.

This victim was Frickin, a notoriously contrary plowman who instinctively rejected any suggestion smacking of good sense. He had been was one of the poachers who had been detailed to watch the approaches to the village, but he had deserted his post and returned to his hut to sleep in his own bed.

Florio doubled over as if stabbed in the guts and retched violently on the tower's stone floor. He knew that humans could be cruel, but he had never before witnessed such wanton butchery. Wod was a harmless old man. Frickin had been foolish and contentious, but he in no way deserved to die.

Two captives remained—Millie the blacksmith's daughter and her lover, a hulking youth aptly called Rutt. They had obviously snuck back to the village in search of privacy. Florio could not let them be murdered. But before he could act, there came the *thrum* of a bow, and an arrow went streaking from one of the tower's narrow windows. The arrow flew wide of its mark but came close enough that the men beside Gavin raised their shields and all three stepped backward out of arrow range. Another arrow flew. This one fell short.

The knifemen did not wait for a signal, but slew their captives at once.

A great outburst of shouting and wailing came from the other end of the hall. Frickin's adolescent son, Little Frickin, stood at one of the slit windows. He was about to loose a third shaft, though his targets were now out of range.

Florio barked in his direction.

"Frickin, hold! They are too far! Don't waste your arrows. We need them all."

The boy turned, his eyes filled with a mad burning for vengeance—mad enough perhaps to turn his weapon on the elf.

"Frickin, I said hold! Now hold!"

Little Frickin stood for a moment, then his eyes regained focus as his mind cleared. Two slow, fat tears oozed down his cheeks. Several other boys, Little Frickin's friends, slapped his back and shouted approval, congratulating his fine shooting and cool nerve.

"Attaway, Fricki! You showed 'em, you did."

"Made 'em shit all over theirselfs, I'd say. Good shootin', old lad."

"Yay fer good ol' Fricki. Done right by yer poor dad, for a fact."

Caught in the moment, these boys seemed entirely unaware that their friend's rash shooting had hastened the deaths of Millie and Rutt. They praised his skill with a bow even though none of his arrows had come close to their targets.

Yet Florio was encouraged. The lad had shown an eagerness to fight, and his friends had responded with enthusiasm. So maybe the villagers would stand up. But he knew not to expect too much. These were serfs, and as such, they were by law and custom forbidden the use of arms. Their bows were short, homemade affairs of the type favored by poachers. They had neither the range nor the penetrating power of the heavy war-bows carried by professional archers.

He knew he needed help—help from someone with experience in war, from someone with a host of armed men. But to whom should he appeal? The Earl? The Sheriff? Neither of them would lift a finger to aid a penniless elf. Besides, he had no way to get word to anyone. He had to rely on his own resources.

Vilnos was livid. This arrogant boy—Master Fortunae he called himself—was a liar. He said the door would be easily smashed, but it was thick and strong. He promised there would be no soldiers inside, but the tower dwellers, whoever they were, were shooting arrows and dropping rocks on his men. The boy was no warrior—he was awkward in his armor and stood in the rear like a coward while Vilnos and his men took the risks.

Who was the boy really? He looked like a soldier, but Vilnos could tell he knew nothing of war. Maybe he lied about the elf treasure, too. Or maybe he wanted to keep it for himself. Maybe, maybe, maybe. Vilnos wondered why he had ever allowed himself to be persuaded into this doubtful adventure.

The mercenaries gave a loud shout as they raised a corner of the battering ram's protective shed to attach a heavy wooden wheel. Several of these had been scavenged from the carts and wheelbarrows scattered about the village. They were all of different sizes, causing the shed to tilt to one side and droop precariously at one corner.

The makeshift axles that held the wheels were barely sufficient to carry the great weight of the roof. They would have to push the shed up to the keep's door without the heavy log that would become the actual ram. Once the structure was in place, they would haul the ram beneath the roof and suspend it with ropes and chains. The war sow, for all its crudity, would then be a formidable weapon capable of smashing through the strongest door.

While the last wheel was being fitted, men hung shields along the open sides and front to provide protection from arrows. That done, the mercenaries took positions inside, grasping the posts and crossbars that supported the roof. Pushing against these, they drove the engine forward. Vilnos joined his men beneath the roof. He cast a disparaging look at Gavin, who continued to hold back. The young thief read the look and knew for certain the mercenary captain was now his enemy. So be it.

Gavin knew his own life was much too valuable to risk in such reckless foolishness. But if that grizzled old soldier wanted to lead the attack, so much the better. It would be much simpler if he were slain doing so. As he was sometimes wont to do, Gavin called on Lady Fortune to grant him a boon— *Dear Mother, may Vilnos catch an arrow in his eye!*

With an exultant roar, the mercenaries pushed the sow forward. Its unmatched wheels made it hard to manage. It skewed to one side, lurching drunkenly, awkwardly. But the men, sweating and cursing, shoved and yanked and pulled until the great unwieldy structure swung back to its proper path. Arrows poured from the tower's windows, most striking the roof and hanging shields. Occasionally one found its way inside, but the heavily armored mercenaries escaped unscathed. Vilnos screamed for his men to push harder, and they drove the sow forward with a savage vigor.

Then they were at the door. From the village, other mercenaries came dragging the heavy log that would serve as the ram, its end cut to a blunt chisel edge. Shield men ran before and beside them to guard against arrows. Everyone was shouting, screaming. Large rocks pummeled the engine's roof, the dull *thump* of their impact sounding like a monstrous drum.

The log was hauled beneath the roof and hoisted on the shoulders of the men inside. Then it was tied to thick ropes hanging from the framework above. The ram was ready. The mercenaries took places and sought whatever handholds they could find on the rough, bark-covered length. They began to swing the log back and forth, back and forth, building momentum for the first devastating blow.

CHAPTER 51

FLORIO'S VALIANT STAND

Florio looked on in dismay as the attackers brought beams and boards to assemble the battering ram. He was not sure how long it would take to complete, but he knew he had no time to waste. Fortunately, the villagers were showing some spirit, shouting insults and threats at the men who had slain their friends and family. Their wrath grew as the raiders demolished their homes for building materials. The village was their entire world. Its destruction was a devastating blow to their sense of order and certainty. Florio had no doubt that, given the chance, his people would wreak a horrific revenge.

He called together Frickin and his young friends—they would be his archers. Gripe, the dour fletcher, was appointed as their leader. Hopefully his stubborn, unflappable nature would temper their chaotic youthful excitement. The old-timer took his position seriously and immediately set to work, checking the condition of their bowstrings and the straightness of their arrows.

Big Tam the blacksmith, nearly deranged by the murder of his daughter, was detailed to lead a party of the biggest, strongest men. These descended to the storeroom on the tower's ground floor to stack beer casks and grain bags against the inside of the door. They would also stand ready to repel any attackers who might penetrate this barrier. Armed with nothing more than hammers and farm tools, they stood little chance against the well-equipped, well-trained soldiers that would come bursting through the broken door.

The circular stairs would be the next layer of defense. They were narrow, allowing but one person to come up at a time, and the right-twisting spiral was specifically designed to hamper the sword hand of an attacker. But without proper weapons or armor, the villagers would be hard put to hold even this barrier against a determined assault.

Florio took another look at the men in the yard. What could he do against the ram? He needed to break its back by dropping a great weight from the tower's roof, but the archers would feather anyone attempting to heave such a thing over the parapet. He had an idea—Roscoe's three long dining tables. They were nothing more than long planks laid across supports at either end. When not in use, these were taken down and stored along the walls of the great hall. They could be turned into a protective cover, not unlike the roof of the ram. Florio called for Sulk the village carpenter. The man was slow of wit and not overly skilled at his trade, but he would be adequate for the job the elf had in mind.

"Sulk, see those tables there against the wall? Get some men and carry them upstairs to the roof. The planks are long, so it won't be easy getting them up the spiral stairs, but you've got to do it somehow. Cut them shorter if you have to. Understand?"

Sulk nodded.

"You gonna have dinner up there, Master Florio?"

Florio gritted his teeth, trying to remain patient.

"Nay, Sulk. Those men out there are shooting arrows, and anyone on the roof right now is likely to be killed. That wouldn't be good, would it?"

Sulk shook his shaggy head.

"Nope, that ain't good."

"Right, so I want you to set up those tables to protect us from those arrows. As long as we crawl underneath them, we'll be covered. Understand?"

Sulk nodded again.

"But, Master Florio, what's gonna protect me whilst I'm a-settin' up the tables?"

Sulk was smarter than Florio had thought.

"After you get them all up there, you come get me and I'll help you set them up. We'll have to keep low and be very careful, but we'll be all right. Understand?"

Sulk nodded one last time, his eyes stupid but full of trust. He trotted off to fulfill his mission.

Florio took another quick look out the window, this time at the two men who seemed to be the leaders. They were some distance away, well out of arrow-shot, but elf eyes are keen, so Florio could see something of their features. The shorter one was older, darker. It was he who gave the orders to the men building the ram. The taller one—there was something about him. His ungainly stance suggested discomfort, as if he were unused to wearing armor. He was not a soldier, not really.

Then it struck him—the friar! The Black Friar who had initiated all this turmoil—he, too, had been an impostor! The mock soldier and faux friar were of equal height. Could they be brothers? Or had the black robe of the one been exchanged for the armor of the other? He had no time to think of that now.

Bodo's wife Bess was sent to prepare bandages and poultices, while Florio gathered available chirurgical supplies. Roscoe's uisge was requisitioned for the wounded. Space was cleared to serve as a makeshift surgery.

The elf wondered if he should break the lock on the young witch's occult workroom. There might be something useful inside. He decided against it. He knew nothing of magic and had no idea how to employ anything he might find there. He could inadvertently release an evil presence into the tower. Besides, the villagers were utterly terrified of the room and refused to even approach the well-secured door. If he opened it now, he might drive them into a frenzy. The workroom must remain locked.

It was time to help Sulk on the roof.

Florio was surprised to discover the carpenter had the job well underway. Staying low and keeping quiet, he and two others had managed to set up the trestle supports without attracting the attention of the archers below. They now waited for Florio to show them where he wanted the covers positioned.

The most important place was the section of parapet directly above the door. From that spot they could drop large rocks on the roof of the ram. The area next to Torgul's siege-kettle needed a cover so its fire could be tended and the water replenished. The third and final table would be set up halfway between the stairs and the parapet as an intermediate refuge from a sudden hail of feathered death.

The men were not so careful as before, standing too straight and talking loud as they rested the broad planks across the supports. Arrows immediately started to fall amongst them, forcing them to abandon their work and seek shelter. One took a bad wound when a broadhead point slashed into his forearm. Screaming and bleeding, he fled down the stairs.

From below, a shout of triumph heralded the coming of the ram. There was nothing else for it—Florio leaped to his feet and dragged a trestle toward the parapet. To survive on the roof, they had to set up the tables. He hoped the others would follow his example. They did. Sulk and the others jumped to their feet, all caution abandoned as they threw the planks haphazardly across their supports—not without cost. The dim-witted carpenter went down in a welter of blood, a shaft sunk in the base of his neck.

Seeing their foes in the open, the archers redoubled their fire, driving Florio and his three surviving helpers beneath the tables. Arrows *thunked* into the tabletops. Needle-sharp bodkin points broke entirely through the soft pine boards to project from their undersides. Other shafts struck the rooftop all around them.

A throaty bellow from below drew Florio's attention, but the table was too low for him to see over the parapet. To stand up for a look, he would need a shield, but he had not thought to bring one up to the roof. The clumsy, ill-conceived things his men had made were all below with Big Tam and his men.

Florio bobbed up anyway, risking death for a quick peek between two crenellations. The ram, he saw, was on its way, sliding a bit sideways at first but then straightening toward its target. He saw a volley of arrows fly from the tower's windows, striking the engine's roof and shield-hung sides.

No need to risk another look over the parapet—he had only to look down through the opening over the door. In what seemed like an impossibly brief time, the ram hove into view. Florio signaled his men, who bombarded it with great chunks of shale, schist, and basalt. These landed with the satisfying *crack* of breaking timber but failed to punch through the sturdy roof.

The defenders lifted their largest stone, a jagged piece of flint as big as a cyclops's eye. It was their best chance to break the ram. They discovered that it was too big to fit through the machicolation. Braving the arrow fire, they stood, heaved it up into the crenel, and pushed it over the edge. The immense flintstone smashed into the ram's roof with an explosion of splinters as the boards beneath it shattered. But the stone rebounded harmlessly away, bouncing high into the air like a child in a game of blanket-toss. The ram and the men inside remained unscathed.

There came now a deep, thundering *boom* that made the whole tower shudder. The ram had found the door. It struck again and again, each subsequent impact louder and more forceful than the last. The men below chanted as they swung the ram—back and forth, back and forth.

The arrow fire slackened, then stopped altogether. Vilnos's bowmen were moving their mantelets closer to their target. Time for some hot water. Florio gestured toward the siege-kettle now boiling heartily over its fire. The villagers hooked special handles to the iron loops on its sides and dragged it forward on its rails. The handles were then moved to different loops set into the rim. With one hard tug, the vessel pivoted forward and dumped its scalding contents on the roof of the ram.

There was a *gasp*, and the booming ceased. Then came a raucous laugh. Far from being hurt, the attackers, well protected beneath their heavy cover, were amused by Florio's feeble efforts. The laughter did not last long, however. One sharp command from Vilnos sent them back to work.

Florio also issued commands. The ram had survived rocks and water, but there was one more weapon he could bring to bear—at least if the door held out that long. He pointed at his three men.

"Drag the kettle back, and keep the fire burning hot. Throw on all the wood you can. I'll be right back."

With that, he ran down the steps toward the great hall. Even before he entered the room, he was shouting as loud as he could.

"Bess, get to the kitchen! Fetch all the oil you have—whatever kind it is—and bring it all! Bring me suet, butter, lard, fatback—anything you've got! Hurry!"

He turned to the men and women who cowered in the corners of the hall.

"Bring me every candle you can find, every drop of lamp oil, every scrap of tallow or beeswax! Make haste! Our very lives depend on it."

Not one of them moved.

"Go! Now! Or I'll unlock the demon that lurks in the witch's chamber of magic! Do you want to see its fangs and claws?"

That threat was sufficient. Bent-backed crones and stiff-legged gaffers, pregnant housewives and toddling children suddenly found their legs and sprinted to fulfill the elf's demands. As fast as the required items could be retrieved, he sent them upstairs to the siege-kettle.

The pounding of the ram continued, louder in the hall than on the rooftop. He heard splintering of the door with each successive blow. It could not endure such horrible battering for much longer, and once it fell, every person in the tower would die.

Florio grabbed a shovel from the stack of farm implements and ran back up the stairs. He was followed by women and children bearing cooking oil, lard, and candles, which smoked, spattered, and flared as they hit the hot metal of the cauldron. When the last of the fat was in the pot, Florio's men pulled the kettle down its rails and dumped it on the ram's flat wooden roof.

The hot, greasy mess hissed and sizzled when it struck, soaking into battered wood and oozing down through the many cracks, but it failed to ignite. Florio anticipated this and quickly used the shovel to scoop red-hot coals and burning brands into the smoking cauldron. The attacking archers again turned their bows on the tower. The elf heard a cry as someone behind him was hit, but he had no time to wonder who it was. He signaled his men, and they again raced the kettle down its rails and dumped its content. The burning embers landed directly in the middle of the grease puddle spreading over the top of the ram.

And then it ignited. Just a small flame at first, but then with a *whoosh*, it burst into an intense blaze that ran the length and breadth of the engine's roof. The pounding stopped, and a few of the raiders emerged from the ram, intent on extinguishing the flames. These were driven back by a deluge of smaller rocks launched from rooftop baskets. The ram's grease-soaked timbers began to burn. The attackers attempted to push the engine away from the door, back to where they could fight the fire without fear of the rocks. But the weight of the heavy log frustrated their efforts. One of the makeshift wheels snapped from its axle, causing that corner to sag into the mud. The ram would move no more.

Rather than be roasted alive, the mercenaries abandoned their blazing contraption and bolted from all sides. The more thoughtful ones grabbed one of the hanging shields as they made their break. Those less cautious were struck by the arrows that now poured from the tower's windows.

With the ram fully engulfed in flame, the raiders withdrew to the village, dragging several of their number by arm or leg. Whether these were dead or wounded, Florio could not say. Vilnos's archers unstrung their bows and followed. The elf retrieved his own bow and sent shaft after shaft after the retreating men. He was gratified to see one bowman stumble, hit directly in the buttock.

Four villagers were dead, and two were dying. Many bore wounds. The final arrow storm had caught the rooftop crowded with people, and there were causalities in the great hall as well. One of Florio's young archers had been hit by a lucky shot while standing at his slit window. The arrow still protruded from the lad's pierced lung. A woman had cracked her skull as she ran up the stone steps and slipped in a pool of spilled lamp oil.

The surviving villagers, oblivious to the deaths of their friends and neighbors, sent up a tremendous, triumphant cheer. They sang and boasted and ululated. Several threw their hands above their heads and danced a strenuous jig. Some thanked God, while others kissed. All smiled.

Florio was thankful to be alive but took no joy from the day's events. He had faced armed enemies and driven them from the field, but he could find no glory in their destruction. He discovered no important insights, learned no wonderful truth. Battle was just killing, nothing more. He could only hope that they had killed enough of the bastards to make them go away for good.

CHAPTER 52

ROSCOE'S WILD RIDE

From the distant tree line, the adventure party watched as the ram burned and the bloodied raiders fell back to the village. Roscoe was aghast. What was going on in his demesne? Who were these people?

Sarah had been entirely correct—something very bad was happening.

He had been so certain her predictions were unfounded, nothing more than a young girl's hysteria. But now he saw her wisdom. How foolish he had been to doubt her. How glad he was now that he had yielded to her reason. She was, after all, a witch. Witches have uncanny ways of finding things out—everybody knew that.

Sarah was hunkered down next to Pozi. Her dream, or whatever it was, had been a timely warning. How much better it was to be here now rather than in two days when the tower would have been taken and all the villagers slain. Sarah felt guilty about what she had done to Roscoe, but he had been so stubborn and condescending he left her no other choice. Still, it was distinctly unprincipled to use charm spells on one's friends and allies—was it not? Thurmond had dismissed her qualms—sometimes there was no good way to make the old Adventurer listen to reason.

Thurmond knelt next to his mentor, watching the battle from a thicket of hazel.

"Whoever these people are, Roscoe, I count near two score of 'em. They're well-armed and look like real soldiers. What are we going to do?"

Roscoe snorted.

"Well, them boyos ain't gettin' inside anytime soon. Florio's doin' a fine job of defendin' my property. We got time to ride into Gorgonholm and pay a call at The Severed Head. I'll find plenty old friends there who owe me a favor. I'll come back leadin' a gang of battle-mad Adventurers, so I will."

Roscoe's expectations proved to be overly optimistic. At the Head, he did find a large number of friends and acquaintances who owed him favors, but only three were willing to come to his aid, and they demanded payment in gold. They were, at least, experienced fighters who bore the terrible scars of edged weapons.

The first was Gomez, a black-bearded, thickly muscled man built like a tree stump—short and nearly as broad as he was tall. Alphonse was lean of build and sleek of movement, more skilled with knife and bow than with sword or spear. Black Adam was a haunted, bilious man, a defrocked priest who kept his own counsel.

Returning to Grimsgard, Roscoe and his followers sharpened their weapons and adjusted their armor in preparations for battle. Sarah was aghast. As he tightened the cinch strap on Millie's saddle, Thurmond overheard her confronting the old Adventurer.

"Have you lost your wits, Roscoe? Even with your three friends, there are only nine of us. Eight really, because I'm not having Pozi take part in your crazy scheme."

He gave her his most winning smile.

"We're in complete accord there, lassie, so we are. The child must be kept well away from any danger. And as to me losin' my wits—well, there may be some truth in that, too. An Adventurer has got to have a touch of madness in his soul."

Once again he refused to take her seriously.

"That justifies nothing, Roscoe, and you know it. I don't like any of this. You might be ready to die, but I'm not!"

Her words hurt him. His smile faded, and his voice went wistful.

"That's just as well, then, because you won't be joinin' this nightride. I've got somethin' more important for you to do, somethin' more in line with your special skills."

Sarah was doubtful.

"What are you planning?"

"We don't have to kill all them boyos campin' out in my village. They had a bad day, saw their friends dyin', so they'll be scared. Can't be much fight left in 'em. All they'll be doin' tonight is gettin' drunk. We just gotta spook 'em real good, and they'll run off. Maybe you know a spell or two that will help us out."

"I could do that. I mean, I *will* do that. You know I will, but you have to listen to me—this is sheer madness."

Roscoe cut her off with a wave of his hand.

"And don't be tryin', lassie, to change my mind with another of your charm spells. It took a bit of thinkin', but I finally come to see what happened the other day. It ain't nice to be slappin' your friends with magic."

Caught! Sarah felt her cheeks burning with shame. She recovered quickly and turned the conversation back to the issue at hand.

"There'll only be seven of you on the ride. Facing…what…forty of them?"

"Seven, aye—seven against forty. Won't it be magnificent?"

They certainly did look magnificent as they prepared for what they now jokingly referred to as Roscoe's Wild Ride. Cloaks spread wide over armored shoulders, weapons drawn, horses in line abreast, champing in anticipation. Pozi gave each rider a lighted torch before withdrawing into the shadows of the forest. She would play no further role in the coming conflict.

When all was ready, Sarah began to cast illusion spells. Instead of seven torches, there would seem sevenfold that number. The ground would shudder beneath the pounding hooves. The night air was to be rent by a hellish, cacophonous din, perhaps the shrieks of demons in torment or the mortal screams of dying children.

With the remnant of psychic energy remaining to her, she produced a flock of black flapping shapes resembling huge bats. These should inspire terror, so long as no one looked too closely and disbelieved. Then with the very dregs of her power, she fashioned a gawky, skulking creature with absurdly long arms and legs. It was, in sooth, little more than a vague outline—her energy being so low—but it was large and weird enough to be frightening.

Afterwards, Sarah was drained. Her head throbbed as if struck with a hammer, and her stomach writhed like a skewered serpent. Gasping, she sank to her knees in an effort to keep from fainting. It was never wise to reduce one's psychic vigor to such a degree, but she seemed to make a habit of doing so.

They rode at moonrise, coming on hard, whooping like maddened ghosts, waving their ensorcelled torches, sounding for all the world like a squadron of heavy cavalry. Roscoe's Wild Ride should have been truly magnificent, would have been had it gone as the old Adventurer expected. Unfortunately, he was once again overly optimistic in his expectations.

Vilnos's mercenaries were not, as anticipated, lying in a defeated, drunken funk, but were instead vigilant and angry. There was plenty of fight left in them. Consummate professionals, they were disciplined and methodical in their work. Sentinels were posted both around the village and in the adjacent paddock that held their horses.

Before retiring to the huts to rest and recuperate, they had constructed a barricade of overturned tumbrels and the dismembered remains of doorframes, furniture, and wheelbarrows. Weak spots were reinforced with a hedge of sharpened stakes.

The men on watch were properly alert and blew their warning horns as soon as Roscoe's riders burst from the trees on the far side of the field. Mercenaries poured from their billets, donning armor as they ran. Bows were strung, arrows loosed.

Things went badly for the Wild Riders almost from the start. Sarah's skulker took no more than a dozen wobbly steps before fading to nothing, her power too depleted to sustain it. Then an ill-fated arrow, fired blindly into the dark, struck Gomez square in the chest, punched through his mail, pierced his heart, and killed him instantly.

The flapping bat-things swept down on the village as intended, but their color rendered them next to invisible against the night sky. The mercenaries, intent on their human targets, never even noticed them. They fluttered harmlessly about until, their magic expended, they went the way of the skulker.

Worst of all was that damnable barricade. The companions had been off to Gorgonholm during its building and were therefore unaware of its existence until they ran against it in the dark. Torgul's mount impaled itself on an unseen stake, pitching the dwarf to the ground.

He landed on his shoulder, rolled twice, and was on his feet in a twinkling—unhurt. Two spears immediately jabbed at him from over the barricade, and before he could unsling his axe, they were joined by two more. Torgul could only step away from the darting points.

Thurmond spurred his mount forward, searching desperately for an opening in the barrier, but it was defended everywhere by growing array of spearmen, swordsmen, and archers. Seeing Torgul unhorsed, he leaned low, grabbed his outstretched hand, and pulled him up behind. The dwarf's voice was raspy in the young man's ear.

"This ain't no good, boy, there's way too many of 'em. We ain't got no chance. Ride off."

These words confused Thurmond.

"I can't! What about Roscoe? The others?"

"They ain't fools! They'll see things for what they be. Now ride off before we get feathered."

Thurmond felt an arrow strike his mail. It did not penetrate but struck with sufficient force to be painful. That was enough. He turned Millie's head and galloped back into the dark.

They heard the thudding of hooves approaching swiftly from behind, then Roscoe and Alphonse were beside them, the latter cursing steadily and angrily. Roscoe said not a word but sped on toward the distant trees. The others fell in behind him.

They found Sarah where they had left her. She was shaky and weak from the energy drain of spell casting, but she was able to stand. Bodo and Black Adam rode up, both on the same horse. They had been detailed to open the paddock and stampede the mercenaries' horses, but it had been too well guarded.

Black Adam's mount had collapsed beneath him, after an arrow severed the big vein in its neck. Bodo, bending in the saddle to open the paddock's gate, had been taken by surprise when a man with a falchion came out of the dark. He received a terrible cut just above the right knee, and then another to his body as he tried to draw his sword.

He would have undoubtedly been slain, but Black Adam had come up from behind and cut the swordsman's throat with his dagger. He had then mounted behind the reeling Bodo and held him in the saddle while they retreated under a barrage of arrows.

Bodo's leg was bleeding badly, and it seemed likely he must die unless they stopped to tend to his wound. But there could be no stopping at that moment. The mercenaries might well mount up and pursue their attackers, so they must get further away.

Roscoe rode close beside Bodo, his brawny arm encircling his shoulder to keep him from tumbling to the ground. Thurmond led the way through a tangle of underbrush in an effort to disguise their trail. Pozi rejoined them at a small clearing, where they were finally allowed to rest.

They laid Bodo carefully on the ground then stripped off his mailshirt and gambeson. The heavy-bladed falchion had obviously broken his ribs. He groaned loudly when Roscoe touched the injured spot, and his breath came in short, ragged gasps.

The leg wound was far worse—a large section of meat and muscle had been scooped away just above the kneecap. It continued to bleed heavily, quickly sopping the bandage that Roscoe tied around it. In desperation, he tied a strip of leather tightly around Bodo's thigh, just above the wound. He then inserted a length of stick beneath the leather and twisted it until the flow of blood was reduced to a trickle.

The old Adventurer looked Thurmond straight in the eye.

"Bodo's bad hurt, so he is, and like to die unless he gets help right quick. There ain't nothin' we can do for him here, but them Gray Friars up the road can help him."

Healing spells were a jealously guarded prerogative of the church.

"We've got to cut some branches to make a litter for him—he can't ride that far. We'll tie one end to his horse, the other end can drag on the ground. Bodo's my man-at-arms, so I'll be takin' him. I might need some help. Alphonse will come with me."

It was at that moment they realized that Alphonse was no longer with them. Neither was his horse. The stealthy archer had slipped away unseen.

Thurmond was outraged.

"That's not the way Adventurers do things! Roscoe, you always told me Adventurers stick by one another. That foul bastard left us as soon as things went bad. You oughta kick him out of the Brotherhood."

Roscoe shrugged.

"He's a disappointment, so he is, but we ain't got time to be botherin' about him at the moment. Bodo needs lookin' after. Black Adam, you'll come with me. Thurmond, I'm leavin' you in charge, so figure out what we should do next."

"Me? I don't know what to do."

"I don't either, so you better start thinkin' hard, laddie."

"But Torgul ...."

"Torgul's a great friend and a true adventurin' brother, but he ain't so capable when it comes to things like this here. Tends to get a mite carried away, don't you know? Ask Sarah what she thinks. She's smarter than any of us. Now hurry up and make that litter. Bodo's layin' there dyin' while we're runnin' our mouths."

And so it was that Thurmond found himself leader of a very dispirited and diminished coterie. He had no idea what they should do next.

Roscoe's Wild Ride was not, however, quite the complete disaster it appeared to be. Earlier that day, when the mercenaries were heaving the war sow toward the tower, Gavin had begged Lady Fortune to send Vilnos an arrow in the eye. That plea had been heard, though in her typically capricious fashion, the Good Lady held off granting it until it served her own obscure purpose.

Gavin's prayer was answered during the Wild Ride. As he crashed through the dark, Alphonse, an agile rider, released several arrows from the saddle. These were aimed at nothing in particular, so Lady Fortune must have been guiding his hand. One fateful shaft entered a peasant's hut from which the door had been removed to construct an archer's mantelet. This was the very hut Captain Vilnos selected as his billet for the evening. Said captain was buckling on his swordbelt and preparing to rush forth to battle when Alphonse arrow struck him squarely in the left eye. He was instantly slain.

This was no particular hardship at the time because Vilnos's men were sufficiently battle-wise to carry on without him. Indeed, his death was not even discovered until sometime after the fray. It did, however, prove distinctly problematic the next morning. Many of the men were disgruntled, because Vilnos had promised them an easy job—the takeover of an undefended village, the chance to pillage and rape to their hearts' content. One fell swoop to secure the tower, and then all the feasting, swilling, and screwing they could ask for. But their only reward so far was a cluster of empty huts.

They did not particularly trust their employer, the young man calling himself Master Fortunae, but he had promised them a bounty of ten gold sovereigns per man when the tower finally fell. That was a goodly sum and seemed a fair offer at the time. But now it looked as if, despite their brave efforts, that payment might never come to pass.

With Captain Vilnos dead, command fell to his lieutenant, a big, blond northerner named Hrolf. Vilnos had been a wily and capable leader. So why, Hrolf wondered, would he ever have agreed to this venture in the first place? Always before he had demanded half payment up front—so why not this time? What secret deal had he made with their employer? Hrolf did not believe anything Master Fortunae had to say. The fellow wore fine armor and carried an elegant sword, but he was most clearly not soldier. He stood in the rear, refusing to share the risks of battle with the men in his employ. The battle-hardened mercenary saw him as a poltroon and a deceiver.

Hrolf was in favor of simply killing him, claiming his fine armor as his own, and riding away. But that sneaky prick had spent the night talking and talking to the men, making new promises until he won several to his side. Many were willing to believe him. They were his men now. The bastard was clever. If Hrolf moved against him, his men would end up fighting each other—not good. There was nothing to do but disband the company. Soon after daybreak, Hrolf and his loyal followers decamped, leaving behind a rump force of sixteen men.

Gavin was beside himself. The sense of betrayal cut so deep he thought he might actually weep. What was the matter with people? How could they live with themselves? Was he the only one what understood the meaning of loyalty? Of honor?

Vilnos had sworn an oath to deliver the tower. Though his efforts were far from satisfactory, he had died while attempting to fulfill that sacred obligation. But that hulking churl Hrolf had taken most of the men and deserted without so much as an apology. Didn't they see that under the ancient laws of custom, their master's word had bound them as well? Or perhaps they just did not care.

What was he to do with sixteen men when forty had failed? Sixteen who had no real belly for a fight, who had refused to renew the assault until they could rest? Who claimed to need sleep after being kept awake all night? What good were these?

The day was as cold and gray as his mood. He strode to the village common and stood, hands on hips, looking up at the tower. To his surprise, he saw the elf looking down on him from the battlements.

He moved closer and shook his fist.

"Know this, elf—if your walls were hard as dragon bone, yet would I take them!"

His foe, unmoved, hollered back.

"If these walls were soft as marzipan, yet would I hold them!"

CHAPTER 53

A CARTLOAD OF WANTON DOXIES

As soon as it was light enough to see, Thurmond raised his head above the fallen beech tree. He was, in approaching the tower so soon, defying all common sense, disregarding all instinct for self-preservation, but he had to see what the men in the village were up to. A large group, he counted nearly a score, was busily packing gear and saddling horses, obviously preparing to depart. A second group of roughly equal size stood to one side, watching but making no effort to assist their comrades.

What could be happening? Half the attackers seemed to be leaving, while the other half were determined to remain. The crunching of leaves and snapping of small sticks interrupted Thurmond's thoughts as Torgul came up beside him. They watched as the first group mounted, formed column, and headed off toward the Royal Highway.

The dwarf spoke in a raspy whisper.

"Them horses is all loaded with gear. Looks like they be leavin' for good. Hey listen, I was thinkin' maybe I oughta rig up a catapult an' throw some fireballs into the village. That'd root 'em out o' there."

Thurmond saw what Roscoe had meant about Torgul getting carried away.

"Might be you're right, but I think we'd better just watch. Ask Roscoe about the catapult when he gets back."

Torgul grunted his assent.

Sarah and Pozi came through the trees and joined them. The presence of his friends worried Thurmond. If they did not keep their heads down, they would be spotted for certain. He was trying to be a good leader. Roscoe had placed him in charge, which meant he had to watch out for the entire party, had to keep them from making mistakes that could get them all killed.

He also had to be decisive. Roscoe had told him to determine their next course of action, but try as he might, he could come up with nothing. He took Roscoe's advice and asked Sarah.

"What do you think we ought to do?"

The girl was pale and haggard, still not recovered from her exertions of the night before.

"I think we need to get smarter."

"What do you mean by smarter?"

"I mean exactly what I said—we need to get smarter. Roscoe's ride would have been all fun and glory if it had worked out, but it was foolish because it was much too risky. I'm surprised any of you are still alive."

"All right, how do we get smarter?"

"There's too many of them for us to fight, so we need to be tricky, find their weakness."

This confused Thurmond.

"What weakness? They're not weak. Those are real warriors, who know how to fight."

"Not weak like that. I mean…I don't know…what do you think they're wanting right now? What do they need? Besides getting into the tower, of course. Food? Drink?"

"Well, soldiers always need more food and drink, but I don't think that's a weakness exactly."

"*Women!*"

This came from Torgul.

"Real fightin' men is always hungry for women, 'specially after a battle. There ain't none left in the village or we woulda seen 'em. Them boys will be wantin' some soft time, wantin' it desperate bad. I'm bettin' they'd do 'bout anythin' for a cartload of wanton doxies."

The ancient farm cart was drawn by an equally decrepit donkey. It was not a comfortable ride and the cart stank of cabbages. Sarah walked alongside, guiding the tottering beast around the worst of the potholes. This was not Sarah as anyone had ever seen her before. Her rugged adventuring garb had been exchanged for a gown of crimson scarlet. Her face was heavily caked with white powder, her lips painted red with rouge. Bells jangled from the belt slung low around her hips.

Four more women rode in the cart. The first was quiet, perhaps even sullen, yet her raven-black tresses lent her a mysterious and exotic charm. The next was quite tall—a buxom redhead well into middle age but retaining a lively, winsome smile. Beside her, a lithe and attractive girl of perhaps twenty summers tugged at her gown and shifted about as if nervous and distracted. The fourth was squat and ugly, with a wisp of beard along her jawline suggestive of an internal imbalance.

The tall one spoke to her young, lithe companion.

"The child—she's safe?"

"Aye, back in the woods with the horses."

"Where'd you find the cart and mule?"

"Some old farmer hauling his cabbages to market."

"You didn't just steal it, did you now?"

"Of course not. I paid him."

"How much?"

The girl knew her answer would not be well received.

"A gold piece."

"So much? See here, Prospect, you had no business givin' a king's ransom for a broke-down old cart and a swaybacked donkey."

"When he saw us come out of the bushes, he thought we were bandits. He got so scared he peed himself. I wanted to make it right."

"Well, I suppose that was the proper thing then, so it was."

The tall woman now turned to Sarah.

"You was looking pretty raggedy last night, lassie. How'd you get your power back so quick?"

"Paid a visit to the Goddess Spring. Whisper helped me. He doesn't have near the power he used to, but he's still a creature of pure energy."

"And you're sure the illusion will hold up? It won't suddenly fizzle out at the worst possible moment?"

Sarah was offended by this suggestion, her reply was huffy.

"I think not! Illusions are my forte, as you of all people should well know by now! We'll be fine as long as none of you do anything stupid to arouse suspicion and make them disbelieve. Anyway, the illusion won't have to last that long. As soon as we get them to gather around us, I'll put 'em to sleep. Then you'll do the rest."

Like a flask of overcharged beer popping its cork, the short, ugly woman suddenly blurted out.

"This ain't no good! I can't act like no female. It ain't right, me paradin' around without a proper beard. I...."

But there was no more time for discussion or protest, for at that moment, the cart arrived at the barricade surrounding Grimsgard village. Sentries, seeing its approach, sounded the alarm, but discerning the gender of its passengers, the mercenaries lowered their weapons.

They shouted and crowded around the cart.

"Whooooo! Looky here what we got! Wenches!"

"Well, bless my soul. It's a miracle!"

"Hallo, little ladies. What brings you here?"

"You bring us any wine?"

All was going according to plan. Sarah was about to unleash the first of a barrage of sleep spells when Lady Fortune, who never liked schemes to proceed exactly as intended, gave a wink and a nod.

Contrary to all reasonable expectations, the short, heavyset, bearded woman commanded the most attention. Eager hands reached through the cart's railings, to grope, paw, and caress. At first she just glowered and knocked away the offending fingers, but this only seemed to excite her admirers. When they tried to unlace her bodice and lift her skirts above her knees, she rose up and plowed a meaty fist into a groper's eye. The others looked on in amazement as their comrade was knocked from his feet.

One of the men complained loudly.

"Here now! That ain't called for! I don't believe a girl in your line of work oughta be so high-handed!"

As soon as the fateful words *I don't believe* were out of the man's mouth, a remarkable transformation occurred. Instead of a hard-favored human female, there suddenly stood before them a very male, very angry dwarf, who reached beneath a blanket at his feet and withdrew a most lethal-looking axe.

The mercenaries jumped back, their faces clouded with fear, confusion, and doubt. This shattered the remaining illusion. In a trice the cart was filled not with wanton doxies but with men, men who were busily filling their hands with weapons. Seeing their plan had failed, Sarah immediately started throwing sleep spells. Unfortunately, things did not go as well as she had hoped. The wood sprite had indeed renewed her psychic power, but the illusion spells she had cast over her companions required substantially more energy than she expected, so her sleep spells were weak. She felt that as the first left her fingertips.

The spell struck the three men standing closest to her. One dropped, but the other two merely stood as if dazed and then shook their heads as if coming out of a dream. The spell should have put down all three. The next was aimed at the rear of the cart, at the group who had been accosting Torgul. The distance was not great. The men were easily within range. But today, in her weakened state, the spell fell short. None of the targets seemed to feel it.

She turned again to the first two, who had regained their senses and drawn their weapons. The range was point-blank, enabling her to throw the spell directly in their eyes. Both dropped, but Sarah knew the last of her energy was expended. She reached frantically into her shoulder bag and withdrew one of the scrolls taken from Castle Sathas. It held four spells. They might be anything, there was no way to tell. But this was not a time for undue caution. She read them all as fast as she could. The results were immediate and profound.

Small orange fireballs spiraled through the air and then exploded in showers of white-hot sparks. Some struck the thatch of a hut, setting it ablaze.

Then came a torrent of tiny lightning bolts, each delivering a tremendous wallop. One struck a mercenary in the side of his face, blew clean through both cheeks, and sent a bloody spray of teeth and tongue out the other side. The third spell invoked a horrible sonorous chanting—almost unendurably loud—as if a chorus of drunken ogres were singing a sacred hymn. The fourth called down a rain of skinks—small, silver lizards looking exactly like snakes save for stunted vestigial legs. They were malicious creatures, possessing a nasty, stinging bite.

Sarah hoped the mad medley of spells would cause enough confusion that she and her friends could escape. There was nothing else to do, for they were outnumbered three to one. It looked for a moment as if they might get away. Roscoe and Torgul jumped from the back of the cart, driving the surprised mercenaries before them. None was eager to face the dwarf's axe. But then things went awry. As he clambered from the cart, Black Adam received a blow to the head that sent him reeling into Thurmond, who lost his balance and landed with his face in the dirt. Before he could rise, a spearman raised his weapon, intending to pin the hapless lad to the ground.

Fortunately, Sarah's spells had not yet run their course. The fireballs continued to shoot sparks, and the diminutive lightning bolts maintained their painful barrage. Thurmond was saved when a free-falling skink sailed down the open neck of the spearman's gambeson. Bitten again and again, the spearman hopped about, beating wildly at his belly and chest. The battered reptile was forced to seek refuge in the man's small clothes, biting all the while.

Thurmond found his feet, grabbed the insensible Adam by one foot, and dragged him beneath the cart. The mercenaries were for the moment too involved with the magical assault to concern themselves with human foes. They clustered together with their weapons ready, but they did not move to the attack.

Sarah was about to leap from the cart when a random lightning bolt exploded on the rump of the geriatric donkey. It brayed loudly and launched itself forward with more energy than it had known for years. Tossed headfirst to the ground, Sarah struck hard and almost lost consciousness.

The magic ended as abruptly as it had begun. Fireballs, lightning bolts, chanting, and skinks suddenly ceased. The mercenaries prepared to renew the battle. Swordsmen raised their shields. Archers strung their bows and notched their arrows.

Sarah raised herself from the mud. She had one final gambit. If it failed, she would have to draw her sword and join the others in a hopeless battle. She fished the leather box of glass globes from her bag. There were two left—blue and black—she chose the blue one and threw it into the midst of the mercenaries.

Blue being the color of cold, Sarah expected ice or snow, but she got water. A rainstorm of epic—nay, *mythic*—intensity. It was like something from the end of days. A downpour so extreme, with raindrops so fat and heavy, that the combatants were forced to kneel under the force of the impact. Fighting became impossible. Vision was limited to inches, and breathing could be accomplished only with the utmost care. Yet for all its intensity, the storm was quite small in girth, encompassing an area of no more than fifty yards across.

The spell, like those on the scroll, was short-lived. Within minutes it slackened, diminishing at first to a deluge, then winding down to a cataract, a monsoon, a torrent. When it lessened to a cloudburst, the fighters rose and looked to their weapons. The sodden strings rendered bows useless, so the archers drew shortswords and long daggers. When the rain dwindled to a shower, the mercenaries reformed their ranks and advanced. Thurmond faced a pair of sword-and-shields with a spearman coming up to join them. He knew he could not last long against this deadly combination. The storm continued to wane—he would die in a gray, hazy drizzle.

Sarah prepared to hurl the last glass sphere. This was a desperate act. She was certain the black globe held some form of death magic, but she knew nothing of its range or power. It might kill them all. Then out of that drizzle came Florio, leading a mob of villagers armed with scythes, grain flails, and kitchen knives. Distracted by the storm, the mercenaries remained unaware of the impending threat until sickles were severing their tendons and blacksmith hammers were caving their skulls. The elf was in the forefront, wielding his weapon of choice, a large iron toasting fork.

When the mercenaries spun about to face this new, unexpected assault, they were taken in the rear by Thurmond, Roscoe, and Torgul who immediately leapt to the attack. The dwarf's mighty axe rose and fell with the same even rhythm of a musician beating a drum. The fighting lasted no longer than had the rain of skinks.

Any mercenary who fell to the ground was slain by the vengeance-hungry villagers, as were those who threw down their arms and begged for quarter. A few managed to escape to the paddock, fling themselves upon unsaddled horses, and flee across the fields, but even those did not get away unscathed. For at that moment, the wayward poachers, who had remained in hiding since the arrival of the invaders, rose up from the weeds and loosed a volley of arrows at the invaders' backs. One fellow, struck in the base of the neck, fell sideways from his mount. Another, caroming against a beehive in his desperate flight, rode off in a cloud of outraged insects.

The killing done, Florio approached Roscoe, whom he saluted with his bloody fork.

"Welcome home, milord."

He gestured toward the ravaged village and corpse-strewn grounds.

"I'm afraid I've been rather lax in my duties. Things have become somewhat...disarrayed. Had you sent word ahead, I would have tidied up. My apologies."

The old Adventurer stared in disbelief, then grasped the elf by the shoulders and kissed him on both cheeks.

Gavin had watched with disinterest as his men ogled the cartload of lowborn sluts. As the son of a goddess, he would never consider defiling himself with such base creatures. When the fighting started, he watched intently but took no hand in it. Let the soldiers take care of it! That's what they were for. When the elf led the sortie from the tower and he saw his soldiers slain, Gavin slipped off unseen. He could not guess why Lady Fortune would allow such an enormity to occur, but he assumed it would work out to his liking.

CHAPTER 54

DISTURBING CONVERSATIONS

"So, Prospect, what great lesson has this adventure taught you? Your mentors included Bukovian bandits, an old witch and her minions, a false wizard with a pack of wolves, and now these…well…whoever they were. Did I leave anyone out?"

"I found the tutorial of Baron Melgwyn to be quite instructive."

"Aye, the good baron. I quite forgot him, so I did. Now tell me, what was gleaned from the curriculums of these fine instructors? Speak up now!"

The old Adventurer was feeling fine. He had enjoyed a great night's sleep in his own bed. After the strenuous demands of the last few days, he had really needed that. From the kitchen came the smell of Florio's wonderful cookery. The breakfast menu included poached fresh-water hagfish garnished with young frogs, a zesty stew of badger paws and ferret livers, and the collops of a creature Florio could only identify as a *squeezle*—this was later found to be a porcupine.

Roscoe and Thurmond sat in the great hall, which bustled with activity as things were, in Florio's words, being put to right. The livestock had been driven back to the pastures, their dung was now being scraped from the floor. Pozi, having been fetched from her hiding place in the woods, was busy with a stick, prodding chickens and geese down from the beams and chandeliers. The arrow-gouged tables were carried down from the roof.

There was, at the moment, no place to sit in the hall except on the floor, but Roscoe accepted this inconvenience with the best of humor. He was now—goblet of mead in hand—subjecting his Prospect to a challenging examination.

"You aspire to the Black Hat, and that's a fine thing, so it is. But there's more to bein' an Adventurer than fightin'. You gotta have the right kind of thoughts in your head and feelin's in your heart. I ask you again, what did you learn on this adventure?"

Thurmond was loath to answer. He was pretty sure Roscoe would not like what he had to say, but finally he began.

"I learned more from my friends than from my foes. I learned there are different kinds of Adventurers, and that not one of them truly lives up to the ideals you're always preaching about. Since I can't rely on anyone else to show me how to act, I have to trust myself to make the right decisions."

Roscoe frowned.

"What do you mean by *none of 'em live up to their ideals?*"

"I mean when you really needed help, only three of your so-called friends would come with you. They're supposed to be your *adventurin' brothers*, but they didn't act like it. The three who came weren't moved by any sense of loyalty. They wanted your gold. And that scurvy Alphonse deserted the first chance he got."

"Well, I can't argue with any of that. Not all who wears the hat honors their obligations."

But Thurmond was not finished.

"And you, Roscoe, you left me and Sarah alone on that bloody mountain after Torgul was hurt, and again when you took Bodo to the friars."

"You think it's wrong, then, for me to look after my friends? I would've done the same for you, boyo. Don't ever doubt it."

"But you abandoned us like we didn't matter, and both times you insisted I had to carry on with the adventure. I didn't know what I was supposed to do."

"Consider that part of the test, boyo. Seems to me you did right fine on both occasions."

Thurmond paused and took thought before continuing.

"All right, I see what you mean. Maybe that's why I have to trust myself. There won't always be someone older and wiser to show me the way."

The old Adventurer smiled.

"Just so, laddie, just so."

Thurmond did not return the smile.

"There's one more thing, Roscoe. You're not going to be happy when I tell you."

Roscoe's smile faded, his tone grew sharp.

"Out with it, Prospect! Say what you mean to say!"

"Like I said, I've learned I have to rely on my own judgment...even when other people may not like it."

"You're meanin' me, are you not?"

"Not just you—anybody."

Thurmond was getting nervous, flustered.

"Anyway, I have to tell you—if I ever become a full-fledged Adventurer, I'm making Sarah my Prospect. I want you to know this ahead of time, in case it makes a difference."

Roscoe stood up abruptly, all trace of emotion erased from his face.

"Indeed it makes a difference, Prospect. Now go find Torgul, and ask him to please come talk to me. Then see what you can do to straighten this place up. The mess is distressin' me somethin' fierce, so it is."

Thurmond found Torgul outside where the light was better, stitching a ragged gash in Black Adam's brow. He delivered Roscoe's message and then moved to Sarah, who was now back in in her accustomed garb. They watched two peasants disassembling the charred remains of the ram. On the far side of the field, others were digging a large pit for the dead mercenaries.

Sarah looked a bit less battered today, but the dark circles under her eyes betokened a deep state of exhaustion. The excessive draining of her magical energy had taken a serious physical toll.

"I talked to Roscoe."

"Did you tell him?"

"That I did."

"How'd he take it?"

"Not so good—about like I expected. He seems pretty offended, like I'm betraying him."

Sarah heard the gloom in his voice.

"Look, Thurmond, if this will affect your chance of joining the Adventurers, let's just forget about it. I'm not going to come between you and your dream. Anyway, the Adventurers are like the wizard's guild. It's just another men's club. I'd never really be accepted."

Thurmond exploded.

"Nay, nay, nay! I've always believed—like Roscoe always told me—that if you're an Adventurer, you're bound by a code of honor. That you have to stand by your brothers no matter what. Well, he's not standing by you now. It's not right to push you away just 'cause of how you pee."

"What?"

"How you pee—you told me you couldn't be an Adventurer 'cause of how you pee, remember?"

"Oh, that…"

"If Roscoe and Torgul can't see that, after all we've been through together, then they might as well refuse me, too."

Sarah was deeply touched by his loyalty. She knew how he had longed to become an Adventurer since childhood, how he struggled and suffered to prove himself. And now, on the verge of success, he was willing to throw it away on her behalf. She reached out and touched his arm.

"Let's get away from here for a little while. Let's take a walk to the Goddess Spring. It's a peaceful place. That's what we both need right now. Maybe Whisper will restore some of my energy. I haven't rested enough yet to get my power back."

The path to the spring was deliberately convoluted, winding through groves of trees, between dense patches of undergrowth, and around moss-covered boulders. The journey there was not intended to be a straight course because nothing in the world really followed the cold, hard line of logic.

The twistings and turnings of the path offered a chance for calm reflection and self-centering before arrival at the shrine—at least that may have been the intention—but Sarah and Thurmond were anything but quiet and reflective as they made their way along it. They were deeply engrossed in another important topic.

"… Dollop, he was my gaoler, he said the nobleman, the one who told Melgwyn I was a princess, was young and tall. The false wizard also was tall, and he wore a false beard, so maybe he was young but trying to look old."

"I think you're right. I was talking to Florio last night. He said the false friar who threatened him was also young and tall, as was the false soldier who seemed to lead the attack. Florio thinks those two were the same man. I think they were all four the same man."

Sarah threw up her hands in frustration.

"Who is this poxy blackguard? Why does he hate us so much?"

"Whoever he is …."

Thurmond did not have a chance to complete his thought because something heavy crashed into the back of his head and knocked him from his feet. As darkness closed around him, he was vaguely aware of Sarah screaming.

When Thurmond came to, it seemed Black Tam the blacksmith was pounding his head with a hammer. But that pain paled compared to the biting agony shooting through his arms and legs. Struggle as he might, he was unable to shift his limbs to a less excruciating position.

Opening his eyes, he found he was locked to a heavy iron bar that ran the length of his back. A collar at one end went around his neck, while thick bands along its sides constrained his wrists and ankles. The peculiar placement of these bands was forcing his body into a most unnatural and painful posture.

Movement on the other side of the room drew his attention. Sarah lay on her face, apparently unconscious, her hands and feet tied together behind her back. A tall figure stood over her, using a knife to cut the lacing from the back of her gown. Thurmond fought to rise, but could not.

The tall figure noticed his thrashing and turned toward him.

"So, boy, you're awake. Excellent! Just in time—I didn't want you to miss the show, but I have to admit I was getting restless, a bit overeager perhaps. But no matter, since you're awake now."

It was Gavin! The lying thief who had tried to violate Sarah months ago. Who had tried to kill them at the Goddess Spring. The thief chuckled.

"Surprised to see me? You shouldn't be. I've been with you through most of your travels."

He affected the stooped posture and quaking voice of an old man.

"Remember the venerable Buyuk ve Korkunc Sihirbazi? Well, he was me."

He straightened his back, and his voice assumed a woebegone timbre.

"And the sad young nobleman who encouraged the good Baron Melgwyn? Me again."

Thurmond struggled against his bonds.

"How do you like the bilboes? That's bilboes, not bilbo—always plural, you know. A bilbo in the singular is, I believe, some kind of a sword. But bilboes are a droll little gadget, aren't they? Actually, I brought it for the elf. I thought it would help hold him still while I peeled off his skin one little strip at a time. That's a reward I do not intend to deny myself, by the way.

"But in the meantime, it was just lying there collecting dust, so I thought, why not try it out on the boy? Those loops holding your hands and feet— they can be adjusted to make the experience more…diverting. What do you think?"

Thurmond rolled and flopped, but this only caused more pain. Gavin, never hesitant to shout his own praises, continued his monologue.

"For a while, I could not understand why my mother—that's Lady Fortune—I'm a demigod you must understand—why she let you kill my soldiers. There had to be good reason because things always go my way.

"But then I understood. She allowed you to escape all my traps just so we could have this time together alone. I knew that if I was patient, your whore would be coming along that path to her stupid shrine, but Mother Fortune sent *you* along as well—like a gift to her favorite son.

"It all works out. Once I enjoy my revenge with the whore, you'll be next. Then I'll devise a new plan to take that tower away from the fat oaf and his disgusting elf. I always win."

Thurmond was so shocked, so horrified, that he knew not what to say. His response was discouragingly trite.

"You...bastard...I'll...kill you!"

Gavin grinned, he was clearly savoring all this.

"How clever! Did you think that up all by yourself? Maybe I should write it down. You won't object if I steal your line, will you? But enough of this! Time to get down to business. I've got to wake the little bitch up. I don't want her to miss any of what's coming."

Thurmond's mind raced. He needed something to distract this lunatic.

"You say you're a demigod. What does that mean?"

Obviously irritated by the interruption, Gavin snapped haughtily.

"I told you, Lady Fortune is my mother. I'll explain it all after I've had my pleasure."

Thurmond desperately tried to find something to prolong the conversation.

"Wait! If that's true, it changes everything. We didn't know who you really were. We wouldn't have...we would never..."

Gavin ignored him and turned his attention to Sarah. Thurmond thrashed painfully and futilely against the iron bands that constrained him. But then he heard the lock that secured the bilboes go *click*, felt the bands that held his hands, feet, and head loosen and fall away. Sarah opened her eyes, looked over at him, and winked.

CHAPTER 55

SHOWDOWN

Thurmond took stock of where he was—a simple wooden hut with a dirt floor, perhaps a shepherd's cottage. It was small and cramped, not a good place for a swordfight. His blade and swordbelt lay on the floor perhaps six feet in front of him. Gavin's battle-gear was in a heap on the room's other side—mail, breastplate, helmet, sword, crossbow. The only weapon he had at the moment was the dagger in his hand.

Absorbed with the removal of Sarah's bodice, Gavin failed to notice Thurmond's release. The thief rolled her onto her back and grabbed a handful of her hair.

"Wake up, slut. You're about to receive the greatest thrill of your life—the greatest and the last."

Thurmond sprang to his feet and grasped the bilboes by one end, like a great iron club. He was dreadfully aware of his opponent's skill and speed with a knife, and of the awkwardness of his own weapon. His chances, he knew, were slim.

Though taken by surprise, Gavin was blindingly fast. In one graceful motion, he released Sarah's hair, pivoted, and lunged at his adversary, his knife at throat level. The fight might have ended right there, but Thurmond had anticipated just such a response.

He dropped low and swung the bilboes horizontally to crack Gavin hard across the shin. The thief shrieked and stumbled backward. Thurmond used the opening to pull his sword from its sheath. He expected Gavin to draw his own sword, which was near at hand. Then the real fight could begin. But Gavin, always tricky, surprised him. He jinked to his left, putting Sarah between them, and again snatched up a handful of her hair. The edge of his dagger was pressed to her throat and a thin line of blood appeared.

"Want to see her die, boy? That what you want?"

"Nay, don't! Let her alone. Come outside, and fight me man to man. I'm the one you really want, isn't that right? That's why you were saving me for last…hmmm?"

Thurmond slowly backed away until he was up against the hut's sagging door. Never taking his eyes from the thief, he fumbled it open with his left hand and stepped outside. He needed room to fight, and he had to draw Gavin away from Sarah. Thurmond's voice was jeering, spiteful.

"Come on, Gavin! Don't be afraid! Or maybe Sarah ruined you as a man when she kicked you in the stones! Sodding coward!"

Gavin was immune to such taunts. He had absolutely no sense of personal honor nor felt any obligation to his own manhood, so the insults might well have been delivered in an unknown tongue.

Then, by great good luck, Thurmond tried a new angle and found the one soft spot where the crazed thief was vulnerable.

"You say you always win. Well, I haven't seen you do anything but lose. I could have killed you in the stone circle. You've still got the scar I put on your face. Loser! We left you for dead at the goddess shrine. You call that winning? Your schemes all fail. You always fail. You're not a winner—you're a loser! Loser! Loser! Loser! You say you're the son of a goddess. Nay, you're more like the son of a common strumpet!"

These last words did the trick. Gavin came flying out the door in a blind rage, sword in hand.

"Don't talk about my mother!"

With that, Gavin was on him, wielding his sword in both hands. Its blade was long, narrow, and tapered to a sharp point. A deadly weapon capable of delivering a lethal thrust or debilitating cut. Thurmond's broadsword had a much heavier blade, which could cleave through leather and mail. But neither fighter wore armor, so Thurmond's weapon put him at a disadvantage.

Gavin was supremely confident that he could defeat this upstart whelp quickly with scant risk to himself. He would, he decided, disarm him rather than kill him outright, then he might still have his fun later on. He had good reason to be cocky. He was superbly trained with edged weapons, his sword was lighter and faster, and he was a much bigger man with a longer reach. This luckless boy would soon be his.

Thurmond did not wait for Gavin's attack but came on quickly with a three-blow flurry, one shot to each side of the head followed by a third aimed at mid-thigh. Gavin parried all three, smiled, and took a quick jab at Thurmond's face with his weapon's point. As Thurmond lurched back to avoid the thrust, Gavin stepped forward, continuing his attack, pressing in with a series of light, fast head shots, taking his opponent's measure rather than making a determined effort to kill.

Frustrated, Thurmond tried to kick Gavin in the groin, but his boot struck only the meaty part of his opponent's thigh. Gavin sneered at this failed attempt.

"Is that truly the best you've got, boy? The little harpy in the hut kicks better than that."

Then Gavin came on hard, slicing rather than hewing at Thurmond's unarmored flesh, sending him reeling backward in an effort to escape the unrelenting attack. Thurmond's parries were ragged, and he received long, nasty cuts up and down his arms. His broadsword was a highly effective weapon when used behind a shield, but it was not designed for this style of sword-on-sword combat. Thurmond finally managed to slide out of range, and both fighters paused to take a breath. Gavin, Thurmond realized, was not trying to slay him, but to bleed him, weaken him, disarm him.

It was time for a new tactic.

Thurmond jumped forward, crowding his opponent chest to chest. This was risky because Gavin's superior size gave him a great advantage at such close range, but Thurmond did not intend to stay there long. Before the bigger man could respond, he pushed the edge of the broadsword into his opponent's forehead and left cheek, opening them to the bone. It was certainly not a debilitating injury. The force of the blow was insufficient force to shatter the skull or jaw, but it was enough to make Gavin gasp and spin away. The pompous thief was always astounded, outraged, indignant even, when an adversary hurt him. Superficial though it was, the wound bled heavily, forcing Gavin to use one hand to wipe the blood from his eyes.

This was Thurmond's moment. He glided into range, preparing another three-blow flurry, this one ending with a blow to the side of the neck. But before he could take his first shot, Gavin dropped his sword and staggered backward. His hand reached convulsively and closed around a crossbow bolt protruding from his chest. He pitched forward, seemingly dead, but Thurmond wanted to be certain. He drove the point of his sword through the man's body again and again, unable to stop himself.

Then Sarah was with him, one hand still holding Gavin's crossbow, the other trying to hold up the torn remnants of her gown.

"That's probably enough, don't you think?"

Thurmond turned to her, his eyes wild with battle-madness.

"Damn it! I had him. Why did you do that?"

Sarah was startled by his reaction.

"What?"

"I had him. I wanted him, and I had him. He was mine, but you shot him. Damn it, Sarah!"

Then he sank to his knees as the fury drained from him and was replaced by pain and exhaustion. Sarah helped him back to the hut and inspected his wounds. The cuts were long but shallow. Clearly Gavin had been toying with him. She took a shirt from the dead man's effects and tore it into strips for bandages. She found a skin of wine, which they passed back and forth until it was empty.

When Thurmond said nothing, finally Sarah spoke.

"Aren't you the slightest bit curious how you got unlocked...or how I got loose? When you left the cabin, I was still hogtied."

He looked at her with tired eyes.

"Aye, tell me. How did all that come about?"

Unlike Thurmond, who was dazed and worn out, Sarah was filled with nervous energy. She was eager to talk.

"Magic! Only I didn't intend for it to happen like it did. Remember my knock spell—the one I used to unlock the cathedral gates the night we snuck in there? That's how I unlocked that metal thing you were trapped in. I'm pretty proud of myself. I cast it from clear across the room. Didn't even have my wand.

"Anyway, that knock spell was so powerful it worked on my bindings as well. As soon as I cast it, I felt the knots loosen. I didn't dare make a move while that horrible pig was standing over me, but as soon as you lured him outside, I started working myself free."

This puzzled Thurmond.

"I thought all your energy was expended, that you didn't have anything left after yesterday."

"I thought so, too. But while you were unconscious, I was lying there and listening to that madman go on and on about all the things he was going to do to me. I started thinking about all the terrible things he had already done. How he lied to me, betrayed my trust, took my coin, tried to take my body. He had me locked up in a stinking cell and tried to take our home from us.

"Remembering these things, I was bursting with anger. I've never hated anyone like that before, not even my brother Bart. Hate's such a strong emotion, I thought maybe I could use it to empower a spell or strike him with a curse. I tried as hard as I could to stop his heart or fry his brain, but I was just too weak. I used so much magic during our adventure that I wore myself down to nothing.

"But then you woke up, and he started taunting you. In knew I had to do something or he'd kill us both in some slow, hideous way. I tried my knock spell on that iron thing he had you locked in. It worked."

Thurmond raised an eyebrow.

"So how come you could suddenly do that? What was different?"

Sarah's expression suddenly softened.

"It had to be the strength of my feelings."

"What feelings—your hate?"

"No, Thurmond. Hate wasn't enough. It was something else."

The young man's eyes gleamed with a winning sparkle his mother called his *bing*.

"You mean your feelings for me? Is that what you're saying?"

Sarah's deep crimson blush was all the answer Thurmond required. He gave a tired little laugh.

"You're a dangerous woman. I must remember never to make you angry." Sarah also laughed.

"That's right. You had better be careful."

"Why did you have to go and shoot Gavin? I was just about to kill him. I wanted him so bad, but you took him. You stole my victory."

Sarah was not nearly as certain about the battle's outcome, but she was not about to tell Thurmond that.

"I'm sorry, I really am. I just had enough of the dirty arsehole. I had to shoot him. Anyway, we should be getting back. Do you feel well enough to walk? If not, I could go bring back some help and a cart."

"Do you know where we are?"

"Certes, in an old, abandoned shepherd's cottage. I've been by here before. It's not very far from the Goddess Spring."

"I can make it, but I have to do something first."

"What would that be?"

"I gotta make sure that Gavin stays dead this time. Then I want to lie down. I need to rest a bit before we head home."

Sarah was suddenly as tired as he was.

"Go do whatever you're going to do. I'll look for a blanket or a cloak in Gavin's gear. I'll curl up with you until you're ready to head back."

They returned to the tower in the late afternoon, Gavin's head dragging on a rope behind them. Sarah carried the dead man's fine, bronze-trimmed helmet, which Thurmond claimed as his own. Their arrival aroused an explosion of excitement and curiosity, for no one knew where the couple had disappeared to, and all feared the worst.

While Florio cleansed and dressed his wounds, Thurmond related the story of their captivity and the fight in the woods. The mystery of the tall imposter was solved at last. The tale told, Torgul departed to retrieve the rest of Gavin's equipment. A careful inspection of his remains revealed no kraken tattoo, so he had not been of the Brethren after all. His head was displayed atop the tower's battlements, much to the enjoyment of all.

CHAPTER 56

AT THE SEVERED HEAD

After three days, Florio had Grimsgard pretty much back to normal. The dead had been buried, and the burned ram had been cleared away. Torgul and a gang of village men were repairing the damaged huts. Others were back at work in the fields. Butter was being churned and chickens fed. Black Adam returned to the city. Florio mixed up a batch of a special salve that had a marvelous healing quality, so wounds were coming along nicely. His meals were, of course, superlative.

But all was not well. Roscoe and Torgul remained conspicuously aloof from Thurmond and Sarah. They were courteous, but their usual warmth and good humor was distinctly lacking. Something was definitely on their minds.

Then one afternoon, the old Adventurer summoned his Prospect.

"Tonight there's goin' to be a gatherin' of the Black Hats at The Severed Head. I'm thinkin' that cowardly Alphonse is like to be there, and if he is, I intend to settle the score for his runnin' out on us and all. If your cuts are healed sufficient, it would be most convenient to have you there. He may have friends with him."

The Severed Head, properly known as The Old Traitor's Head or sometimes simply The Head, was a notorious drinking den where the Adventurers customarily met to swap lies and plan expeditions.

Thurmond heard the unspoken challenge in Roscoe's invitation—was he willing to stand by a friend in spite of his own injuries?

"Certes, I'll come, Roscoe. My wounds are minor."

"Very well—and would you speak to Sarah for me? She'd be welcome as well, if she's willin'.'"

The excessive formality, the indirectness—this was not the playful, kind, affectionate Roscoe who Thurmond loved so well. What had changed? Had his own stubborn resolve to bring Sarah into the Adventurers driven a permanent wedge between himself and his mentor?

Sarah would certainly be willing to accompany them. They all wanted a crack at Alphonse.

As Roscoe predicted, The Head was jammed that night with men wearing the huge black campaign hats that denoted membership in the Brotherhood of Underworld Adventurers. There was also a full complement of Prospects, hang-arounds, and eager young women whose fondest dreams were to win the affections of such legendary figures. These were not men who held back, so the mead, wine, and ale flowed copiously. Large flasks of illegal uisge were passed from hand to hand. The revelers told obscene jokes, swapped outrageous yarns, and bellowed incomprehensible songs. Some even tried to dance.

Now one might assume that at an event attended by such colorful individuals, a certain degree of bloodshed was to be expected. Such a supposition would be mistaken. Even in a highly inebriated state, the Adventurers displayed a remarkable degree of courtesy and self-restraint. In a company of professional killers, civility was the key to survival.

When a great, lumbering, hairy bruiser tromped on Thurmond's toes while attempting to execute a complicated *estampie*, the fellow immediately begged his pardon and offered to buy him a drink. Moments later when a swaggering young Prospect made a rude remark to a young lady, the same bruiser lifted him by the throat with one hand and pinned him against the wall so his feet dangled several inches from the floor. The misguided fellow was instructed in proper deportment until he saw the error of his ways. Restored to his feet, he apologized to the lady and offended no more.

Nonetheless, Thurmond and Sarah were looking for trouble, and were disappointed when Alphonse was not in attendance. With nothing else to do, they joined in the raucous festivities and were soon feeling the effects of the uisge. After all the hardships they had endured, it felt good to let go.

They were surprised, therefore, when the gathering became something more than a wild revel. The clanging of a bell called the assembly to order, and the Black Hats pushed through the crowd to take positions at the front of the room. Roscoe stepped up onto a low stool and addressed the crowd.

"We are gathered here tonight for a most momentous occasion—the admittance of a new member into our sacred Brotherhood, so we are. He has fought alongside Brother Torgul and myself more times than I can recall. His skill with arms—well, in sooth it ain't quite what it should be, but he's gettin' better. His courage and loyalty are beyond question. His wisdom—he's workin' on that, too.

"But a finer adventurin' brother none of you will find anywheres. And most of all, he has an uncanny knack of findin' treasure. Brother Adventurers, I now summon Thurmond of Grimsgard to join our ranks."

Rough hands grabbed Thurmond from all sides and propelled him forward. All the details of the initiation ceremony may not be described in this narrative, as they remain closely guarded secrets, and it would be deadly dangerous to reveal too much. Let us just say it involved an element of personal embarrassment, a modicum of physical abuse, some extended and pointless ritual, and much swilling of strong drink. Few of the individuals witnessing the ceremony would remember much about it the next day.

After a great deal of smiling and congratulating and backslapping followed by more drinking, Thurmond, now wearing Roscoe's hat, was released to rejoin Sarah in the crowd. He presumed he would spend the rest of the evening carousing with his new brothers, but other important business came first.

Torgul now stepped upon the stool but, even so, lacked the height to make himself seen above the crowd. After some grumbling, a table was pushed up, and he mounted it. He spoke in typical gruff, dwarven fashion.

"I ain't much one for fancy words. I say what I mean to say, and that's about it, so maybe it's better that I'm the one doin' the sayin' now, 'cause there's some things that gotta be said.

"Our Brotherhood's got many fine traditions, and them are important because it's tradition what binds us together. But there's times when traditions gotta change. Some of you might remember when no dwarf could wear the black hat. I'm mighty glad you was smart enough to see how stupid that was."

Torgul took a huge swig of ale and went on.

"Well, tonight we're gonna make a change that needs to get made. Roscoe and me, we got us a Prospect here that's as brave and loyal as any of you brothers out there. This one ain't maybe that great with a sword or a bow, but plenty deadly when it comes to flingin' magic. There ain't no doubt this Prospect earned a hat, and if any of you thinks different, you can take it up with me later."

Roscoe rose from his bench and stood beside his friend.

"You can take it up with both of us right now, so you can."

Torgul resumed his speech.

"Sarah Staynes, come forward and join our ranks."

The assembly was shocked speechless as Sarah made her way forward. She was a girl—a female woman! How could this be? This could only be a jest, surely, or perhaps some mistake. Thurmond looked at Roscoe, who returned his gaze with a broad, self-satisfied grin.

And then the newest Adventurer, standing in the back, gave a great triumphant cheer, and the crowd responded in kind—*wahooing*, clapping hands, stamping feet, raising flagons on high. Maybe it was all the alcohol, possibly it was Sarah's natural poise and beauty, or perhaps the old ways were not as sacred as expected, but nobody took any noticeable exception to Sarah's initiation.

The particulars of her ceremony, like Thurmond's, must remain shrouded in mystery. Suffice it to say that it was very similar save that the ingestion of a live frog was substituted for the bare-bottom paddling. At the end, she received Torgul's absurdly wide-brimmed hat, which spread out over the tips of her shoulders.

The rite complete, she rejoined Thurmond, who threw his arms around her neck. He looked into her eyes.

"You officially belong somewhere now—feel good?"

"Aye, it does, but I realized something a while ago where I really belong— with you. We belong to each other."

And then they kissed for a long, long time.

This intimate moment was brought to an abrupt end when the couple was forcefully pulled apart. It was time to get their tattoos. They were led to a table at which sat a leather-faced, one-eyed man. Spread before him were pots of ink and an array of bronze needles laid out on a cloth.

Roscoe handed them both a goblet of uisge.

"Best drink up—this is like to sting a bit. Thurmond, you was initiated first, so you goes first. This here is Squinty. He's been tattin' new Adventurers since before you two was born. His hand might be kinda shaky, and he ain't got but one eye, but when you're wearin' genuine Squinty ink, well then, you're a real adventurin' brother, so you are."

Sarah, too drunk to be subtle, blurted out in a slurred voice.

"Or sister…nothin' wrong with bein' an adventurin' sister."

Roscoe took the reproach in stride.

"Just so, an adventurin' sister. You'll have to forgive me until I learn a new way to be sayin' things."

Thurmond, too, was feeling the effects of promiscuous drinking.

"You gotta tell me one thing, Roscoe. These last three days, when you and Torgul was actin' all mad at me. So that was just play-actin', huh?"

His mentor laid a meaty hand on his shoulder.

"That was a mite cruel, so it was. I beg your forgiveness. The dwarf and I thought a charade was needed to bring a proper spice to the ceremony tonight. We wanted you both flabbergasted, and I think we succeeded."

"We weren't really lookin' for Alphonse tonight, were we?"

"Nay, that craven has flown away to parts unknown. If he knows what's good for him, he'll not be showin' his face in these parts ever again…well … not for a while anyway. Now drink up 'cause you gotta get your ink. But before you do, I gotta say a few things."

The two new Adventurers hurriedly downed their goblets of uisge. Roscoe waxed grave.

"If you've any reservations at all regardin' your commitment to the brotherhood —uh, sorry, Sarah, I don't know what else to call it. Maybe… commitment to our association…then you'd best speak up at once. 'Cause after you get your ink, it's too late to turn back.

"Once you're inked, you're in for life, permanent, just like the ink in your skin will be there till the day you die. From this hour, you'll be expected to act like an Adventurer, to think like one and feel like one. If you ain't up to it, speak up now."

Both Thurmond and Sarah remained silent. Roscoe beamed.

"Then let old Squinty do his job!"

Adventurer tattoos were always given on the sword arm, just below the elbow. As Roscoe had promised, Thurmond was the first to feel the needles. The old Adventurer was correct. It was painful in spite of his deep alcoholic fog. Very soon, the emblem of the Brotherhood…uh, association…took form on his arm—a wyvern, a fearsome two-legged dragon grasping a battle-axe, ready to strike.

It was Squinty's artistic conviction that no two tattoos should be alike. Thurmond's wyvern was skinny and mean, its fangs were bared and the axe was raised as if ready to strike. Sarah's creature was more subtle, with its axe held low in a position less threatening. But its long, sinuous tail, terminating in a vicious barb, was bent beneath its body, poised for an unexpected sting.

The formalities concluded, they all got down to some serious reveling.

The witch-queen's gold allowed Roscoe to pay his taxes, and so Grimsgard was saved from forfeiture. The tenants did not starve that winter and, under Florio's watchful eye, were far more attentive to their duties. For his heroic efforts during Gavin's attack, the elf was richly rewarded with gold, and his position as reeve was ensured for as long as he wanted it.

With his injured hip repaired, the gouty, sedentary Roscoe of yore was no more. He was replaced by an ardent and invigorated sportsman who spent most of his days strutting about his fields, hunting in the nearby woods, or angling in the river. His single regret was that his once-bulbous belly, sorrowfully reduced by the privations of their adventure, stubbornly refused to return to its previous magnificence. The short, embroidered tunic and splendidly cross-gartered hose remained folded in his clothing chest, but his friends made secret wagers about how soon they would make another appearance.

Torgul, a fundamentally simple soul, was content as long as he was mending or constructing something. The devastated village provided ample opportunity for the fulfillment of this passion. He forged door hinges, experimented with diverse styles of thatching, and replaced ceiling joists. And he always found time to sing gloomy dwarven songs to his bees.

Torgul and Pozi became fast friends, both sharing a fascination with mechanical things. But while the dwarf was most interested in designing and building contraptions made of gears, springs, and pulleys, the girl was devoted to taking them apart. She became highly adroit in the opening of all kinds of catches, locks, and latches.

Sarah finally belonged somewhere. She was formally, definitely, officially, perpetually enrolled in something established, recognized, enduring, and at least somewhat reputable. She was, naturally, proud of being the first female Adventurer, but had to wonder from time to time what inner quirk had led her down that particular path. She could only shrug—she had signed on for life.

In typical Sarah fashion, she set to work to identify the vast array of occult implements retrieved from Castle Sathas. She sorted through stones carved with talismanic runes, potions in stoppered vials, fat little jars holding pungent balms, bundles of scrolls and parchments, rings of power, and periapts on golden chains. There were weird bundles of feathers and bones, desiccated body parts of unknown beasts, cryptic sigils burned on swatches of dried skin, and even an assortment of reptilian scales that changed color when subjected to different degrees of light.

To accurately gauge the function and value of each item, she would have to master a number of complicated divination spells—a branch of occult science with which she had little familiarity. This would require substantial time and effort, but she would persevere without complaint. They might need some of this junk for their next adventure.

Her efforts were not without mishap. One errant enchantment caused her to compulsively blurt out her most embarrassing secrets. Roscoe and Torgul were greatly amused during the three days of the spell's duration. Thurmond figured prominently in many of her confessions.

Thurmond had finally attained his fondest dream, full membership in the Brotherhood of Underworld Adventurers, Gorgonholm chapter. He had earned the black hat and wyvern tattoo he had yearned for since childhood. But ironically he realized he was still at the beginning rather than the end of his personal journey. Roscoe and Torgul routinely referred to him as a baby Adventurer. This was done in a good humor, certainly, but it was also intended to remind him that he must continue to look inward to truly abide by the ideals he was sworn to uphold.

During his initiation ceremony, Roscoe promised the other Adventurers that Thurmond was *workin' on* his wisdom. What did his mentor see in him that had prompted that remark? Thurmond could ask, but he had learned long ago that he was expected to puzzle things out for himself. As always, being an Adventurer was more about the inner quest than hunting treasure or slaying monsters.

More troubling was Roscoe's remark that his fighting skill *ain't quite what it should be*. After his successes in Castle Sathas, he had felt like a young god of war, but his recent battle with Gavin brought his feet back to the ground. As much as he hated that fellow, he had to admit that he had been a superior swordsman who merely toyed with him during their encounter. Most likely, Sarah's timely crossbow bolt saved him from death.

He must practice, practice, practice with sword and spear and bow. Roscoe had never been much for grappling or close-in work with a dagger, but Torgul would instruct him in that. The dwarf was wicked fast with his scramasax. Thurmond knew that, sooner or later, a new adventure would present itself, and he did not want to die a baby Adventurer.

Oh, and about his relationship with Sarah? Well…that would be telling.

EPILOGUE

After a prolonged search of the ancient family records in her father's library, Sarah discovered that Lady Agnes de Roache had indeed been married to the great-great-grandsire of Lord Percy Staynes and was, therefore, her own great-great-great-grandmother. The blood of the witch-cult did truly run in her veins.

Bodo survived his dreadful wounds, but the Gray Friars were unable to save his injured leg. This put an abrupt end to his career as Roscoe's man-at-arms. In sooth, he was happy to embrace a different line of work. The death of Lars and the sight of so much of his own blood soured his enthusiasm for adventuring. At Roscoe's suggestion, he replaced Sulk, the village carpenter who fell during the siege of Grimsgard. Bodo's father had been a carpenter, and he had as a child served as his helper, so the change was an easy one. His skills turned out to be far superior to those of dim-witted Sulk, and he made for himself an excellent peg leg beautifully carved with floral motifs.

Bodo's wife, Bess, left Roscoe's service to start a small poultry run on the outskirts of the village. Her sister Maybelle departed with a troupe of traveling

mummers who passed through Gorgonholm the next spring. She eventually
sent word that she had married a tall, blond soldier named Hrolf.

Though soundly defeated by Baidan's bandits, Baron Sir Melgwyn de Pudni
did not perish in the whelming of Castle Skynslip. He and his knights fled
in the final stages of the battle, abandoning his common soldiers to a painful
fate. Escaping through a secret passage, he made his way west to another of his
feudal estates, where he gathered his strength and prepared for the reconquest
of his ancestral home.

With Castle Skynslip in his grasp, Baidan quickly assumed the behaviors
he thought fitting for the self-styled King of the Hills and Forests. These
mostly consisted of drinking incessantly, squandering the substantial treasure
he had wrested from Melgwyn, and abusing everyone around him. Within
a year, his gold was gone, and Baidan's royal guardsmen, disgruntled by the
constant abuse, began to slip away. This was welcome news to Melgwyn, who
immediately attacked the castle after bribing a disaffected guardsman to open
the gates, thereby regaining his birthright. The baron lived the rest of his life
in smug contentment.

Baidan miraculously survived Melgwyn's surprise attack, but his failed
leadership aroused the ambitions of Ouichi. On the way back to their hidden
mountain fortress, the once-loyal henchman challenged the discredited chief
for leadership of the much-depleted bandit gang. This of course involved a
duel to the death. Baidan somehow lived after a blow from Ouichi's axe staved
in his helmet and left him stretched on the ground, for all appearances quite
dead. Regaining his senses after a period of several hours, he found himself
alone. Ouichi and the others, believing him slain, had long since ridden away.

Disenchanted with the vagaries and vicissitude of the outlaw life, Baidan
gave it all up and returned to his native village, where he married a widow,

sired a litter of children, and took up basket weaving. He remained as irascible and brutish as ever, frequently beating his wife, terrorizing his offspring, and threatening his clientele. These qualities brought him the admiration of his neighbors, who deemed him a man of uncommon perspicacity.

Ouichi proved to be a worse leader than Baidan, but his tenure in that capacity was happily brief. The ever-fickle Skrot, acting on impulse, rejoined his old comrades to resume a life of banditry. Shortly thereafter, he pushed his knife into Ouichi's liver and assumed command. Under his leadership, the outlaws prospered beyond their wildest expectations. Word spread that they were no longer mere bandits but a revolutionary army dedicated to resisting the unjust oppression of the lower classes by the predatory nobility. The rapine and pillage they so frequently indulged in were now trumpeted as great victories committed for the cause of freedom and universal brotherhood. For this, the peasantry rewarded Skrot with undying love and support, seemingly unaware that none of his efforts brought any material improvements to their lives.

As the battle raged on Castle Skynslip's broad stairs, the kitchen girls, who proved to be quite amenable to a change of scene, begged Dollop to lead them from the doomed edifice. Despite his reluctance—the gaoler was a creature of rather fixed habit—Dollop eventually was persuaded. He found it exceedingly difficult to refuse a woman's tears.

Well acquainted with the castle's secret passages, they made their escape just prior to the flight of Baron Melgwyn. As she passed by a sideboard, pregnant Maggie had the good sense to snag several silver goblets, which they later bartered for food and travel gear. The group headed west and, after a number of narrow escapes, made their way to the city of Vistu in the kingdom of Poitiers. That they arrived unscathed is nothing short of miraculous, for the road through the forests of Bukovia abounded with malefactors.

Following a period of struggle and indecision, Dollop and his girls opened a tavern on the city's outskirts. This establishment, rejoicing in the name of The Willing Wench, proved highly lucrative. The good food and clean bedding made it very popular with travelers on the Golden Road. Lonely men far from home greatly appreciated the spirited and exotic diversions available in the upper rooms.

Moments after Thurmond and Roscoe rolled it over the edge of the cliff, the fearsome snow beast known as a hyut was released from Sarah's short-lived twining spell. It scrabbled futilely through space until it struck the rocks far, far below. Its shattered corpse was later discovered by a hunting party of shaggy snow goblins, who had for generations lived in mortal dread of the nearly unkillable creature. They had at first fled in squealing terror, for the hyut had taken a special delight in goblin meat. But when their sensitive noses detected the true aroma of death, they returned to stare in awe at their fallen nemesis.

After a prolonged argument with much gnashing of teeth and brandishing of weapons, the goblins carried the hyut back to their cave, where its flesh and entrails were eaten raw. Thus did the goblins acquire the strength, ferocity, and invincibility of their old enemy. The skin was tanned, stuffed with mountain heather, and hung from the cave's ceiling. It became their guiding spirit, their protector, their provider.

Ghleet never returned to the company of men. His mournful howling eventually reunited his broken, scattered pack, which he led on pitiless forays against any human unfortunate enough to enter their domain. In time, he chose several of the largest females as his mates and raised a brood of mongrel offspring noted for their savagery even by the rapacious standards of the wolfpack. Together they added a whole new chapter of pain and misery to the already blood-soaked history of Carpat.

Father Hieronymus had long dreamed of possessing Castle Sathas and establishing a religious community renowned for its simple piety and fundamental goodness. It would be the Beacon on a Mountaintop that would inspire others to follow his example of rejecting wealth and worldly power in favor of the spiritual virtues of truth, charity, and devotion. When Thurmond and Sarah cleansed Castle Sathas of Old One, he saw the fulfillment of his dream finally realized.

First and foremost, he conducted an extended ceremony of exorcism to rid the castle of any lingering malevolent influences. Satisfied that his efforts were successful, he moved the villagers into the edifice and set them to work restoring it to its former grandeur. The dilapidated outbuildings were repaired, the dusty chambers swept and scrubbed, the rotted furnishings replaced with the simple, practical appointments in keeping with his austere monastic tastes.

Their next task was to clear the fallen boulders and other assorted rubble from the dilapidated road leading down from the mountaintop's northern side. This was then widened and improved to allow the passage of full-size wagons. For the first time in decades, the castle was readily accessible to people other than intrepid mountaineers.

With the castle rejuvenated and its spirit of evil purged, a new name was imperative. Castle Sathas was reborn as the Abbey of Saint Olive, named for an early martyr of the Charonite church and a patron of wayfarers. Although usually portrayed as a large human with a club, most primary sources described him as a three-headed ogre, nine feet tall. He was, in addition, a hermaphrodite, though church doctrine forbade the mention of this detail.

The wisest and cleverest of the villagers were designated as Canons of the Order of Saint Olive and donned the dark blue robe of their leader. The most intelligent and attractive women became Vestals of the Blessed Saint, and were garbed in habits of azure.

With all necessary details attended to, Father Hieronymus announced that the abbey was open for business. He sent messengers far and wide to spread tales of the wondrous healing and spiritual solace to be found within the abbey's walls. The Holy Father's slightest touch, they claimed, allowed the lame to walk, the blind to see, and the mad to find their reason. Possessing demons would be cast out. Those damned by sin would be washed clean and forgiven.

In short order, the long twisting road up the mountain was filled with pilgrims eager to exchange their gold for the easing of their pain and guilt. The Holy Father was especially adept at discerning the particular needs of each petitioner and sending them home happy and satisfied. As word spread, more and more pilgrims made the arduous trek to the Abbey of Saint Olive.

But then a strange thing came to pass. Hieronymus and his minions abruptly cast off their blue habiliments, replacing them with robes of dark crimson. Soon after, the popularity of the abbey waned. Instead of a constant influx of eager pilgrims in large, boisterous companies, there now came solitary individuals, often arriving under the cover of night.

Very little is known from that period.

ACKNOWLEDGMENTS

Many, many thanks to the people who helped me get this written: my wife Christine for her insightful suggestions, careful proofreadings, and infinite patience with a husband often lost in Thurmond World; my daughter Dr. Kate MacKenzie for a most excellent proofreading; my friend and colleague Loren Preuss for a diligent proofread and for the good humor that kept me sane on a day-to-day basis; Sam Brown, Larry Penland, and Charles Buchanan for more than forty years of fun and inspiration…and quite a few bruises. And finally, a profound and robust thank you to Kathy Meiss and Shilah LaCoe of Bublish publishing platform for their knowledge, skill, and congeniality. Working with you is always a pleasure!

Coming Soon!

Turn the page to read the first chapter of

The Battle of
Gorgonholm

Chronicles of the
Medieval Underworld
Vol. 3

CHAPTER 1

THE CALL OF THE
BLACK STONE

The stars twinkled merrily overhead as they do, entirely unconcerned with the comings and goings of men, and yet inevitably intertwined with their destinies. Their influence was undeniable.

Consider for a moment the unlikely alignment of three certain stars directly over Skut, a tiny hamlet nestled deep in a forest glen several leagues south of Gorgonholm and a few more to the east. What else could account for the strange events that occurred there?

Skut was so far removed from the other villages of the county of Avincraik that few nonnatives were even aware of its existence. Over the generations, the lack of fresh blood had caused its inhabitants to develop certain unique physical characteristics—curiously narrow heads, fishy eyes too far apart, ridiculously long arms, hands with fat, stubby fingers, and a loose-kneed, shuffling gait. Their intelligence was abysmally low, the result of too many cousins marrying cousins.

One such specimen was a woodcutter by the name of Slow Pate. He had never in his life exhibited any traits suggesting ambition, authority, or nimbleness of mind. Yet when the combined light of those three stars beamed down upon his filthy hovel, he was a man transformed.

On that remarkable night, he awoke from the most compelling dream in which a deep and fearsome voice had commanded him to dig beneath an ancient oak, where he was to find a wonderful treasure. With uncharacteristic zest, the woodcutter was, in an eye-blink, out of bed, on his feet, and through the door with a shovel in his hand. But his frantic delving revealed not a golden trove but only a flat, black stone—square cut, some four feet wide, and three times as long. Immensely heavy, it was just the thing a man might set in place to thwart the removal of a buried hoard.

Poor Slow Pate! Lifting the huge stone would demand the strength of many men and require tools he did not possess. Great wealth was almost within reach, but he could think of no way to bring it into his hand.

Thus, the luckless woodcutter did what he and his neighbors always did when faced with a problem—he sought out Uncle, the headman of the village of Skut. This decision would be costly, for the headman was certain to take a large share of the treasure for himself. But only Uncle could muster the resources to pull the great stone from the earth.

Despite his congenial nickname, Uncle was no blood kin to Slow Pate, nor did he exhibit any of the warm, nurturing qualities one might expect from a close family member. Rather, he was greedy, self-serving, and cruel. His position as headman was secured neither by his sage advice nor mature discernment, but by his immense size and ready willingness to use fist, club, or knife to enforce his dictates. Uncle was a dangerous fellow.

Slow Pate approached Uncle's cottage just as the sun was climbing above the treetops of the surrounding forest. This was perilous, as Uncle might be suffering the ill effects of the previous night's drinking. Or he could be taking his pleasure with one of the village women. In any case, he would not be pleased with a visit from a hapless dimwit like Slow Pate.

Before knocking, the frightened woodcutter paused and listened at the door. Loud snoring within confirmed that the headman had not yet risen. Slow Pate hesitated, afraid—waking Uncle would most surely rouse his ire.

Slow Pate summoned what little courage he had and knocked. When the snores continued uninterrupted, he knocked harder and called out softly. When this failed to elicit a response, he pounded on the door and shouted.

The snoring ceased, and after a few moments, the cottage door swung open. Uncle stood there, naked, hairy, and huge. His scarred, bearded face twisted with disgust upon seeing Slow Pate standing at his threshold.

"Whadda you want, you little piece of snot? Why'd you wake me up? You better have a damn good reason, or you'll get beat like you never been beat."

Slow Pate stated his purpose as best he could—verbal expression had never been his particular gift. Uncle listened with growing irritation until he at last grasped the meaning of the words. Then his response was explosive! He ran fully nude down the length of Skut's single street, bellowing for the villagers to come forth.

And come they did. The magical word *treasure* filled the normally lethargic serfs with unprecedented enthusiasm. At Uncle's command, they sprinted to fetch spades for digging, ropes for hauling, wooden timbers for bracing, oxen for pulling.

Slow Pate cursed silently, for he now saw that his share of the treasure— *his treasure*—would be woefully small. Uncle would not care that it had been his dream that brought such good fortune. Nay, he would claim all gold for himself and then dole out pitiful handfuls to his favorites. Slow Pate had never been one of those. He might receive nothing at all.

Regretfully, the woodcutter led the entire population of Skut to the site of his discovery. They fell to work at once. By midmorning the dirt had been removed from all four sides of the stone, revealing a slab about a foot thick. The village carpenter and his sons erected a stout wooden tripod at one end of the excavation. A heavy rope was then passed beneath the stone, run through a block and tackle atop the tripod, and attached to a yoke of oxen.

At Uncle's signal, a plowman gave the beasts a smart blow with a switch, driving them forward. Ever so slowly, the black stone was drawn from the ground until it stood upright, twice the height of a tall man. The exultant villagers jumped in the hole, shovels flying, lusting for the riches that would soon be theirs.

Yet nary a single bronze farthing came to their avaricious fingers. They dug and dug, but nothing did they find. In his disappointment and frustration, Uncle turned on Slow Pate and beat him bloody.

Tired and resentful, the villagers unyoked their oxen, coiled their rope, shouldered their spades, and headed for home. None seemed aware that the great stone, no longer supported by rope and tripod, continued to stand, seemingly of its own volition.

Nor did they note the cold, leering visage in the stone's rough texture, fashioned not by any human hand but formed naturally from the living rock.

That night, another strange thing occurred. Slow Pate's dream voice returned. It was different this time, promising not treasure but something even more desirable—revenge upon the odious Uncle. Without hesitation Slow Pate took up his reaping sickle and slipped silently from the door of his hut.

The woodcutter was not the only one to hear voices that night. The diggers, the builders, the plowman—all who had lent a hand in the raising of the stone—were roused by a call to cast off the restraints that kept them in want and degradation, to know the bliss of limitless power.

Late that night, in the darkest of the dark, drawn by some uncanny instinct, they gathered around the stone. Some brought gifts for their new idol. Slow Pate laid Uncle's severed head reverently at its base.

ᚱ

In his private chamber in Castle Skut, Lord Ubo Futz awoke with a start. Somebody was whispering in his ear, but when he looked about, no one was there. A woman's voice, he was certain. But who would dare to disturb his sleep in such a manner?

Certainly not one of the sluttish servant girls he often pulled into his bed—they knew better. And not his wife, that sorry sack of bones—she was smart enough to keep her distance. *Who then?* No one in his household would be so foolish.

He shouted into the darkness.

"Who's there? Come forward! Show your face!"

When no one appeared, Ubo began to have doubts. Perhaps it had been a dream. Or a ghost. The castle abounded with unquiet spirits, many of whom bore him an abiding grudge. Putting the matter from his mind, Lord Ubo turned over and closed his eyes.

The whispers returned at once. Alarmed, Ubo attempted to rise but found himself pinned, as if something heavy had oozed onto his chest. He tried to shout, to command the unseen presence to be gone, but no sound came from his throat.

Ubo, the dread lord of Futz, began to panic, afraid that this thing—whatever it was—was about to stop his breath. But when his lungs continued to draw air, he gradually regained his composure. The whispering thing, it seemed, did not intend to kill him, but it did to want to be heard. So he listened, and as he did, he slowly comprehended.

The voice was soft, teasing, seductive—the voice of a beautiful woman. It revealed several stark truths Ubo had never before considered, urging him to rise and act upon this new knowledge without delay. To be the man he was born to be.

He resisted at first, but the whisperer continued to tempt, prompt, and prod until he could stand it no longer. At last, he flung himself from bed, donned his clothes, and strode to the stable. There he kicked the sleeping groom and bade him saddle his favorite palfrey, a chestnut mare of great speed and agility. Then he rode into the gloom of the night.

Ubo's arrival at the stone filled the worshipers with trepidation, for he had never been a mild or understanding overlord. Indeed, they expected the most severe of punishments for their forbidden devotions. Idolatry was, after all, a crime against all decency or reason. Heretics were sometimes burned alive by the holy church.

They were surprised and confused, therefore, when Ubo did not drive them back to the village with a whip. Rather, he dismounted and, leading his mount by the reins, approached slowly and quietly until he stood directly beneath the great, looming slab. Then, to the utter astonishment of his tenants, Ubo drew his dagger and slashed the great veins in his mare's neck, causing its blood to gush upon the stone's black surface.

As the beast collapsed, Lord Ubo Futz bent his knee and pledged his faith.

The assembly began a slow, tuneless chant. Hands clasped in supplication, eyes squeezed shut, they repeated it over and over, over and over. And the harder they prayed, the greater the stone's power waxed.

Its call reached deep into the forest, so that uncouth, skin-clad woodsmen emerged from the shadows to join the villagers. Next came a cluster of clannish, reclusive charcoal burners.

At dawn, the call was heard upon the Royal Highway, causing wayfarers to turn from their journeys to seek the source of the summons.

The Gray Friars in their monastery heard it too, and some few forsook their holy vows to answer the stone's more pressing call.

In the village of Grimsgard and in the streets of Gorgonholm, in country lanes and in the mansions of the wealthy, an ancient summons was boring into people's brains.

www.ingramcontent.com/pod-product-compliance
Lightning Source LLC
Chambersburg PA
CBHW020231110726
47898CB00004B/1226